THE SHADOWS

Laevatein's Choice

The Shadows: Lævatein's Choice

ISBN-10: 1-7325704-3-4
ISBN-13: 978-1-7325704-3-6

Cover and interior by E. Kathryn
Edited by Victoria Miller

ekathrynsshadows.com

Because what you have done takes such enormous strength,
Learn from it, do it again, grow, until you reach your dream.

THE SHADOWS

Laevatein's Choice

E. KATHRYN

1
HEART STOP

March 2, 2031

The unoiled door screeched as it opened to the crisp air, and Emilie grinned at the cold pinching her nose. There it sat among the pebbles in the walkway, just as she had expected, and the red-tailed hawk perched upon the iron hook above the mailbox. Kneeling to the cobblestone, Emilie lifted a single white rose with delicate fingers, and she blushed with the warmth of the cold air nipping at her cheeks. "He sent you again?" she chirped at the hawk, and cautiously reached out to it.

The hawk's cool blue eyes sized her up from the iron hook, assessing her stance, reading her soul to sense any fear or insecurity. Winter ruffled her feathers, puffing up and squawking at Emilie. She was unable to trust Emilie, but the bird would still deliver items at her master's behest, even if she was anti-social and didn't like to be touched. Her wingspan forced Emilie to draw back and watch as the hawk took to the sky over the roof of the little house, but Emilie couldn't let the call to the sky carry her away.

Following after the bird, Emilie's feet left the ground, allowing her Shadow to awaken and course through her veins, demolishing gravity's grip over her form. The sting of the cold air caused her body to beg her to find warmth, and the thin tank top she wore as a nightshirt let the lingering winter cold bite at her arms. She couldn't help herself; flying was all she lived for. She wasn't getting enough of it. The last months had confined her to this house, a smaller space than she had grown up in, and her heart felt boxed in.

The wind called her, and the invisible path the hawk trailed as she disappeared into the distance led to the only other home she truly knew. Winter followed after him. Regretfully, she let herself sink, and she drifted from the air just over the roof of the house, to the snow dusted gravel at the front door. Her heart called her away, but her blood held her here. With air in her stride, Emilie returned into the little house, a place she still couldn't consider home, and sank into the day.

Pale peach curtains drawn back from the corners of the front window allowed pure white light to flood into the sitting room. The once musty studio room was now open and inviting, hiding Emilie from the truth she'd buried as she cleaned. With a little Mason jar, Emilie placed the white rose into water and set it upon the counter by the kitchen window and smiled at it before her attention was drawn to the one room which stubbornly remained dark.

Before a television, which was perpetually on, a woman laid in several thick comforting blankets which concealed her face from the glaring light of day. Pressing her lips together, Emilie tried to ignore the entire room, and hurried off to the small studio space connected to her bedroom. She had been working on the clutter in the studio, passing her time with going through everything and making it neat while getting rid of as much as she could. Emilie liked cleaning and organizing things, but she'd lied to herself. She wasn't happy here. Every room she worked through and made to look inviting and bright, satiated her heart, but nothing satisfied her.

Water in the kitchen gushed from the old faucet, and Emilie tensed, hurrying about the corner. The couch had been vacated, and her mother stood in the kitchen filling a shimmery silver coffeepot with water. "You're up!" Emilie gasped.

The woman with dark bags under her eyes gazed bitterly onward until they locked upon the pure joy exuded by the silky petals of the rose in her windowsill. "He sent another one?"

Offering a smile, Emilie's feet left the hardwood, and she weightlessly soared over her mother to the opposite side of the sink. "I'll get one for every room!"

Her mother frowned, distraught by every step Emilie made toward making the house her home. Hellen preferred the darkness, bitter with a heart full of sorrows she couldn't let go of. Hellen had lived on them for years, and Emilie knew that. Letting go of it was harder, and Emilie was determined to help her. "We should go visit Mark this week," Emilie declared cheerfully, getting out a skillet to make brunch, knowing her mother hadn't eaten much in the last day or so. "I could use a little time with the Shadows, and we have an open invitation!"

Hellen scowled at the prospect of leaving the house. "You just want to go see that boy," she murmured.

Offering a fake laugh, Emilie wouldn't let her feet touch the floor as she whipped up some scrambled eggs. "If I wanted to visit Sil, I'd leave whenever I want." The half-threat was met with a cold glare from a woman who was so utterly dependent on her. "In fact..." she murmured softly as she seasoned the eggs, "I was planning on flying over today."

Almost immediately, the woman shuddered, visibly distressed. "B-but... what about dinner? I thought we planned—"

Emilie glared at her, pushing around the eggs in a small frying pan. "This is a strange time for you to care about seeing guests. You hate people, remember?" she jabbed, offering a wry smile as she adjusted the heat on the stove, which was cooking the eggs too fast.

Hellen deadpanned, making her way over to the coffeepot, irritated and overtired. "Fine, do what you want, but just be back in time to help me with dinner."

Shaking her head, Emilie smirked to herself as she took the pan off the heat. "Like you'll do anything to help," she spat under her breath, now admitting to herself that she was getting a little hostile with her mother. She didn't hate Hellen, but she wouldn't let the woman try to control her. Plating up her breakfast, Emilie floated gaily over to the small dining table. Half of this table was clear and set for two people, decorated in light floral placemats with clean white plates and silverware folded into a matching floral napkin. The other half of the table was still piled high with junk.

Emilie ignored the clutter, focusing on the pretty painting she had found and hung on the opposite wall, lying to herself that this half of the room was all that consisted of the dining room. The floral patterns and the warming winter light were all she was aware of as she ate her breakfast. She loved Hellen, but she was a packrat and refused to clean anything. Over the past few months, Emilie had found herself making whatever mess she could find as tiny as possible, having grown up in a very clean and spacious environment. She tried not to abuse the poor woman, but she couldn't get away from the feeling that she was an intrusion into her mother's life and cleaning up after her intensified that feeling.

The eggs were gross and burned, but she ate them out of spite, proving to her mother that anything could be good if just a little effort was invested into it. Her mother stood there in the kitchen behind her, staring blankly into the coffee pot as the black liquid dribbled into the well, hopefully contemplating her own mundanity. Emilie couldn't stand coffee. Caffeine didn't do her any good as it only made her flighty and restless.

Scarfing down the last of her eggs and swallowing them without tasting the spongey, bland rubber, she got up quickly, taking her plate and rinsing it off. She opened the dishwasher with a loud, "Hey look!" and while gesturing exaggeratedly, she placed the plate into the dishwasher as if her mother didn't know how to use it. She didn't act like she did anyway. She slammed the dishwasher and stepped lightly—so lightly most of her steps didn't touch the floor—to her room.

Huffing, she sat down on her bed and got dressed with the door open. She hated closed doors, locks, boxes, tight spaces, or anything that made her feel trapped. This whole house was a box, but she made herself more comfortable with the little things, and Hellen didn't even come back here so she had no need to worry about privacy. The woman slept on the couch with the TV on, drowning out all thoughts of how alone she was. Emilie scoffed, bending down and slipping a pair of knee-high boots over the black leggings she practically lived in. The boots had tall heels, and she had gotten them for herself for Christmas, showing off mostly, since she would never be able to walk in them. The shoes were mostly for warmth, as she had no meat on her skinny legs, and it was bitter outside.

Floating up rather than standing, she pushed off the bed springs to her closet where her jacket hung on the door, and while she was still in the air, she slipped on a flowing skirt over her leggings, enjoying how it flew in the wind when she soared. "I'll see you later!" she yelled from the front door, zipping through the halls without even touching the dusty runner carpet.

The door whined, its old springs protesting as it whined open and then slammed shut. The cold air hit her again, and every fiber of her being froze. She closed her eyes and inhaled a sharp, deep breath of the frigid air. This was her home! Her eyes flashed when she opened them, and gravity let her go like a slingshot giving way. The wind whizzed around her ears as the clouds came around her in a fog. She thought nothing of the thin air as she let herself go free into the morning light.

What was a fifty-minute drive became cold fire on the tip of her nose, hitting seventy miles per hour at least as the neighborhood came into view within twenty minutes. She plunged down through the air, declaring herself in the Realm to see him down here, waiting for his hawk to return. He looked good in the cold of early spring, helping the winter to keep its icy grip on the New York suburb. It suited him, and she was happy for him, in that melancholic, jealous way, that kept her own predicament quiet.

"Sil!" she yelled down through the air, catching his eyes just as the wind picked up.

He shuddered at the harsh wind, unaffected by the cold, but surprised to see her when she fell out of the air, throwing her arms around him. She latched around his waist and playfully locked her joints. Sil pulled away, struggling to push her off him. "Emilie, let go."

"Nope!" she declared gleefully. Her arms pinned his two-foot long, spider-silk-like white hair, and she noticed that it was wet and weightier than usual.

Rolling his eyes, Sil's arms fell limp at his sides. "You can let go now…" Not amused in the slightest, he let her legs float up parallel with the ground.

"Nope!" she blared again, perfectly happy to hang there.

"I have to go braid my hair before it's a tangled mess! Let me go!" he finally shouted, and the moment he got angry, she released him, snickering evilly. Sil gave a sigh, a slight smile on his lips as he pushed her away. "What are you doing here?" he asked with muted sarcasm as he started fighting with his long hair, struggling to work it into a tight braid that would last him through the day.

She watched the skill of his hands as she floated behind him. "Getting out of chores, of course!" she sang, obnoxiously soaring across the backyard to one of the clustered oak trees. She took a perch in a low branch and spied Mark Halo below her. "Oh, hello hothead, how are you?"

All Mark's attention was absorbed into his quivering right hand. Fire died away in his palm and his ardent eyes were fixed on Sil as his friend returned. Breathlessly, he pushed the flames down, his black hair falling into his face as his whole body trembled.

Sil chuckled as he tied off his braid. "We're working on refining his Shadow." He dodged a cluster of chickens which roamed the yard led by a single rooster, and he avoided their muddy path. "It's a pain keeping clear of getting burned again," he murmured, scratching the scar along his jawline, "but we're getting there."

Mark's feet were caked in mud six inches up his shins, and his knuckles were blistered. "I'm sorry…" he cringed, grinding his teeth. All he could remember was his own fire flashing through the air and striking Sil in the chest. With cold weather, Mark couldn't see them now, but he knew Sil had extensive scars on his neck and right shoulder. He winced just thinking about it, utterly ashamed.

Emilie snickered, dangling over the tree branch. "You need to stop letting your emotions control your Shadow."

"That's all I got!" Mark nearly yelled, his fists trembling to hold back the conflagration.

Sil tied his braid into a knot to keep the weighty thing from flying around. "Yeah, yeah, we've been over this." His feet spread apart, the mud latching onto the soles of his shoes to strengthen his foothold. With a smooth, level-headed breath, he goaded Mark on, raising his fists.

Mark's shoulders fell and he grumbled, but he made an effort to steady his heart. He closed his eyes, softening his senses, inhaling fully before he dared to exhale. He had to be calm. Emilie swung back and smiled sadistically as Mark struggled to ignore her. He opened himself in the Realm, and that's what Sil wanted, a free-flowing connection between them, so that Mark would sense it the moment Sil lunged at him.

The icy fist swung through the air, aiming primarily for Mark's face, but not with intentions to truly hurt him. At best, Sil just wanted to rattle him up. Sil's knuckles impacted Mark's forearms and Mark put his weight into it, pushing Sil back. Mark was older and just a tad bigger than him, but Sil knew what he was doing. Emilie hovered above them leering over Mark's lean frame like a crow, waiting for him to snap.

Sil swooped in under Mark's defenses, aiming to score him firmly in the gut, but Mark rightly buckled, bashing Sil's fist down into the muck and tripping him. Sil stumbled but flicked the dirt off his knuckles and caused his hand to freeze over. He slipped behind Mark, his back to him for a brief second, then he elbowed him into the small of his back as hard as he could.

Gasping, Mark scrambled away from him, a little winded, and still panting. "Dude... I told you I have a bad back!" he groaned, stretching out his shoulder, but Sil wouldn't let him rest yet.

Icy tendrils sprayed out at him from the ground like blades of diamond grass. They fired up into Mark's muddy shins, and again the flames within him burst. Giving a yell, Mark swiped his left hand across the air, not at Sil, but at his ice. Sil had used his Shadow. It was only fair for him to respond in kind.

Sil's eyes twinkled when his ice melted. "Better." Each shoe scuffing the mud, he paced slowly. "Keep your mind open in the Realm. If I can feel your intentions, and you can feel mine, we won't hurt each other."

"I do," Mark insisted indignantly, "all the time."

"You talk to me all the time." Sil raised an eyebrow, faintly amused. He tightened the knot in his braid which was already falling loose. "Let's do it again. You have to wait longer."

Gasping for air and still rolling his shoulder, Mark quelled the flames. "How is not using Fire supposed to help me refine it?"

Sil spread out frost on the ground to harden it, inevitably making it more slippery. "It's not abstaining from using it. It's using it at the opportune moment. Easily, I could have used those icicles to actually hurt you, and you had to find out what it felt like to get shanked in the leg before you melted them."

"So, why'd you say wait longer!" Mark burst again, already yelling at every breath. "I should have used it sooner."

Cool and collected, Sil just lowered his gaze to the ground and shrugged. "Fighting is a great way to practice, and you rely on adrenaline to get your Shadow flowing in your veins. So, if you can hold off the flames even when your adrenaline is high, it accomplishes two things." He held up two fingers with his count. "You learn to control your Shadow under pressure, and you learn how to fight without your Shadow. Let's face it, fighting me isn't a real challenge for you, 'cause we're not really trying to kill each other."

Mark resigned himself to heave a sigh, ready for the next round. It was only a few motions each time, but he could feel himself getting stronger, maybe not in his Shadow, but it felt good to land a hit whenever he did. Opening himself in the Realm, he read Sil's intentions, feeling every movement of the ice Shadow before it happened.

Abruptly, he clenched his fists, quieting the fire and before Sil was prepared, Mark side-stepped, ducking Sil's initial haphazard swing and dashing firmly into Sil's blind spot. "What!" Sil gasped, unsure why Mark had jumped the gun. Jumping up, Mark raised his left arm and sank his elbow deep into Sil's lower back as sweet revenge.

Sil tripped right to his knees, and Mark gave a little laugh as he rolled his shoulder more. "Wow, I didn't think I could hit that hard, and with my left arm!"

Saving his fall with his hands, Sil cringed as the mud seeped between his fingers. "You sure you're right-handed?" Before Mark could answer, Sil swiped his foot to send Mark flying.

Purely reactionary, he sprang, missing Sil's leg by a hair. Sil found his footing, and Mark lurched back from his fist. The icicles started to rise from the ground, and Mark's shoes were slipping. He needed to get out of the area Sil had frozen.

Sil threw his fist again, missed, and threw another, his left.

Mark blocked it with his right forearm, his dominant arm, and with his left, he grabbed Sil's wrist and yanked his weight out of the perimeter of the firm ground.

Sil's heel sank deep into the mud. Mark watched his eyes widen, his balance gone to the wind. Sil's other leg got caught between Mark's, his weight worked against them and pulled them both down.

Crying out before he hit the ground, Sil landed flat on his back in the mud, followed by Mark, whose face hit the muck before the rest of him did.

He groaned in disgust as he sat up. "Dang it, Mark! I just took a shower!" Sil tried to shake off the mud, but it caked his arms, his whole backside, and it saturated his pure white hair.

Even more unpleasant, Mark tried to wipe the mud out of his eyes, but with his hands filthy, it was perfectly useless. He was equally sickened, but when Sil finally caught sight of his face through the muck, Mark had a wide and wild smile. "That was awesome!" Mark cackled, using the sleeve on his left shoulder to wipe his face.

"I hope you're proud of yourself!" Sil lifted himself from the squelching muck, cautiously feeling at his braid and shivering at the slimy awfulness soaking it.

Mark's red eyes shone brighter, enthralled and exhilarated. "Let's do it again! I didn't even use Fire at all!"

"You're kidding, right?"

"It's working!" Mark nearly shouted, "I didn't rely on my Shadow."

Rolling his eyes, Sil continued attempting to clear some of the mud off his arms. "Not today, I need another shower, and you do too."

Hoisting himself out of squishy clay, Mark laughed to himself. "Fine, but we have to do it tomorrow."

"Whatever…" Sil groaned, leaving reddish footprints across the patio. "But we need to find a better place to do this. Or wait for the ground to dry out." He kicked off his shoes at the doormat and heaved the sliding door aside, leaving his friends behind.

"Hey, thank you." Mark called after him.

Sil paused at the door a little surprised. He seemed perfectly amused by how dumb Mark looked in a mask of rusty mud, but he couldn't imagine he was thankful for that. With just a small smile, Sil nodded as his only response.

11
LUNGS

Mark ran home to keep the adrenaline up, the crisp wind and subtle warmth of early spring was making him stir-crazy, and staying active was the only way to keep himself from going mad. One last winter snow melted away on every dark curb, but the air was finally getting warm, so he hoped the snow would go away soon. He loved the good jog to and from Sil's just as much as hanging out with his one Shadow friend. How had it already been four months since he found out he was a Shadow? And how had nothing changed yet?

His house was about a mile from Sil's in the community and several winding blocks away, far enough that he wouldn't hear his mother screaming from all the way from Sil's backyard. He dreaded coming home lately, sometimes his mother was unbearable to be around. He was sure he looked ridiculous running down the street with mud all over his face and clothes, but he didn't care about the neighbors. He had a much more unpleasant lecture in store for him at home.

Being home only brought with it one comfort: the Realm. When he wasn't around Shadows, he entered the Realm to be as close to them as he could. That was the only reason he ever came home other than to sleep. He slipped in through the garage to not incur the fanfare that the front door would create. The cold concrete made him shiver as he skirted around the family car, and to the squeaky kitchen door. As slowly as he could, to keep it quiet, he went inside. Glancing frantically about the kitchen, he made sure his mother wouldn't spot him.

The coast was clear. He shut the door, latching it without a sound, but as he turned about, his spine crawled.

"You can sneak around, but you're not going to avoid me," his mother said, a terrifying scowl in her voice. Mark jumped but he couldn't see her, not in the kitchen, the hall, or the laundry room. Her voice came from the living room.

"I do not want to get into this," another voice came. Mark peeked his head out of the kitchen. His father stood in the threshold of the front room. Despite the Halos' one car being in the garage, his dad looked like he had just walked in the door a moment before Mark.

January's distressed brow refused to soften when his wife glared at him, and Mark hastily slipped into the Realm, turning invisible so he could sneak past them. Marissa poised her hands on her hips. "You can't keep avoiding this!" she insisted, going to a harsh tone abruptly.

Mark froze at the entry to the hall, but January cowered, turning away from Marissa and to the stale living room. "You want to talk about me avoiding it. How about you?" His gaze suddenly shot to her. "Did it ever occur to you to tell me that our son was a Shadow? Why did you wait until after he destroyed the ASH? Why didn't you call me the moment you found out, instead of them?"

"Because I knew you'd do this!" Marissa screamed.

Mark tensed, listening to his parents fight. It hurt, but he was getting used to it. He tried to keep his ears to himself, as he had in the various minor fights his parents had had over the course of his life. This wasn't minor. His mother could never speak about Shadows around January before now, and Mark could tell by her voice that she was emboldened. They had a Shadow in the family now. She felt safer, but that didn't change how January felt about the subject. From the quiet avoidance of anything Shadows, Mark didn't know if he was hiding something or just prejudiced.

January gestured to his chest, infuriated. "Didn't you think I wanted to know? That maybe, I'd want to be a part of permanently changing our son's life."

Crossing her arms, Marissa scoffed. "You didn't seem to care before."

"You need to talk to me, Isa!" his father shouted, attempting to talk her down. "We just need to work through this."

"'Work through it?'" she shrieked. "You're kidding right? If you're so scared of the Shadows in the ASH, then why weren't you here? Why didn't you want to talk then?"

"So we can talk now," January pled. Mark was terrified by the desperation in his father's eyes, so broken by Marissa's anger.

"It's a little late for that." Marissa glowered, falling silent for a few moments. Her crossed arms drifted to hug her sides, and the miles between them grew wider. "Our son is gone... talking through it isn't going to change what the Shadows did to him."

Mark stumbled back, a step escaping his shaking legs. They were fighting about *him*. They had been at it for months now, and it was all about him. He slipped into his room, closing the door as soundlessly as possible in spite of how his hands were trembling. He locked it, almost certain the noise would have alerted his parents, and he sank down onto his bed. Exhaling sharply, he let out an unexpected pressure in his chest.

One of them knocked on his door, trying it to find it locked. "Mark? Are you in there?" his father asked through the wood panel.

Mark turned his face away, toward the window. It didn't help that his mother had known he was a Shadow all his life, and she had been lying to him from the moment he discovered his fire.

January's heavy sigh hit the door. "Look, I know you heard all that." Mark seethed, his red eyes flaring brighter, completely certain his parents were annoyed by his ability to turn invisible. "Listen, I don't want you to think we don't love you. We do. It's just... complicated."

Mark scowled. What was complicated? January either cared or he didn't. Was it harder now that his father knew the truth? He didn't respond, ignoring him completely as he pulled his legs up onto his bed. He adopted a meditative posture to enter the Realm, and fully immersed himself into it. He let the dark world rush over him and allowed himself to sink deep into the starfield.

It was always peaceful here, quiet, and the absence of Shadows always calmed Mark's raging heart. He breathed slowly, the rate of his heart falling as he opened his mind to the hidden world. Within moments, he was aware of Sil's presence, and he could almost see him tending to his animals. Emilie was still flying around aimlessly just to stay away from her home. The Shadows he knew best glowed like gems in firelight, and Mark sensed there were more Shadows out there.

The human world was bland by comparison. All physical objects, his bed, the possessions in his room, the door, the hall, the kitchen, and the house shimmered with wavering white smoke. Corporeal bonds didn't affect him when he was in this state. He could see right through his door at his father still standing with his fist to it. January looked like any other inanimate object, wavering white smoke, which shone brightly against the darkness.

Unlike most Shadows, Mark didn't have to enter the Realm and turn invisible to see clearly through the secret world. He was a bit stronger in the Realm than most. But, with his newfound freedom, Sil was starting to rival him. They were equals at best, and Mark loved it when he could hear Sil's voice over the distance of the community yelling at him to mind his own business.

It was so fun to communicate telepathically.

Sil was reserved most of the time, but he was quick to beat Mark over the head when he was irritated, sometimes going as far as freezing Mark's hair or shoving blunt icicles into his hands or back. Mark knew better than to retaliate. He had learned that lesson the hard way. Sil was just anti-social, not mean-spirited.

Somedays it felt like Sil was the only Shadow who Mark could talk to. Using the phone over the distance to the ASH just wasn't the same, and Emilie was... Emilie. But other days, he heard a twinge in the Realm, like his range was expanding. He caught a glimpse of a familiar place far from here, and the soft airy aura of another Shadow.

She appeared in the distance, a vision of some exotic place behind her back, and then she spotted him, calling him to her mind, and using his presence in the Realm to home in on him. Mark felt a rush of cool air and opened his eyes.

His room seemed too dark to contain her. The closed blinds dimmed her bright soul, and Mark stood up abruptly to bring some light to his bedroom. "Rita! Where'd you come from?" he declared, not in the least startled by her appearance. It didn't matter how she appeared. He just wanted to know where on Earth her Shadow had carried her from.

Rita fluffed her red hair, dusting the green mist her Shadow created off her clothes. "Florida," she stated, rolling her Rs and exaggerating her accent. "You still sulking?"

Mark shrugged and adopted an easy smile. "What else is new?"

Rita cackled, her deep chortling laugh filling Mark's heart with hope. Rita was much like Emilie, with a deep desire for freedom, but unlike Emilie who had to travel actual distance, Rita could teleport wherever she wanted. She was completely on her own, stopping at the ASH when she got hungry, and Mark legitimately couldn't pin down a time when he had seen her sleep. She was usually on European time anyway, since she spent so much time in her homeland of Scotland.

Rita sported light summery clothes although it was still quite chilly up north. She didn't carry a suitcase or backpack of any kind. She didn't bring any supplies on her adventures. She just went freely. Mark envied her—no ties, no family, no reason to look over her shoulder and care.

"So, where do ya want to go today?" she asked, plopping down onto his bed and nudging him in the shoulder with hers.

Smiling helplessly, Mark closed his eyes and breathed, imagining the scents of Scotland or the warm beaches of Florida. With her, he could go anywhere, if even for a day. And no one would ever know he was gone. "Anywhere you want to go, that's fine with me."

Rita deadpanned playfully, "You have no creativity. Give me a hint or I could drop ya dead into the middle of the ocean."

Mark's shoulders fell, revealing his frustration. "Just... out of here, that'd be nice."

"What's wrong?" Rita's brows drew together, and she draped her elbow on his shoulder. Somehow, she always seemed so relaxed. Rita had nothing, she was an empty person always ready to be filled by the wonders around her and she was never sad.

He liked how relaxed she made him feel, imparting that freedom onto him and giving him glimpses of other worlds. Mark couldn't admit it, but he wasn't brave enough to let her take him to more far-reaching places on the Earth. He just wanted to get out of this house.

"Normal stuff. Family stuff." He wouldn't admit to anything else.

Rita didn't have a clue what was going on with Marissa and January. She'd never heard how they fought. She'd never seen how January spent more and more nights on the couch. Mark wasn't ready for this. He didn't want to think of the possibility that the strains in his parents' marriage were too deep to repair.

"I got it!" Rita burst, accepting his evasiveness, like she always did. "You wanna put your shoes on or just dive into this?"

Awkwardly, they simultaneously glanced down at Mark's feet. He was already wearing shoes, which were thoroughly caked in mud. "Are we going swimming or something?" he puzzled.

Rita chortled ecstatically. "No, it's too cold for that. How about I give you a bit to clean up, and then we'll go."

"Sounds like a plan," he said with a relaxed sigh.

She beamed madly and teleported away, leaving him alone with his thoughts and his dark room. The lightbulb was dead, of course, so the only light came in through the window. Mark stood up and started by kicking off his shoes, then grabbed a change of clothes. He hadn't even noticed how his hair was still coated in clay and there was dried dirt on his face. Rita wouldn't have pointed it out either, not unless she intended to mock him for it. She was snarky, that was probably why she avoided all adults if she could.

Cautious, Mark unlocked his door and peered out into the hall. January was gone. He would have said something if he had heard a girl's voice in Mark's locked room. He snuck out toward the bathroom to wash up and clean the mud out of his hair.

As the dirt dripped off his face under the warm water, he frowned, and peace and quiet around him wasn't enough to steady his heart anymore. It beat too rapidly. It needed constant adrenaline, and it took every trigger to fill Mark's veins with fire and make him want to hit something. This was especially so when his parents fought. He closed his eyes again, and let his mind sink into the Realm.

There was another presence now, in the distance, he could feel it distinctly. It felt like the water flowing over his face, warm yet crisp, like rain on a summer day. He could see the blue aura before he identified the Shadow.

Ocie... he whispered through the Realm.

Her form became clearer, a song in the darkness, sweet as always and gentle. *Where are you? Are you near the ASH?*

Mark sent a tone of denial across the void. *No, I'm at home, how can I hear you if you're all the way in Virginia.*

Ocie hummed. *You must have finally expanded your range far enough to reach the ASH. That or our ranges are meeting somewhere in the middle.*

How far is your range? He asked, his fiery form stretching across the Realm.

Giving a benevolent laugh, Ocie's visage expanded, vast as the ocean and almost completely enveloping Mark's mind. *Larger than yours. Like you, I was never hindered by the ASI. However, I spent my time in the ASH expanding my range for far longer than you have.* Nothing about her voice was cocky or goading. She was more powerful than he was. She was Shadow Hope. Every breath she breathed was grace and kindness.

From what Mark understood, Shadow Hope was one of the Orchestrators, a Shadow with the ability to act outside of its wielder's will and to push events into place. Shadow Hope had triggered the Exodus, and Ocie had used Mark to inspire the Shadows to escape. It was Mark's sense of freedom which fired up all of the Shadows: Rita, Sil, and Emilie. However, the one thing Mark thought had made him special was a gift from an even more powerful Orchestrator called Shadow Trust.

Since the Exodus, Mark had not heard anything from the godlike Shadow who had spoken to him telepathically over a much greater distance than this.

Who knows... Ocie brought him out of thought. *You may yet become more powerful in the Realm than me, if you keep practicing as much as you are.*

Being in the Realm didn't feel like practice. In Mark's mind, practice was a strenuous thing, but sinking back and shutting his mind off to enter the Realm wasn't hard at all. He did it when he was frustrated, like now, when he was alone, when he was trying to sleep, and really during any hour of the day that he didn't feel like paying attention. Entering the Realm in his mind was as second nature to him as staring off into space.

Mark's fiery form in the Realm warmed their two souls. *Well, I guess I'll talk to you again soon, now that my range is big enough. I have to go.*

She made no visible response other than her form spilling back into the blackness as Mark turned off the water. Opening his eyes, he smiled to himself. He liked Ocie for what she offered the Shadows. Even after the ASI was taken down, she had encouraged the Shadows to stay, to take advantage of the safe haven in the ASH while they searched for their families. She was brutally honest and a good listener.

Throwing on clean clothes, Mark sneaked back to his room, locking the door securely and once more clearing his thoughts to call out in the Realm. *I'm ready, Rita.*

A flurry of green mist burst into his room. She hadn't gone far, to stay within range to hear him. Mark was pretty sure she didn't spend nearly as much time in the Realm as he did, but what did he care? She was having way more fun than him.

"That took forever!" she blared, but when she saw his face, she cackled hysterically. "Dude, make up your mind now, grow it out or cut it off!" she mocked, pulling his long black bangs over his eyes.

"What!" Mark complained, "I've always hated cutting my hair, and Mom hasn't gotten on to me about shaving it off, so I've been growing it out!" The red strike fell between his eyes where Rita tugged it, and he brushed it away uselessly. Of course, Marissa hadn't been paying attention. She was too busy stressing over her husband.

"Fine, I tried." Rita snickered and grabbed his arm. "All right, surprise it is. Ya ready?"

Mark nodded eagerly, bracing himself for the sudden disorientation of teleporting, which was getting easier to handle each time Rita dragged him along. The mist cleared around him, but the green didn't fade, and suddenly all he could see around him were the green buds along the trees and the open grass of a park. Mark shook off his perplexity and took a few dizzying turns at the world around him. It wasn't warmer, so it wasn't like she had taken him to some tropical place like Florida. But as he turned to the skyline, he knew exactly where he was.

"This is Central Park! This is like fifty miles away!" he gasped excitedly but smirked and gave her a firm nudge in the shoulder with his fist. "You didn't want to take me to the other side of the world? Aren't there more interesting things to see?"

Rita shook her head and punched him back, a little harder. "I've been wantin' to explore this place, and you know it best, so I wanted a guide! Is that too much to ask?" she raised a brow, not really asking.

A spark of hope alighted within him. She had been waiting to do this for ages. They had talked about exploring the city together right after the Exodus, and it was the first time Mark had been in New York City in almost six months. January worked in Brooklyn, so he was in and out of town every day. The commute killed him, but Mark knew he thrived on routine.

"Okay..." Mark breathed, satisfied. "To the lake, there's something I've been wanting to try."

"All right?" Rita puzzled as Mark picked up his feet and started running toward the nearest body of water. The ground was muddy and the grass was brown, but even with the patches of snow everywhere, the air was still quite pleasant for once.

Running up along a shallow pier and scaring away a flock of geese, Mark stopped close to the edge and waited for Rita to catch up. "Every time I get near water lately, I can feel Ocie." He stared out over the still lake, taking a glance at Rita. "It's like, through that element, I can connect with her, even over the distance. Like her Shadow is in all water."

Rita's brows drew together curiously. "I still havenae forgiven her for selling us out to Keller. She knew the whole time what we were plannin', and never even told us she was Shadow Hope."

"I know..." Mark sighed, sitting down on the wood. "But Shadow Hope had control over everything. No matter what she did, it was all going to work out for Hope in the end."

Gradually, Rita sat down with him. "It makes me wonder why she let us escape in the first place if it was all going to end at the ASH anyway."

She was quite close, so much that their hips almost touched, and she crossed her legs as Mark leant back. "Trust told me we were doing the right thing."

"Still bankin' on that Shadow?" Rita scoffed.

Mark pressed his lips together and nudged her shoulder playfully. "I'm done trying to convince you he exists. Even Keller said so." Getting up stiffly, Mark strode to the bank and knelt along the muddy grass to reach into the shallow water. Rita watched him with narrow eyes as he selected a single algae-covered stone. He shook the water off it and returned to the dock, using a little fire to kill and dry out the remaining algae.

"What are you doin'?" Rita asked as he plopped down beside her happily.

Mark dusted away the dry dirt on the stone. "I'm working under a theory, humor me."

"You are about as far from scientifically minded as they come!" she blared, making fun of him as he dipped the clean stone into the dark and dirty water.

"Here's the idea," he ignored her. "If Ocie can control any water, and I can sense Ocie through any water, then her Shadow must be in it. Think about how far-reaching that power can go."

Rita crossed her arms. "And I can travel to anywhere in the world. My Shadow reaches pretty far too. So what's your point?"

Chuckling, Mark laid a hand over his heart. "The concept should be the same with Shadow Fire. And that means, our Shadows are within all things, and all things pertaining to our Shadows are pure and unaffected by them until we come into contact with it."

Rubbing her temples, Rita dizzied. "You've been spendin' way too much time in the Realm."

With his eyes closed, Mark pressed his hand to his breastbone and removed his own Shadow. "If I'm right, I can put a Shadow into an inanimate object."

Rita shivered at the sight of the intensely black orb within Mark's palm, spinning tirelessly and lashing out at every droplet of dew in the air. Mark's Shadow was a wild monster, full of rage and endless conflagration. But he loved it. Nothing was a more perfect power for him.

Mark compared the two spheres, the stone and the Shadow, and drew them closer together. Shadow Fire felt the slick droplets clinging to the rock and its black tendrils lashed out at them, lapping up the water and evaporating it.

"Mark… I'm not sure this is such a good idea," Rita warned him softly, watching as Shadow Fire grew more violent the closer it got to the wet stone. It was like a raging black hole in the depths of space, angry and all-consuming. Mark was immune to the heat, but he could tell Rita felt it growing hotter.

Pressing the two together, Mark ignored her, fire sparking in his eyes as, when Shadow Fire touched the stone, it burst with flames and the intense white light of a star. In a bright flash, Mark felt his hands catch fire, and his Shadow protested, fleeing his palm and dashing back into its safe haven within his heart. What was left was a shimmering, polished, white stone.

Mark's eyes lit up excitedly. "Oh my—"

"It worked?" Rita burst up onto her knees. "Is it hot?"

Shaking his head, Mark held the stone with both hands. "It's still cold, but it's empty, like whatever Shadow it could have connected me to is gone and it's..." He hesitated, his flames searing inside him. "It's a vessel. I can put any Shadow I want into this."

"Hold up!" Rita leant back, keeping her distance. "You're goin' to do it again, aren't you?"

With a smug, lopsided smile, Mark affirmed with his eyes. The stone was smooth now, clear around the edges, but opaque in the center like ice. With no hesitation, he dipped the stone back into the water and closed his eyes, entering the Realm in his mind.

The water was black in the Realm, wavery, and it no longer had the sensation of being wet. It just felt like air, a cloud of white fog resting on a level plane in this dimension of the Realm. It had no color as Mark perceived it, not until he reached out in the Realm, for that feeling Ocie gave him. It was blue, bright and oceanic, it was warm and showered up from the depths rather than down over him. There was no gravity in the Realm, and every sensation was otherworldly.

He latched onto the blue, feeling it pass over his palm, and he held it tight, drawing enough of the Shadow into his hand to press it against the stone and pray. The light burst once more, much brighter in the Realm, and Mark had to leave the Realm just to be able to stand it.

He had indirectly harnessed Shadow Marine. He might not have been able to levitate water like Ocie, but he could still feel her Shadow in all things. The light faded abruptly, and Mark lifted his hand out of the murky water. It was dim at first, but when the water dripped off its smooth surface, the stone glowed, shimmering and blue.

Mark smiled triumphantly. It worked. He had somehow managed to infuse Shadow Marine with a stone and it was so beautiful. The blue stone looked like polished glass, mostly circular and deep blue in its center. It seemed like a galaxy in of itself and Mark was quite proud of what he had made.

"So…" Rita hummed. "What are you goin' to do with it? It's got to be good for something."

Shrugging, Mark dried off the stone with his sleeve. "I was planning to give it to Ocie, if it worked. I guess it could amplify her powers, or let me or someone else use Shadow Marine."

"This seems kind of wrong." Rita's eyes darkened, more than just a worry deep inside them. "Ocie didnae help us escape the ASH. If anythin' she made sure we'd stay there. I don' know why you feel so grateful to her."

Mark drew his brows together. "Why do you assume it's gratitude?"

At this, Rita stood up abruptly. "Well, it's that or you like her!" She chortled, punching his shoulder in jest. "Come on! Let's go explore. I'm gettin' cold just sittin' around."

Rising, Mark chased after her. "Don't worry, I've got plenty of fire to keep you toasty!" He lit his hands on fire, making her squeal and run away.

III
GOLD

The March sun struggled to peek through the clouds between the skyscrapers. Mark hadn't been to Central Park in almost a year, but it wasn't hard to find some of his favorite things. The lake was one of them, and of course, any street vendor selling pretzels. The Mall was another, but it was barren and ghostly this time of year. It was always nostalgic, bringing him back to a time when his father brought him into the city, before his sister was born, before he knew January bounced in and out of depression.

It was hard not to become melancholic, but Rita was here, so she made it much easier to ignore that pang of reality. When it was just them, and he could forget about everything else, Rita made everything happy. Her thick Scottish accent turned heads, garnered questions about whether she was visiting, and reminded Mark just how new everything was to her. He got the impression she never did anything twice, and the tininess of Mark's hometown bored her.

She stomped on his foot and boldly insisted on paying for a snack.

"How unladylike," the vendor patronized her, playing along with her snark. Mark gaped at his bruised ankle from how hard she had crushed his foot, but watched as she forked over a couple dollars. Mark barely had any money on him anyway, so he couldn't guess why she was so defensive. "Don't worry little lady, you keep him in check and he'll be buying you the nicer things one day." The man winked.

Rita smirked proudly, brandishing the two pretzels with no shame. Mark had to play along and nudged her back. "Yeah, Rita, why you gotta be such a tomboy?"

A sparkle appeared in her face, as if he had challenged her to a duel. "I don' know, Mark, why you gotta be such a weakling?"

Mark's feet glued to the ground as she left him in the dust. Sometimes, her snark and sass frustrated him to no end. She led him back out to the grass and waited with an amiable grin for him to dry a spot for them. Mark tried to be discrete about his fire in the slightly more populated area. He didn't want to cause any sort of panic, or to actually set the grass ablaze.

"So what is this, exactly?" Rita asked, lifting the twisted dough knot out of its paper cover.

Mark took his own out of her lap. "Hot, soft pretzel."

"I can read, you know," she mused, biting into the pretzel.

"Then doesn't that answer your question?"

Nodding a little, Rita lost her snark for a moment. "It's good though."

Mark sighed happily. He didn't care about her playful physical abuse—he got that from Sil too—and besides, it was her language. When they were nudging up against each other, the little bruises she left him with made him feel warm inside. Even in the damp grass, he couldn't be happier to explore with her.

"So when are you going to take me to Scotland?" he asked, watching her devour the soft pretzel as if she hadn't eaten in days.

Rita froze, her shoulders arched, and she swallowed slowly. "You'd freeze over there. You're not ready!" She played it off with a smile.

Mark frowned. "You're still not ready to go home?"

Gazing into her lap, Rita's emerald eyes dimmed sullenly. "I mean... I want to..." Her voice cracked a little. "I've seen them, but family just feels like another prison." She lowered her snack and gazed off across the park. "I was locked inside the ASH for four years, and more than wantin' to see my family again, I just wanted to be free. I wanted that before I left too, and I finally have it." She blinked away a faint tear, misty-eyed. "So why would I go back?"

No part of him wanted to pressure her. It was bad enough knowing how emotional it made her, and Mark let off immediately, hastily changing the subject. "So, um..." He massaged his neck awkwardly. "Sil has been trying to teach me how to fight. I told you that, right?"

She nodded, drying her left eye.

"I finally beat him today!" he declared excitedly. She smiled dreamily as he spoke, accepting everything he said and letting it flow over her. She didn't care, but Mark didn't mind because she liked listening, and it made her smile. Mark went on about his day and how he had fallen in the mud, losing himself in her big green eyes.

"Oh, I wanted to ask." Mark stopped himself. "Since you know my family has that spare room. If you needed a place to crash, we could easily—"

"I have a place to stay," she interrupted.

"Is it the ASH?" he asked without an extra thought.

Rita shook her head, her golden bronze hair falling around her shoulders. "After you left, a lot of older Shadows and people who cared for us came to the ASH and offered a lot of the kids places to stay. I was skeptical at first, but I checked on those who went with them and I guess they were trustworthy, so I found someone who was all right with me coming and going."

"A Shadow?"

"No, but he knows a lot about Shadows, and he has a lot of old tools and weapons made by Shadows—stuff like your stone."

Mark raised an eyebrow. "He?"

"Yeah, he's a guy!" Rita blared, hitting Mark in the arm. "But I trust him. He's given me a lot: food when I'm hungry, a safe place to sleep, a little spendin' cash. And he doesn't take any crap! If I want that bed, I'm to show up and use it at ten o'clock sharp." She smiled tenderly. "You'd like him."

Finishing off the last of his snack, Mark elbowed her. "Then why don't you introduce me sometime?"

Rita looked up startled, but she didn't waver, those gem-like eyes so sure of herself. "You sure?"

"Yeah, if I'm not intruding. You know I'd rather go with you than back home."

"All right…" Rita hummed, crumpling up her paper and taking Mark's to do the same. "Hold onto your socks." She grabbed his arm and instantaneously carried him away.

The great mist cleared over him and a rush of senses overwhelmed him when he realized he now stood indoors. Rita stepped away from him, dusting herself off, and Mark blearily looked around, orienting himself to the room. The space was mostly open with hardwood floors, and they stood in the foyer right inside the door, giving him full view of the dining room, living room, and kitchen, as well as the hall and closest bedroom, which was left open.

Everything was bright and inviting, warm and quiet, and it smelled like breakfast. In the kitchen, he spied a big silvery kettle on the stove, and even over the distance, he could sense the heat coming off it, not quite ready to boil. Taking a turn, he stepped across the wood floor and pivoted to the wall behind him, and his jaw dropped.

Across the windowless wall, upon racks and hangers of all sorts, rested an arsenal of weapons. Mark had to take a step back just to get a grasp of it. There were swords from all eras: rapiers, broadswords, and cutlasses alike, with gems and stones on their hilts: gold, silver, and bronze, a myriad of Shadows singing out to him in the Realm. He could feel it, each hilt on every sword had a Shadow infused gem of some kind making the blades powerful.

"Geoffrey!" Rita called, teleporting over to the stove to make sure the kettle hadn't been abandoned. While she was there, she crumpled up the parchment paper from the pretzels and tossed it in a nearby bin.

Mark stood with his back to her, in awe of the wall of weapons. It wasn't just swords, there was also an array of machetes and long daggers, decorated knives with intricate sculpts on their hilts, maces, and bludgeons. It was too much to take in.

"Whatcha-need?" a voice came from the back room, growing closer. "It's not like you to be here this early."

Mark turned slowly as a man entered the open space, pausing in the archway to the hall when their gazes met. The man was startlingly tall, with long brown dreadlocks and a thin scraggly beard. He looked a bit like a Viking. That might have explained all the weapons. He was quite tan, and even in the cold weather, he wore a light tank top, exposing his coppery shoulders, which were more sun-kissed than the rest of his arms.

Mark shuddered a little when he took note of a pale white scar traveling down the length of this man's left arm. Mark felt his own arm tingle with false pain at just the thought of how the man received that wound. He hugged his arm awkwardly and forced himself to step closer.

"Hello," he forced through his helpless stammering.

"This is Mark," Rita said for him, and Mark breathed a sigh of relief.

"Ah, so you're the Exodus!" Geoffrey sang excitedly. "Wow, a fourteen-year-old kid really did stick it to Keller."

"I'm fifteen actually!" Mark insisted, puffing up his chest.

Rita teleported next to him. "Not when you did it."

"So, uh... who are you?" Mark forced out quietly.

"Geoffrey James," the man introduced himself, sticking out his right hand to shake even though Mark's was locked on his left arm.

"Mark Halo." His grip was pathetic as he shook Geoffrey's hand.

"I know your name," Geoffrey scoffed with a broad smile. "I'm pretty sure Shadows in Asia know your name by now. The Exodus is a pretty big deal, and it has less to do with you blowing up the ASH than the way humans' perception of Shadows changes after the event. And there's a running bet, through generations of Shadows, over which Orchestrator is going to get to pull it off."

"But... you're not a Shadow?"

"Nope." The man seemed quite amiable as he explained, "But I've got friends in high places, and I've been in charge of guarding all these weapons while the rest of humanity doesn't fully trust Shadows."

Mark's eyes sparked with curiosity. "Who gave you all those swords?"

Geoffrey shrugged, admiring his wall of weapons. "It was my father's profession. I've gathered them with him over the years. People gave them over to me for safe-keeping, especially during the ASH years. And now that the Shadows are free, I'm getting rid of a lot. One by one, their owners are coming back to claim them."

"So..." Mark pressed his lips together a moment. "There are Shadows all over the world, older than the ASH, who were free this whole time?"

Laughing loud and heartily, Geoffrey dropped a heavy hand down onto Mark's back. "There's fifty years of

Shadows behind you, kid. You're on the tail end of the Generation."

"How old are you exactly?" Mark asked bluntly, guessing the guy couldn't be over thirty.

"Twenty-five," Geoffrey stated. "It was my father who started the weapons collecting and his father before him. Most of them Shadows, but I didn't get the lucky gene."

Mark shrugged. Close enough.

"You want a weapon of your own?" Geoffrey offered suddenly, light-footed as he rushed over to the wall. "You look like you could handle something small, I could—"

"No thanks," Mark got out hastily. "I'm good!" He glanced nervously at Rita then swallowed hard. "Besides…" He cleared his throat. "I'm more of a hand-to-hand guy myself." Maybe it was pride, because he knew he couldn't hold a candle to this guy.

Geoffrey raised an eyebrow and smirked. "You can't lie to me, kid. You've never fought anyone in your life."

"I have!" Mark insisted. "My friend Sil is teaching me how to fight, and I'm actually getting good at it."

Crossing his broad arms over his chest, Geoffrey shook his head dismissively. "And who trained him?"

Mark mimicked the taller and much stronger man. "He taught himself, refining his Shadow and spending hours in the Realm."

Finally, Geoffrey laughed. "Spending your life in the Realm and reining in a Shadow is not going to teach you how to fight." The man neared, standing tall over him intimidatingly. "You might get good at burning stuff, Shadow Fire, but what happens if someone who can't be burned or has a high tolerance for pain gets too close, what then?"

Mark felt tiny as Geoffrey demolished any notion of personal space Mark thought he had. "Who would I fight?" Mark's voice came out like a kitten's. "Why would I need to learn?"

Staring deeply into his crimson eyes, Geoffrey read into his soul, confident and overbearing as he smiled. "I think you've already answered those questions in yourself," he mused. "You don't have an enemy, but you want to conquer yourself. Refining a Shadow is an obstacle for you because you know it'll take forever, and sitting in the Realm makes you stir-crazy no matter how much you enjoy being lost in there. Am I right?"

Mark didn't have to say a word. His eyes conveyed everything, and Geoffrey walked away from him with a smug grin. It was only then that Mark realized the ringing in his ears was the hiss of the kettle, and Geoffrey had left him to turn it off.

"Are you staying for dinner, Rita?" Geoffrey asked as he began retrieving mugs from a cupboard.

Rita shrugged. "I just ate, so I'm gonna go back out. I gotta take him home any—"

"Teach me!" Mark burst, silencing both of them.

Geoffrey placed the kettle on a stone holder and looked up from the shining metal with a gleam in his eye. "No."

Mark paled. "But you just—"

"I never offered to teach you. I offered you a sword," Geoffrey snapped. "And besides, I don't do hand-to-hand, and I'm in no position to take a student. But let's face it, you don't weigh enough to be any threat in a hand-to-hand situation."

Mark's stomach writhed inside him, his frustration growing hotter. "So teach me to use a sword!" he yelled this time.

Geoffrey chuckled. "No. Get your head out of its furnace, kid. You should keep learning from your ice buddy." Still bemused, Geoffrey poured the hot water into each of the mugs. "You're mad now," he sensed, "you need to cool off, and when you get tired of losing to someone who's younger and lighter than you, you know where to find me."

"I don't actually." Mark fumed. "Rita teleported me here. I have no idea where this is."

The man ignored him a moment, selecting a box of tea from the cupboard. "You've got Rita to take you places, and it's only ten miles from your house, I think."

"How do you know that?" His suspicions rising, Mark couldn't tell if he shouldn't trust Geoffrey or if he was just mad from being told *no*.

Rita raised her hand a little, revealing she had told the man. Mark sulked but figured that was how Geoffrey knew so much about Sil as well, knowing he was cryokinetic and that he was younger than Mark. Rita sank her fingers into Mark's hand and dragged him back. "I'd love to stay for tea, but I should probably get him home before his head catches on fire."

Geoffrey grinned. "You do that. I'll see you around, Mark!"

Mark seethed, but he forced himself to mutter, "See you," before Rita teleported him again. He gasped a little when his room appeared around him. "I don't like him," he snapped under his breath.

Rita laughed easily. "You just don' like him because you didnae get what you wanted. He's willin' to train you if you play by his rules. He's been tryin' to teach me, but I havenae given him the chance."

Mark's hands tightened into fists, one still clasped around Rita's.

"Hey, relax!" she insisted, gazing deeply into his eyes. "I'll come by tomorrow. You should try a cold shower. That'll cool you off." She pried her hand out of his grip and stepped back to teleport. Even in the dim light of Mark's room, her ginger hair still looked radiant and Mark caught his gaze lingering on her. She paused before leaving him. "Thank you for today. I had fun," she admitted softly.

A fine green mist rose up around her, and she faded away as if she had entered the Realm, but Mark could no longer feel her presence. He collapsed down on his own bed, disoriented by the abrupt change. It was getting dark now, and Mark resented his musty room. He slipped into the Realm again, restless even as the comforting world wrapped around him.

He searched for Rita in the Realm to see where she had popped up, and within moments he found something. Across town, barely ten miles away and one development over, her form appeared. She had gone back to Geoffrey, to share a cup of tea with him and to quietly mock Mark from the distance. Mark smiled to himself. It seemed fitting that Rita had found someone equally as aggravating as her to give her *a safe home*.

IV
A LITTLE HUNGER

Sinking low among the garden, Emilie noted how much the snow had melted in the last twelve hours. Even in the dark, the fine starlight didn't illuminate quite as many patches on the ground, leaving the air damp. She sighed heavily as her feet touched the ground for the first time today. Sometimes it was so hard coming down, but she convinced herself this was addiction and it was here where her responsibilities lied.

Shadows aside, she loved her mother. Hellen needed her.

Summoning her tallest stance, she hurled aside the screeching screen door and entered the dark abode. "I'm home!" she called.

She could see the light on in the kitchen, but as usual, the house was bleak and rank. A few steps in, and she heard the television was on. "You're alive, right?" she asked to the air, heading straight for the fridge to start on dinner.

The TV switched off and this was confirmation enough that her mother wasn't lying dead in the living room like the couch potato she was.

"What do you want for dinner?"

"Pasta's fine," Hellen finally responded.

Emilie breathed a sigh of relief and grabbed a half-empty jar of tomato sauce. In the pantry, she scanned the shelves for a kind of noodle they had not yet consumed, and she grimaced. "No pasta, how about chicken?"

"Do you need money for groceries?" Hellen muttered, entering the kitchen groggily.

As Emilie suspected, she had slept the day away. "Here we go," she rooted through the freezer for some old chicken. "I can try to get into town for groceries if you want." She wasn't totally sure how Hellen had any money left, or where she got what she had for that matter. The woman had a mountain of coin jars in her room, and bills she got in the mail, so certainly the money came from somewhere.

Emilie never dared ask Hellen for much. Occasionally, she found twenty bucks left on the table intended for groceries, but that was never enough for the two of them. Emilie occasionally asked Sil for a little extra money, usually five or ten dollars, but she scantily ate. Eggs and leftovers—which was terrible because she could have a ravenous appetite.

Hellen stood in the dining room staring at the half-set table and the white rose in the sill, contemplating reality and the meaninglessness of life no doubt, and Emilie got on with dinner. The pickings were slim: chicken, some tomato sauce and cheese, stale bread underneath which she pretended was breading, dusty herbs, with a side of canned succotash. Only enough food for two people, but at least she'd eat tonight.

Hellen trembled as Emilie set the skillet and small saucepan on the table among designated burn marks where pan holders had long been abandoned. Emilie sat down without any patience and glanced coyly at her mother. "What are you so worried about? It's just dinner."

Flustering a bit, Hellen turned from the window, her mouth hanging open.

As if Emilie had tempted fate, her heart pounded with the loud thud of four knocks on the door. Like cannon fire, Emilie paled.

Hellen was a shut-in. She never had visitors. No one could be visiting. No one but the postman. Hellen stood up straight for the first time in Emilie's relationship with her. She pushed back her hair, released her wrist she had been pinching with anxiety, and went to answer the door.

Emilie stood up, too cautious to follow, but at least from the kitchen she'd be able to see the door when her mother summoned the courage to tear it aside. The creaky door protested, and before she saw anyone's face, she heard her mother say, "Come in."

Beyond the dark, a man stepped through the threshold, leaning in to give Hellen the briefest of hugs. "It's so good to see you."

"You too," Hellen mustered, masking the normal shakiness in her voice.

"You look good," he murmured, finding a grasp on her hand and keeping it. "How long has it been? Fifteen years?"

Hellen nodded and gestured past the hall, hastily hitting one of the well-obscured light switches to illuminate the hall and reveal the heavy dust over everything. Some of the lightbulbs were out, but just enough of them came on to cast a pale golden light onto the man's face. He didn't look anything like Emilie expected, maybe a little taller, maybe he had the same eyes as her, maybe he was where she got her wild spirit, she couldn't tell. But she knew who he was.

"Emilie?" he murmured with a hopeful voice, but cautious eyes. "Do you know who I am?"

Pressing her lips together, Emilie pretended to be cocky and poised, her hand on her hip. "You're my dad, aren't you?" she guessed confidently.

The man froze, pausing after one step into the house, then his eyes grew tender and he nodded. "That's right. How did you know?"

Emilie crossed her arms over her chest and let her feet leave the floor. "Lucky guess." She wanted to float up higher, but with meeting all-new people, she didn't want to freak them out. "What brings you here?" She wove her farce around her. She never wanted to be sociable. She wanted to fly.

Stammering a bit, the man gestured over to Hellen. "Your mother—"

She stepped up behind him and touched the edge of his arm, a brief contact before drawing away. "I invited him over for dinner. We got into contact a few weeks ago, and we've been talking about getting together so he could meet you."

Her spine stiffening, Emilie felt her knees straining and ankles burning as she put too much weight on them, but she couldn't make herself rise up. How thoughtless of her mother! How dare she! There were no groceries in the house and she'd just scoured the kitchen to make barely enough food for two people. This was an insult. She couldn't bring herself to scream at her mom. "Do you think we could go out to eat? Maybe someplace more fitting to have a family reunion," she suggested, hiding the shakiness in her voice.

Confused, Hellen looked up at her old boyfriend. "Why, dinner's all ready, isn't it?"

"Yes..." Emilie murmured grimly.

"So..." Hellen sang, her voice rising out of the depths of despair for the first time since Emilie had met her. "Why don't you put another plate down, and I'll show Greg into the family room."

The flaccid and useless woman pulled that man into the dark and musty living room where she searched for a light switch, lost for a few minutes, leaving Emilie behind, seething. What was Hellen thinking? And what kind of a name was Greg? She scoffed and flew into the kitchen, kicking herself off the wall to gain a little more speed indoors.

Irritated, she grabbed a plastic plate out of the cupboard and slammed it down on the little dining table as loudly as possible. She hoped dinner was disgusting, because as soon as the light came on in the living room, she shot for the door. Hellen wasn't perceptive enough to hear the latch open until the creaky screen door slammed shut.

"Emilie? Where are you going?" she burst, running for the cold front walkway.

By then, Emilie was already on the roof, hiding out in the dark. The little one-story house was barely a height, and they were surrounded by trees so she could go higher, but in spite of wanting to leave, she also wanted to eavesdrop.

"You didn't tell her I was coming by?" Greg's voice sounded beneath, still within the house.

"I wanted to surprise her."

Emilie scowled. *Some surprise.* Hellen couldn't even think far enough ahead to get some food in the house before asking anyone over. Not that they ever had company. In the midst of her anger, trapped down in the middle of the whirlpool of emotion somewhere, Emilie became aware of her hunger. It didn't usually bug her, but right now she was starving. She had flown all the way to Sil's and back, and she couldn't even come home to a hot meal.

She hated this place. She should have just stayed with Sil tonight. He didn't mind sharing a bed with her.

"Emilie?" Greg called, spotting her silhouette on the roof.

Emilie floated up a bit, moving slowly to the highest point of the roof.

"Hey, it's okay if you're upset. I guess you probably want some answers," he said, stepping into the damp garden to search for her way up onto the roof. "Listen, your mom broke up with me soon after you were born, she didn't want me in her life and—" He tripped over the rosebush and Emilie found herself smiling as he struggled. "—but she does want me here now. She wanted me to meet you. I'm not going to judge you for being a Shadow, and maybe, with some work, we can be a family."

"*Judge me*?" Emilie rose up abruptly. "I didn't make some choice to be what I am, and there's nothing wrong with me. What's wrong is the world, pretending Shadows are evil or something, but I don't care about them. I just want to be able to fly wherever I want." Floating down, she leant over the edge of the gutter, upside down and into his face. "I don't want anyone getting in my way! Got it?"

He looked up dead into her face, shocked to see her hanging above him, but in the moonlight, she could see his eyes. Even in the darkness they shimmered, the palest blue and she gasped, reeling back a few feet higher. "Oh my— you're a Shadow!"

"I'm not here to get in your way, Emilie. I just want to help your mother and take care of you," he assured, maneuvering through the rose bushes to come around towards the old brick chimney, which was in complete disrepair. He dug his fingers into the gaps between the bricks and with some effort he climbed up onto the roof after her.

"No... wait!" Emilie shook her head, jumping backwards across the far end of the shingles. "If you're a Shadow, how were you not taken to the ASH?"

"If you listen, I can explain everything," Greg coaxed, avoiding a patch of snow on the roof as he traversed the dangerous space. Emilie just kept backing away. He kept his voice low, not disturbed by her surprise. "There are plenty of Shadows who never went to the ASH, older Shadows who had more refined powers. And many Shadows who hid from Keller in settlements of their own."

"And, of all people in the world, you're my dad? What's your Shadow?" she demanded, the tips of her feet barely hanging onto the edge of the shingles.

"I don't care about Shadows," he insisted. "All I care about is your mother and helping her heal. Isn't that what you want?"

"How would you have any idea what I want?" She rose up, her feet leaving the roof though she remained level with him, trying to seem taller now that she was floating.

In the darkness, all she could really see was his eyes and the tender gentleness in their pale color. It was hard not to admit to herself he was being sincere. "I don't know. And I know that. I'm not going to try to get between you and your mother, or get in your way. But if you need anything, if this family needs anything, I can give it to you. I can be there."

Emilie paused, the air beneath her feeling like a thousand miles. He drew closer, paying less attention to where he stepped.

"I know she's struggling with money," Greg whispered. "She doesn't have much left. All I want is to help her."

Raising an eyebrow, Emilie smirked, hiding her defensiveness. "You'll do anything for us? Even give us money?" she confirmed cautiously, to sound as if she were easing her way into the offer.

Greg nodded confidently, "Anything!"

"Anything?" she blared skeptically. And he nodded again. Finally, she smiled with a sadistic grin. "Give me ten bucks."

Greg's shoulders dropped, shocked. "What, why?"

"You said anything!" she leered over him, rising up higher than he stood.

"All right, all right, fine." He heaved, reaching into his back pocket and retrieving his wallet. Without much fight, and clearly in an effort to gain her trust, he produced two fives and handed them over. "What are you going to do with it?"

She pocketed the cash and sneered, "Enjoy your dinner!" Then she took off to the sky, only waiting long enough to see if he'd fall off the roof or not. She didn't care if her mom was connecting with him, Hellen could do whatever she wanted. What Emilie really wanted was a nice big meal, and ten dollars would be enough for that.

V
RUBIES

Wanting nothing more than to skip dinner, Mark sat in silence at the table, surrounded by the awkward glares of his parents and his little sister's dumb smile. Mark's fire welled inside him the louder June scraped her fork across the plate. Silences like this were unbearable. Dinner was unbearable.

Marissa got up first, carrying her plate, and this gave a noticeable breath of fresh air to the table as January hastily scarfed down the rest of his dinner so that he'd finish right when Marissa closed the laundry room door within the kitchen. He got up, then June got up, and Mark stared at his plate restlessly.

All he could think about was Shadows, how he was supposed to be doing something bigger right now—not sitting quietly at dinner between his parents who hated each other. They had probably been growing apart for years now, and they weren't hiding it anymore. Mark slumped in his chair. At this rate, it was only a matter of time.

After dumping his plate in the kitchen, January hurried down the hall toward his bedroom. He was graying. His hair was getting noticeably grayer in the months since Mark had found out he was a Shadow. He could only imagine how much stress he was putting on his parents and how this was probably his fault.

He excused himself, giving June a playful look as he picked up his plate. Leaving it in the sink, he was two steps into fleeing when he heard his mother yell, "In the dishwasher," and he had to turn around and move his dishes. He took the quiet gesture to also put his dad's plate and utensils where they belonged to maybe save January from a petty argument later.

With this, he escaped to his room and to video games. Now it was just a tool, no longer a game. He couldn't lose himself in it like he used to because now he had the Realm, and in the midst of mindless motor control—his fingers acting for him—his thoughts slipped into the Realm. He covered himself with his over-ear headset and a blanket of loud music.

The beat of the song matched the pound of the gun he was using and the buzz of the vibrations within his controller. Everything was so loud he seeped into it, sank away, and was oblivious to a similar thudding that originated in reality. He only noticed it when, suddenly, his bedroom door opened and his father appeared.

Tensing, Mark hastily paused his game and batted his headphones off his ears whilst January was mid-sentence. "—need to talk to you. Can you just give me that for two minutes?" January asked, clearly trying to get through to his son.

Mark skulked and took the headphones from around his neck. "I'm all ears…" he forced, despondently.

Gradually, his father made his way into the tight space and sat down on the end of Mark's bed, blocking his view of the television. "I know you have concerns, but your mother and I are not going to get a divorce. It's just not going to happen. I need you to know that. Even when we fight, we still love each other."

Pressing his lips together, Mark adjusted himself in bed so that his back was to the windowsill. Anything to distract himself from facing his dad. He lit the tips of his fingers on fire, just to use his Shadow and maybe scare January away.

January eyed the crimson flames, but he made himself lean a little closer. "Mark, your mom and I made a promise, call it what you want, but we're never separating." Somehow, he was completely confident. "I need you to know that."

"I know," Mark snapped, half-heartedly.

Clearing his throat, January tried to do anything he could to prolong the conversation. "Your mom and I are trying so hard to get through this, but it's much more complicated than just a little fight. I'm... fighting... to figure out whatever I can about my past. I want to be able to tell you stories about my childhood and answer all your questions, but I've never been able to do that. I feel like I can't really be a father unless I tick those imaginary boxes."

"It doesn't matter." Mark shrugged, cradling his controller within his palms. "After all, what life lessons could you teach me now that I'm a Shadow?" he mumbled, not really thinking twice before he realized how hard he struck his father.

January's deep brown eyes were just like Mark's had been before he discovered he was a Shadow. They had that shock in them, the pain, everything Mark felt for those first few days in the ASH. Mark dismissed it, knowing he was being rude. January was an amnesiac. It was like living with someone with a long-term medical condition. Some days were better than others, and January thrived on only routine. However, Mark was more than a little suspicious his father's memory loss had something to do with Shadows.

"Do you really want to get your memories back?" he blurted out suddenly.

Startled, January's back became very straight. "Of course. Why wouldn't I?" Mark didn't respond, always wanting more out of his dad. "I'm sure I have a family out there, grandparents you've never met on my side of the family. Maybe I had brothers and sisters, but whoever they were they probably live over in Scotland. Obviously, Halo isn't a very Scottish name, and it's probably not my original last name. I can only guess some of the details about my childhood, and I barely remember where I was or what I was doing when I was eighteen."

Admittedly, this was the kind of information Mark wanted to know. Where had his father been when he lost his memory and started suffering from this amnesia? How could it be connected to Shadows, if at all? What pieces was he missing because his father couldn't remember anything. Mark sighed to himself. He needed answers, but he wasn't going to get them out of his dad.

"Hang in there..." January murmured. "Just be patient. I'll figure this out."

Mark nodded but grumbled. If he had a nickel for every time he heard *be patient*...

He wanted his life to be filled with crazy Shadows. He wanted every day to be an adventure, and he knew it was possible. Those adventures were just outside his reach. Maybe he wasn't strong enough yet, or smart enough, he just knew he wasn't getting what he wanted, and that made him antsy. Sure, there was a value in sitting still, being in the Realm, and growing stronger, but it was driving him crazy. The Realm wasn't enough.

January left him, closing the door behind him, but it didn't latch. Mark got up to slam it harshly, then collapsed back onto his bed. *Why wasn't this good enough? Why wasn't having a family good enough?* He was lucky! January didn't have an earthly clue where his family was, or who they were, and for one fleeting week, Mark thought he would never see his family again. Why did he take them for granted now?

He closed his eyes and entered the Realm. *Hey, Sil,* he called out, feeling across the neighborhood to his friend's house at the end of the cul-de-sac.

What? I'm trying to sleep, Sil's voice came, plenty irritated but it didn't bother Mark.

Can you do me a favor?

Not at this hour, Sil's crackly voice moaned, like ice being scraped with a sharp blade. Mark liked the sound of it, just feeling another Shadow filled him with excitement.

You've got that psychic power right, for reaching into minds? he confirmed. Sil didn't really like telling people about that, but he had a strange ability to feel into other people's thoughts and he had used this ability to locate and identify who his family was. Mark gulped, grasping the covers beneath him. *Do you think you could use it on my dad?*

Sil's voice in the Realm grew much colder and more callous, as if all at once he was very angry at the mere suggestion of doing this. *Why?*

Mark's heart raced madly. *You know he's an amnesiac. I was just thinking, you could reach into his mind and maybe find out something—anything—about his past.*

Again, why? Sil blared at him. *That's such an invasion of privacy.*

Sitting up abruptly, Mark opened his eyes, but his mind remained fixed in the Realm. *You're the one who always says if it's your power as a Shadow, you have a right to you use it.*

Falling silent for a long few minutes, he could tell Sil was thinking things over, and Mark found himself staring at the backlight of his TV glaring over his dark room. He hated it right now. He didn't want the distraction of video games. He wanted answers. He wanted to be with the Shadows.

Fine, Sil muttered half-heartedly. *But I have to be around someone to do it, and I'm not coming over right now.*

That's okay, Mark assured excitedly, jumping up from his bed. *I can connect you to him through the Realm, all you have to do is feel through me. Make sense?*

A tone of surprise rippled through the blackness. Mark couldn't see his friend, but he figured he would have been staring at him with cold cat-eyes, lecturing him without words. *No, but you have a knack for the Realm, and I trust you to figure it out.*

Mark laughed softly as he left his room, tiptoeing out to look for his dad. *You've got your psychic powers, and I'm a genius in the Realm. Maybe it's just what we're special for.*

I would not go as far to say genius, Sil mocked him, bemused.

Many of the lights in the house had been turned off, but the back-porch light was still on, and he spied his mom out there, standing in the cold. Likewise, his dad had gotten a cup of tea, a bitter green tea, probably the sencha, and he had passed out on the couch in front of the TV. Mark frowned when he saw him, not sure if January was totally asleep yet, but one thing was certain: his whole family was way addicted to television.

Mark didn't get too close. He didn't want to disturb him, but he took a seat in the reading chair, and opened himself up in the Realm, welcoming the wave of black as he closed his eyes and felt out to his father's presence. January's form in the Realm was an intangible pillar of smoke. Most inanimate objects were like that, they glowed with a strange light, and wavered when Mark got near to him. His form, however, was a statue of red fire, burning brightly.

Seeing his father's wavering form in the Realm was the only thing that assured Mark that January was human and not somehow a Shadow. It still disappointed him. *Can you feel him yet, Sil?* he asked out.

Yes... Sil's voice was soft and relaxed. *He is asleep,* Sil assured, easing his way into the use of his power. *He's dreaming. Maybe his subconscious is a good place to start.*

With a few moments, Mark waited, watching as January's constant stress melted away and he sank deeper into sleep. The hot tea on the coffee table gradually cooled, completely untouched. Marissa came in through the back door, and Mark vanished into the Realm, hiding what he was doing from her. She trudged through the house, hitting the porch light and shuffling off to bed without checking on either of her children.

I see a forest, Sil said softly. *He's in a forest. It's not dark. It's daylight, but it's cold. He's not alone, but he seems afraid.* Sil peered around in the dream world and conveyed all he could to Mark. He could see it. A heavy fog shrouded the woods, and moss coated the soft roots of all the trees where January's dreaming self sat. He wasn't alone, but in the presence of a young boy, probably less than four years old and level with January's vision. The boy had black hair and wouldn't look at January, focused on something out in the woods. The four-year-old was alert and primal, worried, but not scared. If the boy was scared, it was for January's sake.

Mark watched these images, utterly confused. This boy was protecting January. He awed. This had to be an image from January's early childhood, and Mark wanted to bet the boy was his father's sibling. He smiled to himself. His father had a brother! The boy got up in the dream, gathering Mark's attention, and hastily looking around, Mark finally saw his face.

He was dirty. Everything about him was covered in muck—his clothes, his hands, even his face—and it occurred to Mark, this boy had likely been out in the woods for a while and so had January. They were lost in the woods together. The boy's agitation heightened. They heard a twig snap and both the boy and January looked into the fog. Something was nearing them.

Mark saw the movement in the fog. A little head bobbed up from beyond a root, and a pair of tall, pointed ears. Puzzling, Mark realized it was a cat, a big one. Not much bigger than a house cat, the creature had gray fur and black stripes, and this wildcat was probably from Scotland. So, this forest was in Scotland.

Suddenly, January's head whipped around at the sound of rustling beside him, and outside of his vision a larger, black bobcat pounced over him and dashed at the wildcat, chasing it down. By the time he looked over, his brother was gone, and the black bobcat killed the wildcat.

"We got food!" the boy's voice echoed in the Realm through January's dream.

January's eyes followed the noise, and standing over the root, the bobcat looked at him with a limp animal in its mouth. The larger predator, which was clearly not native to Scotland, walked closer to January, not prowling, not stalking, just comfortable to be near the human child. It sat down and transformed suddenly, back into the four-year-old boy.

Mark covered his mouth as Sil lost focus and the dream world dissolved. He jumped up, getting out of the Realm and staring down at his sleeping father, doing everything in his power not to make any noise. *A Shadow!* The thought rippled through him and out through the Realm. January's brother was a Shadow.

Sil's voice finally reappeared through the Realm. *It seems they were lost, and it was this Shadow, his brother, or something, who kept him alive. Looks like a physical Shadow and a shape-shifter.*

I have to tell him! Mark burst out, taking a brash step toward waking his father.

No, Mark! Listen... Sil sighed, his cold breath slipping across the distance between them like the fog they'd seen.

We have not proven that his amnesia is caused by Shadows. You can think that, but it's not proof. This is not enough to determine who he was or what happened to him when he started suffering from memory loss. Let's take it slow. I can keep trying to reach into his mind. But I don't want him to realize I'm doing it and shut me out, then we'll never get anything out of him.

He can do that? Mark muttered worriedly.

Sil affirmed, *That's why I'm afraid to do this. It's an invasion of privacy.*

Can you at least—

No, Mark, Sil snapped coldly, denying any further argument. *I need to go to sleep. You should too.*

"Fine..." Mark whispered aloud, barely realizing he had spoken because he felt it again—his anger rising, the flames forming within his hands, and that rage overflowing.

VI
INHIBITION

March 3, 2031

Rita arrived bright and early, plopping down on his bed while he was still passed out. Mark jerked up at the rude awakening, but was met by her bright smile and a scream of, "Up and at 'em, lazy bones. Let's go terrorize the Shadows!"

He couldn't help but smile. He needed a good day, and her effortless cheer quelled his flames. She bounced on the bed springs, smacking him a couple times. "Let me get dressed! Leave me alone!" he yelled playfully and pushed her off the bed, prompting her to teleport away.

She reappeared outside his window, banging on it until he opened the blinds. The bushes outside his window were coated in frost, and surely it was freezing out there, but the best part was knowing she could handle it since she could teleport anywhere. He closed the blinds but couldn't stop himself from smiling. It was the uncomfortable alternation between miserable and overjoyed that he was able to forget when Rita was around.

He wrapped himself up in warm clothes, slung on a coat, stuffed his feet into warm shoes then peeked out of his bedroom door to yell, "I'm going to hang out with

Rita!" He didn't think twice when he got no answer, and she had already teleported back into his room.

"Why do you take so long to get ready?" she complained, her thick accent warming his soul.

"To the ASH?" he invited with a smile, offering her an arm.

Her eyes lit up and she bit her lip, a little intrigue in her posture. "Of course," she sang, looping her arm under his.

Mark loved having a friend to teleport him all over, but as much as he initially hated the ASH, he loved being around Shadows. Such a brief contact with Rita was all she needed to spirit him away, not just miles, but across states; all the way from New York to Virginia. When the green mist cleared, he was surrounded by white marble and the industrial architecture of the ASH.

A pair of hands came over his eyes. "Guess who." He thought they were Rita's at first, but she still held onto his arm. The hands were warm, and Shadow's power pulsed through them. The only thing that threw him off from their identity was how completely girly the accompanying voice sounded.

Reactively, Mark's shoulders tightened, and he elbowed his friend in the stomach.

Kip yelped and reeled back, laughing as Mark whirled about. "Dude, seriously!" he gasped, holding his ribs and displaying that big smile.

Kip's strawberry red curls were wild today. He didn't seem to know what a comb was or how it worked, but his golden eyes shone as bright as the sunshine outside. It was still early, but it was quite a few degrees warmer down south, and less cloudy. The nice weather gave Kip's eyes a sunny glow, and the extra light gave him energy.

Rita broke away from them as Mark gave Kip a big hug, surely cracking the younger boy's ribs in the process. He tried not to think about it, but Kip was very breakable.

"So," Mark forced, trying to figure out how to naturally have a conversation with Kip that didn't involve Shadows. "How are you feeling?"

Kip smirked, a little snark in his posture as he leant away. "Come on, Mark. Don't pity me. I'm fine." Mark inhaled to protest but fell quiet when he remembered how sick Kip had been, and how close to death the escape had brought him. "A little stir crazy." Kip chuckled. "But I'm good."

"You and me both," Mark blared, knowing he was being a little too protective.

Kip dragged him along, guiding him through the long, curved halls over the old building. "I haven't been sleeping that great, but I think that's just all the rain we've been getting. It's been too long since I've seen the sun." He sighed and closed his eyes, soaking it in through the windows. He looked a little overtired, and still really pale, but that might have just been because he was a redhead.

"You hungry?" Kip spun around. "I was waiting to get breakfast until you got here. Rita said she was gonna get you." He gestured over to her.

"Sure!" Mark smiled. "What's for breakfast today?" he asked as they entered the mess hall and the craziness of the early morning meal. So many Shadows lived here even now that the doors were open, and Kimberly still got up early every morning to make breakfast, lunch, and dinner. The kitchen window was open, and she had mass-produced eggs, waffles, and sausage, pitchers of morning drinks, and cereals ready for the taking. It looked like a huge amount of work, but she plugged away happily.

"Hi, Kimberly!" Mark called through the window as he served himself.

Her spine stiffened, his voice startling her as usual. "Oh, good morning!" She caught Rita's gaze first, garnering an explanation for his appearance. Mark smirked, Kimberly was still completely caught off guard by him.

The three of them slipped off to a table, stole some seats from some littler Shadows, and dug in. "Oh, guess what!" Kip burst, right after they started eating. Mark's attention piqued. "Today's my birthday!"

"And you're…" Mark hummed expectantly.

"I'm fifteen. I thought you knew?" Kip burst hastily.

He laughed. "Sorry, I just couldn't remember for sure because you look and sound thirteen."

Kip gaped sarcastically. "I am offended by that!"

Mark snickered. Every moment with Kip was fun. They were two Shadows of fire, and despite how different they were, he felt that was what made them fit together. Mark was friends with Sil, but there was always an air of friction between them since their Shadows were contradictory. Kip, however, was a couple months younger than both of them, and his voice still hadn't dropped, making him sound so girly.

One of the double doors opened loudly, echoing throughout the huge room and Mark looked over at a very tired, hunched, old man staggering in, surely in search of coffee. Keller looked even grayer than January. He hadn't shaved, and his hair had grown out some in the last months, but he was still a head shorter than Mark. The man took no notice of him as he joined Kimberly in the kitchen. Mark caught the smell of coffee and his suspicions were confirmed.

He shuffled out, finally catching a glance of the black-haired outsider among the young Shadows. "Oh, Mark. What brings you here?"

He had food stuffed in his mouth and just managed a loud, "Who," and pointed at Rita.

"Ahh," Keller grumbled exhaustedly. "I should have known."

"Hey, can I bug you about some Shadows stuff after breakfast?" Mark asked, taking into account that Keller likely couldn't function without caffeine.

"Sure, sure…" Keller waved him off, heading back to the double doors with his mug. "I'll be in the records room. I've got finances to deal with. Ocie will show you how to get there."

Mark scanned the room for Keller's daughter, but couldn't find her among the crowd. "Don't worry." Kip elbowed him. "I can show you where it is."

"Is he okay?" Rita asked from across the table.

Kip shrugged. "Just stressed. He had grants or something while the ASH was keeping the Shadows under lock and key, and he lost those when you blew it all up. So, I guess the ASH is a little tight on money." He ate a few bites quickly. "But don't worry, Keller's got this benefactor who's visited a few times. I think they were old friends. And I think this guy is loaning him money or something."

"He's sketchy if you ask me," Rita murmured, twirling her fork in eggs, "and Kimberly doesnae like him."

Sitting back slowly, Mark stared into his plate, burying his worry. "That's not terrifying at all." He had to fight a smile. He wasn't worried. He was anxious for an adventure. It just wasn't coming his way. As much as he wanted something grand, a conventional adventure wasn't his fate. He had *powers*! He guessed he was expecting something a little more exciting, like a superhero's job, fighting crime in New York City or some quest. But at the end of the day—all day, every day—he was just a fifteen-year-old kid who couldn't do jack, even with his powers.

They brought their plates up and Kip followed him around until Mark prompted their group toward the records room. Kip knew this maze like every sunspot on his face, and took Mark and Rita down the hall and into a library-like room with many flimsy shelves of boxes and books. Keller sat at a desk in the middle of the room, doing some paperwork and peering over a pair of reading glasses.

"Hey... I'm not bugging you, right?" Mark checked, still a little wary.

"No, not at all," Keller sighed, throwing aside his pencil and crossing his arms over his chest. "What can I help you with?"

Mark found a seat and Kip beside him, barely taking note of the rather old and velvet-embellished reading chairs he scooted across the concrete floor. Not everyone was used to Keller being a Shadow, and being the one they could talk to, but to Mark that thought was burned into him after Keller had so completely overpowered him. He hated Keller's Shadow, but the man was still a much older and wiser person, so he thought he'd take advantage of that.

"You know about older Shadows, right? Ocie told me you lived in a Shadow settlement and there was a lot of powerful Shadows. I guess, I'm starting to realize there's a lot of Shadows out there who weren't in the ASH, and I'm really curious about that." Mark kept his query topical, not yet delving into what he really wanted.

Keller threw aside his glasses and massaged his eye sockets. "Yeah, Shadow settlements were everywhere when I was younger. I lived in one of the bigger ones. And I'm guessing she told you I tore that place apart when I built the first ASI."

Mark managed a little nod.

"I didn't destroy it. The house still exists, but it's a private property and the owner closed it and stopped accepting Shadows because the ASH had taken its place. There was no need to keep an older, more volatile collection of Shadows packed together in a smaller house when the ASH was so close by. At first, Shadows came here willingly. Well, some of them did. The others ran or went into hiding."

"Hiding? Really?" Mark gasped, his thoughts going straight to his father's brother. Could that have been what happened? The brother had gone into hiding and maybe taken January's memory with him to protect himself.

Keller chuckled at his enthusiasm. "I'm thinking about getting a hold of the property to restore it, but I don't have enough money to keep this place going as it is."

"But don't you have that friend who's helping you?" Kip put in. Mark liked this, it reminded him of the first talk they'd had with Keller over tea. Mark could still remember the taste of that creamy breakfast tea Keller had given him.

"He can only give me so much, and he acknowledges that I got myself into this and I need to figure it out." Keller folded up his glasses, opening them again, and fiddling with them.

"So, I wanted to ask, do... do you know anything about Shadows from Scotland, other than Rita?" Mark asked a little hesitantly.

Suddenly, Keller's eyes lit up. "As a matter of fact..." He grinned. "Back at the old settlement, my best friend had come over from Scotland. There's a pretty big colony over there. Right, Rita? You're from that settlement?" he confirmed, looking over to her.

Rita shrugged and nodded. "But I hate it there. That's why I left. They're all eedjits, isolationists, and I have the Shadow of Teleportation. I hate walls." The pride in her voice was hard to miss.

"Did your home have... connections to this place in Scotland?" Mark eased his way in.

"Mark..." Rita hummed. "If you want to visit, you can just ask me."

"No, no, I don't want to—I mean, I'm just curious."

"Sure..." Rita sang, long and slow.

She knew him too well, able to see right through his façade. Hastily, he cleared his throat and got back on track. "I want to see if I can find a Shadow who could—"

"I didn't get the chance to answer the question, Mark," Keller chuckled. "No, we didn't have connections because they are isolationists. They have a very old settlement with many secrets they certainly wouldn't share with me. The few I met who lived there—" He gestured to Rita. "—were running away."

"Now…" Keller leant forward and folded his hands over the table. "I have records on over three hundred Shadows from this settlement and my old home. If you're looking for a Shadow, Mark, I can find them for you."

Sulking, Mark frowned. "No… I don't think you would know this Shadow."

"Well, why don't you describe them?"

Giving a floppy shrug, he thought about blurting everything out, but in the end, he wasn't looking for some uncle who obviously didn't have a clue about his American family. He wanted answers for his dad. "He…" Mark felt all the words forming on the tip of his tongue. Everything he had seen, everything he thought he knew for sure.

Seeing his hesitation, Keller exhaled slowly through his nose. "A lot of terrible things happened when I lost my first home. I didn't have anyone, or any place to stay, but I didn't just destroy my home, I ruined everyone else's. They hated me. I tried to track them down, to apologize and somehow live in peace with them, but even my best friend left me. He disappeared, and I haven't heard anything from him. No evidence of his powers, not even in the Realm. I am worried… he probably died."

Kip tensed, but Mark focused on Keller's misty eyes. He was so filled with sorrow. He had driven his own friend away, likely to his death. "He relied on me," Keller said, on the edge of tears. "He couldn't survive without my power, and I did it all for him. I made the ASI to protect him. I thought, of all people, he'd come be in the ASH and help me guide and raise the Shadows. But ultimately, he was afraid of me."

Mark gulped hard. He had been just like Kip, and the Recluse. He could see so much sorrow in Keller.

"And he was right." Keller cleared his throat and hid the emotion. "Protecting you all like that: one kid built up an immunity to Inhibitor, and the other can't go without it." He gestured to Kip.

Opposite of what Mark expected, Kip smiled brightly. "Well, then that's what I gotta do!" he declared excitedly. "I just have to go out of the ASH more. Maybe if I get out more, I won't need to be inside the ASI at all times. I can build my strength up."

As Kip glowed, Mark fell quiet in thought. Almost inaudible, he found Keller's gaze. "What exactly—"

"The lights on the third floor are out again." A girl's voice came in, and the four of them reeled around. Ocie's long brown hair swirled around her as she shut the door. "Oh... hi, Mark." She smiled, and blushed.

Keller got up and uttered a colorful curse word, shoving past her and out without a final word. It was abrupt, and Mark figured he'd lost his chance. He hated being the new face around here. The Shadows were free, he'd served a purpose, but shocking everyone when he showed up was getting old. Ocie grasped the door to follow her dad.

Mark gulped down his senses and panicked. "Ocie, wait."

She whirled about again, that long hair dancing around her, and he froze. Again, all the things he wanted to say were there, but they got stuck in his mouth. She was so perfect. He couldn't explain it. He couldn't rationalize why he froze. She was older than him. She was also a heck-of-a-lot more powerful than him as Shadow Hope. He was nothing next to her. But still, she was pretty, wise, magical, and her big blue eyes were enchanting.

"I—" he stammered, hurriedly thrusting his hands into his pockets, both of them, not sure which pocket held the blue stone. "I-I made something for you." He presented the rock, suddenly feeling stupid.

Yep, he was crushing all over a girl, and he offered her a rock. This was great...

"Oh... thanks," she managed, taking the glittering stone, which to Mark now seemed dull and completely unworthy of attention. "Wait... what is—" she stopped and gasped, giving Mark permission to look up and see her face. "This is Infusion! How did you learn to do this?"

"What?" Mark gasped, realizing his breath had stopped. "I don't know. I—I just imagined your Shadow, and I put the rock in water and it just happened."

She smiled so bright, her being seemed to ripple, her very essence like water. "Mark, this is an incredibly useful skill, and I'm impressed you figured out how to do it on your own."

"What's Infusion?" Kip asked, coming up behind Mark.

Ocie observed the gem carefully. "It's putting a Shadow into something to imbue it with our power. All Shadows come from natural things, like water and fire. You can latch onto those elements, and contain the Shadow within something like a rock or glass. Things like gems, but the most powerful vessel to contain a Shadow is a human element. Shadows might be attracted to infused objects, but they latch onto a new element. And that's how a Shadow is born."

"Okay..." Kip hummed, still confused. Mark stood in dumb silence.

"Infusions are also good for other things." Ocie played with the stone in her hands and that was all Mark paid attention to. "They're divided up into classes. This is a class one, the simplest form. It's putting a Shadow into an object. Class two is infusing knowledge or memories. Sil is good at those. And Class three can be used for healing, but you need a lot of Shadows to do that." She sifted the gem between her thumbs, rubbing and polishing the shimmering surface. She liked it. Mark could tell. It felt like it belonged in her hands.

"Here!" she said suddenly, breaking Mark's trance. She stuffed the rock back into his hand but held it steady and closed his fingers over it. "You made it, so this should be easy. Feel into it with the Realm. Focus on water, think about its shape, its movement, its color..." She inhaled deeply and slowly let him go, allowing Mark to seep into the Realm.

He could feel it. Even with its bright color, it reminded him of the murky lake water. It was very cold against his hand, and as much as he wanted to heat it up, his fire was completely cold. The stone felt wet, and he opened his eyes to water dripping through his fingers.

"Oh, look out!" Ocie jumped, spreading her hands under his to catch the water, manipulating it and levitating it up around her. "You did it! You created that water all by yourself."

Mark pressed his lips together. He didn't like her tone and he felt patronized, like he was nothing but an ignorant child to her. Still, she wasn't doing it to be mean. It was just how she talked. He calmed his heart. There was nothing to get worked up about. He gave the stone back to her hastily, before she got any ideas about letting him keep it.

"Thank you," she said with a wide smile. "I'll cherish it forever." Mark thought she was still mocking him, but the more he read into her voice, the more genuine it sounded.

He blushed. His face felt hot like rage.

"I don't mean to blow you off." Ocie grabbed the door again. "But I really need to help my father, unless you guys want to join me?"

Mark flustered and looked to Kip and Rita for some kind of support. They glanced at each other and finally Kip nodded. "Yeah, I'll help." It empowered Mark to join him, but he lagged behind, quelling the fire inside him at the thought of spending any more time with Ocie.

Menial work wouldn't have been quite so intense with Ocie around if it weren't for Mark's clumsiness. He wasn't typically an uncoordinated person, but Ocie's presence made him fumble, even dropping one of the long fluorescent light bulbs and nearly shattering it. He couldn't do anything right with her around.

Rita, however, was always there for him, catching him when he stumbled and teleporting him to his feet when he nearly fell. After twenty minutes of fixing light bulbs, Mark said his goodbyes to Kip and let Rita take him home. Rita drew her brows, fastidious and staring at the ground as they walked toward the lobby once more. It didn't occur to Mark until the circular desk came into view that Rita had no need to walk to any particular place before she teleported.

Her shoulders arched, unrelaxed, hurried to get away from people, and Mark slowed, growing worried for her. "Is something wrong?"

Rita stopped, her feet bound to the ground and her knuckles clenched at her sides. "It's nothing." With her sharp words, she started walking again.

Mark stayed. "Hey, you can talk to me, you don't have to—"

"Am I anything to you other than a mode of transportation?" she burst suddenly, whirling around at him.

"No! Why would you be—" The words came out wrong and Mark stammered, "I mean, yes, you're my friend. You're the one Shadow I get to spend time with."

Rita scoffed. That wasn't what she wanted to hear. "You've got Sil and Emilie, and they live close to you."

"You do too," Mark blurted out, now knowing where she was staying.

"That's not the point!" she snapped, turning her face away and growing more frustrated.

"Rita..." Mark reasoned. "I just love being around you. You're fun, and sassy, and yes, I do like traveling around with you." His mind scrambled as he tried to think of as many nice things about her that he could summon, but nothing changed that scowl on her face. Hastily, he stepped across the distance. "Listen, I care about you, and if something is going on, I'm here for you."

She dismissed him, but he grabbed her arm gently, just a brief contact, and with it she teleported him away. When the green mist faded, he was in his room again.

"Do you like Ocie?" she demanded with her back turned to him.

"What?" Mark gasped. "I-I mean, I do, she's—she's amazing, and powerful, and—" So beautiful. He stopped himself from saying this when he finally saw Rita's face. Her bright red Scottish cheeks were burning. He'd never seen her so angry before.

Rita stuck her hands on her hips and huffed. "And being more powerful than me makes her prettier now, does it? You don't have to say it!" she stopped him when he opened his mouth. "I saw how dumb you get when she's around. You're head over heels, and I'm invisible to you! Just a way to get to her!"

Mark didn't even notice how his jaw was hanging open. "I—that's not true, you're—"

"Your friend," Rita whispered, turning away from him again, toward the door. *Just a friend.* Her green mist enveloped her, and she was gone.

He forgot to breathe. For a few seconds it didn't make sense to, and his lungs had to remind his head to get it together. Mark deflated like a balloon and sank down onto his bed. Before he had a chance to process, just a few seconds alone, his door opened and his mother stormed in.

"Where have you been?" Marissa demanded, holding his door from slamming into the wall.

Mark hesitated much longer than he should have. "The... ASH."

His mother huffed and immediately whirled to storm out, but she paused and white-knuckled the doorknob like it was the only thing keeping her from screaming any louder. "What about school? It's Monday, and apparently you have no priorities. What? Did you just ditch the whole day to hang out with Shadows?"

The thought had completely escaped his mind. School, what was that in regard to the world of Shadows he had gotten sucked into? What was he doing? Rita had woken him up so early, he had totally forgotten.

"Isa, please…" January's voice came from behind her, soft and barely bold. "Don't take this out on him."

Marissa's mouth dropped open, appalled. "Are you seriously defending him for skipping school? Are you kidding?" Mark's heart dropped even lower when he saw his mother turn around and verbally attack his father.

"Maybe public school isn't the best thing for him anymore. Maybe we could look into other things that let him spend more time with Shadows. Because I'm sure there's a lot he needs to learn about them too." January could barely raise his voice, but Mark was shocked by his words. January hadn't the smallest knowledge about Shadows. In fact, he was terrified by them. Mark couldn't believe his father was encouraging this.

"And what? Homeschool?" Marissa blared, driving the fight back out into the living room. "And make him more of a social outcast?"

"Mom…" Mark's voice peeped out, but she took no notice. Scurrying to his feet, Mark raced out to the hallway. "I won't miss school again, I promise. You don't have to worry about me!" he tried to yell after her, but all at once he felt completely exhausted. Two arguments at once was a shock to his system, and he felt the urge again, the need to go into the Realm and hide from his problems.

Marissa reeled at him like a beast, glaring at him in the threshold of the hall and fuming as the final words fell out of her mouth. Words Mark hadn't heard in years. "Go to your room!"

Dejected, Mark's feet froze to the floor. He felt so empty, and suddenly, he felt his lungs forcibly expand and breath rush into him. He had forgotten to breathe again. Without even lifting his feet off the carpet, Mark shifted backward, and inched his way into his bedroom. Why was breathing such a conscious effort for him? Why did this make it hard to breathe?

He sank onto his bed, not even aware of his hand going for the video game controller until he realized how hard he was shaking. He dropped the controller and gaped, covering his mouth. Why was he panicking this hard? The red strands in his hair fell into his eyes and the first voluntary movement he managed was pulling back all his hair and almost working it into a ponytail.

Had Rita just walked out of his life? Just like that? For no reason? What just happened?

He could still hear his parents fighting in the other room, and no matter what he thought about, no reaction or words he could summon in his head would heal the situation or make either of them shut up long enough to cool off. The shouting only got louder, and finally, Mark heard the kitchen door slam through the thin walls. The engine of the car started. Whoever had stormed out, they hadn't left yet because he couldn't hear the clanking garage door opening.

There was a faint knock on his door, and Mark knew it was his mother who was in the car. Slowly, January turned the doorknob and peeked into the room. "Hey... I'm really sorry you got dragged into that."

Mark immediately hid his disgruntled posture and sat up straight. "It's fine, really. Thanks for defending me."

January looked worse in the light, with bags under his eyes and his shaky fingers fidgeting through the new silver hairs he'd acquired in the last few days. "Honestly... I get it." He sighed heavily and closed the door behind him. "All your life, all your memories, you've known one thing, and then suddenly it's something different. I would want to know the truth too, and I do..."

Mark nodded off slowly. "Right... your past." His thoughts flashed with the vision he and Sil had taken from his dreams. "Do you think there's anything you haven't tried yet, to maybe jog your memory?"

Smirking, January shrugged. "Go back to my first apartment, retrace my steps or book a plane to Scotland, and get lost somewhere looking for something I don't remember."

A little smile was allowed to him. "Well, you wouldn't need a plane with Shadows. We've got Rita." His voice caught, his words stung, and he remembered her outburst. Had that really just happened? It hadn't sunk in yet. Was Rita not coming back?

Within January's eyes, he was mulling over what happened. Mark had skipped school, run off with a girl who could teleport, and there needed to be consequences. He could see some kind of mild punishment on January's lips before he even spoke. "How do you feel about homeschooling?"

A little surprised, Mark sat up straighter. "You're asking for my opinion?"

January nodded floppily. "You've just had a major change in your life, and we haven't really taken time to adjust. You're old enough to make this kind of decision on your own, and regardless of what you decide, you've gotta own it."

Mark hid a scoff, poorly masking his sarcasm. *Since when were fifteen-year-olds given the agency to decide on their own education?* He did know one thing: he wanted to spend every moment with the Shadows, even if that meant leaving this family behind. He thought it over. *Okay... not totally leaving them behind.* Being able to come and go without being nagged felt better, but what kind of world would that be?

"Think about it..." January broke into his thoughts. "You don't have to decide now. But you can't make today a habit, got it?"

Mark nodded profusely, and his gaze gravitated to January's hand, firmly on the doorknob, almost leaving, but not quite. January hesitated, as always. Silence resonated between them, and Mark was able to hear the hum of the fan whirring within his game console under the TV.

"Are... you and Mom going to..." he trailed off, forcing himself to speak.

His eyes widening, January turned pale as ice. "No!" he insisted breathlessly. "We are never going to split up. Fights like this only happen because we really love each other."

Mark couldn't accept this in the slightest. Nothing about the words he had heard his parents exchange sounded like love, or even working toward some kind of resolution. He nodded, even though he didn't mean it.

"What do you say..." January left the door and knelt down in the small bedroom beside Mark's bed "...we go meet up with the Addisons like old times. We'll drag Zachary along and do something fun."

Mark smirked, not by the offer, but by Sil's birth name, which no one used except his parents. "Yeah," he breathed easily. "Let's get out of here."

VII
ARROW BLADES

Avoiding Marissa was like escaping prison, but in the fun, cinematic way. Mark and his father hadn't done anything together in well over a year, and leaving behind the girls for an afternoon was more than exciting, especially on a school day. They waited until she turned off the car and came back inside, then slipped out the front door to the garage.

As a family, they only had one car that was functional. Mark did feel a little bad for leaving his sister behind in the wreckage, but what she didn't know couldn't disappoint her. January opened the garage door and barreled out onto the street in a hurry, doing his worst at avoiding the mailbox as he scuttled them down the cul-de-sac toward Sil's house.

Barely into the Addisons' driveway, Mark hurled himself out of the car before January could even park it and dashed around the house, into the backyard. Sil was always out there, tending to his animals and enjoying the cold air. Mark grinned when he caught sight of that silver-white hair out in the tree line.

Sil jumped when he spotted Mark charging toward him. "Will you ever use the Realm to announce yourself?

How'd you get here so fast? I would've been able to sense you—"

"My dad drove me," Mark cut him off, trudging through the mud as Sil's dog came bounding after him with a big smile. Mark gave it a moment of affection, petting its joyful face until it left him alone and took off to the fence to say hello to January. "We're going out to town. Want to come with us?"

Sil spared a glance past him at January, and all at once Mark remembered what they had done last night and the visions Sil had imparted to him. "To do what?" he asked a little nervously.

Mark smirked and crossed his arms. "What, are you still nervous about being around normal people with your white hair?"

At this, Sil glared at him lividly. That was all the confirmation Mark needed. Sil was anti-social as ever, and he was still a bit of a secret the Addison family kept quiet from the neighbors. Sil seemed happy, but Mark would die in that situation.

Finally, January slipped into the backyard and immediately to the porch. "I'm going to check with your father about going out for an old favorite."

"What?" Sil deadpanned, not nervous but a little irritated.

With a little flight in his step, Mark ushered Sil toward the house. "We used to go to this shooting range, the three of us, and do archery. It's been a while, and I thought maybe you'd enjoy it."

At the back porch, Sil kicked off his muddy shoes. "Archery? Me?" he rolled his eyes at Mark's eagerness.

"Why not? You know I have a bad back and bad aim. You can't possibly be worse at it than me."

Sil smirked a little, scratching the faded burn scar on his cheek. He hesitated in the doorframe but smiled. "Fine, you have me curious."

January had already made his way to the open space of Sil's welcoming home. The Addisons' house was bigger than the Halos'. Mark always wrote off the thought with the fact that Mr. and Mrs. Addison had more children, but up until last November they'd even had a vacant guest room, which Sil now filled. Mark didn't know why he was thinking this way. He didn't lack anything materially, it was just the other holes in his life he desperately wanted filled.

He spied his father in the living room, talking in a hushed voice to André Addison, and not about scurrying off to frivolity, definitely not. Mark frowned, his muddy feet falling still on the doormat. He just wanted to escape it, just for an hour, just for a day... with Rita. His lungs protested and he realized abruptly he'd been holding his breath once more.

"Hey..." Sil murmured, elbowing him in the arm. "The day's not awful yet."

"You reading my mind again?" Mark raised a brow.

"No," Sil said, adopting a half-fake smile before treading off. "I don't have to."

Sil was effortlessly relaxed as usual, and Mark wanted nothing more than to get him to yell or do something that wasn't *cool as ice.* He wanted to fight him, to spar hard, to fall into the dirt, to laugh and breathe hard. Not stand here, stagnant as he watched his parents' marriage fall apart.

André glanced at Mark and Sil, a stern expression, before he met eyes with January and nodded. André was a good deal taller than January and he towered over his son and Mark. Sil wasn't that much taller than Mark. He only looked like that because he definitely had his father's genetics, and he was thinner and nimbler than Mark. He didn't like that thought, solely because of the fear of being overpowered or weak by comparison. Mark couldn't shake it, wanting nothing more than to have some kind of control over his situation.

Adopting a bright, warm smile, André stepped across the carpet toward the boys. "You guys ready to go now?"

"Yes!" Mark blared instantly, so loud Sil jumped a little at his eagerness. He pulled Sil along to the front door, barely giving him any time to put on clean shoes and a half-decent hat to cover up his silvery tresses. In the car, Mark watched Sil, bemused as he re-tied his long braid and wove it tightly into a knot that he could hide within his coat hood and under the hat. It might've been March, but it was still plenty cold enough that Sil didn't look odd.

Naturally, Mark was freezing, but he could tell Sil was sweating under all those layers. He was able to lighten up and forget his troubles when he was with a friend, any friend at this point, but he had to laugh at how different he and Sil were. It was a wonder how Sil put up with him at all.

Twenty minutes in the car made Sil antsy, but Mark loved it. Sil didn't like the claustrophobic space after growing up confined in the ASH, but really it was hard to see the long-term effects the ASH had on Sil. In spite of having freedom, Sil was a shut-in, he didn't socialize well, and he was much keener to meditating in the Realm or reading a book before any other activity. As far as Mark had seen in the first few months, Sil's only hobby was his animals, a chore he'd taken from his sisters and genuinely enjoyed.

The gun range was situated far outside of the city on the edge of the woods, making a safe firing area for the various enthusiasts. January was too much of a city person to care about hunting or self-defense training, but archery was simpler, less aggressive, and peaceful in a sense. Mark knew his dad loved it, and so did Sil's dad, but Mark had never been good at it himself. It had probably been two years since they'd come here last, and Mark found he could now use a full-size bow, and thus, so could Sil.

At the counter, Sil took the sleek recurve from his father, nervous and wary of the weapon he was renting for the day. Mark took his own bow and laughed. "You've never held any kind of weapon before, have you?"

"Of course not!" Sil snapped, sending a fierce tone in the Realm afterward to remind Mark, *The closest thing I have to a weapon is Frost.*

Mark held up the heavier bow and let his hand slip tightly into the carved wood. It was only forty pounds. He wasn't sure if he could draw anything heavier. But then, he was older now, and a bit stronger if Shadows counted for anything. After their fathers got a hold of their bows, each sixty pounds, they were led back to the range, and Sil got his first look at the targets and gulped.

The range was outdoors, but a tall wooden wall cut off any stray arrows from flying into the woods and an awning prevented them from flying over the wall. The only natural light beamed in from above them, and they couldn't even see it, as from where they stood, they were still under the roof of the main building. To their right was a separate range for guns, but it was quiet over there, and on a cold weekday, it was unlikely they'd be disturbed by the louder weapons.

"Well, this is gonna be fun," January grumbled sarcastically, as he slid a glove over his hand. "I can barely move my fingers. It's so cold!"

Mark laughed out loud. "Not a problem for me!" he declared, briefly lighting his hand on fire.

"Or me," Sil said in a softer voice. Of course the cold didn't bother him.

"Well, that's just not fair," André chimed in. "I never thought your Shadows would be that convenient."

January stepped up first, evidently as eager as Mark to exert a little energy, and selected one of the many provided arrows. Mark smiled a little at his promptness and the immediate change in his demeanor. January was a disheveled city person who was clearly running away from something, but as soon as he drew back the string on the sixty-pound recurve bow, he was still as ice.

January wasn't a very strong person generally, or disciplined, but he was good at this. He still was after months of drowning in everyday life. He was patient, lining up the shot and training his breathing. Mark was in awe of him, enamored by any attention his father paid him, but this was different. January was completely immersed in the target.

He loosed the arrow, and Sil's jaw dropped. It whizzed silently through the cold air, untouched by outside wind, and flying surely across the range. The muted *thud* was assurance, and January only lowered his bow after the sound resonated. They all gawked downrange at the bright red feathers stuck deeply in the third circle of the target, almost into the outermost ring.

"Well, I'm out of practice," January murmured, still quite satisfied with the shot.

"Show off," André played along, selecting an arrow for himself.

At this, Sil pushed himself onward, taking an arrow gracelessly and holding it to the right side of the bow, trying to figure out how to properly hold the darn thing.

"Hold on…" André laughed, lowering his bow, and setting it on the table before them. With care in his hands, he came around his son, exuding love as he took Sil's arms and gently guided him to place the arrow on the left side of the bow and nock it on the string. "All right, now stand up straight, pick a target." He pushed Sil toward the table about five feet off from January.

Mark grinned to himself. He hadn't seen Sil this nervous since he first met his father, and he could tell Sil was both in heaven and dying inside.

"Focus on the target in front of you, not the arrow," André whispered closely to his son's ear. "Now draw the string back, all the way to your cheek." He guided Sil but did not help him. Sil's arms shuddered, barely able to manage the forty-pound bow, his left elbow locked, and

André chuckled a little. "If you fire that now, you're going to whip yourself in the arm. Rotate your elbow."

"Do what?" Sil gasped, the tips of his fingers turning red. His right arm wasn't strong enough to reach his cheek.

"Stand up straight," André reminded him.

Sil tried but it was a pathetic effort.

"Inhale," his father chuckled. Once more, Mark caught himself breathing sharply, the frigid air biting a little more. Frost curled around the awning posts as Sil's stress lowered the temperature of the whole range.

Sil didn't listen and held his breath. His grip was shaking, the arrow twisted away from the bow, and his fingers gave out. The arrow flipped out to the left, into the dry grass, spinning like a helicopter blade, and landed on the ground ten feet from the target. Simultaneously, the string swatted Sil's left arm, and he nearly dropped the bow to examine the welt.

"Well, that was depressing," Mark blared, coming over in an attempt to reassure him, if he could.

Sil stared at his shaking right hand, across his first two fingers, the redness burned despite his ice Shadow. "You're no help," he spat.

"Trust me!" Mark cackled. "I'm worse at it than you."

Gritting his teeth, Sil tried to laugh it off. "Wanna bet?"

"I'll prove it!" Determined, Mark returned to his own bow, snagged an arrow, and aligned it, already aware of what to do, just not how to do it. Holding the bow forward, he aimed before he drew it, his left arm protesting at just the weight of the bow itself. He inhaled firmly and drew the string back. He was just aiming for the target, didn't matter where, he just had to hit that. At this rate, he'd be doing better than Sil if he only hit the back wall.

His fingers burned. The cold made it worse, and nervously he let his hand get a little hotter. For the first time, he tried to use his Shadow to assist him in archery, to make his hand a bit more relaxed, but he didn't dare actually set it on fire. That was an injury he wouldn't dare inflict on himself in Sil's presence.

He adjusted his left hand, guiding the arrow with his finger pointed at the target, or at least close to it. He could barely focus beyond the tip of his arrow, much less aim. His arm was about to give out when, suddenly, thunder struck the sky and he jumped, letting it go, letting it fly. "What the—"

He heard the *thud* and smiled, but when he looked up, he realized the arrow hadn't stuck. It had hit the wall, but it was somewhere behind the targets now. Someone was in the range next door and had fired a gun, scaring the wits out of all four of them.

"Lovely…" January blared, his accent coming out and making André laugh heartily.

"Nice shot," Sil mocked him.

"I'd like to see you do better!" he jeered in return.

Proudly, Sil took another arrow and straightened his back, smugly. "I think I will!"

"Oh, that's right," André sang, digging into his coat pockets. "I grabbed these for you guys." He tossed a pair of gloves and a pair of bracers at the table before the boys, and both Mark and Sil deadpanned. Gloves to protect their fingers, and bracers for their arms, just a few seconds too late.

They tried to ignore the loud interspersed gunshots from beyond the wall, which made a poor attempt at muting the sound. Surprisingly, after André had thoroughly shown off, Sil raised up his bow again, followed his father's instructions, and patiently drew back the string. It struck his arm again, but the guard protected him and the arrow sank firmly into the bottom of the target, in the white, but on the target nonetheless.

Mark gaped at it in disbelief. It wasn't so much that Sil had good aim, but he had the strength and discipline to catch on to archery. Sil was nothing if not temperate, Mark had known that since he met him, but he'd always seen the ice—as he did his fire—as a wild untamable thing.

They stopped taking turns, and for January's next few shots, he landed consecutively closer to the center of the target.

André played off January, elbowing him with a snarky, "Clearly you haven't lost your touch."

January took it humbly, letting André prove his worth with a couple shots, and Mark stood on, watching his father smile for the first time in a while. He didn't get out enough, letting work consume him and his wife beat down his fire. January hadn't done anything he truly loved in ages.

Mark could only focus on his dad as he kept remembering the vision he and Sil had taken from him. A very young child, alone in the woods, protected only by a Shadow. Was that really where his father had come from?

He forced himself to join them, to shoot a few more times, but as Sil did better and better on his own, Mark continued hitting the wall. His back and shoulders ached, and his hands were getting hotter in frustration. With the echo of another gunshot, Sil yelped suddenly and lowered his bow.

"Oh, my gosh…" he stood gaping, and Mark looked downrange at Sil's target. "I hit the center!" Sil gasped.

It wasn't quite dead center, but who could tell at this distance? Mark managed a smile and dashed over to his friend. "That's awesome!" He said it, but he didn't mean it. His father loved this, it was his connection to André, and Sil was actually good at this, but Mark was left on the sidelines, quietly hating it. He didn't have the patience for archery, or the strength in his back to wield such a useless weapon. There was no point to it, and it didn't expend enough energy for him to be satisfied.

It was just standing still, hurting, and aiming for the center of a stupid circle. It wasn't fighting. Sil was having a blast, and quickly lined up another arrow, but his excitement threw him off and he missed, laughing it off. "Maybe it was beginner's luck," he assured, and tried again, this time taking it slow.

Mark felt the breath rush into him again. A sour taste in his stomach had stopped his breathing again, and all at once, he was jealous.

Hiding his furious step, Mark charged back to his bow, ripped out an arrow, and aimed. As soon as the target focused in the center of his vision, he drew back, angry enough that his thumb graced his cheek and he barely even noticed he had the strength to draw the bow all the way. He'd hit the target, this time for sure.

He waited, the gun was going to throw him off, so he chose to use it, listening for the prompt, for that man over there to fire off his weapon, which used even less energy than a bow. Mark practiced patience. His arm didn't even tremble, and for all of a second, he felt completely still. The gun boomed over the wall and Mark released, his eyes sparking with crimson flames, and suddenly, the string snapped.

The vibrations of the bow knocked the solid fiberglass clear out of his hand, and the string whipped through the air, striking him across the neck as it flipped out of his grip and to the ground. Mark jumped back, not shrieking at the pain, but touching the welt and realizing his hand was on fire.

"Whoa! You okay?" Sil shouted, setting aside his bow and rushing over.

Forming a fist, Mark stifled the flame and glanced down range. "I'm fine." He could see his arrow, the very first one to hit the target. The red feathers rested to the left of the center, in about the third ring, but he couldn't really tell. He'd hit it, but he didn't feel satisfied.

Sighing, he gathered up the broken bow and trudged backwards. "I'm gonna go get this restrung," he murmured, backing away gradually.

January nodded, the slightest approval, but mostly worry. "Here," he tossed his wallet over.

Mark caught it easily, tucking it into his coat. He was thankful for a moment that January trusted him with his money because he knew for a fact there were other members of his family he would never trust with money, specifically Emilie. The doorbell rang as he swung the glass open and he was met with a rush of blessed heat within the gun shop.

Nervously, he placed the bow on the counter and looked around, alone in the shop. He glanced at the register, and the various guns chained together on the wall behind the counter, then at the silver bell and the words *ring for assistance.* He thought about ringing it, but his feet had other ideas, guiding him backward and out into the parking lot.

His breath fogged as he trudged across the asphalt, wincing at the bitter sting. January had given him his wallet but not his car keys, so he was stuck out in the cold, wishing for sunlight. He couldn't hear any more gunshots, but he did hear the muted thuds of each arrow as his father, with Sil and André, continued at it.

Alone, Mark sat down on the parking block and shivered. His life was a disorienting balance of insane, and way too quiet. If he was with people, someone was yelling. If he was alone, he wanted to dive into the Realm and never come up for air. Whatever he wanted in life, it was intangible, just as the need to exert himself, the need to fight for *something,* the need to breathe.

VIII
AMBIDEXTERITY

He sighed. There was a rock in his stomach he could do nothing about, but at least he was alone for a few minutes.

"Mark?" A voice called over, and Mark groaned. Thirty seconds and his moment of peace was gone. "Is that you?" the man asked.

He looked up abruptly and spied a man at the threshold of the shop with a long rifle case. Mark perked up a little. "Geoffrey?"

"Oh, look at that. It is you." Geoffrey smirked and stepped lightly across the parking lot. "What are you doing out here in the cold?"

Mark smirked. "I'm pyrokinetic, remember? The cold doesn't bother me."

A gleam in his eyes, Mark couldn't help but see the laugh Geoffrey was trying to hide. "Mhmm, sure, that's a lie."

Admitting it as his shoulders fell, Mark stood up and leant against his dad's car. "Me and my dad came here to do some archery, but I snapped my bowstring because my fingers were cold. There's the truth, you happy?"

Geoffrey chortled, almost the same sound Rita made when she laughed. "Wow, didn't see that coming."

Mark rolled his eyes. "What are you doing here?"

Geoffrey just raised the case. "Making sure this bad-boy doesn't get rusty."

Drawing his brows together, Mark stared at the old case. It didn't look like a modern gun case, didn't have the same locks or safeties, but it looked old and probably contained an even older weapon. Mark didn't have to ask to know that the thunder he had been hearing through the wall was not for Geoffrey's sake that he was practicing. It was for the weapon.

"What is it?" Mark asked curiously. "Aside from a really old gun."

Geoffrey slapped the case over his shoulder. "Shadow-Infused gun, a trinket my father and I picked up over the years."

"Infusion?" Mark's interest piqued.

"Oh, you know what Infusion is? I figured Keller wouldn't be spreading that technique around the younger Shadows."

Mark pushed off the car and crossed his arm. "I figured out how to do a class one Infusion all on my own, then Ocie Keller told me about Infusions."

"And that..." Geoffrey hummed without a breath in between, "is why you don't teach teenagers how to do Infusions. There's potential for them to make insanely powerful weapons that can end up in the wrong hands."

"It was just a rock!" Mark assured, getting defensive. "And it's in the ASH now, so it's not like it's a danger to anyone."

Geoffrey cackled. "I'm just messing with you, relax." He slammed a heavy hand down on Mark's shoulder. "But seriously, don't experiment with Infusion. It's dangerous."

"Fine..." Mark glowered, making the first motion to go back inside.

Bemused pity appeared in Geoffrey's expression, rash and sly, but he set his hand on his hip. "How about you put all that untapped power into something a little less dangerous?" he offered playfully.

"Like what?" Mark asked without hesitation. Now his voice came out irritated and gruff.

Geoffrey rummaged through his coat pockets, and while Mark assumed he was about to reveal some small Shadow-Infused object, what appeared was car keys, and Mark's hopes lowered with his expectations. Geoffrey unlocked his car and popped the trunk to stuff away the gun case, but he returned with a pair of full-length wooden practice swords.

"What do you say to playing around with these?" Geoffrey offered candidly.

Mark's heart pattered excitedly. "You said you weren't going to teach me!" he gasped, the words falling out faster than he could stop them.

Geoffrey smirked. "This is just for fun. Come on, let's give it a try!" Abruptly, he tossed one of the wooden staves across the blacktop at Mark.

He barely caught it, fumbling with the weight and grasping it just before it hit the ground. "First rule," Geoffrey stated loudly and Mark looked up to see him rolling his wrist with the other sword flying about him effortlessly. "This is my way. Don't question me. Don't seek out fencing terminology and doubt me. I know what I'm doing, and I'm better than you. Got that straight?"

"Um… what?" Mark flustered.

Geoffrey didn't hesitate, taking one certain step forward and leaving the other foot behind. "Second rule…" He pointed the end of his sword skyward and tucked his left hand behind him. "Don't whine like a baby when you get hit in the arms, because it's gonna happen."

He motioned for Mark to emulate the stance, and Mark did his best to mimic him. "Third," Geoffrey reached into his collar and pulled out a small, shiny, blue object: a metallic tube with a single hole cut into it. He took it off from around his neck where it was attached to a lanyard, and he proceeded to take off his coat, chuck it on the ground and stuff the lanyard into his pocket so that the object dangled out. With a smirk he met eyes with Mark once more. "Get the whistle."

The ominous words hung over Mark like a curse. His eyes locked on the blue whistle and he gulped. What was he getting himself into? His cold fingers clung to the polished wood, unsure, trembling, and causing him to doubt himself. He gripped the sword with both hands, his feet spread apart and glued to the ground, and he kept his eyes locked into Geoffrey's. He was as prepared as he could be.

Geoffrey didn't rush at him. He raised his sword, and Mark adjusted, preparing to receive the blow, but Geoffrey stopped. A twinkle appeared in the man's eye, and he stepped back. No words, not even a hint of his intentions. Geoffrey swung again, this time from below, and Mark adjusted once more, his arms twisting and fumbling awkwardly to bat the wooden sword away.

He hit the other blade, and Geoffrey parried him off, driving the tip of Mark's sword into the ground. "Easy!" Geoffrey warned as Mark tripped, and he grabbed his arm to steady him.

Geoffrey stepped away, and without waiting for Mark to acquire his stance, he swung at Mark from the opposite side, at his left, and this time Mark firmly swat Geoffrey's sword and pinned it there lightly. Mark tensed, but Geoffrey relaxed and smiled. "Are you left-handed?" he wondered.

Mark shot a quick glance down at his hands, the left above the right. "No..." he switched quickly.

Geoffrey hummed, eyeing up his stance, but rather than testing him, he swung at Mark in exactly the same way, at his left. The tip of the sword jabbed Mark in the elbow, not very hard, but Mark still jumped back nervously. "Keep your feet planted. I'm not gonna hurt you."

"What was that then?" Mark demanded a little too nervously. "If that were a real sword—"

"Go back to left-handed. You're obviously ambidextrous," Geoffrey interrupted him with a flat voice.

"What?" Mark gasped, switching, but his gaze lingered on his hands. How could Geoffrey learn that about him after just a few seconds? How come he hadn't even known himself? "If I'm... ambidextrous... shouldn't I be training with my stronger arm?"

Geoffrey smirked and relaxed his stance, flippant and a bit irreverent. "Your left is your stronger arm."

"Really?" Mark beamed a little, slightly proud of that fact. But as he thought about it, he remembered he had beaten Sil with a fist from his left arm. Archery was awkward, pointless, and his aim was awful. Maybe Geoffrey was on to something.

"Okay..." Geoffrey breathed, taking one step closer and raising his sword. "Hit me as hard as you can. I want to see how strong you really are."

Gulping, Mark nodded and raised his wooden blade. He couldn't hold back. Geoffrey could take it. Mark wanted to hit that other sword so hard it would snap in half. He held his sword like a bat and jumped a little, light-footed and springing closer. The two rods cracked against each other, but they didn't break, they reverberated, rattling into Mark's bones, and the vibrations hurt his hands to hang onto the sword. The wood fell out of his grip and onto the pavement, clattering against the asphalt pathetically.

Geoffrey sighed, unfazed by the impact. "You can do better than that." He groaned, picking up the wooden sword and handing it back to him. "Again?" he offered as a question.

Mark nodded, determined and level-headed, but he could feel the fire in his eyes. He took a step away from Geoffrey, adjusted his grip, consciously tightening his left hand and loosening his right. Like a baseball bat, he swung it, beating against the other sword and letting his hands remain firm in spite of the pain. It was immediately easier.

Geoffrey pushed back the sword, throwing Mark's balance and forcing him to take several paces away. "Come on, I know you can hit harder than that!" he jeered, a growl in his voice.

Grinning, Mark pulled back even farther, giving himself enough space to go at it from a run and to drown himself in the adrenaline. In the last second, he switched to his right, changed the direction of his swing and tried to blindside Geoffrey.

The man reacted within an eighth of a second, deflecting Mark's blow behind his right shoulder and sending Mark's sword flying into the air, but Mark held on. He wouldn't be disarmed so easily. He let go with his left hand, swinging around the sword with his right and guiding it, to strike at Geoffrey again from below.

In the same motion, Geoffrey's hilt collided with Mark's, and he jammed his shoulder into Mark's right, throwing him back down. "Oh, you think you're quick, do you?" Geoffrey mocked, only making Mark smile with elation. He wanted more.

He ran again, holding the sword left-hand first again, and swung at Geoffrey's other side, hopefully his weaker side, assuming he was right-handed. Mark barely took note of it, catching that Geoffrey's right was over his left before he put all his muscle behind the blow. Geoffrey parried him off like it was nothing.

"You're just a child," he aggressed, "drunk on the power of your new Shadow!" This time he swung at Mark and forced him to raise up and take a defensive position. "Swinging around a toy like it'll teach you a life lesson!" Geoffrey yelled, driving Mark back toward the car.

Geoffrey's sword came at Mark's left side again, where he was certain he was most comfortable, and he met the blow perfectly. Feeling the vibrations rattle through his hands filled him up with rage and fire, and he loved it. He pushed forward, throwing himself into Geoffrey and trying to fight back against someone who was obviously wildly stronger than him.

"Now!" Geoffrey threw him off, his sword between his eyes. "Hit me like you mean it!"

Mark didn't hesitate, swinging the sword back and forth madly.

"You have no technique!" Geoffrey insulted him. "You don't have a clue what you're doing!"

The blades came down on each other again, and each time it hurt Mark's palms more.

"Is this as hard as you can go? Come on!"

Now Mark was aiming for his head, a sweet rage filled his veins just like the fire rushing through them. He wasn't mad, he wasn't even frustrated. He was loving this. Geoffrey was letting him take out all his anger without any consequences.

His blade missed and struck the blacktop. Mark only had a second to process before the other sword came down on his right arm. The hit sent him to his knees and the pain shot fire across his flesh. The crimson flames spread out from him, driving Geoffrey back just one pace. Mark didn't yell. He let his Shadow react for him. The fire was his response to getting whacked in the arm.

With his left arm guiding the sword, he tried to hit Geoffrey back, but the man deflected the weak blow effortlessly. He was wide open and below his opponent. He scrambled backward. It was the only thing he could do to get good ground again.

Ever so slightly, Geoffrey hesitated, letting him get away, letting him recuperate and strike once more. Geoffrey let Mark be the aggressor, to come at him and come down on his shoulder. Geoffrey did not, however, let him land the blow. He moved, only an inch or so, freeing his right arm from the range of Mark's swing and them coming down with the hilt right onto Mark's back.

Crying out, Mark stifled a scream. He wasn't winded, but the heavy end of the sword had landed right on his spine. Mark stumbled to his knees, the sword falling free from his hands that clung to the pavement. His bare hands shivered and pain washed all over his back unlike any other.

Geoffrey stepped over him, ready to beat him one last time, expecting him to jump up and deflect it. Mark wanted to, he tried to go for the sword, but he knew he wouldn't make it. He grasped the hilt, but his breath stopped, preparing his body for the pain.

"Mark!" January screamed, sprinting out of the gun range faster than he had ever imagined his father was capable of.

"Wait..." Mark gasped. "Geoffrey, I'm done!" he pled, trying to get up before his dad did something brash.

Geoffrey immediately lowered his sword and offered Mark a hand, yanking him up to his feet.

January stormed up, fists bared even though Mark was fairly certain his dad didn't have the slightest capacity for violence. "I don't know who you are or what makes you think you can—"

"Dad, it's fine! I'm fine!" Mark shrieked, writhing to his feet even though his back ached. He couldn't make himself stand up straight, and he winced, not helping his case or Geoffrey's.

Sil and André appeared, rushing out toward them, and Mark took the distraction to pick up Geoffrey's other wooden sword. He caught the look in his father's dark brown eyes, ready to explode, ready to protect his son, and Mark groaned. After today, he'd never be able to see Geoffrey again, and he'd never get the chance to learn how to fight. He gripped the sword, his knuckles shaking, but his eyes lit up with fire.

"Teach me how to sword fight!" he demanded, thrusting himself between his father and Geoffrey.

Pausing, Geoffrey's smirk vanished, and he sent January a quick, stern look.

Mark looked from Geoffrey to his dad. "You want his approval, seriously?" he yelled through the parking lot with no regard for anyone who might hear him. "You just beat me to the ground without his permission. Just teach me! You've obviously been training with swords all your life, and I want to learn too!"

"Mark..." January murmured, his timid nature returning as Mark disregarded him.

He pushed down a little regret. He didn't really want to hurt his dad. But he was done seeking January's approval. "I've spent the last four months trying to figure out why I don't feel satisfied! Why I can't be happy with the Realm or Shadows, why nothing makes me feel like I'm doing what I should be. And nothing but fighting makes that go away. I'm supposed to be fighting! I'm supposed to be able to protect the Shadows, and you can teach me!"

"I'm not a teacher." Geoffrey crossed his arms over his chest, unflinching. "Go into a Kendo Dojo. You'll have better luck there."

"I'm not taking *no* for an answer!" Mark yelled. "You were teaching me just now, and you know it! In five minutes, you figured out I'm ambidextrous, that I can always hit harder, and I don't know when I'm beat!" He wasn't without a touch of pride in that realization. He raised up his sword, brandishing it as his own. "You don't live far away. You know all about Shadows. I want to learn from you!"

Geoffrey scoffed softly. "You're too young to know all the things I've learned about Shadows."

"That's a load of crap! I'm *Nova Liberanti!* I've spoken with Shadow Trust. I can handle it!"

"That doesn't matter!" Geoffrey insisted, brutally firm. "I don't believe in age to determine wisdom, only experience, and *you are not ready!"* He snapped, his inflection an abrupt staccato.

His hands tightening around the sword, Mark's nose wrinkled up and he raised it. "I'll fight you again! There has to be a way to prove to you I'm ready!"

Geoffrey leant on his sword and laughed. "And get beaten down again? You really don't know when to quit!"

Mark mimicked his stance. "I'm stubborn. Get over it!"

At this, Geoffrey cackled. "All right, all right, I've heard enough!" he reached out and snagged the wooden sword from Mark's hand. "If you're that dead set on learning swordplay, come over tomorrow, and by then I'll have figured out some kind of entry lesson for you."

Mark's heart dropped. "What?"

Smirking, Geoffrey wrapped the two swords together. "And I'll get you a practice sword to be all your own, but I need you to not blow up at me like that when you don't get what you want immediately."

"What..." Mark's psyche exploded.

Turning to January, Geoffrey reached out and shook his hand. "I guess we need to be properly introduced. Geoffrey James."

Suspiciously, January raised an eyebrow. "January Halo..."

"What!" Mark screamed, a smile starting to work its way across his face.

"I don't suppose you'll be wanting any kind of compensation for lessons, will you?" January wondered.

"Oh, of course not!" Geoffrey insisted. "I'm not a teacher, but I learned by experience and so can he. As long as you're fine with it?" he asked for approval.

Pleased, January crossed his arms over his chest. "Actually, I think this will be great for Mark. We were just talking about some educational alternatives now that he's a Shadow."

Mark nearly shrieked in happiness. "Is this happening?!"

Geoffrey laughed and finally acknowledged him. "Yeah, yeah, you'll get your wish. You know what..." He unwrapped one of the swords again. "Why don't you hang onto this, since you seem to be so attached to it already."

He handed it to Mark, and all he could do was tremble. He couldn't grip it, red blisters were forming on the inside of his palms and his knuckles trembled as it gingerly fell into his grasp. "Really?" he whispered, enamored by the smooth carved wood.

Geoffrey winked at him playfully. "I'll see you tomorrow, eight AM sound good?"

Half-consciously, Mark nodded, letting January work out the rest of the details as he stared at his first practice sword in awe. This was real. Geoffrey was really going to teach him. His hands were so sore, his heart was charging, and his lungs had barely caught up with the war horse that had become his soul. He was ready for this. He'd never been more ready in his life.

Geoffrey dropped a heavy hand on his shoulder, offering a warm smile, and Mark finally acknowledged it was time to leave. "I'll see you tomorrow, Mark." Geoffrey patted his left shoulder a few times, giving a snarky wink, as if to praise him on his prowess with his *stronger* left arm.

Geoffrey turned his back on him, and January nudged Mark to the car, laughing quietly at how shocked he was. "All right, mister fire-in-your-pants, let's get home."

Mark let himself be pushed along to sit in the back of the car with Sil, but he wouldn't let go of the sword. He clung to it, putting all his hope in it because, somehow, he felt like this was his purpose, and for once, everything seemed clear. Time blurred around him as they drove home. Even Sil's sarcasm was muted as his friend nudged him with a playful, "You look like one happy little warhead!"

IX
FREE GIFTS

March 4, 2031

"What are you doing?" Emilie blared the moment she set foot outside of her room. The first time her feet touched the ground was all the way down the hall and around the corner from her room, and she sank down to the floor the moment she saw the state of the living room.

The musty, dark curtains had been ripped down to let in an abundance of light into the space and many of the hoarded boxes had been dumped out and organized into trash and donation piles. This was a dream. This vision was completely impossible.

"Cleaning," Hellen declared easily.

Emilie glanced nervously at the trashcan placed in the middle of the living room and the dusty rags piled all the way to the top to conceal many picture frames and knick-knacks that Emilie knew Hellen wouldn't want to look at after committing to get rid of.

"Okay, who are you and what have you done with my mother?" Emilie joked, bemused as she drifted down to the floor near a pile of assorted ceramic figures.

Hellen smiled, effortless and bright as she threw the old curtains into the trash, balling them up and pushing them down to be rid of them. "I don't know how to explain it. I just woke up this morning, and I decided it's time." She opened a new plastic bag and started shoving paper and foil wrappers, disposable plates and napkins inside. "No more clutter, no more TV." She unplugged the old screen, which was already off and sported a thin crack across the corner.

Emilie eyed the television, taking note of the new crack in the screen, and fairly certain it hadn't been there yesterday.

Spinning about, Hellen stared at the couch where she normally slept. "Can you help me get this disgusting thing out of here?" she wondered.

Her brows shooting up, Emilie placed her hand on her hip. "You're going to have to start thinking about selling some stuff because I'm pretty sure you don't have the money for a new couch."

"Just help me," Hellen insisted in a slightly coarse tone Emilie had never heard before.

Hellen acting like a parent? That was unheard of. Emilie rose up, her shins leaving the floor last, and she drifted to the old couch. Its embroidered, beige and red fabric was mostly brown from dirt and wear, and Emilie couldn't imagine what treasures and trash had been absorbed into its depths. With a touch, she relinquished gravity's control over it, and with a shudder, the wooden frame inside it relaxed and some coins fell out the bottom. In addition, a stack of mail that had been leaning against it fell into the clean spot on the carpet.

To call that spot clean, however, was an insult to the word, and the dirt and coins underneath coated the floor. *Clean* only implied there was space to walk there.

"Where do you want it?" Emilie asked, holding up the beast with one finger.

"Outside, get it out of here!" Hellen sang, proud to be rid of it.

Maneuvering the couch carefully out the hall and to the front door, she had to be especially careful not to tip out any more trash. She had to get under it and to the door, maintaining contact whilst opening it, but she bumped the doorframe and the wood inside the couch shattered, leaving her to carry a huge lump of polyester and mildew out into the frosted front garden. She dropped it there on the side of the road where it sagged, as depressed as Hellen had been yesterday.

She whirled about, twirling in the air to rush back inside, but upon reaching the door she halted in midair at the sight of Greg there, watching her. "Oh... *you're* still here." She groaned, trying not to sound bitter.

"She already got rid of the couch?" Greg awed, peering over Emilie's shoulder and through the bushes.

"Yeah..." Emilie scratched her head. "You wouldn't have anything to do with that, would you?"

Greg gave the slightest smile, just enough to affirm, then returned into the living room and began helping Hellen declutter. He gravitated straight to the TV, picking up the old flat-screen and placing it into a cardboard box of about the same size. Emilie watched from the corner with wary eyes. She wouldn't go as far as asking aloud, *"What are you going to do without it?"* But Hellen had spent every day that Emilie had known her in front of it, often depressed and sobbing, but mostly just to numb herself.

Hellen perked up when Greg reentered the room, and he laid a hand on her shoulder. "I suppose we probably should tell you," he said. Emilie felt herself rise up to get her head above them, closer to the ceiling so she could feel bigger than she was. He was touching her. His hand wasn't just on her arm, it was deep into her soul, and she was letting him get closer.

Only briefly she glanced down into the box where the TV rested and at the crack on the screen. It hadn't been there before. She was sure of that. Why was it the TV and the couch she was so eager to get rid of?

She didn't know how, but Hellen seemed brighter, as if her soul had been set on fire within her. "Greg and I have been talking, and he invited us to come live with him in the city. It'll be closer to the Halos, and you'll have more space."

Emilie's shoulders dropped in disbelief. "Isn't that a little too fast?" she blared. "I thought you two hated each other."

"We never hated each other," Hellen assured. "We just didn't know what to do after you were taken to the ASH. We had been broken up for several weeks when you were born, and we tried to get back together, but it just never worked... until now." She gazed up into his eyes and Emilie finally saw it. Beneath his short, curly, red hair, the smirk in his eyes, Hellen loved him.

"Hold on!" Emilie nearly shouted. "You freak out when I put flowers in vases, but you let him convince you to throw out the couch? How did this happen overnight?"

"It wasn't overnight." Greg seemed cautious to do much talking for Hellen. "We've been in touch since you got back, and we felt it was finally time to bring our family back together as one solid piece. What do you think?"

Crossing her arms, Emilie steadied her frustration and glanced about the cluttered living room. It wasn't that she had any attachment to this house, and she hated living so far away from Sil. She didn't want to cling to any of Hellen's bad habits for sure, but there still seemed to be something wrong about forcing Hellen out of her old ways so quickly. Hellen was a packrat. She couldn't let go of her things.

"Living closer to Mark and Sil would be nice..." she admitted, heaving a sigh. "But if we're moving, how are we going to get all this stuff dealt with?"

"That's why I'm here," Greg offered quickly. He slipped his hand over Hellen's and gripped it tightly.

"We're going to do this together and leave behind what we don't need."

Hellen's skin crawled. Emilie could tell this was hard for her. "I'll try my best," she strained, but in looking at the progress she had already made, she seemed relieved.

"Well…" Emilie murmured, sinking toward the pile of mail. "How can I help?"

Hellen managed a smile when Greg finally took his hands off her, and she rushed over to her daughter, laying a gentle though feeble touch on her arm. "That's my girl…"

Emilie scowled and glared at Greg with piercing eyes. At no point did she even slightly trust him. Last night, Greg told her he and Hellen had broken up after she was born. It might've just been the number of years that had passed that blurred her mother's memory, but the inconsistency was a red flag.

Hellen quietly went back to cleaning, dumping piles of items into the trash until the whole bucket was filled. Emilie could see how her mother's heart broke with every precious trinket she threw away. As much as she couldn't stand the hoarding, Emilie couldn't hurt her mother, and this was utterly painful for Hellen. It was more than just being a little reluctant to get rid of something. Hellen looked at her knick-knacks and old mugs and died inside, like something was compelling her to get rid of them.

Scowling as she let one fall into the bin, Emilie kept a wary eye on her *father*, utterly uncomfortable and wanting nothing more than to get out of here. The smells of the mold they uncovered started to fill the air, and Greg opened a few windows, further illuminating the normally dark living room. The cold air seeped into Emilie's toes, making her already useless legs feel numb. She wanted to fly. She felt cramped, and for the first time, getting cleaning done felt like a chore.

She couldn't do it out of spite anymore. She couldn't quietly antagonize her mother, hoping the woman would change. This man, this person Hellen had once loved, had done it in a matter of hours, and scrubbing the baseboards no longer satisfied her. She normally liked the effort. Without gravity, exerting force was different, easier in some ways, but now, all she could focus on was Greg's blue eyes sending a chill shooting up her spine.

She wasn't sure how, but she had to get him out of here, to get him away from Hellen. Things had to go back to the way they were.

Emilie let out a sigh, certain at this point her bad attitude was more than evident. Maybe that wasn't the right thing to do. Maybe this was good for Hellen, and she needed another sudden change to break her out of the depression she'd been locked in for the last decade and a half.

Part of her thoughts went into the Realm, calling out to Sil. Her heart was so torn between him and the Shadows, and her mother and family. This wasn't who she was. She didn't settle for ties. All she wanted was freedom, but even outside the ASH she couldn't have that.

Mark couldn't get his father awake and moving fast enough. He had gotten up at six-fifty-five on the dot, getting ready in a flash and waiting outside his parents' room with his practice sword until January trudged out. His graying father stood in the doorway, a little startled, blinking confused then smirking. "You know we have an hour, right? And I need to get some tea before I can function."

He playfully pushed Mark out of the way and yawned as he shuffled his feet slowly across the carpet. Mark laughed, January's hair was insanely frizzy in the mornings, he normally tamed it down before emerging, and Mark didn't know why he didn't just cut it. But then,

Mark was also growing out his hair, and he could see the fun in fighting with it.

January set a silver kettle upon the median of the sink and filled it, almost falling back asleep as the sound of water lulled him away. Every movement January made was slow, and Mark wanted to scream, run out into the car, and drive there himself. This was so frustrating. January sat down at the kitchen table and checked his phone, which was left there every night.

Mark glanced over to the kettle on the stove, hating it, wishing the water would just boil faster. Between his father and the kettle, he was going to lose his mind. The stove wasn't even on! Stifling a growl, Mark left his father to check his phone and wandered closer to the stove, just to turn it on for his half-present dad. Just as he touched the knob, Mark hesitated, reminded of the fire in his heart, and he smiled a little.

That's it... I'm the most impatient person I know! He pressed his empty palm to the side of the kettle and very slowly raised the temperature of the metal without setting himself on fire.

A gentle vibration started to roll around inside the aluminum, steadily growing faster, but Mark didn't really notice the heat. He was used to temperatures like this, almost all the time. So when it started rising, he was just focused on making sure he didn't create any flames that would potentially set off the smoke detector. Suddenly the kettle started to whistle loudly, the steam coming out faster than it ever did when January boiled it naturally, and his father jumped.

It took a second for January to realize what Mark was doing and Mark reeled away, letting the kettle calm down as he hastily got out. "Sorry... I just wanted it to go faster!"

Perfectly bemused, January fetched a mug. "Well, if I could get the water to boil that fast every day..." he trailed off, measuring his tea and pouring.

Mark stepped back as the smells of the black tea rose. He wanted to say something snide, like, *"You could get an electric kettle,"* but he held his tongue. He had to stay in his dad's good graces for now.

January put the faintest sweetness in his tea, stirred it around and removed the loose leaves before huddling over the mug at the table and drinking it slowly. Mark couldn't make himself do anything other than stare, too impatient to move on. "Do you ever put milk in your tea?" he forced himself to ask.

Perking up and slowly becoming more awake, January shrugged. "Sometimes... why do—"

"Keller gave me tea with milk in the ASH," Mark interrupted. "It was good, so I was curious."

"Do you want some tea?" January offered, ready to get up.

Mark clung to the wooden sword, wanting to get out of here more, but being impatient wouldn't make eight o'clock come around any faster. Pressing his lips together, he nodded shakily.

January lit up, a warmth in his cheeks Mark hadn't really seen before, when Mark showed interest in the one hobby or collection he held onto. As always, everything January did was habit. Mark set aside his practice sword, January took down another mug, and he tenderly showed him how to prepare loose tea. January had a collection of infusers. It was basically the one inspired Christmas gift he ever received—a new infuser. He set the fine sieve in the mug so its handles sat over the rim, and then he measured the black, wrinkly, dried leaves.

"You only need a teaspoon. I don't really measure. Just eyeball it," he demonstrated. The hot steam clouded Mark's face as he filled the mug. "You can decide on the strength you like, but I'll make it my way this time, sound good?"

"Okay," Mark managed softly.

January pushed around the leaves with a spoon, coaxing them to open up, and adding a very small amount of golden sugar to the cup. Mark could see him basing it on the smell and the color, sensing the moment the tea was perfect and not timing it. He removed the leaves, letting the infuser drip slowly until all of the golden tea had strained out, then he set the hot mug into Mark's hands.

Once more, the hot ceramic didn't bother Mark. His Shadow made it easy, and he sat down at the kitchen table with his dad to sink into that cup of tea. It was darker and not as creamy as what he had tasted in the ASH, but it was smooth, and he could see why January collected it. He was glad for it. With the hot tea absorbing his thoughts, the time passed a little quicker, and by seven-forty-five, Marissa emerged with the aim of coffee.

That certainly motivated January to get out of there. He downed the last of his tea, used as few words as possible to explain their plans, then ducked out into the cold garage.

Finally! Mark let out in the Realm, stuffing the wooden sword into the car with him.

"Geoffrey's place is a couple miles past the Addisons', so you can hang out there if you want," January offered as they pulled out. "I'm not sure how long his lesson is going to take, but this afternoon, I want you to seriously think about what actual studies you want to focus on. Okay?"

Mark forced a nod. "So… you're actually going to let me quit going to school?"

January scoffed. "Heck no! We're going to get you some homeschool books of some kind, so you *can* focus on Shadows and training with Geoffrey, but you've got to own your other studies. No skimping on any subjects. I'm okay with you prioritizing Shadows because that's clearly where your life is headed, and I think you have the maturity to figure out your goals. Do you think I'm right?"

Panicked for a moment, Mark's eyes followed the passing houses. "Uh... I think..."

"Don't answer right now." January turned away from the street that led to the Addison's cul-de-sac. "But what do you want to do with your life? Shadows are important to you, but what do you want to do with that?"

Mark fell quiet, he was pretty sure that's what his father wanted. How could he apply his Shadow in a practical way? Fighting only went so far when he didn't have someone to fight. He needed to focus. He was too manic right now to make any kind of decision. He just needed to think it over. But first, he was going to expend that fire inside him.

January pulled into the driveway of an industrial looking house, a newer build with one story and a sweeping, inverted roof. It looked like a giant hammer had smashed it in. Mark had not seen the house from the outside until now, and it didn't occur to him how small it actually was. He rushed out of the car and up to the front door, sparring sword readied. At this point, he expected Geoffrey to attack him upon answering, and do something unexpected to train him.

The blank slab of the front door opened to a very groggy, pajama-clad Rita. She became lucid the instant she saw him and gasped, vanishing in a puff of green cloud before Mark could make a sound. "Rita!" he shrieked right as the mist faded, sending out a wave in the Realm in the hopes that she was still in the house. He dashed inside, not waiting to be invited into the familiar living room and the wall of Shadow-Infused weapons.

"Make yourself at home, I guess," Geoffrey blared sarcastically from the kitchen.

Mark scanned the house, peering down the hall for evidence that Rita was still here. He heard shuffling in the backroom. She was hastily gathering up items, probably a change of clothes for the day, and then in another puff of green light from under the door, she was gone.

"And she's off…" Geoffrey hummed.

"Ugh… what did I do?" Mark groaned as January hurried in behind him and touched his shoulder. The temperature in the house was much hotter than back home, and the lighting made Mark feel like spring was actually here. The living room had very little furniture, two vintage chairs from the seventies, but no TV anywhere. Much of the wood floor was open and warm, save for what looked like a pair of yoga mats. Mark drew his brows together, the thought entering his mind that maybe Geoffrey was teaching Rita something too. However, the thought of Rita sitting still long enough to do yoga was absurd.

Geoffrey drew no attention to the hormonal teenage girl living under his roof and laughed heartily. "You're a bit early, that's good. You're an early riser."

Mark scowled, his heart racing even as he tried to bury his bitterness. He always had been an early riser, and Geoffrey had once again made an accurate assumption about him.

"I hope it's not a bother that we're early. I have to get to work," January murmured from behind him.

"Not a bother at all," Geoffrey assured happily, striding out of the kitchen for Mark to realize he was already wearing athletic clothes. Mark tensed, regretting his choice of jeans and a plain T-shirt.

"What time do you expect you'll be done?"

Geoffrey shrugged with that confident grin. "Likely when Mark sets my house on fire." He shot a wink at Mark, instantly quelling the flames in him. No way was his unrefined Shadow going to ruin this. "Probably about noon," he amended.

"Okay." January nodded off and patted Mark's left shoulder briskly. "So you can go hang out with Zack afterwards?"

Mark nodded, white-knuckling the wooden sword.

"See you tomorrow then," January held out his hand and shook Geoffrey's before excusing himself. Mark's spine straightened when the door latched shut firmly.

"All right!" Geoffrey beamed, perfectly happy. "Let's get started!" He led Mark out into the living room and to the yoga mats. He gestured Mark to one of them, and Mark cringed, unable to will his feet forward. "Are you okay?" Geoffrey chuckled.

"Fine!" Mark snapped. It was just enough energy to push himself forward a few steps. "I thought you were going to teach me sword fighting, not... yoga."

Geoffrey took a seat readily. "First, I want to figure out where you're at with your abilities as a Shadow."

Confused, he managed to sit down as well, and he emulated Geoffrey's posture stiffly. "B-but... you're not a Shadow, so what does it matter?"

Geoffrey reached out and adjusted Mark's shoulders, aligning his chest with his crossed legs so that his posture was as symmetrical as possible. "Just relax. Are you comfortable?"

"Not really..." Mark fretted. He needed to burn energy! He needed to burn something! The last thing he wanted was to *center himself.*

"So you're Shadow Fire and *Nova Liberanti*, right?" he asked to confirm.

Mark nodded. "So that's... Fire, obviously, and *Nova Liberanti* allows me to defy all of Keller's devices that utilize Shadow Inhibitor, except when he used his Shadow directly."

"Oh yeah..." Geoffrey mused. "Your friend mentioned he *owned* you in your first fight." Mark shrank at the condescending tone and emphasis on his utter insignificance the instant Keller chose to fight him. "Do you know anything about *Nova Liberanti?*" he asked, and Mark denied. "It's a recurring title that comes with a small variety of powers, mostly temporary, and the title is intended to aid one of the Orchestrators in the Exodus."

"Ah, yeah, got that."

Geoffrey placed his hands on his knees and inhaled sharply. *"Nova Liberanti* is also known as the perfect Shadow. That doesn't mean perfect control, or perfect period. It's just perfect intent. I'm sure you're aware of the purification among Shadows that protects them from hurting each other."

"I still don't get that!" Mark hastily interrupted. "If the Shadows are supposed to be pure, how did I hurt Sil? I didn't mean to, but he attacked me and I—"

"You just proved it to yourself," Geoffrey said. "You have no intent to harm another Shadow, and your powers were immensely unrefined, weren't they?" As the assumptions Geoffrey made continued, it was almost as if he already knew everything about Mark's time in the ASH. He probably did through Rita, but it was still frustrating. "The Exodus and the Purification go hand in hand. They were the two recurring events in every generation. However, what I'm trying to get across, is that your title of *Nova Liberanti* is just that: a title. And all the powers you got through that are from the Orchestrator responsible for the Exodus."

"So... Shadow Hope." Ocie. That meant she could defy the ASH as well, and always had. She had never been imprisoned by her father's machines.

Geoffrey raised an eyebrow. "How many Orchestrators have you heard of?"

"Um..." Mark hesitated. "Well Hope, of course, Shadow Trust, and... Shadow Love. I'm pretty sure she's an Orchestrator."

"Okay, three outta five, that's good." Geoffrey's posture didn't relax even as he spoke personally, "Those are indeed Orchestrators, but that's not their main function. They are three of five sentient Shadows, with the ability to control and communicate with their wielder. Like if Shadow Fire could talk to you and influence you. Orchestrators, as a broad term, refers to Shadows with enough power in the Realm to manipulate events. And, at its core, any Shadow can become an Orchestrator with enough time in the Realm. That doesn't mean *any* Shadow can become an Orchestrator unequivocally, but an Orchestrator can be any Shadow. And believe me, it's an extremely difficult skill to hone. It's just easier for the sentient Shadows since they bear the consciousness of a Shadow that has hundreds of years of experience in the Realm within the body they currently possess."

Mark's eyes widened as the wealth of information poured over him. "How do you know all this?"

Geoffrey leant back comfortably. "Because my father was one of those five, Shadow Strength."

"Was?" Mark breathed.

Nodding solemnly, Geoffrey glanced up at the wall of swords behind him. "So much changed twenty years ago. I'm sure you understand why."

"Keller…" he scowled.

Laughing, Geoffrey shook his head. "No, not just that. The Shadows scattered. The ASH is one of the last places where Shadows gather together." Suddenly, he shook off all sincerity. "Enough about that! I need to know about your level in the Realm. What's your range like?"

Sighing, Mark felt much more comfortable. "I can reach to the ASH with Ocie's help. Our ranges about meet in the middle."

Impressed, Geoffrey raised a brow again. "That's pretty good for someone your age."

Mark was almost tempted to ask, *"What about you?"* This guy knew so much about Shadows. How could he not be one? "Am I… stronger than other Shadows?" he asked, trying not to sound haughty.

Thinking it over for a moment, Geoffrey crossed his arms. "Well… considering you didn't grow up with the restrictions of the ASI, which certainly adds to your prowess, I would say yes. And taking into account that you've only been able to use Shadow Fire for the last few months, with no knowledge of the Realm, other than peripheral—yes, I know you've had a peripheral knowledge of it. All Shadows do even before they learn to enter the Realm."

"Oh!" Mark perked up, excitedly. "And I can add to other people's ranges like Ocie can add to mine! I... connected my range to Sil's the other night, to let him use his... um, psychic powers... on my dad..." The shame set in. Why had he revealed that?

"Okay..." Geoffrey chuckled, struggling to hide his amusement. "That made next to no sense. It sounds like you're picking up on a lot of Ocie's skills since she is Shadow Hope. Which makes sense as *Nova Liberanti*, but it can't affect your Realm ability. So you're legitimately learning, not using some power or effect of *Nova Liberanti*. And as far as psychic powers... isn't Sil Shadow Frost?"

Mark nodded.

"And he doesn't have a second Shadow as far as you know?"

Mark denied.

"Okay... so here's my theory. How familiar are you with a Shadow's third ability?"

Instantly, Mark drew his brows together. "Third? But I have one—"

"Not the number of Shadows you have, doofus," Geoffrey interrupted. "You've got your one Shadow, the Realm, and..." he dangled expectantly.

Mark cringed, searching his brain for the right answer. "The... Purification?"

Shaking his head, Geoffrey laughed. "Wow... either Keller really sheltered the Shadows, or you would have benefitted from growing up with them. The Shadows have three abilities. The Realm, the Shadow they were born with, and their Understanding." He didn't really wait for Mark to comprehend anything. "Your Understanding is something you have to figure out for yourself. For some, it's unique to them, and for others, they can share the same Understanding. This is the only thing that's occasionally hereditary in the Shadows. Family members who are Shadows tend to have the same Understanding. Now... If I had to guess, from what you've told me, your Understanding could be in the Realm, but that might just be my blind optimism. And Sil's... definitely more cut-and-dry. You said psychic powers, so that might be it."

Mark thought it over nervously. "He calls it... reaching into minds, and he's always had a connection to animals. So... that's his Understanding?"

"Could be."

"What about Ocie's?" Mark wondered.

"I don't know. It sounds like it could be the same as you and Understanding in the Realm. Sometimes they're unique, other times not. It's a roll of the dice, and has more to do with your personality than your Shadow."

"Can we get on with fighting?!" Mark interrupted suddenly.

X
STRENGTH

Geoffrey raised his brows in surprise. "Forward as usual." He adjusted to sitting on his knees and chuckled. "I want you to do something first. It's going to take a lot of concentration, and that'll get you in the right headspace for sparring."

"Okay…" Mark squeaked out very softly, hiding his mild annoyance.

"Okay… close your eyes and enter the Realm, just in your mind. You do know how to do that, right?"

Guffawing, Mark sat up straight but couldn't make himself close his eyes, too stubborn and insulted. "Know? I'm good at it!" He forced his eyes shut to comply. Entering the Realm was hard this time. He couldn't focus, and for a moment, all he could catch was vague sightings in the Realm, flashes of smoky objects. "All right," he lied, not really ready.

"I want you to give me a number, to how many Shadows are in your range."

Mark laughed dumbly. Everything about this was absurd, but he wanted to get to sparring, and he didn't have to tell the truth. He sent out a wave in the Realm, touching Sil, Ocie, Emilie… and another. He drew his brows together.

"What is it?" Geoffrey broke into his thoughts.

"There's… another Shadow near Emilie. I can feel it."

"Good…" Geoffrey hummed. "But there's a lot more Shadows near you than you're picking up."

Pinching his pants, Mark cringed but felt around him, feeling for Rita's presence or another Shadow. Maybe Kip was here somehow. He did have to focus, and the smoky figures became clearer. The wall behind Geoffrey lit up with sparkling stars. The tangible objects were wavering and unsteady, but at their hearts were many colorful orbs within each weapon.

"W-wow…" Mark gasped a little and opened his eyes. "Every one of those weapons has a Shadow in it!"

Geoffrey crossed his arms over his chest and nodded. "Not all of them. But—" he grunted, rising to his feet. "I'm impressed. It's not always easy to tell if objects are Shadow-Infused. You're definitely very skilled in the Realm. And you might specialize in low class Infusions, considering you performed one without knowing what you were doing."

Mark stammered a bit more, standing up starkly and quelling his enthusiasm. "Is that an insult?"

"No," Geoffrey laughed. "Low class, as in, class one and two."

"And class two is…" Mark trailed off, trying to remember what Ocie had told him. *One, two, and three. Powers, information, and… healing!* He smiled, pleased with how quickly he was learning. "So, if there's three classes, and I can specialize in the first two, that means I'm good at a majority. Why'd you say low—"

"There are five classes of Infusion," Geoffrey said in short, stepping over to his wall of weapons and picking up a simple wooden sword just like Mark's. He didn't say anything more about it.

"What are the other two?" Mark asked, but his gaze finally locked on Geoffrey's sword and he didn't care. He whirled about madly for his own sparring sword and found it behind where he'd been sitting. He didn't even remember setting it down.

"I trust you haven't totally forgotten what you learned yesterday?" Geoffrey acknowledged his forgetfulness, swinging a small whistle around his finger. "We didn't really get to finish our game before you screamed 'mercy,' so here's how this works." He tucked the lanyard into his pocket so that the lightweight metal whistle dangled out. "You have to do everything in your power to get this whistle from me. You can play as dirty as you like, just no fire please. At any cost, get the whistle, and you win."

"That's not hard," Mark murmured, unwrapping his sword.

"Isn't it? And how are you going to stop me from beating you in the head, or your *weak little* back when you dive in to grab it," he mocked.

Mark scowled a little. Talking wasn't going to help, and he needed to strategize. Obviously, he couldn't *dive in* as Geoffrey suggested. He had to get into his blind spot, out of the range of the sword so he wouldn't get whacked. He bore up his wooden sword in both hands, readying himself and praying he didn't look ridiculous. He didn't feel ridiculous. This felt good, natural, and staring down Geoffrey's brown eyes was never more exciting.

Spreading his feet apart, Mark eyed up Geoffrey's nonchalant posture, how he leant on his wooden sword and didn't even seem to care. He wasn't prepared for a blow, not the first one at least. Mark would have to be quick.

He sprung forward, diving for the whistle, but as he suspected, Geoffrey calmly stepped out of the way, dodging the strike effortlessly, but Mark wasn't aiming for the whistle. Geoffrey didn't whirl about because he expected Mark to stumble when he missed, but Mark smiled. It had worked. He got to his knees, yes, but he used the distraction to get under Geoffrey's reach and swipe for the whistle.

He touched it, his fingers caused it to swing, but Geoffrey reeled away, light on his feet and perfectly bemused. Mark slammed a fist on the wood floor.

"Not bad!" Geoffrey sang. "Not too shabby!" The chipper voice irritated Mark. "Pretty good strategy, but you are not a sneaky person, Mark."

"How do you know?" Mark scowled.

Geoffrey shrugged, a plain insignificant smile. "Your eyes told me everything I needed to know about your plan. Especially because you're a Shadow." He stood up straight and slowly circled Mark as he rose from the floor. "Those red eyes..." he hummed close to Mark to send a shiver up his spine. "They tell me so much about you. It's how I figured out you were *ambi*, and how I knew you'd fake-out and try to get behind me. I let you do it."

With his wooden sword, Geoffrey lightly tapped Mark's ankle, startling him into deflecting it like a blow. Portraying confidence, Geoffrey continued circling him. "As a Shadow, your eyes flare. It happens all the time, mostly involuntary, and they can give away your intentions, emotions, and they communicate for you. All you can do is suppress your Shadow and pray because some Shadows are innately stronger than others."

Geoffrey threw Mark's blade off of his, sending him back stumbling, and just as he'd said it, Mark's eyes locked on the whistle once more. He rushed at Geoffrey, swinging the sword at him with his left hand controlling the weight. Maybe he could use that ambidexterity to mess with Geoffrey, and thus *get the whistle*. Mid-swing, he let go with his right hand. He left his chest open, hoping to control Geoffrey's deflection, leaving a free hand to grab the whistle before Geoffrey blew him back.

Geoffrey didn't deflect, he just held Mark at a safe distance so that his right-hand swung and missed, nowhere near the lanyard. "Dude! You did it again!" Geoffrey yelled, startling Mark just before he was shoved to the floor with a forceful foot. Geoffrey didn't hurt him, but his frustration was getting hotter.

"What am I supposed to do? Close my eyes!" Mark screamed back at him defiantly.

"There's your spirit!" Geoffrey sang in a gruff voice, encouraging Mark's madness. "I'm not looking for you to outsmart me!" He laughed suddenly. "You're not smarter than me, you're not going to be smarter than me. Right now, you're just a dumb kid!"

"Shut up!" Mark growled, fire constricting around the handle of the sword, but he wouldn't let it burn the wood.

"What?" he continued mocking. "You think you can get smarter than me? You think with enough trial and error you'll eventually outsmart me? We'd be here all month! And even then, your victory would be a fluke!"

Mark sprung at Geoffrey again, this time going for his head. Geoffrey was willing to kick him, whack him, and beat down his self-esteem. He deserved a good bludgeon to the head. The man deflected effortlessly, one-handed, left-handed, which was clearly not his dominant arm.

Geoffrey grinned with all his teeth. "There you go, there's the rage I want! You want to overcome me, not the stupid whistle!" He pinned Mark's sword with his, threatening to shove him to the floor. Mark only had one choice: push back and pray he was strong enough. Geoffrey leered into his face. "You're just about to drop out of school. This means that much to you, and you know it! Forget learning! You'll be learning, all your life, there's always time for learning. But this right now is what's important: getting stronger, that's all that matters!"

Mark's eyes widened and flared to a bright crimson. It was never about the whistle. It was never about fighting smart or dirty, he just had to beat Geoffrey. For a second, in a flash of red, the fact that he was fifteen years old and trying to beat a grown man with a glorified stick was absent from his mind. Geoffrey's words didn't demean him, they reinforced him—they empowered him!

He pushed harder, assessing his grip, left hand over the right, knuckles white, fingers red, whistle blue. He had all the clarity he needed. He kicked Geoffrey as hard as he could in the knee, sacrificing his footing, but determined it was worth it. He ducked under Geoffrey's pommel, dove for the whistle, and collapsed.

His knees hit the floor. He maintained his balance but only by releasing the sword and letting it fly over his head. He hadn't been struck, but he couldn't breathe. It hurt to inhale, and on both sides of his lower ribs, in his back, everything ached. He hadn't taken a hit. He was sure of it. Geoffrey laughed again and stepped away, paying him no heed. "There's a lesson in that. Don't sacrifice your footing."

Mark touched his stomach and gasped. It wasn't his footing—it was his spine. He let out all his breath and dropped his palms on the floor, trying to wait for the pain to subside.

"All right, get up and quit whining, you're fine!" Geoffrey nudged his shoulder with his knee.

Groaning, Mark's hair fell over his eyes as he shakily denied. "I can't... my—my back hurts."

"Pulled a muscle already?" Geoffrey raised a brow.

Continually, he quivered on his hands and knees, shaking his head. "I have a bad back... it doesn't take much."

Geoffrey plopped down on the floor next to him, offering no sympathy. "You're pretty young for spinal complications. Congenital?"

"How am I supposed to know?" Mark growled, wincing at a sharp pain in his left quarter, only a moment later realizing Geoffrey had poked him.

Geoffrey hummed slowly, rising up on his knees and setting aside his sword. "Ever been to a chiropractor?"

"What's that supposed to do with anything?" He just barely looked up to see Geoffrey glaring at him with that one raised brow. He groaned and nodded. "Four—five years ago."

Breathing was getting a little easier, but he still felt like his whole back was on fire and he didn't want to move, just focusing on the pattern of his own breath. Geoffrey shifted back once more, seemingly disappointed. "Could be a birth-defect, lower-back pain—"

"Can you stop making assumptions about me for like ten seconds. I just need to rest... it's wearing off," Mark assured, ever-frustrated, but migrating to sit on the floor as the pain subsided.

Finally, Geoffrey relaxed and concern appeared in his eyes. "Whoa, you're not exaggerating. You're in a proper amount of pain, aren't you?"

Mark nodded helplessly, his palms still glued to the floor as his only support while he kept his eyes pinned shut.

"Okay." Geoffrey heaved and got up. "Let's see what I can do. Up you go." He offered his hands to Mark, forcing him to take them, slowly by his wrists. He coaxed Mark to his feet and back toward the yoga mats. "You most likely did pull a muscle, and that... I can help with."

Geoffrey held him steady, letting him get on his knees on the mat. He laid his thumbs on Mark's back, rolling down each vertebrae until he felt the slightest tightness in the muscles. "Think you can lie on your stomach?"

Mark complied, but winced. "Sword enthusiast, Shadow expert, and chiropractor?"

Geoffrey smirked as Mark relaxed. "You pick these things up. Now you're going to feel some pressure and a snap. Just gotta stay loose."

Mark tried to hold still, but it ultimately didn't matter. Geoffrey made quick work with two hands on Mark's back and two thumbs between the vertebrae.

"There you go..." Geoffrey sang in a smooth soothing voice.

"I didn't feel anyth—"

Abruptly, Geoffrey pressed down into Mark's back so hard it cracked, kicking the breath out of him, but a moment later, the pain subsided, as if by magic. Geoffrey laughed nervously. "You okay?"

"Yeah…" Mark gasped, sitting up as soon as he could. "Thanks." There were no aches, no stiffness, just a surprising lightness and freedom to move.

"Hey, no problem." Geoffrey shrugged and hoisted himself back up. "Want to keep going?" Without any hesitation, Mark followed eagerly.

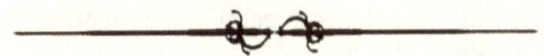

Mark plopped down on the edge of Sil's bed, not tired, not sore, but energized. More than usual. "Do you think he's right?" he asked obnoxiously, recognizing that he was starting to annoy Sil.

His friend stood by the open window, letting the frigid evening air into his room, and completely unbothered by the cold. "My Understanding?" Sil muttered, holding his arm out to receive his pet hawk and bring her inside. "I don't know…" His focus drew deeply into Winter's feathers, her pale blue eyes, and the dried blood on her talons.

"You've always had a connection with Winter, and you spend most of your time around animals anyway." Mark brought his legs up onto the bed.

Sil glared at him over his shoulder. "Stupid chickens don't count."

"Well, what about Mango?" Mark gestured to the year-old lab puppy pretending to sleep at the head of Sil's bed.

Smirking, Sil allowed Winter to climb onto his shoulder and perch there. "Overly happy puppy who likes all new people regardless. And she doesn't care about anything other than food and play." He sat down next to Mark, half-consciously petting his dog.

"You're not helping your case." Mark nudged him on the side with a bird of prey, and Winter flared her feathers, irritable and protective. "You've been in love with animals from the moment I met you."

Uneasily, Sil pulled his braid over his shoulder. "And you're *implying* there's some connection to reaching into minds?"

"Of course!" Mark declared proudly.

Shaking his head, Sil chuckled dismissively. "I refuse to believe all your flukes suggest you're abnormally strong in the Realm." He then sighed. "But at the same time… things that took me years to figure out took you the course of days, that and… Infusion."

Perking up, Mark raised an eyebrow. "You didn't know what Infusion was, did you?"

Sil nodded with a deep frown. "Much less this class two Infusion that I supposedly performed on you."

"Well, not *on* me," Mark smirked. "That was still the coolest thing I've ever seen."

The scowl didn't leave Sil's eyes. "Yeah… my least favorite memory of getting sliced open with one of Kip's lasers was the coolest thing you've ever seen. You're a sadist!"

"Not—I didn't mean—"

Sil started chuckling. "Think about it like this: in the Realm, we can read each other's thoughts, voluntarily, involuntarily, so what if you clumped together a series of thoughts then sent it out to someone to give them a lot of information quickly?"

Mark nodded expectantly. "Like a wave in the Realm, easy."

Sil deadpanned, "You're not helping."

"Okay, sorry," Mark shut himself up.

"Now, imagine those thoughts aren't your current thoughts, but a cluster of memories, sensations, images, sounds. It takes a bit more energy. I just compressed them into my element, and had you touch them. The transfer gave you that vision of what happened."

"Got it…" Mark breathed, then very slowly met Sil's gaze. "C-can I try it?"

Befuddled, Sil leant away from Mark and the puppy sat up, sensing his concern. "I'm pretty sure both Ocie and Geoffrey told you not to mess around with Infusion."

"Come on! What's so dangerous about it? I create a super-powerful, Shadow-Infused weapon, which I can give to Geoffrey for safe keeping, or I give you one boring memory of my mundane life before Shadows!"

Sil inhaled sharply. "The last thing I want is your hotheaded, trigger-happy thoughts in my head."

At this point, Mark tried really hard not to light anything on fire because the room was getting ridiculously cold.

"What I am curious about…" Sil interrupted his fidgeting, "…is why Geoffrey knows so much about Shadows when he's not one, and yet he's concerned about your back problems."

Mark shrugged. "He wants me to get stronger. He doesn't really care how much I can learn from him."

Sil folded his hands together, a tad insecure. "This doesn't sit right with me," he fretted. "The last person who knew a wealth of knowledge about Shadows and claimed to be human was Keller. How do you know for sure Geoffrey's not a Shadow?"

Confidently, Mark flared his eyes. "He had me reach out and look for all the Shadows around me. I was able to see in the Realm, literally every Shadow within my range, including all the Shadows in the weapons on his walls. He's not a Shadow, trust me."

"Okay…" Sil accepted this with a hum. "I trust your Realm ability."

"Dinner time!" André howled from the main floor, cutting off any further conversation.

"Coming!" Sil shouted back, echoing the yells from the other bedroom from his sisters. "You staying for dinner?"

Mark shrugged, hoisting himself out of the bed when Sil went to the window to release Winter. "I should probably head home..."

Sil shut the window quickly and gave a snarky grin. "You *want* to go home?"

At this, Mark beamed innocently, almost manipulative as he rushed to the door playfully. "All right, I guess I can stay."

"Good," one of Sil's sisters sang in the hall right as they burst through the doorway. "You can help us with dishes afterward."

XI
COUSINS

Spying on them through the top corner of the door frame, Emilie slowly hovered up toward the ceiling. The floor of the living room had been mostly cleared, and Hellen sat in the midst of a few final piles of rubble, crying. Emilie scowled a bit, she'd seen this a million times, Hellen's false guilt hanging onto her and making her cling to everything. It disgusted her, and she was glad for the day of cleaning.

The bookshelves had been dumped out, their contents piled and organized on the far side of the room. Greg's truck sat in the driveway, the bed filled to the brim with bulging trash bags. Almost everything in this room had been thrown away, everything Hellen owned, everything she cherished.

The front door closed, and Emilie vanished into the Realm before Greg could see her. Hopefully he wouldn't sense her in the Realm, but she had yet to see him even flare his eyes. Greg walked under her obliviously, startling Hellen as he entered the living room with a solemn expression.

"You did the right thing," he whispered tenderly, kneeling down with her on the dirty beige carpet.

Hellen didn't stifle her tears. "Just give up on everything? Just get on with it? Just... just..." she fell apart completely, and he pulled her into his arms.

The lovingness, his gentleness, he held her up in ways Emilie knew she never could. He shushed Hellen, stroked her hair, and sighed. "Not everything. I want you to have what matters most. A better life than this, and a family that loves you."

"What's wrong with my life..." Hellen groveled. "I have everything I need: a house, my daughter, you. Just depression."

Greg took her shoulders firmly. The love didn't leave his eyes even when he spoke. "You have a hoarding problem." Hellen's eyes widened in terror, alone, cold, and without anything that made her feel safe. "You know it, Emilie knows it, and you need to overcome it. Now, I'm here for you, I'm going to help you, and I'm not going to leave again." Once more he pulled her closer, letting her press her cheek to his chest. "Things will get better once we're in New York."

"But I like it here!" Hellen protested.

Shaking his head, Greg denied her. "You feel safe here. You need to get out of your comfort zone. You have a daughter to raise now, and you're not alone!"

Emilie pressed her lips together, for a brief second thankful for Greg.

"I can't just get rid of everything!" Hellen sobbed. "I paid good money for that couch, and my TV..."

Greg tightened his grip on her shoulders. "The couch is gone," he stated loud and final. "Your TV is cracked. And I have newer, nicer things at my place."

Sinking lower to the floor, Hellen tried to get out of his grip. "You cracked the TV!" she cried out. "This is all your fault! I don't want to leave here. I just want things to go back to the way they were."

"Hellen!" Greg pushed her. "It's going to be hard. I did what I had to do."

Emilie's eyes widened and she gasped, leaving the Realm half-consciously. Greg had intentionally cracked the television screen. He had taken away Hellen's addiction. This was good for her mother, but it hurt. It was ripping Hellen apart.

Hellen shook her head mindlessly. "Just get me my couch back, so we can bring it with us!"

Greg pressed his lips together. "It's gone!" he insisted. "It was disgusting, and the moment it was moved, the frame shattered. Come on, I cleared off your bed. You can actually sleep in it for once." He stood, hanging onto her hands to pull her up.

Hellen refused to budge, weak on her knees in the shag carpet. "I don't want to. It's stiff and uncomfortable, and I want to sleep on the couch!"

"Get it together!" Greg shouted suddenly, grabbing her arms and forcing her to stand. "This is your life now! Do this for Emilie!"

Hellen yelped in pain, unable to meet eyes with him and drowning in her tears. "I can't!"

"I'm doing this for you!" Greg yelled into her face. "We already started. You have to finish it!" He shook her shoulders, making her cry harder, and Emilie sank, close to placing her feet on the floor. Suddenly Greg let out a loud curse and shoved Hellen away, causing her to stumble and trip over an old, dusty lamp on the floor. "Woman, you are just as stubborn as the day we met!"

"Get away from her!" Emilie roared, diving through the empty air and hurling herself at him. He didn't fall with her touch. She relinquished gravity and hoisted him up, shoving him into the window, "Don't touch her! Don't you ever touch her!" Emilie screamed, brute force clouding her thoughts.

Barely registering the motion, Greg raised one arm high above his head, but it stayed aloft. He hesitated. Emilie's eyes lit up like fire, daring him to bring it down.

Daring him to prove he was stupid enough to actually hit her.

He lowered his arm, fuming—shocked. "I'm not the enemy here!" He towered over her. "I'm trying to help you two! There's a better life out there for you, but you have to take it!"

It didn't matter now. He had made the threat. He was capable of it. That was the only proof Emilie needed. "If you lay a hand on her again, I'll drop you from the Empire State! Got it?" She growled, suddenly aware of her incredibly skinny legs, and the lack of strength in her frail body. She could fight him.

"Emilie, Emilie!" Hellen pled, reaching out from across the floor and briefly touching her leg. "It's okay. He's right! Listen to me. He's right!" The tears still in her eyes, Emilie was completely unable to take her seriously. "He's going to give us a better life. I just need to get it together. It's just a couch." Her tears slipped. "I can let go."

Emilie's heart imploded in fear, suddenly feeling very small. She had defended that woman, and she still preferred to be bullied by her ex-boyfriend. "You are so..." she shook her head, her lips quivering. She wanted to say blind, gullible, crazy, but the word that left her lips was, "Stupid!"

Hellen sat frozen, her eyes wide in shock, and Emilie rose up, dusted the dirt from the filthy carpet off her pants, and zipped out the front door. The screen screeched, and she took off into the night. Why had she run away? Why did she always run away when things got hard? She gulped as the cold wind bit her face. She did it because she was nothing like her helpless mother who couldn't get out of her situation without being picked up by a man. Emilie could fly. Fly! Running away was *the most logical* course of action.

Across the darkening horizon she shot straight for Sil's. It was cold, her arms were bare, she only wore jeans and a thin camisole, and in a few seconds her cheeks and nose started to burn, her shoulders grew numb, and every ounce of Sil's unfeeling nature seemed both attractive and unappealing at once. She needed someone to listen, to be angry with her, and try to get Greg out of her home. Sil would talk her down. He wouldn't try to fix anything, and he most definitely wouldn't get angry.

Right now, anger was the only thing that could help, and she knew exactly who would share her frustration. She dropped out of the clouds within the familiar neighborhood, but not in front of the two-story, blue-sided family home. Rather, the small, torn house, clouded with negativity. This was perfect.

As she knew well, the latch on the window in June's room was broken, and she used it to slip out of the cold and into the Halos' little home. She heard a shriek the moment she closed the window tightly.

"He did what?" Marissa's voice sounded from the living area.

Emilie rubbed the warmth back into her arms and shivered for a few moments in the dark to listen.

"I let him! And it's fine. I feel great! I haven't had any pain in my back all day." There was Mark's voice, hopeful and desperate, barely putting up with mundanity as usual.

"This is good for him, a-and he's studying Shadows with Geoffrey," January put in, using the same tone as Mark, only slightly less assertive.

"I don't want to argue about this." Marissa groaned, exasperated. "Just go get ready for dinner."

"I'm not hungry," Mark retorted.

"So what, did you eat over there as well? You're just avoiding home completely?"

"No, I'm just not hungry!" Mark's footsteps stomped down the hall, passing June's room. He slammed his door and Emilie sighed, her shivers subsiding.

She noticed a dull blue light and glanced to the far side of the room where a TV was lit with a violent battle royale game. Jumping, she whirled about when she realized it was being played, not paused, not replaying.

"You here to take him away again?" June's snarky voice came in the midst of clicking buttons on her controller.

"Uh no..." Emilie spat, matching the six-year-old's spunk.

"Mhmm, sure..." June mashed the buttons aggressively. "Take him out to dinner, will you? He skipped breakfast too."

"I'm not Rita. You do realize that, right?"

June raised an eyebrow, not taking her eyes off the screen. "I know, they had a big fight yesterday, and Rita wouldn't sneak in my window. That's totally your style."

Emilie waved her off dismissively, entering the Realm and slipping out silently. She had to keep to the ceiling to prevent her shadow from being cast, but reaching Mark's room undetected was easy. The door was shut tight, and locked upon first testing, but she opened herself in the Realm, to let him know she was there without knocking.

He didn't peek out, just opening the door fully for a second or two, and then locked it once more. "It's not like you to announce yourself..." he grumbled and plopped down on his bed with another game controller. The TV in his room was already on and loaded with the same game June was playing, but he hadn't started a round.

She left the Realm and sank down to the floor. Despite Mark's cluttered bedroom, the carpet was clean. It didn't smell or cake her in dust. It was a relief to get out of that little country house. "So, what was that all about?"

Mark heaved a sigh and started flicking through the menu screens absently. "My parents are talking about taking me out of school because I missed a couple of days. I finally found someone to teach me about Shadows and how to fight, and they think he's creepy because he cracked my back. Did I miss anything?"

Floating about, she collapsed down with him under his window blinds. "Story of my life right there." She groaned. "My dad popped up out of nowhere and convinced my mom to deep clean. She's even more depressed than usual, and I think Greg is shoving her around and bullying her into moving."

Mark perked up and leant forward in bed. "Your dad came back?"

"What? You know something about him?" she deadpanned.

Shaking his head, Mark set aside the controller. "No, I've never met him. All I know is that he bailed on her when you were born."

She crossed her arms over her chest. "That's the gist of the story I'm getting."

"So... do you not want to move?"

"No, moving is fine! It's closer to here! It's fine!" Emilie assured, letting her frustrations out. "Anything to get out of that disgusting, mold-ridden dump. It's just with Greg. I don't think he really wants to help my mom, but I can't figure out what his motivations are."

Mark laughed brightly. "Same with Geoffrey! One second he'll be dumping all this information about Shadows on me, and the next he's like, 'You don't need to learn, you don't need to be smart, just fight me.'" Mark mimicked an older voice playfully. "I can't get a read on what he wants."

"Clearly, you're not getting an overwhelming sense of dread though, are you?" Emilie grimaced, "I can't shake it. I mean, I love her, but I can't stay cooped up in there. I have to fly! I've been waiting my whole life to just fly and do whatever I want. But she's tying me down, and she doesn't even know it."

"What do you want to do?"

Emilie answered without hesitation, "Fly! Duh!"

"No, I mean about Aunt Hellen." Mark gave a little smirk. "Trust me, I've known her all my life, and she's the definition of *toxic personality*. But if anyone can show her who's boss, it's you."

Taking a little encouragement, Emilie tried to smile, but the more she thought on it, she realized that wasn't a compliment. "I don't want to be her boss. I want to be her daughter. Just a normal relationship. Is that so hard? Like, cleaning my room, or *getting ready for dinner*." She slapped Mark's arm. "But I'm not going to get that from her, am I?"

"Sounds like you could though." Mark nudged her back. "Greg gives you a bad vibe, but maybe you could try moving and see how you feel after. Maybe he's just trying to help your mom."

"Tough love." Emilie guffawed. "He's got something right. That's the only way to get her to move." She pulled her legs up to her chest and sulked. "So we both got weird men in our lives. They're trying to help, but they're hard to trust..."

Mark pressed his lips together. "I trust Geoffrey," he murmured with complete surety in his tone. "In three days, I've learned more about Shadows than my entire time in the ASH."

"So, do we wait it out, or make a plan?" She glanced over her shoulder at the fading light and fiddled with the old spaghetti strap of her camisole.

Mark shrugged. "We've got a spare room if you need a place to crash."

"And if you need a flight to the ASH, just give me the word," Emilie offered.

"Why would—"

"June told me about Rita."

Mark's face clouded with bitterness.

"What happened?"

Mark's eyes drifted to the ceiling, searching for words or excuses until he finally growled and let his arms fall limp. "She said I treated her like a mode of transportation!

Which makes no sense because she was the one coming here every day and taking me out places."

Emilie snorted, struggling to keep herself from laughing. "Well, somebody's got a huge crush on you."

"What! No," Mark denied adamantly. "She's my friend, we get along really well, and I like exploring with her, traveling and stuff. It was just when we saw Ocie that she—"

"Oh..." Emilie cut him off and finally cackled. "Don't worry, dude..." She slapped his shoulder briskly. "This is a classic case of jealous female. You got nothing to worry about! Once she figures out you're not into Ocie, she'll—"

"But what if I do like Ocie?" Mark felt his cheeks burning a little, like his blood was boiling, and Shadow Fire was screwing with his body temperature.

"Then *hell hath no fury like a woman scorned!*"

Mark's eyes narrowed. "Thanks, you're making me feel *so* much better."

"Relax, she'll get over it!" Emilie assured, still wiping the tears from her eyes. "Rita is a free spirit like me. She just doesn't—"

"I'm going to have to beg to differ," Mark interrupted in a cold voice. "I know I haven't known her that long, but... Rita just wants a safe place where she's not going to get judged, where she can always come back to. I guess, I was that to her, and so is Geoffrey, but now that she knows I'm kinda crushing on Ocie..." he blushed helplessly, unable to finish.

Emilie smiled, bemused by how smitten her cousin was. "I don't think it's right to tell you this, but I'm gonna warn you now. She's way outta your league." Again, she laid a hand on Mark's shoulder and shook his attention. "Pick one, and be honest! That's the only thing you can do."

"Thanks," he whispered, this time really meaning it. He let his eyes drift to the glowing TV, distracted and silent for a minute. He glazed over, his thoughts running rampant for a while. "Would you talk to her for me?" he asked finally.

"I can try," she shrugged.

"Are you going to stay for a while?" Mark offered, gentle and kind, not as hot-headed as she wanted.

"Nah," she denied floppily. "I'm going to hang out with Sil for a bit, then head home. I have a lot of cleaning to do apparently."

Mark grinned sheepishly. "It would be nice if you lived closer. I know everyone acts annoyed with you, but I really like having you around."

Emilie rose up, yanking the blinds' string to open the window. "Just... keep yourself open in the Realm," she strained. "Turns out my dad is a Shadow and he hid from the ASH, so I'm more than a little suspicious."

His eyes widened a bit, but he wasn't as shocked as she expected him to be. He just frowned and nodded. "I was able to sense him in the Realm. Don't worry, I'll keep an ear out for you."

Placing her legs out the small window, Emilie smiled weakly, tossing her dark hair behind her back. "And I'll do the same for you." She slipped out and he shut the window behind her. Back out in the cold, she immediately started shivering. She should have at least borrowed a jacket or asked for some warming flames, but alas, here she was.

Wide open in the Realm, Emilie vanished for a moment and called out, *Rita?* She was close, always hovering around Mark and nervous, but she didn't come. Emilie heaved a sigh and took to the air, hurrying over to Sil's and away from Mark. *Come on, Rita, don't be ridiculous. I need to go to the ASH.*

A shimmer of green lit up in Sil's backyard and Emilie dropped out of the sky to meet her. "This is a first," Rita declared, snide as always.

Poising her hand on her hip, Emilie tried to pretend she wasn't freezing to death right now. "Just there and back again."

"And you can't fly there?" Rita argued sassily.

"It's frickin' cold! Come on! Help me out!"

A light turned on up in Sil's room, and they both looked up to see his figure in the window staring down at them. He didn't engage, letting them argue among the chickens.

Rita sulked but finally nodded. "Fine... hang on," and extended her arm. Emilie didn't hesitate but regretted it the moment she touched Rita's elbow. She was so used to her own means of transportation that the possession of her gravity, dragging her thousands of miles to the south, flung her clear into suspended air above the mess hall.

About thirty Shadows turned their heads up, staring unblinking at the scantily clad girl hovering above them. "Rita, what the heck!" she swore through her teeth.

"Hey, Feather, you're back!" Kip rose up from his seat, eating dinner with the rest of the crowd.

Emilie growled, struggling to get the attention off herself. She placed her feet on the tile to feign walking. "Save it, sunspot! Just tell me where I can find Ocie!"

Kip smirked and crossed his arms, unaffected. "You're gonna bully me then try to go make nice with Ocie? Good luck!" he mocked, following her as she stormed out.

Emilie shoved him back, unconcerned about how she could potentially hurt him if it would throw him off her trail. She knew where to find Ocie, or at least seven places to look. Emilie's skin crawled. This was the last place she wanted to be right now.

"I'm right here, Emilie," Ocie's sweet and calming voice sounded from the kitchen, and Emilie whirled about, taking to the air and flying over. Ocie's unerring beauty sickened her. *Miss Perfect* only wanted to stay in this prison with her dad, regardless of how Keller had kept them locked up for years. Ocie had never been a prisoner. She had been his accomplice. "What can I help you with?" Ocie sang like a fairytale princess.

Emilie clamped around her wrist and dragged her into the kitchen where they could hopefully speak in private. "You assume a lot in asking—" Her already poor traction without gravity caused her to slip as she gasped.

"Food safety, girls. Please stay over there." Kimberly stood at the helm of the kitchen alone, preparing all the food for thirty rowdy kids and then some.

Letting out a groan, Emilie turned on her heels to leave.

"Hold it. Wait!" Ocie pled. "What's all this about? You wouldn't come back here unless it was something serious."

Emilie glanced out at the Shadows among the tables and then back to Kimberly. "I'm..." She cringed, keeping her voice low. "Moving."

"What do you mean?"

Sighing long and thorough, Emilie's gaze fell. "My dad showed up, and he wants my mom and me to move with him to NYC."

"That's... wonderful, I think." Ocie did her best to hide the unsureness in her voice.

"I just want you to help me pack and clean. Would you do that?" Emilie snapped, unwilling to explain anything with so many Shadows around. Ocie saw right through her eyes, everything going on in her soul, and Ocie's shoulders relaxed, pity in her stance. Emilie hated her, but Ocie's unflinching kindness wasn't why she needed her.

"Okay..." Ocie breathed, her smile disappearing. She already knew that her cheerfulness wasn't welcome.

Wordlessly, Emilie turned away, gesturing Ocie to follow straight to Rita, who had leant against a table and was stealing food off Kip's plate before he got back to it.

"Mode of transportation again," Rita complained, not paying any heed to Kip's realization that his meal was being picked at. She offered her arm once more and Ocie took it gladly, but Emilie was much more hesitant, this time touching Ocie's shoulder to piggyback off of the teleportation.

"To my house," she demanded, offering an image in the Realm for Rita to know where she was going.

Darkness flooded over them, and as soon as Rita rematerialized, she vanished again in a huff. Emilie oriented herself, spinning once and realizing she was standing in the front garden among the frosty foliage. Her safe place, among the ice.

Taking one step toward the glowing screen door, dreading the light inside, Emilie was cut short as Ocie's hand flew in front of her. "All right, Emilie, what is this really about?"

Emilie's feet left the ground, her eye level keeping with Ocie's, but she prepared herself to flee confrontation. "I... I have so much to clean... I just want a little help."

"Of course," Ocie smiled, kind as always, but she still knew this wasn't the issue.

Gulping hard, Emilie slowly pushed past Ocie's hand into the little home. Greg's pickup truck was gone, so that was a relief, and the living room was slightly less disheveled than when she had left it. Emilie peeked into the kitchen where the only light was on, but when she didn't find her mother, she zipped straight to Hellen's bedroom.

She lay there, a lump under the sheets, sound asleep, and Emilie sank. She'd never seen her mother asleep in her own bed, at peace, or actually resting and not just lulled by the noise and light from the television. The silence was comforting, a little reassuring, and just enough for Emilie to not jump out of her skin when Ocie laid a hand on her shoulder.

"You don't have to tell me everything, but I'm here if you want to talk," Ocie assured sweetly.

Emilie frowned, producing a solemn nod. With soundless footsteps, she entered the kitchen and got straight to clearing off the rest of the table. Ocie followed, and through the evening, they cleaned together.

XII
LIGHT BREAKFAST

March 5, 2031

Mark slammed a half-full mug of tea onto his dresser, still managing to spill some as he rushed to get ready. He stuffed one foot into his tennis shoe and took a long, albeit shaking, sip of the hot tea. He had awoken at six-fifty-five again, but rather than pressuring his father, he forced himself to sit down in the Realm. Meditating for a few minutes that turned into forty-five, he successfully shortened the perceived wait.

For the first time, his room was cold, and he didn't really take notice until he realized the window wasn't sealed properly. There was something elucidating about the cold. He could think clearer, move a little faster, and he certainly wasn't as sluggish. Maybe he should keep his window open a crack at night more often.

"Look at you all in a rush," a familiar voice blared from behind him. He whirled about mid-second-shoe to see Rita standing in his doorway, the green mist still drifting off her form.

Mark tensed, but quickly turned away again to tie his shoe. "What's up?" he asked, hiding all hints of passive aggression.

"I want to show you something." Rita took a step further into his room, flustered by the light, the drawn blinds and the cracked window. "I think it might help you find out more about your dad's past."

Though he was sure she expected the opposite, Mark's interest didn't pique. "Where?"

Rita poised her hands on her hips. "You know the house Keller said he used to live in? I think there are some records there that could help—"

"I'm a little busy today," Mark interrupted her coldly. "I don't mean to blow you off, but this means a lot to me."

Her eyes narrowing, Rita shook her head a little. "I thought findin' out your dad's secrets was important to you."

Mark shrugged, a wry smirk forming in his cheek. "This is the first time my dad has really taken the time to do anything with me, alone, without the Addisons. And honestly, it means more to me to just spend time with him than to understand everything."

Rita's breath halted, and she took one wary step back. "I'm serious, Mark, you really have to see this place! It'll change everything we know about Shadows!" She let her voice fill with awe and hope, her eyes wide and sparkling with her power.

"Geoffrey is already doing that. He's teaching me so much. I can only take one thing at a time. So, maybe next week? After Geoffrey's had some time to get me up to speed on his knowledge, at least what he'll share, we can go wherever you want."

Still, strong-willed, spunky Rita wouldn't resort to frustration. "I thought, you'd want to hang out again... now that I've forgiven—"

This time Mark's back stiffened, and he turned about, his eyes so bright red that it startled Rita. "What? *Forgiven me?*" he scoffed and grabbed his cup of tea just to have something to hold onto that he wouldn't set on fire. "Maybe I might have hurt your feelings, but you screamed at me and then left!" He begrudgingly took a sip of his tea, but it tasted bitter and metallic. "This clearly isn't about feeling like a mode of transportation. You like it! This is about you being jealous of Ocie, and I'm not going to get in the middle of it."

Rita's eyes widened fully, shocked by the severity in his voice. Tears began to well up in her eyes. "What… changed?"

Mark picked up his wooden sword, and with his tea, he stormed toward the door, pushing her out of the way. It wasn't harsh, just enough for her to emotionally feel the blow. "You're my friend, Rita, but I'm not going to take sides." He hurried away from the doorframe, not looking back until he heard the quiet puff of smoke when Rita teleported away.

He got to the kitchen, making eye contact with his dad when he finally realized he was holding his breath again.

"Gracious, Mark!" Geoffrey exclaimed as Mark swung his wooden sword wildly like a bat, hoping to hit something. Each stroke flailed, rarely impacting Geoffrey's blade, and when it did, it bounced off harmlessly, doing more damage to Mark's grip than anything. "Control it! You don't need to put all your strength behind it at once."

Mark stopped but kept his feet moving, taking a few smooth strides out into the center of the room. He switched hands and loosened his wrist. According to Geoffrey, he was stronger in his left hand, but he didn't feel it right now. It felt awkward and tiring. "Sorry, I just have a lot on my mind."

Geoffrey's brows furrowed studiously. "Don't let your emotions control you. It'll only make you more uncoordinated."

Switching back to his left-hand, Mark mimicked Geoffrey's method of loosening his wrist, a smooth movement, swinging the sword in a spiral, elegantly. Geoffrey had him constantly train with his left hand, assuring him that the skills would automatically transfer to his right. Mark blew his bangs out of his face, starting to get very annoyed by the red strands.

Geoffrey sighed, seeing Mark's distress, and lowered his guard. "I don't really care what's going on in your personal life, but you have got to do something about that mop." He leant his sword against the wall and proceeded to take out the tiny, black, elastic tie that was holding his dreadlocks together.

Mark was slightly taken aback as Geoffrey thrust the stretched-out hair tie his way. "What about you?" he asked, a little too soon. The moment he took the tie, Geoffrey used two of his dreads to keep his hair together again. Mark stared at the elastic, slightly nervous.

"You know how to use that thing, right?" Geoffrey blared mockingly.

"I do!" Mark jumped, hastily reaching up to tame his hair, and thus dropping his sword and fumbling for it. When it clattered to the hardwood, he just sighed, his shoulders dropping in utter defeat. "I'm not strong enough for any of this yet."

"None of that!" Geoffrey yelled admonishingly. His sheer volume startled Mark. "It doesn't matter if you're strong enough at this point. The skill itself, a teenager who knows how to use a sword, right now, that's what you have going for you. And, in time, you won't need to rely on that sleight of hand. You'll be able to fend for yourself."

"So visually lie!" Mark lamented. "I might be scrawny and barely able to take on someone the same size as me, but hey, I got a sword, so I'm scary for all of ten seconds before I get the dirt beaten out of me."

Geoffrey's brows shot up, barely able to contain his laughter. "Come on, kid, your dad isn't around. You can use a little stronger language than that if you want."

Mark glared at him. "What is Rita's deal?" Completely changing the subject, he didn't really want to complain. There wasn't much to be done about someone being petty without coming off as petty himself. He liked Rita, he missed her, but he couldn't see how much more he could give her.

"None of my business." He sat down on the floor with him. "I still think you can go harder, but part of the risk in that is you're going to hurt yourself. You obviously can't hurt me."

Mark's eyes drifted away, resenting the immediate return to sword-fighting. His gaze traveled along Geoffrey's arm, at the long white scar he bore. "How did..." He cringed, resolving to follow through. "How did you get that scar?"

Geoffrey mused and raised up the hem of his tank top. "Which one?" he laughed, displaying another raised keloid. Mark's eyes widened, flaring brightly at the sight of a grisly wound in Geoffrey's ribs. His laughter faded off, but his smile remained. "Occupational hazard, but this one—" He touched the scar tissue on his rib. "—is from my father."

"He stabbed you?" Mark blared, perfectly perturbed.

"No," Geoffrey chuckled. "I pissed off Shadow Strength, so *he* stabbed me."

Mark gazed down at the hardwood, contemplating. "A sentient Shadow took control of your father and tried to kill you?"

Geoffrey shook his head. "Come on, this wouldn't have killed me; simple medical fix, simple Infusion. Now this one..." He displayed the long scar along his arm. "He was actually in control that time. Training accident, thought I was going to lose my arm for a bit, but it healed."

Mark winced just thinking about it and massaged his left arm worriedly. "So... are you left-handed or right-handed?"

At this, Geoffrey stood up and offered Mark a hand to pull him to his feet. "Right-handed, but like you, I trained with both. Ambidexterity is incredibly important in this field." Suddenly, he slapped Mark's arm even as the phantom tingles were still racing across it. "So here's the plan: you finish tying up your hair, then I want you to let loose, give me everything you got, and forget about control for just a few minutes. I don't care where you aim. Just keep it in your head, somewhere, that you *can* hit me."

Mark forced a nod, leaving his sword on the floor as he worked his lanky black hair into a ponytail. He didn't have much success. His bangs were still in his face, but he did feel a sense of clarity. It might have just come from seeing his mentor's vulnerabilities and their similarities.

Breathing deeply, Geoffrey bent down to pick up the wooden sword for him, placing it gently into Mark's right hand. Mark eyed him curiously, but Geoffrey only offered a playful grin. "Let yourself out. Don't think about it. Just let your actions show your feelings."

Surprised, Mark gripped the hilt, right over left, surprisingly comfortable now. Geoffrey's offer wasn't open. There were dangers in the proposition, suggesting violence over reason, emotion over precision. And worst of all, Mark could still hurt himself with a wooden stick if he wasn't careful.

Mark sucked in a breath, making sure he wasn't holding it again. The roaring fire inside him was growing hotter and without a second breath, he launched. His strokes were graceless, more like swinging a bat or mallet then wielding an elegant blade, but this was only wood. For a second, he didn't care if he shattered it. He beat down on Geoffrey' blade, trusting his mentor to deflect everything, and for a moment, not to strike back.

Mark gave him five good hits with all his might, stronger than he had ever dreamt of out in the cold when they fought outside the shooting range. After those five hits though, Geoffrey retaliated. With a twist of his wrist, he swept the blade at Mark, aiming to strike him evenly across the chest. Mark kept his vulnerabilities secure and deflected, doing his best to prevent the contact from sliding up to his fingers—and slicing them off were it a real blade.

He pushed it back, and Geoffrey retreated a pace, just one, enough for Mark to return to his mad frenzy. In two days, Mark was already stronger. He could feel it. Maybe it was his time in the Realm that was making him more mindful, or the utter frustration from dealing with Rita and his squabbling parents. This was his one safe place, the one release. The video games and artificial violence faded away. He needed it to be real!

Geoffrey instated a pattern, allowing Mark to strike five or so times as hard as he could, then he retaliated, testing Mark's ability to deflect. He met them each time more efficiently than the last. Finally, in the midst of Mark's hardest strike yet, Geoffrey pushed back, and he wasn't prepared for the force. His footing was bad, he was off balance and he had to quickly find his center to meet Geoffrey's pressure.

"Good reaction time!" Geoffrey grinned down very close to his face. Their swords pinned together.

Mark cringed, every fiber in his being tense because he knew, even now, Geoffrey only had to *choose* to overpower him and it would be done. Geoffrey was fifty times stronger than him. He was nothing in a situation like this. Any second now he would be blown over. Normally, Geoffrey backed off after a few seconds, but this time, he held, unflinching, the pressure unwavering.

Mark met eyes with Geoffrey, a little scared. With just a look, he begged Geoffrey to let off, to give him a second to restart, to fix his footing, to adjust his grip. Anything!

But Geoffrey just smirked, taunting him, and pushing harder. Mark panicked, giving a little yelp, but he pushed back with incrementally increasing force. He had to meet Geoffrey's strength; otherwise, he'd be pushed over.

For a second, Mark weighed his options. Save for embarrassment, the worst that could happen was Geoffrey would shove him to the floor. That wasn't so bad. But Geoffrey kept his eyes locked in his, unafraid of the crimson glow, his smile disappeared. "Do *not* give up!" he warned. It was the truest thing Mark had ever heard. It wasn't reassuring, it wasn't designed to build him up and energize him. It wasn't even meant to make him desperate. It was a *threat*.

If Mark lost, he'd get a beating, real physical pain.

He couldn't win. He physically wasn't strong enough to win!

At the same time, there was something exciting in the promise of pain.

Pain. Something real.

Letting out a roar, a scream compared to the blaze inside him, Mark's eyes caught fire, and he gave absolutely everything in his body to throw Geoffrey off his blade. In the same motion, he fixed his footing, giving himself just enough leverage to gain a centimeter or two on his opponent. Geoffrey bore down over him, bigger than him in every way.

If he was going to lose this, he wouldn't settle for anything less than absolutely every muscle in his body giving its all to—

Fire raced across his left arm and he tensed, checking to make sure his crimson flames hadn't actually ignited. There was no fire, just heat, a throbbing weakness. His left arm gave out, and Geoffrey stumbled past him, laughing proudly. "That was amazing!" he complimented with only a little mockery in his voice.

Mark dropped his sword again and hugged his left arm, crumpling on his knees as the pain finally hit him.

His fist clamped tightly to his heart, and he gasped, now finally breathing again. That entire time, he had been holding his breath. Steadying his wrist, he looked down at his left hand to see it trembling, and just moving his shoulder a little felt like his entire left quarter was being electrocuted.

"Did you sprain it?" Geoffrey asked from behind him, a blank expression on his face.

Mark winced and looked back. "I don't know. I... I can't move it!" he cried out.

Geoffrey shrugged and knelt by him to check it out. "Could've dislocated it. Weird things tend to happen when you use that kind of adrenaline."

"Like what?" Mark asked, trying to take his mind off the pain as Geoffrey started feeling his shoulder.

"Like punching through glass, headbutting walls, and lifting cars. Only two kinds of crises inspire that much strength: honor or parenthood." Geoffrey pried his arm loose from his chest, and though Mark wailed, Geoffrey grinned. "Not dislocated," he assured. "Probably a minor sprain."

Mark hyperventilated, letting his arm go limp in Geoffrey's grasp. "Is this what it's going to be like every time we fight? I end up with some kind of injury?"

Geoffrey just laughed, clear and bright. "Kid, I have not injured you once. Both of these times now, it has been you getting a little too over excited."

Grimacing, Mark gave Geoffrey a nasty look. "So all my fault then?" he said passive aggressively.

"You just don't know your own limits yet. And these kinds of injuries, little stuff, are going to help you figure that out. It's pushing past those limits without hurting yourself that allows you to know you've grown." Geoffrey touched his elbow, assessing it, and suddenly he knitted his brows together.

"What is it?" Mark panicked.

"Can you move your elbow?"

Mark tried but a sharp pain caused his fist to tighten.

"Ah ha..." Geoffrey said through his lower lip. "Dislocated elbow, pinching the nerve too."

"Is that bad?" Mark gasped. "Do I have to go to the hospital?"

Geoffrey smirked dismissively. "Well, normally." He laughed. "But why do that when you've got me."

Mark paled, almost as limp as his arm, as Geoffrey drew him up off the floor. "You're gonna..." He gulped hard. "Yourself?"

Nodding confidently, Geoffrey sat him down on one of the chairs in the living area. "I'll do it if you think you can handle it."

Pressing his lips together, Mark rested his back against the chair fully. He couldn't extend his arm at all, sharp pain biting his joint at every breath. It had happened so fast he couldn't believe it.

"You're a skinny kid, your joints aren't very strong yet, and this is a lot of new exertion. So it's bound to happen. Shoulder dislocations are just a little easier and hurt less. So, it'll be a couple seconds of *ten,* and then the pain will mostly go away. You'll just be sore for the next few days."

"Ten?" Mark puzzled, nervous as Geoffrey knelt beside him.

"On the pain scale."

Tensing, Mark felt as if the rest of his body had locked in place like his elbow. He needed to go to the hospital, but at the same time, he didn't want his parents to freak out. A few seconds of the worst pain imaginable, then it would be over. He gulped once more, then nodded.

Geoffrey took the consent incredibly seriously. "Okay... this would normally be a two-person job. I'm going to need all the leverage I can get."

Mark nodded aimlessly, not really acknowledging it when Geoffrey firmly laid his palm against Mark's right shoulder, pushing it down against the seat cushion. With his right hand, he maneuvered Mark's arm as straight as possible before pinching tightly through his skin. Mark winced at every little movement, but it was nothing until Geoffrey found his leverage. Mark felt it, the interior bone was the one that was out.

Geoffrey smiled a little and met Mark's gaze. "One of these days you're going to figure out how essential it is to have a good knowledge of anatomy and basic first aid. And by basic, I mean stitches, splints, and..." he trailed off, hoping he had distracted Mark enough that he wouldn't jerk when the sudden pain hit.

With that immense strength, Geoffrey yanked on Mark's forearm at the joint, his fingers pressing into the bones and pushing. In Geoffrey's eyes, there was only technical, calculating force, but for Mark, he feared his arm was about to be shredded apart, fiber by fiber. It took a moment for the pain to really hit, and Mark was caught in silence and terror as he was held down in this position.

He inhaled sharply, but by the time he was able to produce some kind of actual reaction, he felt like a diamond needle had shot up his arm to his shoulder and his elbow popped. Finally, he gave a scream, the pure release ripping through him, and he launched free of Geoffrey's grip the moment it waned. He clattered straight to the floor, stumbling and trying to get to his feet.

"Easy! Easy! Don't put any strain on your arm!" Geoffrey warned, rushing to grab him.

Mark planted his feet, panting, but he looked down to his arm hanging at his side, and finally winced, gripping his shoulder.

"You did phenomenally," his mentor assured, not one for compliments, but it was to keep Mark calm as he handled his arm again, testing the motion of the elbow. "You have a high tolerance for pain," Geoffrey continued making assumptions about him.

High tolerance or not, Mark didn't know how he had kept still long enough for Geoffrey to do that.

"I need you to sit down. I can't have you stretching those ligaments for a while," Geoffrey advised, cautious to guide Mark back to the chair. Once Mark settled down in it, he left to fetch something. "You'll probably be out of the woods if you wear this until tomorrow," Geoffrey returned with a navy-blue sling. It was for an adult's arm, but nonetheless Geoffrey situated Mark's arm without much compliance.

Mark blinked a few times, a little jaded. "Does this mean I can't keep coming over for a while?"

Finally, Geoffrey's confident smirk returned. "Of course not," he assured. "Tomorrow I'll try for a lesson in adaptability. I'm sure your left arm won't be as sore by tomorrow, but I can't have you stretching it for at least a week."

Giving a half-hearted nod, Mark continued to fret. "I don't want my parents to know about this..." he whispered. "Can I take off the sling at home?"

Geoffrey paused, glaring at Mark long and hard as he weighed his response. "If you promise to take it easy, no heavy lifting, no video games."

Wrinkling his nose, Mark managed a smile. "How do you know about that?"

Appalled, Geoffrey reeled back. "Dude! A kid your age. Isn't it a given?"

Mark laughed in return. "Finally, someone who gets it!"

Geoffrey elbowed his uninjured right side. "I've got a million other things to deal with, responsibilities and such, and even I game to wind down."

"Really?" Mark's excitement piqued.

Geoffrey only jeered him further. "So maybe, when your arm is healed, we can play together. I have a feeling you're going to heal fast."

Mark barely noticed how he couldn't sit still, but Geoffrey certainly did, getting up and letting the amusement fade from his face. "You know what, before I send you home, I want to show you something." This made Mark sit back, patient as Geoffrey walked over to his wall of weapons, admiring the diverse collection, but rather than selecting a gilded longsword, or a sharp spear, he heaved up a gray case.

Geoffrey set it on the coffee table, giving Mark a better look at it. It was a very dense material, but it didn't appear heavy from the way Geoffrey carried it, and it was almost three feet long. He unbuckled the latches and opened it to the light, producing a literal gold sheen when the contents were illuminated. Mark peered into the case at a polished, and incredibly elegant sword with a crested hilt.

Geoffrey took two cloths out of a pouch in the case and used them to pick up the blade without getting any blemishes on the gold. "This is a sixteenth century French rapier. The hilt is made of pure silver and gold-plated. It has sixteen diamonds on the crossguard, and one on the pommel. And the blade, though it's made of the toughest steel, is that gold color because of the Shadow Infused inside it."

He carried the incredibly valuable instrument closer to Mark to allow him to get a good look. "What Shadow is inside it?" Mark asked on instinct.

A little smile peeked in the corner of Geoffrey's eye. "This is Morglay, one of the Swords of Strength."

Mark's mouth fell open a little. "Your father's Shadow?"

Geoffrey nodded solemnly. "Shadow Strength, as one of the five sentient Shadows, is unable to go dormant, so rather than *floating,* which is what most Shadows do when their wielder dies, they retreat to their vessel."

His red eyes dashing about, Mark pieced together this information. "So... they need a vessel? Are they Infused to it?"

Geoffrey only gave a half nod. "Technically, yes, but the Infusion of a Shadow of this power is going to be way out of your league by far."

"I got that." Mark smirked. "Infusions are dangerous. I won't play around—wait! Shadow Love is one of those Shadows!"

"Yes," Geoffrey said very slowly.

Mark's eyes widened. "Kimberly told me about this! She said I was the vessel for Shadow Love!"

Geoffrey frowned suddenly, the information filling him with bitterness. Mark tensed at the change, but he could see how quickly Geoffrey pushed it down. "It's rare, yes."

A little taken aback by Geoffrey's sudden lack of expositing, going from freely giving knowledge to hiding something. It was the first time Mark had experienced this since the ASH. He didn't like being ignorant, and worse, being kept in the dark. "So… who has the power to Infuse them?"

Shaking it off, Geoffrey managed a smile, playfully stroking the blade in his hands to clean it of dust particles it had acquired just in the time it had been out. "Shadow Trust, of course. He made those decisions centuries ago, keeping the overpowered Shadows under control. Strength especially," he added with bleary eyes.

"What do you mean?"

Tenderly, Geoffrey replaced Morglay in its case, gently wiping away any marks the cloths had left on it. "Strength… as the name goes, is a lot more powerful than the others, in aptitude, voracity, and hunger. Trust felt threatened by him, so he was split into four pieces. It was my father's purpose in life to bring those parts together, but in a lifetime, he only acquired two," he gestured to a second case beneath where Morglay had been taken from. "I can't finish the journey without a Shadow, but for the first time, I know where another Sword of Strength is."

He closed the case and sighed. "Strength is power hungry—always has been—he takes no weakness, and is driven to perfection until the day his wielder dies, then he has to start over again, unsatisfied. It's the curse Trust placed on Strength. And my father was driven mad by the need to grow stronger." Drifting, Geoffrey went to put away the sword. "Until he found a way to pass on all he had learned."

Standing up straight, Geoffrey stretched uneasily. "Strength can never go dormant, so if a wielder of Strength were able to survive into the next generation, they could personally pass on the Shadow to another wielder. Other Strengths have done it for centuries, so at the end of the generation, about five years ago now, he was about to do it..." Geoffrey's hands formed into fists. "Then he left me to his work..."

Mark could see Geoffrey's distress. He knew what had really happened. For a moment, he could see weakness in the mentor he looked up to. He could see a young man, someone as scared as he was when he first awoke in the ASH, when he discovered his Shadow. It only then occurred to Mark that Geoffrey's father had only died five years ago. The wound was still raw.

XIII
MIDWINTER

Mark stopped outside his house, his tracks falling short in the muddy snow. He hated coming home. Several painful hours of Sil and his family making fun of his sprained arm, an awkward meal Mark skipped with no appetite, and walking out the door still hiding the fact his arm wasn't sprained. He heaved a sigh and slipped around to the garage door where he could get inside quietly. Outside, he took off the sling and tucked it into his coat pocket, wincing as he moved his arm a little.

Ensuring that none of the straps dangled out, Mark entered the cold garage cautiously. A light was on and he tensed, scanning the room worriedly until he spotted a silhouette in the car. It was after six. January would have gotten home half an hour ago, but there he sat, in the cold. It seemed like he had been there a while.

"Dad? Are you okay?" Mark announced himself.

January tensed, opening the car door and throwing aside a small box. "Oh, you're home. Did you have a good time?"

Mark nodded aimlessly, his eyes drifting to the box where it had landed on the seat. He tensed but tried to hide it. Instinctively, he sniffed the air for any hint of smoke, but sighed in relief when he couldn't detect any.

January gulped and glanced back. "Caught me, huh..." he frowned, tears lingering in his eyes. "Don't worry. I didn't smoke any. But I was thinking about it. You saved me just now."

A bitterness welled in Mark's throat. January was lying to protect himself. This didn't happen often. When he was very young, Mark could remember his father smoking. He battled with the addiction for years and occasionally fell back when he was stressed. Mark had caught him before—Marissa had caught him before. That never ended well. He'd still gone out to buy the cigarettes, he'd still contemplated it, and he might've already opened them or had one on the way home. But Mark couldn't smell the smoke. That made him a little hopeful. "Are you okay?" he asked again, softer.

January hastily rubbed his face to hide it. "I'm fine." It was weighing on him too. He didn't want to come home. Suddenly he forced the fakest laugh and gestured at his son. "Look at you with your hair tied back. I bet you and Geoffrey really went at it?"

Mark half-consciously massaged his left shoulder. "Yeah, it was rough. I did have a good time though."

"That's good," January forced a hopeful voice. "Now let's go see what your mom has planned for dinner." He hastily tucked the carton of cigarettes into his coat pocket, hiding something just as Mark was, and scuttled toward the kitchen door.

"Dad," Mark stopped him. "Can I talk to you... for real?"

"You can always talk to me." Every word was a struggle. He fought so hard just to be there for his son, his wife and daughter, this family. It was all falling apart.

Mark gulped. "Sil can read minds, reach... into them." The gut sickness worsened, anxiety, or maybe just the hunger from skipping breakfast and lunch. "A couple of days ago I asked him to do it to you."

Confused, January turned fully at the nose of the car. "Why?" was the only word he could summon.

Continuing to hold his arm, Mark lost eye contact. "To try and figure out your past, where you came from, where your family might be." With every phrase, January's eyes grew wider. "And in a distant, locked away memory, so deep into your past... we saw..." Mark bit his lip. "You have a brother."

"What?" January gasped. "That's—how?"

Mark shook his head frantically. "I don't know, but it was all we could really uncover. We saw through your eyes—you were with someone, really young but your age. You were alone in a forest and—" In the cold, even Mark's teeth felt too weak to finish. "He's a Shadow. You have a brother, in Scotland, who is a Shadow."

"No way..." January dismissed it. "Are you implying that when I was a child I somehow came over from another country?"

"I don't know when you came here. I wasn't able to see that," Mark insisted, growing a little more desperate to keep his father calm.

January shook his head repeatedly, denying everything. "No, I had to have been at least seventeen."

"Why does that matter?" Mark kept his voice low. "You have a brother! More family out there. I'm sure if we looked, we could find him. He's a Shadow, he has the Realm, and he'd remember you, wouldn't he?"

"No," January said again, firmer. "I don't know what reason I had for leaving, but I've worked so hard to have this. I'm not going to go digging around in my past for answers. Mark, this right here is what matters most to me: you, and your mom, and June. You are my family, and I'm not going to abandon you just because I might be related to another Shadow."

Mark tensed, a silence catching in his throat.

January froze, realizing the tone in his voice, and then hastily stepped around the car, back to Mark. "Hey, I'm sorry. That came out the wrong way."

Batting away his caring hand, Mark frowned. "So I'm just another Shadow. You still hate Shadows and... I'm just one of them now."

"No, Mark, that isn't what I meant!"

"Maybe I want to find this Shadow. Maybe I need someone in my family who understands me. Don't you want that? Right now, the only one who's giving me that is Geoffrey, and if I keep hanging out with him, I'm gonna come back here with more than a sprained arm." He chuckled to hide his terror, gripping his left arm still. The dull pain felt like it was getting worse, but maybe that was the anxiety, or the tears clinging to his eyes.

January's eyes widened, a little shocked. "You're hurt?"

"It's nothing. It's fine," Mark snapped under his breath.

"How did you sprain your arm?" January continued fretting.

"I didn't sprain it!" he batted his father away again, retracting his lie. "It was dislocated during our spar and—it was my fault not his!" Reverting, Mark took his father's arm. "Dad, please! I just want you to look! You've never looked before other than a stupid DNA test that I'm sure Mom is the one who made you do it. I can get Rita to take us over—we won't have to pay for a plane ticket—and you can really look for your family!"

"Mark..." January sighed, ready to deny him, but the kitchen door opened.

"What are you arguing about?" Marissa's voice came, bearing over them, a silhouette with a halo of kitchen light behind her. "Come on inside. Dinner's almost ready." For a moment, her voice was calm, it wasn't abrasive, and Mark's heart steadied.

January closed his eyes, but before he turned, he whispered, "I'll think about it."

March 6, 2031

Mark slipped off to his room and went to bed. He locked the door, done dealing with everyone tonight and completely exhausted. It hadn't really kicked in until now—dealing with the social adrenaline of being at Sil's house and the actual adrenaline of fighting Geoffrey. For the first time, the burst of energy left him with a crash, and he was asleep in minutes.

His mind drifted somewhere between the Realm and reality, sending him confusing images and reminders of the insanity he had been introduced to in the ASH. He still got nightmares about that week occasionally, not bad dreams per say, but crazy waking dreams reliving it all. They usually woke him early, but this time it wasn't the dreams, rather an aching pain that had settled all through his body.

His conscious thoughts lingered on what Geoffrey had said in regard to the Realm. It was a peripheral sense, like something was always out of Mark's line of sight. He knew it was there, but he couldn't sense it with his eyes or touch. Realm was a type of sixth sense to Shadows, which made practicing it all the more confusing . Thudding in his ears, the peripheral awareness of the Realm was keeping him awake.

His arm didn't hurt much, just a dull soreness, but the rest of the limbs tingled and ached. He tried to sit up in bed, but the motion made it worse. Curling up on his side didn't help either. Cocooned in darkness, even though he should've felt safe, he had to get up. He flicked the light switch a few times before remembering the bulb was dead and resolved to turn on his TV. The console lit up, displaying the time. Mark pressed his lips together. Five AM.

Suddenly, a blunt knuckle knocked on his door, and he jumped, still standing in the middle of the room. Dismissing his soreness, he unlocked the door then immediately sat down again. January peered in, the silver strands in his graying hair catching the light from the screen. "Are you all right? I thought I heard something."

Mark meant to nod, but instead he shook his head. He hadn't made a sound, and the volume on his TV was always turned all the way down so he could use headphones. He hadn't been tossing and turning, and he hadn't been talking in his sleep. He hadn't made a sound.

January grimaced and invited himself in. "Maybe it was nothing. I just got a weird feeling."

Mark hugged his arm, realizing the window was still open a little, and he was freezing. He reached out to close it, but with his left arm. He winced and recoiled. January stared down at him with a knowing glare, a look in his eyes that warned that he knew everything. Mark gave up, letting his head fall as he produced a weak cry in pain. "Everything hurts, not just my arm. I'm so sore."

Hurriedly, January took a seat beside his son and brought an arm around him. "Your body just went through a traumatic event. Like a car crash where no one got hurt. It's normal to be very tense afterward."

Cringing, Mark couldn't bring himself to shake his father off. "It was only a few seconds. I barely remember what it felt like because it was over so fast... so why am I shaking so hard?"

January rubbed his back. "You're okay..." he shushed lovingly. Mark fell against his shoulder, shudders rippling through his body. Maybe January did sense his pain. For now, Mark was just thankful he was here. For once, for what felt like the first time, his dad was actually here for him. Words spoken could never express how much this meant, so Mark sat there in silence.

Minutes piled on and he waited for his body to settle, his heart to calm down, and the pain to pass. Bathed in the blue light from the screen, he savored this time with his father. His dad's heartbeat was all he could focus on for a minute, that little promise that the warmth he felt was not his own Shadow.

First light appeared outside, and the clock gradually ticked toward six-fifty-five. "You don't have to go today if you don't feel well," January broke the long silence.

Mark denied even though his joints and muscles still ached. "I want to."

Pressing his lips together, January continued rubbing his back, and suggested, "You don't have to leave until seven-forty. You could try to sleep a little longer."

With all the effort he had left, Mark nodded. "Okay..."

January released him, but he didn't want the warmth to leave. His father closed the window and the blinds to block out the light, then turned off the TV. Prompted, Mark laid back down, pulling his covers over his head and tightly closing his eyes. Every fiber in his being was exhausted, and his mind drifted again. He had an hour at best to lay here, to recover, but his limbs throbbed.

Some time slipped away, and he forgot about the pain, only made aware when his doorknob creaked, and January tiptoed in, placing a hot mug at the head of Mark's bed. The smell warmed Mark to the idea of morning, awakening his senses, and he soon realized he didn't feel quite so tense. In a half-hour, just a little tiredness remained.

He rose again, this time welcoming a cup of tea, and he sank into it. Maybe it had been his mindset, not the trauma. After three days of greeting the day excitedly, having a calm morning was what he needed. He spent the last twenty minutes in the Realm once more, acquiring a meditative posture and breath, until his dad broke through his thoughts to draw him into the day.

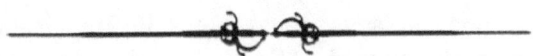

Geoffrey was still eating breakfast when they arrived. Mark invited himself in without knocking, and the man perked up with a bright smile and a call of, "Rita, it's time to skedaddle!" He mocked her ridiculousness, and Mark listened for the distinct sound of Rita teleporting away until Geoffrey cleaned up his place at the kitchen counter.

January didn't leave Mark's side, placing a firm hand on his shoulder to reassure him. "Hey, not to be *that* parent, but could you go a little easier on him? Sounds like this training is a lot rougher than he can handle."

Geoffrey paused with his hand descending into the sink. "He can handle a lot, from what I've seen. It's rudimentary right now, but with a little more exercise—"

"That doesn't matter," January cut him off and Mark tensed. He'd never heard his father being so assertive. "You dislocated his arm yesterday. That's too rough. Can you focus more on pose and precision than brute strength?" he suggested, clearly not knowing a thing about the craft.

"He's going to need a bit more muscle on his bones first," Geoffrey retorted playfully.

"So go to a gym together or something, but he needs to rest in between beatings. Don't you agree?" January raised his voice just a little, startling Mark even more, but he nodded along hopefully.

That queer smile appeared in Geoffrey's eyes, and he gave in. "All right, we'll take it easier today. Peak shape is the end goal, not the first step."

Less than satisfied, January patted Mark on the back and through a nervous gulp he muttered, "Have a good day. Take it easy." Mark chuckled at his father's immediate regret for being forceful. He tried. That counted.

As soon as January was out, Geoffrey leant on the counter and laughed. "So, what did you have for breakfast? Are you interested in *second breakfast?*"

Still grinning like an idiot, Mark led himself over to the counter. "I didn't eat."

"What?" Geoffrey gaped.

"Just had a cup of tea…" Mark said through his teeth.

Geoffrey slammed his hands down on the counter. "You *can't* come here and have your dad lecture me about taking it easy on you when you're not even eating right. You'll heal so much faster and have so much more energy if you actually eat breakfast. You cannot start your day with just tea!"

Taken aback by the outburst, Mark chuckled nervously. "I'm not hungry in the mornings," he assured. It occurred to him he'd been skimping on meals a lot lately, so even if one cup of tea wasn't a problem, lunch and dinner probably were.

"Fried eggs?" Geoffrey suggested, already taking out a pan. "And if you say any word beginning with a *V* when I say bacon, I will beat you with this!" he threatened casually, playfully spinning around the frying pan.

Mark threw up his hands. "Nope, bacon is fine!"

Geoffrey moved like a madman, cracking open brown eggs and carefully lowering them into the pan to form into smooth round shapes. "Over easy, runny, or well done?"

"I don't care," Mark shrugged.

"My way then," Geoffrey triumphed and threw four pink disks into the pan.

Mark puzzled. Geoffrey had said bacon, but—he grinned, Canadian bacon… *okay that makes a little sense.*

Geoffrey was so fast as he pulled it all together, concocting one huge breakfast sandwich with two eggs, four pieces of Canadian bacon, and two slices of cheese wedged in there. He set the giant before Mark with a grin. "Super high in protein, good fats, a little carbs for energy, and of course, quality cheese, not processed junk."

Mark snorted at it. "You're a bit of a health nut, aren't you?"

Geoffrey put his hands on his hips, "Ever heard of CrossFit? Now there's an addiction I'm not introducing you to until you weigh a hundred pounds."

"Hey! I weigh one-fifteen!" Mark retorted, pulling the plate a little closer but unsure if he had the appetite to mow down such a huge sandwich this early.

"Sure..." Geoffrey doubted.

Mark paused before attempting to pick up the thing. Geoffrey implied he had done some weightlifting in the comment. He probably knew what a hundred pounds felt like. And again, it occurred to Mark he hadn't eaten much in the last few days. It was possible he had fallen below a hundred. He ate as much of the sandwich as he could, getting his hands covered in grease and egg in the process, but he couldn't finish it.

Geoffrey saw him giving up and strode out to the living room. "Let's start with some stretches."

Eager to get to it, Mark rinsed off his hands, doing more to clean them by lighting them on fire for a few seconds, then rushed over to the open space. Though it pained him to extend his left arm, the muscles in his arm had recovered, and he didn't have too much difficulty with the stretches. After Geoffrey deemed he had *warmed up,* they switched to wooden swords. And once Mark overexerted himself and dropped it, Geoffrey let him rest. Mark could only use his right arm, which really hindered him against Geoffrey who was favoring his left today.

He was a tad more wary of giving his all, now that he knew how badly he could hurt himself. But, as January had requested, Geoffrey was going a little softer today.

Mark's gaze drifted to the two cases on Geoffrey's wall, the powerful Shadow-Infused Swords of Strength. What did the other one look like? Was it as magnificent as the gold plated Morglay? Was it more beautiful? Did it balance Morglay's beauty with bleak hideous features?

Mark's curiosity was killing him, but he didn't have the *strength* to ask.

"C-can I ask you a question?"

"Depends," Geoffrey said, standing across from him with his wooden sword still ready.

Mark gulped. "About the peripheral Realm." Geoffrey nodded a little, pacing and starting to instigate a fight again, slowly, working Mark into dividing his tasks with light banter. "You told me to count the Shadows within my range, and I was able to detect another Shadow, but I didn't know who it was until yesterday. Is that like, in my peripheral?"

"No," Geoffrey raised his blade, crossing it with Mark's. "Your peripheral sense in the Realm is something that's on standby, you're half listening for voices in your range directed at you, and the only way to stop it is to learn how to block yourself out of the Realm. That skill takes so much practice and so much focus, one little slip up, even slightly entering the Realm will alert other Shadows to your presence, because their peripheral will be looking out for other Shadows in their range. Until that moment, someone blocking themselves out of the Realm could seem like just another human."

Mark took this in, slowly sidestepping to circle with Geoffrey. "That's still not what I meant..." he murmured. "Like, I never knew how to use the Realm when I was young, and you told me I've always had a peripheral sense of it when I clearly didn't."

"That's not possible." Geoffrey smirked. "When was the first time you used the Realm?"

"Easy, in the kitchen the first day I figured out I was a Shadow."

"Hmm... felt familiar, didn't it?" Geoffrey hummed mockingly.

"Yeah..."

"I'll bet you use the Realm in your sleep all the time. You daydream, and your head goes in there, and that's part of the reason you're so good at using the Realm without entering it. Most Shadows figure out how to enter the Realm when they're a few years old, but Shadows I've met who have really young children or babies have said they've felt tones in the Realm from infants, months, maybe weeks old. Shadows learn how to use the Realm around the time they learn how to smile and laugh. You're probably no different."

"So, what? I was blocking myself out of the Realm?" Mark grumbled.

"No way," Geoffrey dismissed it immediately.

"Then it was Trust." Mark gave in. "He forced my Shadow to wait to come out of dormancy, and therefore hide my Realm ability. Make sense?"

Geoffrey shook his head. "Doesn't sound like him..."

"Oh, and you would know."

Geoffrey paused a moment, mulling it over and letting his gaze drift to his swords. "Then again... I guess it's possible for one Shadow to hide another's powers or force them into dormancy. That would prevent your eyes from turning red and flaring."

"How?" Mark burst excitedly.

"The Realm, I guess." Geoffrey swung his sword gracelessly at Mark, testing his reaction time without much weight behind the blow.

Mark barely deflected it, his thoughts wandering. The vision of his father's brother returned. The young Shadow had been alone, taking care of his brother and afraid. What if he had been protecting January? What if he had taken very drastic measures to keep January safe? That word stuck with him, Peripheral. This constant, empathic force connecting him to other Shadows regardless of whether he was awake or asleep.

January had come into his room moments after he had awoken, and it didn't feel like a coincidence.

"Ow!" Mark let out a yell as Geoffrey whacked him in the left arm with his sword, just enough to aggravate the strained muscles.

"Pay attention! You can chat, but you can't let your head go off during a fight, not even to piece together seemingly crucial information."

Mark jumped out of the way of the next swing. "Isn't that basically *shoot first, ask questions later?*"

Geoffrey cackled. "Haven't you learned anything yet? I'm about the living embodiment of that saying. Remember: grow now, learn later. You've got your whole life to learn square roots and algebra, but how are you going to apply that? Pretty pointless in my opinion, and this is coming from a dude who counts calories!"

Mark shook his head and laughed. "You really are a health nut!" He took a swing at Geoffrey, for a moment feeling like he was dancing around him, light on his feet, and never missing the parry. When it wasn't life or a dislocated elbow, this was actually fun.

Mark never heard the sound of Rita teleporting away, yet in his peripheral he suddenly became aware she was watching them.

XIV
TENDER

"Here's an idea! How about after you move into the new apartment, we go shopping for a new couch together?" Ocie suggested, a bright face in the dank front room. Black mold had grown in every corner, and there wasn't much such a soft and elegant figure could do about it. Emilie couldn't imagine Ocie getting on her hands and knees to rip up the nasty carpet. It would have to be gutted once the house was sold. Emilie had washed her hands of the dilemma.

Hellen huddled over a cup of coffee with bags under her eyes, the same color as the joe and the corners of the house.

Ocie wasn't dragged down by the darkness and continued gleaming as she looked around the nearly empty living room. "You can test out every one, and we'll know we've found a winner when you fall asleep on one."

Emilie pressed her lips together. The woman looked like she needed to sleep right now. The bed had not done her any good, but at least she had slept. She and Ocie had stayed up all night clearing out the trash and unsalvageable junk. Emilie felt like she was slowly ripping out her mother's organs and entrails and making her watch. This whole process was excruciating.

"I don't have money for a new couch," Hellen grumbled, burying her face in the mug.

"I can afford it. Don't worry," Greg's voice returned, and Emilie's spine stiffened like a rake. He took off his coat, draping it over a box in the hall and bearing four fancy coffees, which he distributed amongst the girls, even Hellen.

She wouldn't quickly give up her boring black coffee, but Emilie almost rejected it altogether when Ocie slapped her hand. "Be polite!"

Emilie groaned, keeping herself one inch from touching the floor where they sat. The hot coffee seeped into her palms and she hated it, but she held it, waiting for it to get cold so she could pretend it wasn't good anymore.

Ocie sipped hers, wary of the heat, but that innocent and precious smile was glued to her face. "Thank you so much for letting me stay another night," she beamed. "I can help you start packing if you like. I really don't mind."

"We're certainly grateful." Greg smiled, taking a seat behind Hellen.

Emilie glared at him skeptically, noticing how he didn't actually sit on the floor, but rather on his feet, using his thick-soled boots to keep off the carpet. Hellen was miserable. She didn't want him behind her, she didn't trust him, and Emilie could blatantly see that even though Ocie was blind to it. Ocie just wanted to help, especially with people around. She just wanted to be *Miss Perfect.*

Shifting, Emilie made herself float up and leave the group.

"Where are you going?" Ocie asked quickly.

"To my room, give me a sec!" Emilie seethed, flying through the hall and diving into the only other empty room in the house. She had a bed, an empty dresser, and a pillowcase full of clothes she had never unpacked from the moment she left the ASH until now.

Ocie didn't give her ten seconds of silence. "Hey, what's wrong?"

Her eyes widening, Emilie spun about and rose up over her. "How could you leave them alone!" she hissed through her teeth. "I saw him shove her to the floor! I don't want them to move in together, but I do want her out of this house! That's the only reason I'm going along with stripping her of everything she cares about!"

"I see," Ocie responded too quickly, her tender eyes glazing over. "You care about her a lot."

"Don't assume things about me!" Emilie growled. "I'm doing this for me! That man is going to abuse her until she has no part of herself left alive!" It was real effort to keep her voice down.

"Well, he's a Shadow. We're just going to have to trust that his heart is pure. He might be abrasive, but Sil is too. You need to learn to see the good in people."

"Don't patronize me!" she spat, livid and refusing to back down. "He raised his hand to me! If he's capable of hitting me, he'll hit her! I want your help to get rid of him! As soon as all her stuff is packed, we're going to the ASH!"

Ocie raised a brow in sarcasm, "*You're* going to go back to the ASH?"

"We've got nowhere else to go! She can barely pay the electricity bill, much less groceries!" Emilie couldn't contain her anger. She needed to scream. She needed to run away. She had to get out of here and go to Sil's... that wasn't going to solve anything. She groaned, trying to get her heart rate down. "I hate this..." she admitted finally. "I hate being trapped under her roof, and I hate her..." Finally lowering, Emilie collapsed into her springy bed, miserable.

"You don't hate her," Ocie soothed, sitting down beside her like a true sister. "You're not as selfish as you think, stop trying to convince yourself otherwise. You can be as hard as you like, but the walls you put up are only going to make you lonelier."

Emilie slapped her hand away before a hug could be suggested. "Get off your high-horse." She dropped her face into her hands. "I don't want this. I don't know what I want. I know I want to fly, but when I run away I just feel emptier. I miss being around Shadows, being around the people who knew me and didn't skirt around me. Like Kip! I tried to insult him, and he didn't even flinch; whereas, my *mom* would start crying!"

Finally, Ocie's hand made contact with her back. "I know you don't see it, and you're trying to look out for yourself, but you're very protective. I know you think it doesn't matter if he hurts you, but it does. You might not feel an emotional attachment to him, but she does, and it's not your responsibility to save her. You don't deserve to live in abuse, or in chaos. You can have safety, and you do deserve it. You can always come back to the ASH, if you want." Her suggestion was so biased it made Emilie's face sting. Before Emilie began weighing the option, Ocie patted her lovingly. "I know you want to see this through. Let your mom do what she wants, to be with the man who is your father. After they move in, you can come to the ASH, and still check on her. Do you think you can do that?"

Emilie shuddered, her limbs curling close, cold and strengthless. Her core was freezing, but she made a shaky nod. "Okay," she gasped, holding back tears. She wouldn't cry in front of Ocie. She wouldn't cry in front of anyone! She could hold out a little longer, help Hellen, and make sure she was settled before she left the woman again.

"She's never going to forgive me." She shuddered.

Ocie's grin deepened. "Since when have you ever cared?" She wrapped her hands around both of Emilie's shoulders. "I don't pretend to know what's best for you, but I do know you, and I can tell you're not listening to your heart because you want to protect her. You don't have to. She can protect herself, I promise."

Emilie shook her head, unsure.

"Okay... try to think about something else?" Ocie urged, certain driving the nail any deeper would only aggravate her.

Sitting up starkly, Emilie pulled all her hair back and smirked. "Mark's got a crush on you. Is that a big enough subject change?"

Ocie's brows shot up in surprise. "I'm a year older than him," she dismissed with a laugh.

"Does that matter?" Emilie blared sarcastically. "He's head over heels to the point where Rita is completely jealous, and their relationship has all but completely self-destructed because of that. I'm pretty sure Rita hates you."

"Gossip is going to get us nowhere." Ocie stood, maturely trying to push away the topic. She was only sixteen. She wasn't that much older than him.

"*Here's an idea*," Emilie mocked Ocie's *pretty-sweet* voice. "How about you give him a date? Make his day. Maybe when you two work out, or not, Rita and him can finally get back to their normal antics, and Mark can stop moping about."

"That's not the impression I've been getting in the Realm," Ocie retorted with a laugh. "I don't want to step in between them. Rita can be petty, but she'll work this out, probably already has, and now she's faced with Mark's stubborn side."

"That or he's moved on and made his decision." Emilie crossed her legs and reclined in midair.

Ocie reeled about. "Are you incapable of restraint?"

Throwing her arms back behind her head, Emilie cackled. "I just tell it like it is!"

Mark caught himself distracted one more time, his eyes drifting off to the wall of weapons and the various powers he could sense within each. He deflected a sudden blow over his head, instinct driving him more than anything, and he was almost unconscious to the movement. "How do you find all those swords?" he asked curiously.

Geoffrey spared a glance at his trove. "Some of them were being auctioned in private collections. Some of them were made hundreds of years ago by Shadows and have passed hands. My dad is the one who put this together, and those two swords of Strength were the last before he passed."

"No, I mean, how do you detect them? I can only barely pick up on the Shadows, and it's not like a presence, so I imagine it's really hard for Shadows who aren't strong in the Realm."

"Ahh," Geoffrey hummed, testing a series of strikes to keep Mark's focus. One swing tapped over Mark's right shoulder, then the left, then sweeping his legs, and back. The routine was comfortable, allowing Geoffrey to do it faster each time. "The powers are dormant unless a Shadow comes along and activates them, and even then, it's usually only people who specialize in class two Infusions and sometimes only the one who performed it. Others are more innate, like poisons on the blade undetectable by science, but once they bind to the blood, like a Shadow working through your element, that's what activates the poison. These weapons are designed to be clean, quiet, and efficient."

Mark tried his luck and instigated the pattern, putting Geoffrey on the receiving end of the three blows. "So using an Infused object in general puts that Shadow into my element temporarily, letting me use it?"

Geoffrey shrugged. "Or sometimes not temporarily. It all depends on how the weapon was designed in the first place. Shadows build them to serve all kinds of purposes. Swords where one nick will kill the victim, wands to cast wild enchantments, earth-bending staves, water-bending paddles. Or stones in your case," he added playfully.

His eyes caught a twisted and shimmering metal stick on the wall in a glass case. It looked like a wand. "Will you teach me how to Infuse a weapon? Maybe I could have my own sword."

Smirking, Geoffrey quickly dodged Mark's weak swipe. "No, I know firsthand just how dangerous these weapons are, and I can't in good conscience put one in the hands of a kid unless you're properly trained or have a connection to the thing. And I won't let you make one to forge that connection."

Mark smirked. "You know I'm going to try to make one now."

"Do not!" Geoffrey warned, still keeping that nonchalant attitude. "Get good with technique first, then we can move on to boring metal swords that are actually sharp, and then you can up the ante by throwing Shadows into the mix."

Distracted, Mark smiled up at the shiny blades, quietly excited. He wasn't even aware of any soreness anymore, just happy. Keeping his focus into the slow choreography of slashes and parries, he felt like he was actually getting the hang of this. Geoffrey had tested his strength and his knowledge, and now he was actually learning. Happiness, satisfaction, a task—it felt like months since he'd had any of those. And for the first time, this could continue for the foreseeable days to come.

"Do you want to try real swords?" Geoffrey offered suddenly.

Mark's shoulders fell lank.

"You're doing really good keeping up with me, and if we take it slow, I think you could be ready."

"Really? It's only been three days!"

Geoffrey shook his head, bemused. "And, in three days, you're past the point of *beat it with a stick.* You understand how easily you can get hurt, and right now, your caution is at an all-time high. You're in the right mindset for an introduction to fencing."

"Okay," Mark nodded hastily, following Geoffrey with his eyes as the man set down his wooden sword, prompting Mark to do the same. Geoffrey strode to the wall, admiring the blades until he came across a pair of identical short swords. Both made of an old, tarnished silver, but sturdy and similar in weight and style to the wooden swords they were using.

With a sword in either hand, Geoffrey passed Mark the silver blade in his left hand. "This is not a weapon yet," he said. Mark cherished the sword, wrapping his fingers around the hilt snugly, taking in the weight and awing at the glint of light caught on the end. "This is a slow dance." Geoffrey extended his blade away from Mark. "Every movement premeditated, controlled, elegant. You must first find the balance in your sword, and finding that is going to be what connects you to your weapon."

Geoffrey drew the sword back like the string of a bow, secure and balanced. "You're looking for the center of gravity, where the sword becomes an extension of yourself, so natural to you that cutting through anything will feel like paper." Mark mimicked his stance, feeling the tip of his sword weighing down. His arm wasn't used to holding up the weight, but he told himself, it was a part of his body, vital and alive.

Geoffrey's voice grew softer. "Now slowly, just like we practiced." He acquired a stance with his sword directed at Mark's. "This isn't the time for speed, just for precision, slow and accurate." Without the force behind his blows with the wooden sword, Geoffrey led into the first blow, raising up the sharp metal blade and declaring, "Three."

Mark parried the blow as seamlessly as he had twenty times already with the wooden sword, but the moment the metals scraped against each other, Mark's heart fluttered. The gentle clink was no more violent than a pair of teacups toasting to health.

"Two." Geoffrey said loudly, striking at Mark's left in slow motion, giving him more than enough time to react. The clang was louder, and Mark's movement was jerking. Geoffrey had to steady it in the air with a glimmer in his eye. Mark could feel it, the firm stillness in the air when his blade impacted Geoffrey's, unwavering, perfectly still.

"One!" The final slash at Mark's right, a similar motion, a series of responses, and that satisfying sound of metal against metal. "Good..." Geoffrey hummed smoothly, "now let's go a little faster, you ready?"

Mark produced a shaky nod.

They returned to a readied posture, blank and protective of their cores. It did remind Mark of judo, but this was too real, too random and unpredictable. Geoffrey gave him fair warning rather than springing on him, instigating with a telling look in his eye. Mark flared his crimson eyes. "Two, one, three!" Geoffrey sequenced quickly.

It was slower than they had been going with the wooden swords, but every impact filled Mark's heart with nervous shivers. Left, up, right, meeting in the middle each time. The sword was much lighter than the wooden sticks. It took less effort to swing, and thus Mark wasn't sure how much force he could put into it.

Geoffrey guided him carefully, starting another pattern. "One, two, three, one, two, three, one, three, one, two, one, two!" Mark didn't know how Geoffrey could match the sequence and keep count of which one he was planning. Mark only barely understood the numbering assigned to each choreographed movement, but what it came down to was seeing where the sword traveled using Geoffrey's eyes to view his intentions and meeting it. "Two, one, three, two, one." Mark protected his left then his right, raised his sword to parry off the blow to his head, immediately protected his left side again, but had to switch gears very quickly when the metal sword swung for his head.

Mark gasped, the two blades shattering against each other, and the metal ringing out loudly through the room as he raised it up with all his might. "You didn't—" he cringed when Geoffrey pushed down on him harder.

"Anticipate your opponent tricking you." Geoffrey smiled through his teeth before letting off and giving Mark a moment to recover. "One thing you're going to have to work on is not being so stationary," Geoffrey padded lightly on his feet, beginning a slow circle around him. "Be prepared to move, to get away, or to drive in. Decisions you'll eventually have to make. Forget honor in not backing down. You'll have to get to a point where you know there's no shame in running. Your honor is not more important than your life. That was a lesson I had to learn the hard way."

Mark nodded determinedly. "Got it!"

"Again?" Geoffrey offered, and Mark struck first.

XV
RATHER RUN

"I'll see you tomorrow," Mark called as the door latched shut, and he hesitated on the front walkway. Glancing over his shoulder at the window to his right, he spotted Geoffrey about to make lunch, opening up the fridge and going about his day. A puff of green light materialized at his side, and Mark scowled. Rita had been there the whole time watching them. He wasn't oblivious to her in the slightest, constantly aware of her presence in the Realm even while he was fighting.

Please come out. Can we talk? he called out in the Realm, knowing more than anything else she was listening. She would hear.

Through the dim glass, he could see her stop moving, her green eyes flashing, staring at him on the doorstep. Geoffrey gave her a nudge, a gentle, warm smile, and she frowned. She teleported, and a seamless second later, she appeared outside. Bitter sorrow rooted in her eyes, and she refused to look at him.

"Is there something I did to hurt you?" Mark pled, taking only one step closer so as not to prompt her to run away.

Rita hugged her arm, tears already clinging to her eyes. "You just never noticed me..." she cried. "We spent the last few months together, hoppin' around on adventures, but you never once asked me to take you to my home, or why I didn't want to go there."

Mark's spine stiffened, and he gulped, but the words were a relief. "I thought you didn't like the Shadows there because they're isolationists. Isn't that what you said?"

"There's more to Scotland than just Shadows," she mumbled angrily.

"You're not making any sense. Why does it bother you to be a mode of transportation? You didn't have a problem with it during the Exodus even though we talked about it, and you didn't have a problem doing it for Emilie yesterday."

Rita cringed, letting her tears slip away. "Because I cannae run anymore! Okay! I got what I wanted. I got out of my home, I got out of the ASH, and now I can live in the country I ran away to. I want to stay in one place and feel safe. Is that so hard to understand?"

"So why are you avoiding me?" Mark snapped back at her.

"I want to be with you!" Rita sobbed, completely losing the walls she'd built up. "You let me in. We had so much in common, but when we went back to the ASH, you only had eyes for Ocie! I was invisible to you!" Clawing mindlessly, she dried away her tears, unable to make them stop. "You make me feel safe, you make me feel happy and loved. But I have to work so hard to keep you from leaving me!"

"Rita…" Mark gasped, reaching out and trying to take her hands. "I would never leave you!"

"I thought it would be easier if I just left." She whimpered, covering her red face. "I feel safe here too. I could find somewhere else to live."

This time, Mark successfully grasped Rita's hand and refused to let go. "Come with me. We can just hang out, and you can—"

"No..." she glowered. "I just need some time. And your feelings aren't going to change."

Mark gaped, his breath catching again, and for a few moments, he didn't know how to inhale. "Rita! You didn't give me time to say I didn't like you like that. You just assumed I didn't and ran!"

Crossing her arms, Rita hugged herself as if for protection. "You made it pretty clear who you want to be with, with your doe-eyed, enamored, stupid face, giving her gifts and showing off your powers!" she seethed.

Flustering at her anger, Mark stepped away hastily. "Well, maybe I should make it clearer for you. Ocie would never act like this. I look up to her because she's so mature, but you're my friend because we're the same. I can talk to you, and you can always talk to me. I can't approach Ocie! She's on a completely different level from me, and she's Shadow Hope."

"You still worship the ground she walks on!"

"Would you stop it!" Mark pleaded. "I don't want to argue if you're going to be unreasonable!"

"Then just say it!" Rita demanded firmly, her back stiff and straight to hide the fear in her eyes.

Mark inhaled sharply, all his breath coming back to him and fueling the words he would immediately regret. "You'd rather run than have your heart broken! If this is who you really are, and you're going to freak out every time something like this happens, just leave me alone!"

Rita gasped, that little fear turning to terror, but Mark didn't let her continue, turning about with his wooden sword in hand and storming down the walkway. "And don't keep coming by!" he added, not looking back.

He never heard her teleport away, and with all his might, he started to run, not to Sil's house but straight home. The air was nippy and bitter, altogether making Mark more miserable. His strained muscles started to ache, his legs began to feel limp, but he pressed on, running the seven miles. At the turn to the Addison's cul-de-sac, he paused to catch his breath, supporting his hands on his knees and panting. He didn't declare himself in the Realm. He didn't want Sil to know he was close even though that was probably impossible.

Once he had rested, he picked himself back up. Home was close now, and even though fire ripped through the muscles in his legs, he persisted into the garage quietly, through the kitchen and past Marissa, and finally, he closed himself into his own room and collapsed onto the bed. He felt sick, way too physically exhausted to get up, and his heart beat like a war horse. He'd just run seven miles in the cold. He had nothing left.

He slammed his window shut and pulled the covers over himself.

"You're home early," Marissa called through the door, knocking a few times but receiving no answer. She probably assumed he was playing video games and had headphones on, so she left him alone.

Mark let the whole day go by, completely asleep until sunset, dreamless and content. He didn't stir until it was fully dark out. The light of the family car's headlights streaked across his room as his dad pulled in, and he groaned, sitting up slowly and yanking his defiant body out of bed. His legs were cold and he was exhausted, but he pushed himself out of the room and into the hall-bath to take a much-needed shower.

He joined his family for dinner, pecking at the plate and not finishing anything. He scraped his plate sullenly and only managed the soft words, "I'm going to bed," at six-thirty in the evening.

Locking his door behind him, and plopping back down in bed, Mark first turned on his TV, heaving a very long sigh. Just to cool his nerves, and try to sleep a little more, he started a game. The chatrooms were abuzz in his ears, but he kept his microphone off to listen to the chatter and sink into the violent worlds. He met up with some friends and ran a mission, not getting too into it, and leaving the group silently once the round was complete.

A notification pinged in his headset, and he opened the live chat. *"I got your Usertag from Rita -Geoffrey"*

Mark smiled to himself just a little; he did have one thing to look forward to tomorrow, more sparring, and another day with metal swords. Reaching over to his bedside table, he pulled up a small detachable *QWERTY* and plugged it into his controller. *"Is she there?"* he typed.

A trio of dancing circles appeared as Geoffrey typed, *"no,"* followed by, *"I thought I said no video games,"* and an accompanying emoticon.

Quietly, Mark chuckled and reclined deep into his bed. His shoulder was feeling a lot better, and the mobility of his elbow had improved after the stretches, but he wouldn't argue with Geoffrey over texting.

"Would you like to come over tonight for another hour or so?" Geoffrey's words came through abruptly as if he had typed them very fast, and that was saying something on the tiny keyboard.

Mark's heart stirred with excitement. The one thing he was looking forward to tomorrow could happen now? He sat forward instantly, his thumbs tapping madly on the little controller. *"Yes, I'll be there in an hour."* He could make it in an hour, if he ran. He got up too quickly and realized how tired his legs still were. On second thought, his gaze drifted to his roller skates. They would cut the effort in half.

He peeked out of his bedroom door to see the front room virtually vacant, but he still didn't trust it. He locked his door and snuck out the window. In the grass outside, he strapped on his skates and tossed his shoes over his shoulder.

It was barely ten o'clock when he saw the golden lights from within the windows of Geoffrey's house. He tried to barge in but found the front door was locked, and he had to wait for Geoffrey to come answer it. Mark stepped over the threshold and skated out toward the small dining table, taking a moment to switch his shoes.

"Well, that looks remarkably dangerous. You skated here in the dark?" Geoffrey commented in that endearing snark, locking the door behind him.

Mark tucked his laces into his skates and scanned the house. In the Realm, he couldn't sense Rita, and he sighed. She really was gone. One more phrase Geoffrey had taught him was sticking: *"There's no shame in running."* Mark hid his disgust. Rita and Emilie ran away constantly. He would never be that cowardly. Emilie was a little justified—she could fly, she'd been trapped her whole life and this was the first freedom she had tasted, but then, the same could be said for Rita.

Geoffrey took no notice of his brooding and jumped right in, taking the same two swords off the wall. "Let's work on keeping you moving." He passed one to Mark, but the moment he touched the blade he knew it wasn't the same one he had earlier. He wasn't certain how he determined that instantly, but upon closer inspection, he discovered the hilt had a different wrapping on the handle.

Loosening his wrist, Geoffrey began circling him. "Follow my movements," he instructed, pointing out his feet as the dance-like pattern slowly spiraled around the room. Mark mimicked this, orbiting around an invisible axis as Geoffrey trained the tip of his sword at him. "There is a tug and pull with fencing. You'll learn when it's the right time to gain ground or give it up. It'll make you more aware of where your back is, obstacles in your path, and how to get the high ground."

Mark crossed blades with him, making infinite tiny adjustments to prepare for the first routine. Geoffrey ditched the numbers, eliminating the warning of where each blow would land. Thus, he started slow, keeping his feet moving as he dealt five smooth contacts, one after another. Mark met each one, the satisfying clang of the metal confirming his success and preparing him for the next. His feet, however, staggered, and he fought to keep himself from freezing.

"I'm going to do it exactly the same. Keep yourself moving," Geoffrey warned and recreated the exact pattern of slashes.

"Good!" he declared when Mark kept moving in a circle. "I'm going to take some ground now. You have plenty of room. You won't run into anything." Geoffrey tapped the tip of Mark's sword then made the five swift movements again, no faster than the last two times. However, after each contact, he took a step, pushing Mark toward the door.

"There! Easy peasy!" Geoffrey declared. "Now it's your turn to lead."

Mark gulped but was comfortable enough that he wouldn't slip up to practice the new aspect of movement. Five strokes—left, right, over, swipe, jab—but he couldn't get his feet to move but two steps forward. He didn't try to circle. He tried to gain ground.

Geoffrey only took two steps back towards the wall of weapons, nowhere near close to it, but Mark could see Geoffrey's spark of pride in his ambitious decision. There was a swell of excitement in those two steps, and Geoffrey lowered his sword. Mark's eyes didn't flare. He kept them as cold as possible to not prompt Geoffrey's defenses.

Abruptly, Mark lunged forward, making up more than ten strokes, motions he had not practiced, but he let instincts and muscle memory drive him to take a chance. He aimed over Geoffrey's shoulder, coming down on it with all his strength. Geoffrey met it with a loud resounding *clang* and blew Mark's strike off. He reverted, slashing at his side, and again Geoffrey deflected it. Mark swung as fast as he could, recovering from each parry and pushing Geoffrey back.

Abruptly, about three paces from the wall, Geoffrey wouldn't allow his feet to be pushed back any farther and he held his ground. He met Mark's final blow and held it, pressing tight into Mark's crossguard and pushing down over him. Mark felt all his muscles straining. *Keep your footing,* he reminded himself, *don't put your all into it yet. Just hold your ground.* With both hands around the hilt, he did precisely that. He just drew out the hold, standing his ground as long as he could so he had time to weigh his options.

He was so much smaller than Geoffrey, who right now made it more than clear he was only putting a fraction of his strength into pinning him. Geoffrey could easily sacrifice his footing, use one hand, or shove him to the floor if he wanted.

Mark had to use everything he had. He was going to run out of energy soon, either that or strain himself again, so he had to do something.

He refused to hurt himself by overestimating his own abilities. He had to work smarter. He ducked and dodged the full weight of Geoffrey's arms. He stumbled and Mark tripped in opposite direction. Turning hastily, he slammed into the wall, rattling the many swords and knocking one of the sword cases off its shelf.

The priceless gold sword rattled around inside, and Mark winced, praying he hadn't done any damage. "I'm sorry..." he got out, just thankful this time he wasn't injured.

Geoffrey had already recovered his footing and was gazing down at the case with wide eyes. Giving a little groan, Geoffrey went down to his knees to carefully open it and check to see the sword was safe. The glistening glow of the gold caught Mark's gaze, and he realized he had disturbed the second case, not the one containing Morglay. The sword inside also had a gold hilt, but it lacked the many crested jewels except one small ruby on the end of the pommel in exchange for a blade dyed blood red.

"Mark…" Geoffrey exhaled, and Mark prepared himself for a reprimand, hanging his head in shame. "I think you're ready."

Tensing, Mark's gaze shot up in disbelief. "What?" he gasped. "Ready for what?"

Geoffrey picked up the whole case and brought it over to the coffee table. "We didn't meet each other by accident. I didn't move here by coincidence. I was looking for you."

Mark got up hastily, his heart constricting with anxiety.

Leaving the second sword, Geoffrey fetched Morglay, giving Mark a long minute to take in the beauty and elegance of the Sword of Strength. "I have to finish Strength's work, and I told you from the beginning I wanted to give you a sword. Morglay is mine, and Lævatein is the blade that wounded me."

His eyes flashing with fire, Mark stared at the red sword. "Lævatein?"

Very carefully, Geoffrey lifted it out of its case. "Mark, my intention is not just to give you a new weapon, but a new Shadow."

"Wait…" Mark stepped back shocked. "You're going to give me Shadow Strength? That thing is probably worth more than my house!"

Geoffrey smirked a little. "Don't get me wrong. It costs a lot to wield this sword. Strength has passed wielders like this for generations, and one day you'll pass Strength to someone else."

"But, you're not a Shadow! Why are you—"

Abruptly, Geoffrey's posture changed, his twinge of a smile vanished and his eyes flared gold. "You can't sense my Shadow because it's dormant, only my second Shadow Strength is active, and like all *class three* Shadows, they're very hard to detect. I wouldn't expect you, even with your Understanding in the Realm, to pick up on it. So

I made sure, testing your ability to sense Shadows around you."

"But why couldn't I sense you in the Realm? I can communicate with Shadows a hundred miles away!" Mark yelled, not sure what to do in the face of this clearly powerful Shadow who had evaded the ASH.

Geoffrey's smile returned. "Focus, remember what I told you. I was blocking myself out of the Realm, which takes a lot of concentration and practice. You *are* very strong, Mark, but you have four months of practice, and I've been at this all my life."

Mark seethed a little. Geoffrey had been taking advantage of the fact he knew nothing about Shadows the whole time. He stared at Lævatein and pressed his lips together bitterly. "Thank you for the offer, I guess, but I can't accept." He took a few more wary steps backward. "I'm good with Infusions. I'll practice a bit, then I'll make my own weapon." Cautiously, he headed straight for the door, weighing whether or not he had time to put on his skates.

Behind him, Geoffrey sighed and turned away, opening Morglay's case as well. "Maybe one day, but that's not an option right now." Across the room upon the wall of weapons, Geoffrey opened the thermostat hidden among the steel, and when he adjusted it, Mark felt a familiar stir in the Realm.

All through the house, the floor and the walls, a bronze aura tainted the windows, and in the Realm, Mark could sense the glowing cyan pulsing through the structure of the building. He gasped and turned slowly. "You just turned on an ASI. You know that doesn't work on me."

Geoffrey suddenly threw down Lævatein so that it slid across the hard floor to Mark's feet. "It does work on Rita."

Jumping out of his skin at the noise, Mark tensed and sent out a wave in the Realm. Someone had to hear! He wasn't blocked by the ASI! He sent one message, loud and clear. *Rita, help!*

He spotted a bright flash of green in the corner of his eyes, just outside the window. She had been nearby, always listening for him. Even after what he had said to her. "Mark!" she screamed through the glass, muffling the sounds as she banged on the surface. The ASI zapped her powers, sending her fists flying back and preventing her from touching it without a painful jolt.

Mark's eyes dashed to the crimson blood sword, Lævatein, the only weapon within his reach. He summoned his bravery and gulped. "Go get Ocie! She can defy the ASI too!"

Geoffrey closed in on the center of the room, bearing his own shimmering golden Morglay. He didn't show the same care to it as he had before, wielding it just as any other sword. "Lævatein is yours. You don't have to fight back, but it usually makes the ritual a little more interesting if you do."

XVI
LÆVATEIN AND MORGLAY

March 7, 2031

A horrible feeling wrenched through his gut, and January awoke abruptly on the couch. The living room had grown cold as if a window was open somewhere, and he sat up groggily. His heart felt twisted up, beating a little faster even though he couldn't remember dreaming anything. He checked the time and groaned because it was well after midnight.

January trudged straight to Mark's room, worried maybe he was up again, shivering or weathering the pain he had last night. There was a pale blue light under his door, but he hesitated to approach, grasping his heart. He couldn't shake the fear, the bad feeling, the gut instinct that something was wrong, but the other side of him assured Mark was just staying up too late playing video games.

He tried the doorknob to find it locked, and he glanced down the hall at his bedroom where Marissa was sleeping alone. Quietly, he knocked a few times even though he knew it was useless. If Mark had headphones on, he wouldn't hear. Yawning, January shuffled into the dining room, searching a cabinet by the back door for a paperclip.

In the dark, he dropped it and had to feel around, but as he carried it back down the hall, he straightened it into a key.

The lock snapped open loudly and January peered in, his eyes first catching the light of the TV. It was bright, and he needed a moment to adjust, but the console was idling. Mark's bed was empty, and the window was cracked open.

"Mark?" January addressed quietly, scanning the room fully, then peering back down the hall at the bathroom. He called a few more times, and the assumptions flew about in his head. Mark had probably gone over to Sil's or Geoffrey's. Mark had a friend who could teleport. He could be anywhere. That didn't worry January, but for some reason, panic started to rise in him.

He didn't know why he was so worried. He didn't know why the bad feeling was swelling. He couldn't keep still. Hastily, he got dressed warmly and stormed out to the car.

Mark stood with his feet firmly planted to the floor, trying to hold his strength up to the tip of Lævatein. The unfamiliar sword was much heavier than the other metal swords and the wooden ones, and it had a completely different balance. He had to find that balance quickly. He had to make this sword an extension of himself. He gripped it tightly in his right hand, finding the most comfortable handling, and definitely appreciating the spiraling sweepings which curled around the hilt of the rapier.

It was a permeable cage, but it completely protected his hand. Keeping his eyes locked on Geoffrey, Mark touched the length of Lævatein, discovering one side was sharp and the other was dull. He loosened his wrist, never once taking his eyes off Geoffrey. He adjusted his grip, slipping his index finger over one of the cross bars so his hand was more deeply protected. Also, within this position, he found the balance of the sword.

Geoffrey burst forward, premeditated but unpredictable, thrusting the blade at him, and it was all Mark could do to parry it off and prevent himself from getting impaled. The feeling of the one-handed sword was completely new, and he wanted with every power inside him to control it with both hands, but there simply wasn't room on the hilt. He felt open and unprotected; however, that did leave one of his hands free to use Fire.

Without giving him a chance to recover, Geoffrey swung around at him, slashing Morglay at his arm. Mark held up his sword in the nick of time, batting away the weak end of the flimsy blade, but he wasn't quick enough to spare himself the pain. The heaviest part of Morglay's hilt slammed into his right arm, and as he reeled back, Geoffrey ripped it away, making contact with the sharp side of the blade and slicing shallowly.

Mark stumbled, grasping his right shoulder and letting out a yelp. He looked at his left hand and saw blood. He stared at Geoffrey, appalled, horrified, but now silent in shock.

Geoffrey cackled. "Remember what I told you about Infused blades? This one transfers a Shadow permanently, and the more it gets into your blood, the stronger the effect."

Tensing, Mark winced as a searing pain finally hit him. The blade might as well have been poisoned, and Geoffrey had drawn blood, introducing his system to the new and highly volatile Shadow Strength. He got a rush of adrenaline and his hand burst into flame. Allowing himself to be burned, he sealed the wound. It didn't hurt, but it was an odd sight to see the closed injury coated in blackened scar tissue.

Rushing in again, a stabbing blow rocketed toward Mark with one aim, his torso. Mark jumped clear out of the way. He couldn't win this fight. He just needed to stay alive long enough to run. Rita watched from the other side of the glass sobbing. She was his escape. He just had to unlock the front door and get out, and then Rita could teleport him to safety.

Distraction proved risky as Geoffrey swiped high and didn't give Mark enough time to deflect. Geoffrey was far enough away, and he thought he wouldn't reach. Mark thought he was clear, and he had reeled back far enough, but the very tip of Morglay cut deep above his right eye, near his brow. Mark stumbled to the floor, blood soaking down the side of his face. Any lower and he would have lost his eye.

He had to ignore it. He wouldn't bleed to death. It was just a little blood. He got the hit of adrenaline like a drug pumping into his circulatory system, Shadow Strength entering his bloodstream and taking control. He flailed, swiping the sword madly up at Geoffrey and praying to hit something.

He forced himself to get up, to get back on his feet, to get out of the vulnerable position, and his tenacity was met. He closed his eyes a second, felt the tip of Lævatein swipe across something and Geoffrey yelped. When Mark looked, Geoffrey had reeled back, guarding himself with his sword protectively. Suddenly, he laughed, wiping his face with his free hand, and when he lowered it, Mark realized he'd scored Geoffrey with a vertical cut beside his right eye.

"Wow..." Geoffrey gasped in ecstasy. "Haven't felt that rush in a while!"

Mark paled. Little superficial cuts would only make him stronger. Strength triggered adrenaline, so the more hits he took, the more brash and energized he would get. Geoffrey knew how to control it, but Mark... he was too uncoordinated for anything to go right. But he had landed a hit, and some daft, idiotic impulse in his mind told him to keep going.

The blood on Geoffrey's face mirrored his own, and the man was once again fully prepared to strike. In a fury, Geoffrey slashed back at Mark, not giving him a second of victory. Mark quickly parried off the blows, one at a time. The dance came back. The rhythm made him confident.

Geoffrey nicked his left hand, but he let it burst into flame, and he hastily retaliated by throwing fire at him, doing all he could to push Geoffrey back. This was already becoming a very bloody fight, and Mark's confidence waned every time he took a small cut. The one over his eye was still bleeding, dripping down the side of his face and clouding his vision.

Suddenly, he was distracted by the sound of something crashing into the window, and he looked over to see Sil had arrived, wielding a heavy baseball bat of ice. It didn't even crack the window, instead the ice shattered under the power of the ASI, blowing Sil back. He couldn't hear them in the Realm, but he knew they were screaming at him. "Ocie! Go get Ocie!" he pled, hoping they'd hear.

Through the translucent pane, Rita stood paralyzed, and Mark's face darkened. She wouldn't go get Ocie. She refused to ask Ocie for help. "Rita!" Mark roared.

I'm here, Mark! Ocie's voice soared above him, coming in from the sky, and through the window, Ocie appeared with Emilie carrying her. Sil handed her the bat, and Mark could read his lips as he told her to break the glass.

"Don't get distracted!" Geoffrey growled, thrusting at him. Mark had lowered his sword to yell at the Shadows. He'd lowered his defenses, and the quick movement caught him off guard, thrusting the gold blade of Morglay at his shoulder.

Mark wanted to scream. He saw the blade moving toward him, glistening as it met the light of a car, but it didn't lose course. Geoffrey drove it in as far as he could, grabbing Mark's opposite shoulder to hold him from falling down so he could shove it that extra few inches.

The entirety of the thirty-five inches had passed through his arm.

His eyes went wide as he felt the hilt at rest in his left shoulder, perfectly below his collar bone and above his shoulder blade. He got another glance at Ocie to see her hands over her mouth as she screamed. The muscles in his shoulder frayed, and fire ripped through his veins as his Shadow counteracted the bleeding to no avail. Little spurts of flame raced across his arms and face, spasming, and confused. He couldn't otherwise react.

Suddenly, Geoffrey twisted the blade upward, making sure the injury would not heal, and as he did this, he hooked Mark so that he was forced to remain standing.

Mark couldn't breathe. The pain finally hit him.

Geoffrey's face was less than an inch from his, and he sneered, pointing the blade a little higher. Mark's left arm hung at his side, useless. "For the will of Shadow Trust, this was the task I was given," he whispered. Geoffrey took the hilt of Morglay and shoved it into Mark's shoulder, driving him to fall back and slam into the floor as it was ripped out.

After this, he screamed in agony.

Mark laid there, hugging his arm and wailing, utterly exhausted and now bleeding uncontrollably. Blood dripped from the tip of Morglay, trailing the floor as Geoffrey swiped it through the air. His blood. And now, Morglay looked exactly like the reddened blade of Lævatein. Mark still clung to the hilt, but he couldn't move his left arm.

He tried to sit up a little, holding tight to his sword and glaring up at Geoffrey indignantly. The man stood over him, warning him not to try and swing it. Tears streamed from Mark's eyes. For a few days he had thought Geoffrey was his friend, someone who could teach him. He'd never felt his trust so thoroughly crushed.

Geoffrey loosened his wrist, swinging the sword around and smiling triumphantly as he raised Morglay and pointed it down. Mark tensed when he did this. He looked to Ocie, Sil, Emilie, and Rita, desperate beyond the bronze film of the glass.

Mark's breath escaped him. He tried to breathe, but he couldn't. He didn't feel any pain now. He just felt... nothing at all. His gaze slowly drifted up to Geoffrey, but his view was sliced in half by a gold blade... protruding from his heart.

His red eyes went dim, and his chest felt so tight. He couldn't draw air. He couldn't hear either, but he knew for a fact that his friends were out there, screaming his name at the top of their lungs. His face lolled toward the window, but in the dim light he couldn't see them. They were gone.

He felt something forcing its way up his throat, and finding it impossible to breathe, blood poured out of his mouth and splattered over the wood floors. He collapsed on his back, lying quietly in the blood. Somewhat random, broken, nasty-tasting, erratic, terrible excuses for breaths were all he could acquire while Geoffrey held Morglay firm.

All the pain returned in an instant—every time he had been cut, the fire through his shoulder, and the steel in his chest. Morglay retreated. Geoffrey ripped it out and staggered back a few paces with a euphoric smile. This was a ritual, but he had never done this before. Mark realized it then, those scars; Geoffrey had been through this himself, fighting another Strength. He could feel the foreign Shadow inside him, he could feel his heart rejecting it, fighting it off, and the adrenaline Shadow Strength gave him was the only thing keeping him conscious.

Mark's lungs expanded like balloons, and he gasped, sputtering with the blood in his mouth, which drained over his lips. Everything was silent, all he could hear was his own raggedy breathing. Geoffrey just stood there, traumatized and unsure how proud he should be. All that confidence Geoffrey had portrayed was gone in an instant. Mark's energy waned, and his eyes fell shut, only aware of the faint air passing through his throat.

His hearing returned when the window shattered, but more than that, the whole wall was blown down, and Mark saw the front end of a car crash into the house.

"Mark!" Emilie flew in, holding onto Ocie's hand long enough to pass through the ASI. Ocie climbed over the wreckage, followed by another figure, silhouetted by the headlights of the car. Mark could only see a halo of light when he tried to make out a face. He didn't know who it was, until he saw that silver crown.

January didn't charge at Mark, but straight to Geoffrey, firing a fist at him with all the weight in his body behind the blow. Geoffrey took the punch to the face, which sent him to the floor and into the corner of the wall. His head struck it at full force, and he didn't rise.

Ocie went for the controls to the ASI to take it down and let Sil and Rita into the barrier. "Mark! Mark!" Emilie slid down across the floor and grabbed his hand. Finally, the rest of them surrounded him, crowding over, and Sil was the first to examine his injuries.

Sil was as cold and frigid as always, but the fear in his eyes was unmistakable. "He's barely moving air…"

Mark couldn't fill his lungs. There was just a little wind, passing in and out. He coughed violently as he tried to break through the barrier of blood in his lungs, but it hurt so much, and his fearsome cough sprayed blood all over his neck.

Ocie lifted his head into her lap, attempting to raise his back and open his airways, but it ultimately made it harder to breathe and smeared his blood onto her skirt.

"January!" Emilie shrieked suddenly. "You have to call an ambulance!"

January's knees hit the floor with a hard *thud*. His hands were trembling, and he hesitated for a second before daring to touch his son. He could barely summon any voice. "I left my phone at home." His chest filled with horror. Tears started to flow, and he gathered Mark up into his arms in a tight embrace. Mark seemed so light to January, so small, and he inhaled sharply, clearly in pain to be held. He savored it while simultaneously resenting it. He clung to the rapier in his right hand, the only tangible thing he had the strength to hold onto. His eyes fell shut, and a tear of pure blood fell from his cheek.

Emilie glanced between the Shadows frantically. "Somebody find a phone!" she screamed. Sil didn't move, and Ocie sat there in her own tears. Emilie turned to Rita. "Go!" she howled. "Go get him help! You're the reason he's in this mess anyway!"

Rita's back stiffened. "I—" She choked and tears started to fall.

Furrowing her brows, Emilie rose up a little, letting go of Mark's limp hand. "Then get out of here!" she bellowed.

Mark's breaths halted abruptly, and from his father's arms he struggled to exhale, unbearable pain closing his throat. Even within January's arms, he coughed again, and this time what felt like a liter of blood poured out of him, leaving him cold. January grimaced at the blood doused on him. The blood itself was Mark's life, quickly seeping away.

Mark blinked erratically, his crimson eyes dim, still blazing with the fire inside him, but it was fading. His breaths became slower, further apart and softer. He didn't even try to draw air. He opened his eyes just enough to see Ocie's face, just long enough for January to see they had turned completely brown again. He managed to keep his eyes open, but after a few long seconds, his gaze fell distant and dark.

January gripped him tightly, but upon feeling his son's body go completely limp, he released him to see Mark's pale and bloody face. Mark sagged in his father's arms and his empty gaze drifted off to an unknown place. All of the Shadows let out a gasp when they saw his dark brown eyes, devoid of his Shadow.

Sil reeled up on his knees and touched Mark's face, hovering his fingers just over his mouth. "He's not breathing!" he whispered in utter horror. Hastily, he stood up and ran to Rita. "Go to the hospital, right now, and get him an ambulance! I'll tell you the address in the Realm!"

Rita shook through her tearstained face, but finally managed to nod and teleported away. As soon as she was gone, Sil ran out onto the street to get the house number.

Minutes passed. Sil stood over them, staring at Mark and biting his nails. January lifted his son back into his arms, simply crying, unable to save Mark. Sil seethed, grinding his teeth. "We have to get him breathing!" he panicked. "Ocie, can you help me?"

Shakily, Ocie nodded. "What are you going to do?"

Sil knelt on the floor and grasped January's arm. "I'm going to try CPR. That's all I can do." He pried January's grip free to try to force him to let go of Mark, but it was hard. He made Mark lay on the floor as if in sleep, but his wounds were still flowing. Sil crossed his hands but hesitated. Blood saturated Mark's chest. He could potentially injure Mark more by doing this.

Seeing his hesitation, Ocie got up on her knees. "We could try an Infusion?"

Sil's eyes widened, panic-stricken and frozen. "For healing? Do you know how to do that?"

Ocie nodded hastily. "We need more Shadows though. I don't think three will be enough."

His gaze dashing about hastily, Sil quickly opened himself in the Realm. *Rita, get back here! We need you!* The green mist flashed behind January. Rita was even more hysterical.

Ocie stood and gestured her over. "Okay, we all need to take our Shadows out," she instructed looking to the others, especially Emilie who was pained to part with her ability to fly.

Emilie, however, didn't show any reluctance and pressed her palm over her heart, exuding an immensely black orb of dark energy. Sil followed and prompted Rita to do so while January stared in horror. Ocie removed her Shadow and held it out over Mark. "Now, we combine them." She guided Sil's wrist, gently moving the two Shadows closer to each other. Emilie and Rita followed suit cautiously.

January got out of the way hastily and watched, in fear, the bewildering powers before his eyes. But he didn't say anything. If he didn't interfere, they had a little hope in saving him. Each Shadow had its own light, a little glow within the blackness that seemed to offset the inky black hole. January wasn't sure if he should look into them, as if he was looking directly into little stars. It seemed horribly paradoxical, and he found himself taking a few extra steps back as the four Shadows spun and tangled together.

Their auras became intertwined, and suddenly, the blackness burst out in a pure, immensely bright white light. Ocie held tight to it. Sil could barely see her face through the glare, but she was confident. She lowered it, pressing her palms over Mark's heart and holding it there. The light burst, filling up the entire house and blinding January.

He shielded his eyes, but he had to peek, he had to look into the light of four Shadows going supernova within a single heart. He could barely see Mark's body through the white, but he could feel an incredible warmth within it, and he knew exactly what it was doing. The Infusion was deep within Mark's heart, mending the puncture and pushing it gently, urging it to beat again. It was brilliant. It was a pure plea for life.

Ocie fell back to her knees just as the light's intensity waned. Mark still lay motionless, his hand curled around Lævatein's hilt. Sil lowered himself upon the hardwood, staring at Mark and hoping. The wound was still there, open and bleeding, and Mark didn't move.

January took Mark back in his arms, squeezing him tightly and wallowing in grief, utterly unsure how much hope he should allow himself. Mark was only fifteen, how could this be his fate at such a young age? He sobbed, his whole torso shuddering as he came to terms with the grisly scene. Was Mark gone?

Ocie fell into tears again. "I'm sorry. I thought it would work! It wasn't strong enough."

Sil bit his lip. All they could do now was wait for the emergency team, but even then, it was probably too late.

Emilie stared down at her legs, attempting to move them and certainly too weak to stand. Her power was gone, and a panic entered her posture, looking to the others, for any evidence their sacrifice wasn't for nothing. Sil laid a hand on her leg, trying to reassure her, but he shook his head.

January gulped, cradling Mark and glancing between them, at Rita standing five paces behind them covering her mouth, and at the moaning and shifting form of Geoffrey lying on the floor. No one else seemed to notice, but January glared hot hell at Geoffrey as he awoke and assessed his surroundings nervously. Geoffrey locked eyes with January for just a second, and fear entered his expression.

Ocie never took her eyes off Mark, Sil and Emilie held each other, and Geoffrey inched to his feet and scrambled away as soundlessly as possible. January's heart calmed when that monster was gone, and he gazed into Mark's empty face. Tears dripped off the apples of his cheeks, and he looked away, up at the shattered wall. He caught a glimpse of a fire on the horizon. Morning was attempting to break over the tops of houses and trees. Edged with purple darkness and a vibrant gold at its center. The sun began to climb and stream over the smashed wall into the house.

The gold glistened against Lævatein's blade. The fire burst, and something happened.

Mark's chest expanded fully, and he gasped for air as if he had been holding his breath. He came to, sputtering, disoriented, and wincing, but he suddenly started violently coughing again, sending blood from his mouth. However, once his airways were clear, he gaped, breathing deeply, and just trying to get the blood out of his lungs.

Ocie gasped also, actually holding her breath and letting the relief wash over her. Emilie rose off the floor a few inches, and her Shadow returned to her.

Mark's eyes burst open. Confused and hyperventilating, he glanced around, panicked, and he somehow found Rita's gaze, just as she teleported away. Everything hurt, and his memory was a blotchy mess. January held onto him even as he felt him jolt, but he gazed into his eyes to see them more crimson than ever. Releasing the purest tears, January cried, and embraced his son again, relieved. He was still bleeding, and not all his wounds were healed, but he'd live. With time and healing, he'd live!

XVII
SURVIVAL

"Mark! Mark! Stay with me! You've gotta calm down." Ocie called into his face as he gasped, looking around and trying to move. Flashing lights filled his vision, and he panicked as he saw other figures moving around him, dim silhouettes in the morning light, adult figures he didn't know. "You're going in an ambulance. You can't freak out."

Mark felt four pairs of hands touching him and one very shaky voice muttering, "What happened to this kid?" Abruptly, Mark's breath stopped, and eight hands raised him up, transferring his maimed body onto a stretcher and carrying him out the front door. For a few seconds, he saw the sky, then the roof of an ambulance covered him and the loud noises of the doors shutting kept him alert and scared.

His shirt was ripped off, and the paramedics started packing gauze into his shoulder and his chest, sending Mark reeling back, screaming. The ambulance finally started barreling down the road. Mark's heart pounded ravenously as he lay in pain with his eyes clamped tight. He felt someone holding his hand, someone with very cold fingers.

Sil's voice called through the fog faintly. "You're going to be okay. *It's going to be okay.*"

Mark felt an abrupt halt as they reached the hospital, and every pain increased as the light of morning poured over him, a shock to his system only worsened by the fluorescent lights inside. His breaths shortened further, shallow and tight. He was only able to keep his eyes open dazedly, but dancing silhouettes flurried over him like black flames blocking out the light.

Sil was left behind in the emergency room, forced to let go of his hand as several doctors pushed the rails of his bed into an enclosed room. His eyes caught sight of one face, a good distance away, but very briefly. His dad was there, staring worriedly and calling, "I'll be right here!"

Assuring words confused him. His chest was inflamed with pain, and his shoulder hurt more than he knew. It could've been Shadow Strength in his blood still, but that force wasn't energizing anymore. It had changed him. Now it made his muscles feel like sturdy rocks, immovable, and it rushed through his veins like a calming chemical.

He pinned his eyes shut when bright lights directed down over him, and he winced. He felt a few pinches upon his forehead, and he peeked his eyes open to see a man standing over him, threading a needle through the cut on his brow. He didn't feel it when it pierced him, virtually unaware the area had been numbed, but he knew he was getting stitches. Vaguely, he was aware of another pinch on his right arm, and he realized another doctor was applying stitches to the cut there but again, there was no pain.

His breath cut short and he cried out, a deep mournful moan just before he started coughing and more blood flooded his throat. Red spattered everywhere when he coughed and he felt a small cloth being held there, wiping away the blood.

"We've gotta deal with the collapsed lung," he heard one of them say.

"I'll get to it," another replied. Mark's chest was uncovered, and the doctors gaped at his impaled shoulder. His muscles were tattered, but he became aware of someone grasping his left arm and pulling it away from his side. Mark screamed as a pain like no other ripped through the ligaments in his broken shoulder, and he ignited Strength in his heart for the first time.

His muscles locked up, tough as steel and the doctor grunted. "He's… fighting me."

"That's impossible." Another one came around to help, and together they yanked his arm away and began wrapping gauze bandages around it. Mark cried and coughed, his breathing hoarse, and every time he tried to draw on the air, sharp pains fired through his chest. When they finished, his arm was laid to rest up by his head rather than at his side, and the bandages were quickly stained red.

Mostly numb from the blood loss, he lay there gasping, not sure how he was still conscious, or why. It became easier to breathe once the doctors at his left numbed a place on his ribs and sliced in, placing some kind of siphon there, and suddenly his breathing cleared, and he filled his chest with air.

"Can we put him under now, get him prepped for surgery?"

Mark's eyes fell shut slightly, mostly blind to the lights and movement around him.

Someone was examining his chest wound. "I don't think he needs it. There's not a lot of bleeding coming from this."

Mark reeled back, struggling to raise his back and breathe easier. "Whoa, whoa!" They panicked. "Put him under." Once the order was made, it became harder to breathe again, and his ability to fight for it was weakening. His feelings went dull, and as his bleary gaze drifted off, he saw his father's face again, very near to him. January's concerned eyes were the last thing he locked onto as he faded out, letting the exhaustion consume him.

January reached out and touched Mark's hand as he fell unconscious under the anesthesia. His eyes didn't have a trace of the eerie crimson. He fought the drugs, the new powerful Shadow empowering him to push up in the bed, and involuntarily set his hand on fire.

The ten or so skilled surgeons and doctors dashed back, terrified, and January burst up to his feet, "He's a Shadow, don't worry!"

Mark crumpled onto his right side, struggling to get off his left shoulder, and his limp arm lolled over his face as he grasped his heart. His burning hand pressed against his chest, ripping at the bandages but to no avail in tearing them. His body was weak from having lost so much blood, and he seemed to lose strength as they forced him flat on the table.

They glanced amongst each other, then returned to his injuries. Mark finally succumbed to sedation, and they got to removing the packed bandages and stitching up the damage beneath. His breathing got fainter, and January stayed long enough to see them insert a tube down his throat to help him breathe.

January reluctantly rose up, his legs thinner than water as he willed himself to leave Mark. He stumbled out into the glaring white lights of the hospital, face to face with the Shadows and his family. Marissa stood up from a bench with her arms tightly around June, her eyes expectant and terrified. January couldn't look into her eyes, but she dashed at him, leaving her daughter and throwing her arms around her husband. "Emilie came to get us," she whispered into his ear. "We came as quick as we could!"

She released him just enough to gaze into his face, worry written across her drawn brows as she saw her husband's face. January was fairly certain his dark eyes looked lifeless. "How did it go?" Marissa got out in a quivering voice.

January sank, reaching out for the closest sturdy object, grasped the armrest of the bench just outside the emergency room. His knees buckled and he gave in, falling to the sterile hospital floor and clinging to the cold metal for support. "With what he just went through..." January cried, his tears hitting the floor. "Hell would comfort him."

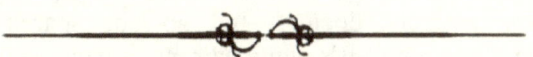

The halls in the hospital were quiet until about seven in the morning, when Mark was taken into surgery. A clamor of doctors spirited him away, and within the crowd, no one caught a glimpse of him. After this, everyone shrank. Reluctantly, the three Shadows took seats as well, but Sil was the last to give in to exhaustion. He stared far down the hall for any hint of them bringing him back. Sil tried to visualize his friend, to link with Mark through the Realm and maybe reach into his mind. He'd never attempted to do it over a distance without Mark's assistance, extending his range.

For a moment, he thought he wouldn't get anything, but then the vision came to him, it wasn't much, but he could feel Mark's chest. The pain became the most prominent, but also every slight movement as his chest rose and fell, every silent breath, assured him Mark would survive this. Sil was knocked out of his state, and the vision vanished when Emilie plopped down beside him, laying her head on his shoulder.

For a mere second, he was annoyed with her, but it passed. He remembered the blood, and he knew that thought was still very present in her mind as well. She looked exhausted, emotionally and physically. Maybe it was due in part to giving up her Shadow for a few minutes, feeling gravity on her atrophied bones. She laid on him tiredly, and in the quiet, he linked his fingers into hers and held tight. She didn't stir, probably not asleep, but he could tell in her aura the gesture had brought her a little peace.

They waited all day with no word. Sil's only sensation was the sterile air, and he was so tempted to fill the hall with ice. A clock ticked loudly above one of the emergency rooms. It was almost six in the evening, and none of them had eaten or moved. People passed—visitors, patients, doctors—but no one spared them a glance. Even with Sil's white hair, no one gave him a side-glance for being a Shadow.

The air was so uneasy, no one fully registered it at first when they were approached by a man in the telling white coat. Sil burst to his feet abruptly, just before the man started speaking, prompting January and Marissa to follow suit just as quickly. The doctor flustered when he saw Sil's white hair and spotted Emilie's feet not touching the floor. He visibly gulped when he made the connection they were all Shadows.

Nervously, he found the parents' eyes. "We have him in the ICU. For now, he needs to be under observation until he wakes up," he said, glancing constantly at Sil's cold, calculating golden eyes. This man had never been around Shadows before. "There is still the matter of paperwork. We'll need a full record of his medical history—"

"How is that supposed to help him?" Emilie interrupted incredulously.

Marissa reached out and touched her arm admonishingly. "I'll take care of it," she assured, shooting a dismissive glare at her husband. For a second, Sil thought it was a jab at his poor memory, but then, what if there was something relevant only Marissa knew now. Sil fiddled with his fingers. Mark had a weak back, and for some reason, right now, that fact was sticking out to Sil.

The doctor retrieved a clipboard and pen for Marissa and led them along the halls toward the new room hidden among the catacombs of the hospital. "You made it sound like his heart was punctured, but there was no evidence of that." The doctor spoke as they walked, sounding very confused. Sil felt air escaping his chest, breathing an immense sigh of relief. They might not have been able to heal anything else, but they had healed his heart, and that was enough.

The doctor had no notion of what Shadows were capable of, but explained what he had observed nonetheless. "His lung collapsed due to a shallow puncture, and that was the only evidence of trauma to his chest. The pneumothorax was putting a lot of pressure on his heart, and it severely lowered his heart rate, so he's still at risk, especially since he lost so much blood." The doctor's tone was even-tempered as he delivered this information sensitively, but it did not end with the chest wound. "Most of the bleeding was from his shoulder. It seems a vein was almost severed through, cutting off circulation to his arm for quite a few hours. We did our best to repair it, but it'll be up to time to see if the damage will have long-lasting effects. Right now, we can keep him on a blood transfusion and wait."

Sil's heart caught in his throat when they turned the corner to approach the new observation window to Mark's room. He felt like he was hit with a blast of sensations and quiet whispers from the minds of the many doctors that still surrounded Mark. They wouldn't say it to the family, but Sil heard they estimated Mark had lost nearly thirty-five percent of his body's blood, and no one could bring themselves to believe Mark had been stabbed in the heart by a sword. Sil could hardly believe it himself.

Then, they laid eyes on Mark. Sil shuddered at the sight. He was covered up to his chest in a thin blanket, and up to his neck on the left side in bandages. He had gauze on the right side of his forehead and his right arm, but worst of all, Mark's breath was completely forced by a ventilator.

When they were finally allowed inside, Marissa nearly fell at his bedside, unable to bear the sight of him like this. Sil moved in to take Mark's left hand, which was cold and clammy. Mark was completely unresponsive, pale, and anemic. There were tubes inserted all over his body, restoring his blood, maintaining fluids, and clearing his chest cavity of the blood and fluid welling inside that had caused his lung to deflate.

Mark's eyelids barely twitched. His only movement was to faintly push himself up higher in the bed and raise his chest. Sil frantically searched for a way to help him, even a little, but only managed to adjust the bed slightly, and only with the nurses' permission. Sil could hear his breaths, air being pushing into his lungs and then being sucked out again. He fought with the ventilator, his ribs shuddering every time he was forced to inhale, but he showed no sign of consciousness.

Sil settled down on his knees, keeping a tight grip around Mark's fingers, if anything, to let Mark know he was there, they were there, they were all watching over him. He laid his head against the mattress and looked about at the Halos. Marissa had Mark's right hand, crying softly. June was whisked away by Ocie and Emilie, finding seats on the nearest bench, and January paced, fidgeting with his hands in his pockets.

One of January's hands was balled into a fist around something. Sil didn't have to reach into his mind to know January was thinking about smoking. Something had to be done to cool their nerves, to give them the smallest promise that, any minute now, Mark would come back to them. January only calmed down when Marissa invited him to sit with her, to share the chair on his right, and though he complied begrudgingly, Sil watched as Marissa let go of Mark's hand, settled into her husband's arms, and fell asleep. With the loud fights Mark had been enduring at home, this was a silent prayer, for their love to bring their son back.

March 8, 2031

Sil's head shot up, and he gasped a lungful of the stale air. He couldn't remember falling asleep, but he became aware of the stiff pain in his knees. How had he let himself fall asleep in this position? His right hand still clung tightly to Mark's left, and he had been sleeping on his own free arm, which had a stream of drool running down the side of it. His legs felt as stiff as rods as he made himself stand, to gauge the room and figure out what time it was.

January and Marissa were gone. He couldn't see Ocie or Emilie through the observation window, and there was no sign of natural light, but he found an analog clock that did enough to tell him it was morning. He was alone with Mark. Finally, his gaze fell down on him. Mark was no better, paler even, and his bandages were saturated from the little gauze on his brow to his left shoulder. Red stains had seeped through the white. Mark was still bleeding.

Drifting a few wary steps back when he stared too long at Mark's shoulder, Sil caught flashes of what he'd seen through the window and he found his way to the one chair in the little room. He collapsed, shuddering, fingering through his hair and smoothing it down. Dazedly, he kept his eyes locked on Mark's sleeping form, unconscious to the bright room around him. Sil had to quiet his thoughts, focusing instead on how frizzy his hair was from the long night.

Restlessly, he pulled out the small elastic tie from the end of his hair and began unweaving the two-and-a-half-foot length of his braid. There was a pinch deep in his chest when people passed in the halls, and he suddenly felt very self-conscious about his ice-white hair, and how telling it was that he was a Shadow. He didn't know why it bothered him all of a sudden. He had been out of the

ASH for months, but he saw the stares he was given, and he never really left home without covering it up.

The gut feeling got worse as he brushed out the length with his fingers and started plaiting it again. The motion calmed him a little, but his breath caught in his throat when the door opened brashly. January entered, his phone to his ear and barely taking notice of Mark's state. Sil could tell he had left, probably to let his wife and daughter go home to rest, to get a little sleep himself—or not—and from the looks of him, get a change of clothes.

"Yes, he's awake," January said, his gaze locking on Mark long and hard, which startled Sil. Mark wasn't even beginning to wake up. But then, January thrust the cell phone at him, and Sil realized he was talking about him. "It's your dad," January mouthed.

Sil took the device awkwardly, all long-distance communication he engaged in took place in the Realm. Sure, the technology of a cell phone was nothing strange to him, he'd just never used one to talk to his parents. "Hey..." Sil got out unsteadily before he pressed the phone to his ear.

"Hey, how are you doing? I just wanted to call to check on you." André's warming voice dribbled through the phone like melting ice.

Sil rubbed his face tiredly, his hair falling over his shoulder in a tangled mess. "Yeah, I'm fine. I'm not the one who got stabbed."

André sighed heavily, his breath hitting the receiver. Over the distance, Sil could see no emotion, nor even possibly reach into his mind, but he knew from the sound of his father's breath that he had picked up on Sil's fear. *"We'll be coming by later. Want us to bring you anything from home?"*

Scratching his arm a little, Sil cringed. "Change of clothes, couple hair ties... maybe leave out some scraps for Winter?"

His father chuckled suddenly. *"Great idea. I'll leave some raw meat in the backyard to attract hawks to our chickens."*

Sil smirked, his first smile in a day. Somehow the sarcasm was welcome. "She won't hurt the chickens."

There was an endearing pause of soft laughter, and finally André whispered something he knew would calm his son, *"Mango misses you. She slept in your bed the last two nights."*

Choking up a little, Sil swallowed forcibly, his thoughts with his animals. He could almost feel Mango's shaggy fur and her enthusiasm, oblivious to all the woes of the world. Sil's nose stung as he fought back any approaching tears. "No way to bring her here?" he murmured, half-jokingly.

André laughed slightly, exhaling long and slow. *"I could just come get you, if you like?"*

Sil's eyes drifted to Mark and he frowned. "No... I want to stay with him until he wakes up."

Understanding him fully, André moved about the house, and that was all Sil could hear of his gestures. *"Okay,"* he sighed. *"We'll be there soon. You hang in there."*

"Okay," Sil assured unconvincingly. "Bye."

"I love you."

The words stung and Sil froze. "I... love you too."

He could tell his father was smiling. The words had been so forced and hard, but they were genuine. *"Bye,"* André said.

"Bye..." Sil repeated as if he could say it a hundred more times and never actually want to let go of this connection to his father without Shadows. Andre hung up, and Sil's sense of dread came back. He blinked erratically, doing all he could to not let any tears escape. January leant at the foot of Mark's bed, watching him intently, seeing everything.

"How are you doing?" he asked, mirroring the voice of his father.

Handing up the phone to January, Sil slumped deep into the chair and slowly finished braiding his hair. "I'm fine," he deflected, returning his attention to his friend.

Mark visibly sank and the movement startled Sil. Was Mark waking up? Sil held his breath, but after a few moments of nothing, he groaned and tried to take himself off the edge. He focused on Mark's arm, at the saturated bandage, and finally he saw it. Along the crest of his shoulder and down his arm, his veins were dark and swollen. Upon second glance, there was a lot of swelling in his left shoulder, compared to his uninjured arm.

Curiously, Sil got up and moved to Mark's bedside, and with January watching, he placed both of his hands on the sides of Mark's head and closed his eyes. Even with his body in shock, Sil could reach into his mind, to sense his thoughts. Maybe he could offer Mark some calming thoughts to help him rest and heal. He couldn't sense much activity in Mark's head, no dreams, no fears, just pain.

Discouraged, Sil sank back and frowned. His own head was in too much turmoil to muster any kind of calming sensation. Mark had been the one to tell him about his Understanding, but he couldn't do anything with it to help him. He could only take. He couldn't give.

"He told me you and him did that to me, to look for my memories," January whispered and also took a seat at Mark's legs.

Sil frowned, worried with the memories he had acquired. "Yeah…" He breathed. "He felt really guilty about that."

January folded his hands together, fiddling with his fingers, nervous, aware that the person next to him had seen a place in his past he had no vision of. "Do you think… any of what you saw wasn't a dream?"

Eyeing him carefully, Sil sighed, hiding how much he was shaking. "I don't know. I... can't know," he murmured, completely unsure. "I can't help you get your memory back... I wish I—"

"Hey," January interrupted, "you don't have to. It's not your responsibility. Maybe you should go home and get some rest," he offered softly. For a second, it was like Mark wasn't even in the room. Sil's chest ached just at the thought of the amount of pain Mark was in.

Before he could speak another word, a nurse shuffled in quietly, moving to check Mark's bandages. His eyes were immediately drawn to the saturated gauze on Mark's shoulder, and his brows knitted together. "How long has this been soaked?" he asked, glancing between Sil and January. They gave half-shrugs, and abruptly, the nurse lifted Mark's shoulder and back enough to see Mark had bled through onto the sheets and the blood had pooled all over his left quarter. January got up fast when the nurse gasped, containing himself to flicking a call button.

Moments later, an array of doctors flooded in. Sil scurried back, pressed into the wall. "He might have a damaged artery," one of them muttered frantically.

"This is a lot of bleeding..." the nurse said under his breath. Then, January and Sil were ushered out, forced to watch from the observation window as the saturated gauze was unwrapped and thrown aside, opening up Mark's shoulder. Sil caught just enough through the crowd of hands to see a larger incision was made in Mark's wound, stitches were broken and reapplied, and though they made quick work, Sil's eyes burned with the flood of red beneath Mark's skin. He had been bleeding internally. The artery was clamped and repaired, controlling the bleed, but it occurred to Sil that Mark's arm had probably had very poor circulation for the last day.

He was already unconscious, and probably only numbed locally, but Sil was left in shock at how quickly the doctors closed up the now larger wound and rebandaged it, changing out the bloodied sheets as well.

"What happened?" Someone frantically grabbed Sil's shoulder, and suddenly he felt another flash, staring through the glass, helpless to do anything for Mark. He had to force himself to not see a bronze tint in the glass. Inhibitor was not separating him from Mark. This was the hospital, not Geoffrey's house. He jumped a little when Ocie suddenly touched his arm.

Sil clenched his fists at his side, a little ice forming. "He was still losing blood."

"Is he okay?" Ocie fretted, staring until the doctors started to file out one by one.

Sil's knees trembled, and he sank down onto the bench outside the window.

"Are *you* okay?" Ocie redirected, moving her hand to his back and sitting down beside him.

Sil shook his head, but otherwise he didn't move, gazing emptily at the sterile floor. January went back in, staying by Mark's side and stroking his hand gently. It was all they could do—sit beside him, give him a little touch, but nothing else. Mark didn't know they were there. He didn't possess any semblance of consciousness.

Ocie tried to comfort Sil, but she blurred in his mind, hardly there. All Sil could see was the bronze film and Mark on his back, eyes wide and blood welling in the small of his chest. Sil didn't know how to acknowledge he was traumatized. But he was fine. Mark was the one who was hurt.

Sometime later—maybe a little, maybe a lot—a new set of hands came down on him, and he shuddered, not really acknowledging who it was until his father's scratchy chin rested on his head, pulling him deep into his embrace. Sil never felt so small.

He buried his face, hiding from the world that he was a Shadow, that he was small, and that he was crying.

André protected him, shushing him softly, stroking his back, and never asking him anything until he was ready.

"Are you sure you don't want to go home?"

Sil shook his head, wiping away his tears, ashamed of them. "I want to protect him…" Sil shuddered. "He did so much for me. He's… the reason I'm here! The reason I'm free! And I'm scared that, just like that, he'll be gone." Looking up into his dad's eyes, Sil broke a little. "I was so terrible to him. I could have done something. I could have… told him not to—"

"Shh…" André pulled him closer. "You did everything you could. You were there for Mark, and you don't have to feel guilty about anything."

Sil's forehead pressed into his father's breastbone. "I'm scared!" he admitted finally. "What if I had been in that situation? I'm not strong enough even with Shadow Frost to have beaten Geoffrey. Mark didn't stand a chance!"

His father sighed long and slow, just like over the phone, loving and understanding. "Oh, Zack, you are only fifteen. You are not responsible for this at all, and you should not feel responsible for taking care of Mark, even now."

"I just want him to be okay!" Sil cried, taking little notice of his birth name. Sil kept himself open in the Realm, and suddenly he felt something. He perked up, and even through the glass, he realized it was Mark's voice. He was no closer to consciousness, but just that twinge in the Realm caused Sil's heart to race.

André saw him sensing something and smiled. "He'll wake up. Don't worry, not much longer now."

Sil pressed his lips together, swallowing the bitter taste in his mouth, and he nodded. "He's in a lot of pain…" he whispered. "That's all I heard in the Realm."

Giving him a little pat on the shoulder, André stood up. "I'll go mention it to January. You gonna be okay?"

Sil nodded hastily, standing right after his father to go into the room. The first thing he was aware of was Mark's breathing. Long, raggedy, and fighting with the ventilator. Sil could see Mark's chest shudder. The pain he could express spiking in the Realm when his lungs were filled. Mark forced himself to exhale longer than the device allowed, and Sil winced, unable to block out his own Understanding.

Mark did it again right as the nurse returned, and the man noticed it immediately. "He's already breathing on his own?"

Sil nodded hastily. "Do you think he can—" He glanced at January, whose eyes picked up from conversation with André when Sil spoke for Mark. January received another look from the nurse, and he became more attentive.

The nurse hesitated, a skepticism in his eyes that made Sil shut up. "Maybe... but his airways were very damaged from all that blood. I'll... try to get him off the ventilator."

Evening was already drawing near again, and Sil kept a close eye as the nurse administered something to reduce the pain, and after eight, he got permission to remove the ventilator. It was nerve-wracking. If Mark wasn't strong enough to breathe on his own, then for a few seconds, he'd be suffocating. For a few moments, he'd be without air!

The larger apparatus was switched off and disconnected, leaving Mark unconscious with a tube in his throat. The silence was unsettling, and two or three seconds were unbearable until Mark's chest rose... and fell... as normal. The nurse smiled a little and proceeded to remove the rest of the tube.

Mark gagged, the muscles in his neck tightening, and the moment it was out, he coughed violently. The tube itself had some blood on it, and immediately, Mark was spraying blood. The nurse tried using a cloth to contain it, but Mark didn't stop until his lungs were clear. That one complete lungful of air as he finally caught his breath consumed Sil with a rush of hope. In his fit, he had shifted a little, now directed more on his right side, but now that he was breathing on his own, he seemed much more peaceful.

Sil was determined now, confident, optimistic even. If he paid attention to Mark's breathing, he would make it through the night unencumbered.

XVIII
BROKEN GLASS

March 9, 2031

Mark awoke lying perfectly still, perfectly flat, in the hospital bed. Vague, mottled memories rushed through him, aware of the swords, the blood, and Lævatein, but the hazy part of his memory lay in the last few hours. Everything was a blur: pain, blackness, whiteness. The one clear memory was how miserable he felt.

Slowly, with his consciousness, the pain in his shoulder increased. He didn't dare move it. He just looked around. The first thing he could focus on was Emilie's feet up on the footrest, and gradually he saw her, sacked out in a folding chair. In the corner of his eye, he spotted Sil's white hair, and as he followed up the right side of his bed, he laid eyes on Ocie, asleep with an open magazine in her lap.

He savored the sight of her stillness, her motherly care, and her wavy brunette hair cascading around her shoulders, barely pinned back. Finally, he looked up, spying the IV stands, the medical equipment, and he became aware of a sharp pain in his side. With his right hand, he slowly felt his ribs, suddenly becoming conscious of the bandages on his arm and his face. Right there between his ribs, he felt a tube secured into his chest, and he winced.

He stared up at the ceiling in pain and breathed sharply, but for some reason his chest tightened and he coughed a dozen times, uncontrollably.

Sil awoke with a start, his eyes dashing about and his hand going for a tissue until he realized Mark was covering his mouth as he coughed. His eyes widened in surprise, and he smiled ecstatically. "You're awake!" he whispered very softly.

Mark tried his best to smile too but even that hurt. He looked at his hand and tensed. It was spattered with blood. Sil hurriedly handed him the tissue, helping him to clean the blood. "How long have you been up?" Sil asked kindly, to not wake the girls.

Mark tried to shrug but only got one shoulder to move. "A few seconds," he guessed as he turned to Ocie, raising a hand. He reached out, his finger catching a curl before he nudged her arm a few times. She too awoke abruptly, tired but alert to any change.

She rubbed her eyes tiredly, but the moment she saw him, she lit up. "You're okay!" Bursting to her feet, she reeled forward to give him a kiss right on the face in relief. With Ocie's outburst, Emilie woke up and flew over, throwing her arms around his neck.

He did his best to hug her back, but he was too shocked for a brief moment over the fact that Ocie had just kissed him. "Um... Emilie." He grunted in discomfort. "Could you—that kinda... hurts."

"Sorry!" Emilie let go immediately. "We were just so worried!"

"You had a collapsed lung and two surgeries. It's been a long two days," Sil explained flatly.

Mark slowly let his right hand drift over his chest and felt the bandage. He gasped shallowly. "Two days?" he repeated breathlessly. The memory flashed through him when he felt the pain—the glint of the gold sword.

Ocie finally sat back down and explained, "You've been here three days now, and you just started breathing on your own again last night. Even after what we did, your heart was healed but nothing else was, and you lost a lot of blood."

Mark coughed again. "Yeah..." His voice was very hoarse for a moment. "How... am I—"

Emilie floated up and put her hands on her hips, spunkier than ever. "Your dearest performed a class three Infusion on you!" She gestured to Ocie, who blushed.

Mark raised his brows and stared at Ocie in awe. "You did it?"

She nodded a little, bashfully. "Well, we all did. Class threes take many Shadows, so it was all of us: Emilie, Sil, me... and Rita..." Her eyes clouded over in sorrow.

Frowning, Mark settled down. "Where is she?"

Ocie couldn't answer and looked to Emilie, who looked to Sil. "She left right after the Infusion. We don't know where she is."

She was gone. Mark felt hollow. She had been there, but she wouldn't help him. He wasn't sure if it was fear, jealously, or petty retribution. It wasn't *that*. She wasn't that angry. She was just afraid. If only there hadn't been an ASI, she could've jumped in and gotten him out of there. They could be in Scotland right now, trying to figure out what to do to stop Geoffrey. They could be coming up with some wild plan to get all the Shadows together, or they could just be alone together, and safe.

"And my family?" Mark managed to direct the conversation away from Rita.

Sil shrugged. "They went home last night to get some rest. But June threw a fit when she found out she couldn't stay with you."

Mark tried to sit up slightly, but it was then that he realized his back was killing him. On top of being stabbed, he had to be stuck with his same old back pain. It wasn't fair. "W-Where's... my dad?" he wheezed with very little voice. He breathed slowly for a few seconds, steadying his lungs. "I... I want him here," he stammered.

He brushed the red streaks out of his face, and Ocie smiled; seeing him fighting with the darn thing made everyone feel more confident he was feeling better. "I can call them if you want," she offered, stepping up from the bed and over to an outdated corded phone on Sil's side of the bed.

Mark shrugged again, this time also just slightly moving his left shoulder, and a jolt of pain shot through his left quarter, and he buckled over. Geoffrey had completely ripped through his shoulder, and now Mark was paying for it. Sil quickly shot up to help steady Mark, easing him back into the pillow as he brandished the sudden pain.

He stared down at his left arm, limp in the covers, and he spent the next few minutes trying with all his might to flex his fingers. He couldn't move them. He couldn't move anything. Geoffrey had destroyed his left arm. He couldn't even catch his breath. All he could do was lie silently, devastated.

"—Yes, I can, as long as he thinks he can," Ocie said brightly and placed her hand over the mouthpiece "Your dad wants to talk to you. Do you feel like it?"

Mark thought about shrugging, but thought better of it and reverted to, "Sure," summoning all he could to not sound out of breath. Ocie handed him the phone, but he didn't know what to say. He didn't want to talk on the phone. He wanted them here. All he managed to get out was, "Hi."

"*Oh, thank god.*" January let out a long sigh of relief. "*What time did you wake up?*"

Mark scanned the room and caught sight of an analog clock pointing vaguely at seven. "Three minutes ago," he answered bluntly and rubbed his throat.

He could tell January was also checking the time. "*Ha! That's six-fifty-five exactly.*" He tried making a joke, but the enthusiasm couldn't last. *"So how are you feeling?"*

Grimacing a little, Mark coughed once. "Really bad." All he could get out was short statements. He couldn't hold enough breath to say more. "I can't really move—" He filled his lungs as much as he could. "—move my arm, and it's really hard to breathe..." The last few words felt like he was running on empty, but it was out and he had a few seconds to catch his breath.

January hummed with a deep frown in his voice. *"Is it any better?"*

Drawing in a slow breath, Mark paced his breathing carefully, but still let out a few erratic coughs before answering, "Not really." Every use of his voice was hoarser. And again, all he could say was a short statement.

January stuttered a second then finally said, *"June is dying to talk to you. Do you mind?"*

"No," he answered calmly, learning fast that if he breathed too quickly, he'd cough again.

June got ahold of the phone and immediately sang as soon as she got her mouth close to it. *"Mark are you there?"*

Mark smiled to himself. "Yes, June, I'm here."

"You're alive!" she screamed euphorically, and Mark could hear her feet stamping around the house as she danced.

Holding the phone away from his ear until she calmed down, Mark chuckled. "June!" he wheezed but couldn't yell.

"June!" Sil broke in, closing in on the phone to hear better. "Mark's in a lot of pain right now. Can you quiet down? You don't want his ears to start hurting too?"

"Oh, sorry, so tell me, what was it like?" she asked without a breath in between.

Mark rolled his eyes. "C-could you... give the phone back?"

A disappointed tone came through the line as June handed over the phone in despair. *"We'll be there in a few minutes,"* January said quickly. *"Did you want to tell me something?"*

Mark felt his chest tightening up. Just talking was exhausting, and he laid his head back tiredly. "N-nothing, I'll tell you later."

"Okay, I'll see you soon," January said lovingly. "Bye..."

Mark thought the silence didn't last as long as it did. He felt his delayed response and the lingering expectant tone dangling above him, but he wasn't sure he should or even could respond. January didn't hang up. He waited. He wanted that response. "Bye," Mark choked, the breath weak.

January hung up after a few more reluctant seconds, leaving the silence hanging. Mark sank in bed, not even handing over the phone but letting Ocie take it from him. He needed to breathe, to really fill his lungs, but everything hurt. He tried expanding his chest, inhaling as long as he could, but it stopped abruptly and he choked, coughing helplessly and sending a little blood to his mouth.

Sil grabbed another tissue and handed it over. Mark took it gratefully, and after wiping his mouth, he spit in it to get rid of the awful taste. "It's going to take a while for you to heal..." Sil murmured begrudgingly, resting his chin on his palm.

Mark nodded and laid his head back again. "I guess that's the price... for getting a new Shadow."

Perking up immediately, Sil drew his brows together. "What?" he demanded sternly. The girls also gasped in disbelief.

Mark glanced between them. "That was the point. Geoffrey wanted to give me Shadow Strength."

Emilie leant forward in the air. "You have a second Shadow again?"

Kip had made such a huge deal of it when he discovered Mark had two Shadows, in addition to an overpowered range in the Realm, and the ability to defy the ASI. Keller had told them it was common outside of the shield, but of course Emilie was still surprised. She didn't know any better. He nodded slightly, saving words and breaths. "The swords were... Infused."

Ocie contemplated slowly. "Shadow Strength..." she hummed, curling a finger under her chin. "That's one of the Orchestrators, like Hope."

"I know," Mark nodded again.

The door opened abruptly, and the nurse came in to stop short at seeing the four of them. "Oh," he started as the Shadows all turned to him. "It looks like the infamous Mark Halo is awake." He slapped on some sterile gloves and approached cheerfully. "I'm here to take a look at your bandages and see if anything needs changing."

Mark didn't bother trying to move or answer, finding that everything he did made his body hurt worse.

"Now tell me," the nurse asked, "what's bothering you the most?"

Mark glared at the man. He had a list! Literally everything was bothering him. He couldn't breathe! He couldn't move his arm! He didn't know why the question was so frustrating, all he had to do was pick something. "My chest," he said quietly, still pacing every breath. As quickly as he said it, he realized how much his shoulder hurt the most. Ocie and Emilie cleared out of the way, but Sil remained latched onto his left hand.

"I had a feeling you'd say that," the nurse mused, trying to be personable and just coming off as phony. He of course started with the small bandage on Mark's right arm, peeling off the tape to reveal seven tight stitches. "Looking good," he noted with a smile and moved on to the one on his brow.

"A sword, huh?" the man asked playfully, trying to start conversation as if he was dealing with a nervous pediatric patient. "There's something you don't see every day."

Very cautiously, the nurse helped Mark sit up, keeping a steady grip on his right shoulder and below the gash on his chest. Mark's breaths grew shallower in this position, realizing just how weak he was from the extreme loss of blood. A fatigue he'd never experienced washed over him as he watched the nurse unwrap the gauze around his limp left arm to replace it.

"You doing okay?" he checked.

Mark heaved. "I can't... breathe..."

"I'll be quick. Maybe after you visit with your family, you can try to eat something."

As he was being held upright, focusing on keeping air moving and weathering the fatigue, Mark heard muffled yelling from the other side of the observation window to his room. The first thing he could see was his little sister jumping up and down and trying to see him at last. She yelled indistinctly through the glass, and with dazed and heavy eyes, he smiled slightly when he saw his family.

"Just let me finish this. Then they can come in," the nurse said to the Shadows, tightly binding up Mark's shoulder with slightly less packed gauze.

When he was done at last, he laid Mark down once more and pressed a stethoscope over Mark's chest in several places to listen to his hoarse breathing and make sure his collapsed lung wasn't deflated anywhere. Mark was exhausted from just sitting up, and he rasped to catch his breath after being held upright, but being awake had to be an improvement. It was only after this that the nurse finally left him alone and let the Halos in.

June sprang on him like a wild animal, throwing herself on the bed and tightly wrapping her arms around his neck. She was just happy to see him alive, but for a few moments, Mark couldn't inhale. "June... please." He let out precious air. "Get off!"

June pulled away just as fast the moment she saw her brother's pain. "I'm sorry, but—"

The cheerfulness in her died as Mark breathed in choppily, which hurt his chest to the highest degree, and as he let it out, he fell into a flurry of coughing. He reeled forward and Sil rushed in to support him, holding a tissue near his mouth as he choked until he was spitting blood. It took a few long minutes for Mark to find his breath, and his family looked on in horror as he gasped like a fish out of water.

June's eyes were wide in fear as the blood coated Mark's chin and neck, and tears welled up in her eyes, cowering into her parent's admonishing arms. Mark started to pace his breathing again, *slower* than he physically needed, but keeping the pain muted. The silence was worse than getting stabbed.

He tried to move his left arm again. All sensation was muted, and he could barely feel Sil holding onto his hand. He told his arm to move his fingers, but all he managed was a faint movement in his pinkie. All he could think about was Geoffrey's scars and his words; he had been scared he would lose his arm. It occurred to Mark that he and Geoffrey had very similar injuries. One to the arm, and one to the chest.

Marissa leant down over him with a smile, beckoning "Good morning," and "How are you feeling?" without expecting much response as she kissed him on the forehead.

January struggled to move closer, slowly managing to find words. "Didn't you want to tell me something?" he asked.

Mark closed his eyes for a moment and took another painstakingly slow breath. "I… remember seeing you. You were there?"

Nervously, January nodded. "Yes… I'm just sorry I didn't get there faster. And even though Shadows couldn't get through that shield, my car could." He tried to smile a bit.

Emilie cackled to lighten the mood. "Did you total it? That's what I want to know!"

Marissa crossed her arms over her chest and gave January a knowing glare. "Yes... but there are things more important than a car." She turned her gaze down to her son.

Mark blinked lethargically, too tired to move. "How... did you know?"

January adopted the seriousness immediately. "I... don't know," he stammered. "I just felt it. Instinct, I guess."

Closing his eyes for a few moments, Mark exhaled slowly. That couldn't be it. There was no way January would have gotten there with that perfect timing. And the Shadows didn't go get him. He couldn't have physically heard the fight.

Mark's energy seeped away, he had to sleep. His thoughts whirled with the swords. He could remember gripping the hilt of Lævatein, hanging on to Shadow Strength to stay alive.

Marissa jumped in, observant to Mark's attention failing, and she stroked his right arm tenderly, which brought him to alertness for a few seconds. "It looks like you need your rest. We won't go anywhere if you need us, okay?"

He nodded a little, barely conscious to her words anymore. He let his eyes close and listened intently until he fell right to sleep.

A doctor knocked on the edge of the doorframe, offering a smile to everyone crowding Mark's bed. "I heard he was awake and talking?" he confirmed, seeing Mark was now asleep again.

"Yeah, for a few minutes," January strode closer, crossing his arms over his chest.

"Could I talk with you both?" he asked, gesturing to the parents only. Marissa sat up straighter beside Mark's right shoulder, but she urgently got up and, with January, they followed him out. "His wounds are looking good, and breathing will get easier when he gets the chest tube out. There's still a lot of healing to be done, but this is a good step for him."

January nodded hopefully, taking it in, but Marissa braced herself.

"His shoulder, however. During the second invasive surgery, they found his superior nerve was completely severed. That kind of nerve damage can't just be sewn back together, so he's going to have limited mobility in his left arm."

January tensed but couldn't say a thing in the face of his wife, who was immediately in tears. He held her tight, but he couldn't be of help to her. He was as traumatized by the incident as Mark was. Neither of them could respond. *Limited mobility* was just a gentler way of saying paralysis. Mark's arm was paralyzed—forever. Worst of all, the doctors had known since yesterday and they didn't say anything.

January glanced into the window every few seconds, keeping a close eye on Mark as he slept again, now with the reassurance that he could be awoken. Ocie stared back at them, knowing they had received bad news.

"He's probably stable now," the doctor assured, "so we'd like to move him into a more comfortable room. Would that be all right?" he asked, breaking into January's thoughts.

"Yes," Marissa got out for him, fighting her fear and the hesitation January was suffering.

"The next milestone he needs is to eat. As soon as he wakes up, you should encourage him to try, and when he seems ready, we'll bring him something."

"Um…" January gulped hard, hesitating to meet the doctor's gaze. "He's been skipping a lot of meals lately. I think it's been a few days since he's had a full meal."

Drawing his brows together, the doctor took note of this as well. "Does he have a history of poor diet, like intentionally fasting to lose weight?"

Marissa shook her head hastily. "No, never!" But January stopped her.

With a deep frown, he met eyes with his wife and grimaced. He gave her a knowing glare and sighed. "The dinner table has been tense lately, and he's been getting up early to train with swords."

"Ah," the doctor hummed, devoid of emotion. "Trouble at home and excessive exercise. He's at risk. You need to get him to eat."

January nodded solemnly, and Marissa interlocked her hands with him, falling into tears as soon as the doctor left them. "Is this our fault?" She trembled.

"No!" January enveloped her in his arms as she started sobbing. "You can't blame yourself for this. He's going to be okay." His gaze turned back to the window, seeing Mark moving onto his right side slightly. Mark's face was devoid of color, white like paper, and still the fire hadn't returned to his eyes.

"Who would do this to a child?" Marissa glowered, a bitterness entering her voice. She'd never seen or met Geoffrey. She had no face for her son's attacker. No one to hate but herself.

Quickly, January took her shoulders and forced a fake resolution. "Speaking of food, why don't we go find something to eat. I'm sure the Shadows are hungry too." He managed to coax a nod out of her before he let go and peered into the hospital room. "Anyone hungry?" he called at the three Shadows, and June was the first to jump up.

Mark shuddered, opening his eyes slightly, disturbed by the noise, but he settled down in a moment. Sil saw the jolt and frowned deeply. "I'll stay with him. You guys go eat."

"Okay." Emilie hovered up. "I'll bring you something." She reeled in and gave him a kiss on the cheek before flying out with the rest of the Halos and Ocie.

"Sil," January addressed sternly as soon as everyone was out. Sil perked up, slightly startled because, more often than not, January called him Zachary. "If he wakes up at all, try to offer him food. Doctor said that's the next milestone he needs to reach."

Sil nodded solemnly and sat back into the chair beside Mark's bed, watching him sleep and listening to him breathe. He stared up Mark's left arm, at the bruising and paleness. The arm had lost circulation for a few hours, in addition to having poor blood flow for many hours afterwards. It was looking less lively by the minute, and he had once felt the extent of Mark's strength in it.

Sighing, Sil did his best to quell his despairs. "You were so excited about being ambidextrous," he whispered, even if Mark didn't hear. "And now…"

Mark's eyes opened, his breathing even and slow. Mark gazed away from Sil, bitterly aware of his friend's words. "Do you think I'm going to lose my arm?" he said faintly above a whisper.

Sil took his left hand again. "I don't know…"

Mark shifted onto his back slowly to stare at the ceiling. "It's numb." His eyes dashed about, searching for sensation. "I can't really move it at all."

"Maybe Shadow Strength will help it heal faster. You did say Geoffrey had a huge scar on his arm, maybe…" Sil cringed. He shouldn't have been making Mark worried right now or giving him false hope. Mark had to sit in the middle ground, uncertain and just trying to heal. He gulped nervously. "Are you hungry at all?"

Mark shook his head, his eyes bleak and apathetic. "Just thirsty," he admitted.

Sil rose up a little. "I can make you some ice chips, if you like?" he offered hurriedly. If there was one thing Sil could provide readily, it was ice, and that filled him with hope. Mark affirmed with a faint nod, and Sil got up, searching out a cup to put the ice into. In one of the scattered cabinets, he found a little medicine cup. It was small but it was perfect to keep refilling.

With a little wave of his fingers he created a fine white snow, keeping it loose within the cup and offering it to Mark. His right hand was shaky, but he took it, holding onto the cold for a moment to let it melt some, then eagerly he drank the one tiny sip of icy water. Sil could tell he let it melt in his mouth, and then with a lot of effort, he tried to swallow it.

He coughed a few times, but thankfully there didn't seem to be any blood. "Do you want another?" Sil offered, taking the cup back. Mark shook his head, disheartening Sil to no end. "Did it hurt to swallow?" he asked, a guiding question to help Mark conserve his words and manage his breaths. Mark nodded a little.

Sil grimaced, there was no forcing Mark to eat. He wasn't ready. The Halos returned in an hour or so, and the nurse soon followed, checking on him with a very concerned expression. Mark spent the time trying to sleep, often disturbed by noise but more or less unaware as a team of nurses came in to move him. The chaos worried Sil, and he was pressed into the corner as the whole bed was pushed out.

His gaze drifted to Emilie, who likewise hovered outside in the hall, fretting over her cousin but ultimately letting this happen.

"Emilie!" someone down the hallway shrieked, and Emilie stiffened like a rod, whirling about in the air to see her mother storming over. "Where have you been?" Hellen yelled, barely taking note of Mark as she passed him. "You just disappeared again! You've been gone three days!"

Emilie seethed, keeping her feet off the floor. "I'm sorry!" she blared defiantly. "But my cousin just got stabbed and could very well be dying! I didn't exactly have time to give you a heads up."

Flustering, Hellen stood up to her, irritated and remarkably assertive for once. "You're always like this. You could at least tell me where you're going so I can have an idea of if you're okay or not. One day you might end up getting hurt, and I won't have a clue."

"Oh, now you care..." Emilie trailed off, getting away from her and closer to Sil.

Hellen poised her hands on her hips. "Come on, you're a part of this family. You obviously care. We're moving tomorrow, and I want you to help. This is your life too, and things will get so much better in New York City."

Scowling, Emilie glanced to Sil for support. "Don't you think Mark's injury is more important than moving to the city?"

Sil nudged her arm. "Hey, I'll keep an eye on him. You should go with her," he muttered under his breath.

She glared at him, appalled. "I'm not leaving him!"

Raising an eyebrow, Sil pushed her through the air, away from him. "Come on, he'll be okay, and I'll keep you abreast in the Realm."

Emilie scoffed, alone in the air and livid, but glancing between her mother and Sil, she groaned. "Fine... I'll be back tonight!" She zipped off, disappearing around the corner and leaving Hellen to stand there in awe, slowly turning to chase after her.

XIX
WHERE BROKEN GLASS GOES

Emilie didn't care much what her mother thought. As much as she made herself love Hellen, every instinct inside her screamed to keep away from Greg. Weighing the pros and cons, even living closer to Mark and Sil, there was no upside to being in the same house with him.

She flitted like a leaf on the wind out to the car, barely following her mother as Hellen plopped down inside and started the cold engine, shivering for a few minutes. Emilie could barely feel the cold. Between flying to fight and her spindly limbs, she was used to it.

Emilie scowled down at the emotional wreck who rubbed her hands together to work the warmth back into them. "Are you going to get in the car?" Hellen blared, her breath fogging.

"Do you not even care what happened to Mark?"

Hellen's eyes shot up to her daughter in anger. "Of course I care. But I've been searching for you for three days until my sister let me know you've been here, in this mess, and I'm just about fed up! Some nights, I wonder if you'll ever come back." Hellen stifled the tears that were already starting to form, and Emilie rolled her eyes. Just how careless was she? Hellen was so quick to cry it was disgusting. "You're only fifteen, and you're roaming all over the Earth getting into things not even rebellious teenagers do."

"In case you forgot," Emilie screamed, "I can fly! And I grew up not being allowed to go anywhere! I'm free for the first time, and I'm not going to let anything hold me back." As she seethed, she caught sight of her mother's hand on the steering wheel and she gasped. "Greg proposed to you?"

The shiny rock on her finger seemed dull in the gray light, and Hellen covered her left hand, nodding indignantly. "He's your father. Why do you insist on calling him by his first name? Why can't we just be a family together?"

Emilie slammed her hands down on the roof of the car. "Because he's an abusive prick, and he hit you!" she screamed. "How can you be so blind? He's going to hurt you!"

Hellen jumped a little, startled by her daughter's fury, but she kept her composure and clung to the wheel. "I know you're not going to get in, but at least follow me." She put the car in drive and started backing out.

Annoyed, Emilie kept her hands on the roof and without gravity, she lifted the whole car, wheels and all, off the pavement. "We're not going!"

Tapping her fingers on the wheel impatiently, Hellen groaned. "Put down the car!" she ordered sternly. "We're going home to finish packing, then we're taking the first trip over to Greg's place. Understand?"

The car lurched as Emilie dropped it, the suspension rattling. "Fine!" she snapped, getting in and slumping down into the leather cushion. "But don't half-expect me to fly out and take my own way home, 'cause it's likely!"

Mark became dazedly aware of the dull silence in his new room as the wheels of his bed came to an abrupt stop. He coughed a little, heaving each breath, but though he remained awake, he was barely conscious to anyone around him. He heard muted conversations and dizzily turned his head to see his parents in the larger room, talking with the doctors. He only understood one word: *procedure,* but he didn't have a clue what that meant.

January gave an approving nod he seemed to regret, and Mark's eyes fell shut again. Keeping his eyes open at all was wasting energy, and his consciousness was only there to remind him to keep breathing. He felt like there was a ton of bricks on his chest, stopping him from inhaling to a certain point, and his breaths remained shallow.

There were figures crowded around him, and above him. His eyes were able to focus on the tube leading up to an IV bag of clear fluid. Someone was touching it. A faint movement brushed his arm, and he spied a syringe injecting something into his line. After a few seconds, he knew what it was: mild sedation.

It wasn't designed to knock him out completely, just to make him blissfully unaware of his surroundings as they performed their procedure. Mark maintained a little consciousness. He didn't know how, but it took the form of rippling nightmares. The swords clashing, the flashes of gold, and the rush of Strength entering his veins. Involuntarily, he felt Strength igniting again, empowering him to use his Shadows and his visibility started flickering in the bed.

He was pretty sure the people around him started panicking as he erratically shifted between the Realm. His mind, however, was completely immersed in it. The consuming blackness rushed around him, a warmth and comfort filling his soul as he sank into the Realm. He lost all sensation in his own body, blocking away all the pain and leaving him floating in a perfect state. He relaxed, fully alone.

He didn't need air, he didn't need to fight with it, and within the Realm, his fiery form, he was able to move his left arm again. He didn't feel completely exhausted, and his thoughts cleared, lucid for once. He was able to bring himself some awareness of the level plane, the view of the real world through the lens of the Realm. He could see seven wavering pillars of smoke with arms and legs, five doctors, and his parents. And the taller of the two pillars, his father, flickered faster as if a harsh wind ripped through the smoke, displaying his nervousness.

The physical objects around him, his bed, the window to the sky, the medical equipment, table and chairs, were all made of this same, illuminated white smoke, the only mundane thing in the Realm. He drifted deeper into the Realm, falling lower into its planes and losing sight of his family above him. He spied the stars beneath him, millions of colorful orbs, each with Shadows of their own, representing the fallen who had gone to rest. Mark was eager to join them, hoping for a touch of peace.

He stopped sinking, somewhere in the middle, and the mundane pillars of smoke returned this time with a vision of five Shadows. At first there were five—Ocie, Sil, Emilie, Rita, and Mark's own—wavering faintly on the floor as his blood spilled out. This was the memory he could not maintain. The moment of his Infusion permanently written into the fabric of the Realm.

There were more Shadows around him, many more. He saw a glistening, gold Shadow, an unconscious form on the floor behind him, and realized he could now see Geoffrey's Shadow since he had stopped hiding it. And from his position on the floor, he looked up and saw the one wavering tower of white smoke, his father. However, January's form was illuminated by ten dozen glowing orbs behind him of many colors, and Mark realized just how many Shadows Geoffrey had collected.

It was against that light, with the darkened smoke behind the wall, that Mark noticed how pure the smoke coming off January's form was, white and bright. He had a glow within the Realm only noticeable when he was surrounded by Shadows, while being almost indistinguishable when he was around other humans. His aura didn't move like smoke, dancing slowly, but rapid and snapping like fire.

Mark gasped, drawing in a rough breath and becoming fully aware of his pained body again. He tried to cough, but the motion was even more unproductive, and he felt like he had something stuck in his throat. He tensed, panicking for a few moments and looking around until he realized he was alone. His breaths were fuller somehow. He could draw in more air, but he was still tired, and his breaths slowed gradually.

Wincing, he felt his side and discovered the tube that had been in his ribs was gone and replaced with a bandage and some stitches. Through the window beside him, he discovered it was almost night now, but he was thankful for a way to tell time. He tried, but he still couldn't move his arm.

After a few minutes, his chest started feeling tight again, and his shoulder ached terribly. Every cut panged, and he felt his exhaustion enclosing on him. Weakly, he tried to swallow, but his throat felt obstructed. Reaching up, he touched his face, going for the bandage but he felt tape on his face. Tensing, he felt more tape on his cheek, holding between them a narrow tube looped behind his ear and feeding into his nose.

Panicked, his eyes dashed around. A third bag had joined the fluids, a blood transfusion. He didn't want to be alone. He called out in the Realm. He could sense Sil was close, but why wasn't he in the room? He gasped, breathing choppily until the door opened and light streamed in. Sil rushed to his side, but hesitated, his steps falling short when he saw the feeding tube.

Sil fell by his bedside and grasped his left hand tightly. "I'm sorry... I'm so sorry... I told them you were having trouble swallowing."

Mark sputtered but couldn't bring himself to speak, too uncomfortable and now frustrated once he could see his own left arm, but couldn't feel it being held.

Sil's thumb stroked across the back of his palm. "You need to get your strength back. This will help you have a little more energy. Mark..." he grimaced, pushing back emotions. "You're so weak. This is your best chance."

Despairing, Mark turned his face away indignantly, struggling to swallow the bile in his mouth. He couldn't tell if it was stubbornness, frustration, or the pain medicine, but for the first time, he was really alert and awake, and he didn't want to be. He breathed a little faster, still shallowly, and he made himself control it, training his breathing, and forcing himself back into the Realm, to meditate. It was the only thing he could think of to cool his thoughts.

"Just got word on the car." January reentered the room, pocketing his cell phone. "Not totaled, but the repairs are going to be comparable to the medical bills." His steps fell short when he saw everyone sitting around Mark's bed, Marissa stroked his forehead, Sil held his hand, and Mark slept through everything. It was almost more unbearable, now that Mark had been awake for some time, to see him like this. There were more chairs in the larger room, and they lounged about, patient for any movement from Mark, but he didn't stir.

Marissa rose, faintly worried. "Is insurance going to pay for the rental?"

January plopped down beside his wife and massaged his temples. "Maybe for a few days. Might just get a new car. The other one was paid off..." He sighed, burying his face in his hands as their debt piled up. "I explained what I could, but I don't think compassion is going to alleviate any of our bills."

Shaking her head slowly, Marissa stared at Mark, supporting her forehead on her spindly fingers. "I can't believe you drove it into a wall."

Eyeing her, January's breath caught as his frustration rose. "The Shadows couldn't break the glass, and I could, so I did what I had to do."

"You could have—" Marissa stopped a moment, refusing to meet eyes with him. "I don't know, grabbed a rock or something! You didn't need to blow down the whole wall."

Growing irritated, he huffed. "Do you want me to apologize for getting there in time?"

"In time for what? Saving him? He's still here!" she gestured at their son.

"Guys!" Sil snapped quietly. "Could you not fight right now? I'm pretty sure he can still hear you."

January sank back, ashamed, and sighed. "It's just a car... it can be replaced." Marissa rubbed her face tiredly and nodded. Unconsciously, she leant against her husband's shoulder, and he wrapped his arm around her tenderly.

Though it pained him to go, Sil's father came at nine, and convinced Sil to come home to get some sleep that night. He slowly released Mark's hand even though he was pretty sure Mark wouldn't feel the absence. He was so deeply asleep, not even the new people in the room caused him to stir.

"I can bring you here tomorrow," André assured, pulling him away into the bright hallway.

"We should get home too." Marissa rose, turning her attention to her daughter, asleep in Ocie's arms. She smiled a little at the two girls clinging to each other in sleep. She nudged Ocie, and she stirred but didn't wake June as she slowly transferred her into Marissa's arms.

"I'll stay with him," Ocie offered, sweetly gaining a weak smile from Marissa.

"I'll stay too," January said suddenly. "I'll call when he wakes up again."

Somehow, Marissa managed to nod and accept this. She gathered up her purse and coat with one arm and carried her six-year-old daughter away. Ocie settled back down, falling asleep again, leaving just January to watch Mark through the night.

March 10, 2031

Sometime into the unholy hours of the night, January moved the chair close to Mark's bedside, unable to sleep, unable to rest, and resolving to keep his focus on Mark's constant breathing. In the moonlight, his face was ghostly, and every motion of his lungs was deathly slow. It was truly amazing that he was still alive after losing so much blood.

He took hold of Mark's right hand tightly, stroking his skin repetitively and drawing hope from the warmth within his hand. Mark cringed, shifting, aware of the sensations. January shuddered, his eyes stinging until finally a few tears fell. He'd done all he could to hold them back in the presence of his family. "I'm so sorry. Maybe if I had been there for you this never would have happened."

Mark opened his mouth and drew in one long, raggedy breath. January thought he was waking up, but after a moment, Mark visibly sank, his breaths returning to shallowly passing air in and out of his chest. Only his brows furrowed, aware of the pain, and that alone. Holding tight to Mark's hand, January pressed it between his palms and prayed, desperate and letting his tears loose. "This is all my fault…"

He had allowed his son to be alone with that monster. He hadn't known the man, and clearly Geoffrey had been grooming him from the start. January scanned over the needles and tubes all over him, but his gaze locked on the feeding tube taped across his cheek. It seemed so demeaning. Once they determined Mark could barely swallow water, it must have occurred to the doctors that he was a lot weaker than he seemed.

In the last week or two, Mark had lost a lot of weight. January could tell. He covered it up with lanky clothes and coats, but he had been skipping meals to avoid confrontation for quite some time. Without nutrients, he wouldn't heal. He needed this, but that didn't make it less painful to look at.

Suddenly, crimson flames raced down Mark's arm and January let go before the fire reached Mark's fingertips. His arm fell limply into the sheets, and when January tensed, Mark opened his eyes slightly. The cherry glow had returned, illuminating the dark hospital room. Nervously, January glanced back at Ocie who slept hunched in the awkward chair.

"Hey…" January whispered, adopting a warming smile. "It's the middle of the night, are you feeling okay?"

Mark gave a soft moan in denial, then coughed a few times before his eyes opened more fully and he stared up at the ceiling. January grimaced at his lifeless eyes, hopeless and in pain. "Sorry…" he whispered, long and slow.

"For what?" January said too quickly, not waiting for Mark to gather his breath.

"My Shadows are a little out of control right now. Might be from losing so much blood."

January perked up happily. That had been the most words out of Mark's mouth since he had first awoken, and it was a good sign his lungs were doing better. That was his hurdle now—getting his strength up with food, and then breathing normally.

"I wouldn't have burned you," Mark said, his crimson eyes finally locking with his father's. "My fire won't burn anything unless I want it to."

"It was just a reaction," January excused his jumpy movements. "Can I get you anything?"

Again, Mark shook his head gradually, ignoring the question. "I've been in the Realm... to hide from the pain. While I'm in there, I feel myself leave my body and nothing hurts anymore." He heaved another hoarse breath, barely able to summon any voice. "But... the deeper I go, the more strange things I see."

Suddenly, he began coughing, sending blood to his lips and turning them just as crimson as his fire. January fetched a tissue and helped him clean his lips, waiting patiently for his breath to return. It took several painful minutes of watching him gasping for air and suffering, and then Mark's eyes dashed around the dull room, disoriented and dizzy.

"Do you think I'm going to die?" he cried out, bloodstained tears drifting out the corners of his eyes.

"No..." January assured, taking his hand tightly again and gripping it to give him something to hold onto. "Y-you're going to be just fine!" Stammering didn't help convince Mark he was telling the truth.

Mark reeled back, his head lolling around as he waited for his dizziness to steady. "In the Realm... I saw the Infusion. I could see Sil, Ocie, Emilie, and Rita putting their Shadows into me, and I saw you." He paused for a breath, his eyes flickering shut for a few moments. "Brighter than any—" He coughed suddenly.

"Don't force yourself to talk. Get some rest," January urged lovingly.

Shaking his head, Mark frantically found his father's face, struggling to stay awake for a little while longer. "You were brighter than any human. You didn't look like smoke..." None of his words made sense to January, and his voice was growing fainter.

He sucked in a breath, pushing himself upward to draw air but to no success. "You… looked like a white…" Mark stopped, raising his chin and fighting to lift his back and fill his lungs. His breath caught, and no air passed through his lips.

"Mark?" January fretted, slowly standing up. With some effort, he brought his hands under Mark's neck and tried to hold him up. "Don't try to talk."

Mark's lips hung open, parting to gasp for air, but he made no sound, barely keeping his eyes open. "I… can't…" the sound was faint, but barely any air escaped. January held him up, panicking and not sure what to do. "I can't…"

"You can't what?" January cried into his face with a much more frantic voice.

His eyes fell shut again, and all the tenseness in his muscles, all the energy he had summoned to raise his chest, faded. January's eyes widened. Mark couldn't breathe! His face fell, and his grip on January's hand relinquished. He shook Mark in his arms, jostling him to try and get him in a position to clear his airways, but he made no response.

"No… no…" Mark wasn't breathing! In a last panic, he punched the call button for the nurse! He pulled himself up onto Mark's bed, holding him tight and crying, praying, sobbing. It was after two in the morning, no one in the hospital could possibly be awake.

Before he could lose hope, the lights were turned on and doctors and nurses flooded in. January was forced away from his son and Mark was dropped onto his back. January watched in horror as the ventilator was inserted back into Mark's throat and beyond that, they started chest compressions on his injured torso.

January's eyes dashed about at the flurry of people, only then taking notice of the monitors beside Mark's bed. "He's going into cardiac arrest!" one of them shouted, and a moment later, Mark's heart stopped. January's knees gave out, and he backed into a chair, stumbling and tearing at his hair, blocking out the sound of them violently performing CPR over Mark's wounds until a defibrillator brought him back.

Mark sputtered, jolting and panicking as he awoke to the second, thicker tube down his throat, completely controlling his breathing. Every time the machine pushed air into his lungs, it expanded them too hard, firing pain through his chest, and he pushed himself deeper into the Realm.

"Did he just have a heart attack?" someone said as they began examining his wounds for the damage they had likely inflicted. The stitches in his chest were tearing, and the wound had reopened, bleeding again, but their attention turned to his shoulder. January saw it through the tangle of hands. The bandage was saturated again. He was still bleeding. They panicked to unwrap the bandage and staunch the bleed, but the moment his shoulder was uncovered, January heard collective gasps.

He rose, gazing through them at Mark's shoulder. His whole arm was inflamed, and the wound was swollen, seeping blood in and through the limb. He was still bleeding internally, and this one had gone on much longer than the last. It had spread, and the bruising had enveloped much of his chest and neck. The sword had been Infused with a Shadow, and that poison was consuming him.

Worse off, without the bandages, the blankets, or anything covering his torso, he looked emaciated. There was no way he had lost this much weight. The muscles in his arms had begun to break down, leaving him thin and weak. It was Shadow Strength causing this, January was certain. The second Shadow inside him was devouring his body, eating away at any muscle he possessed.

Mark was awake through this, terrified and only able to stare as they argued over how to reduce the swelling and fight back against what they assumed was an infection. January rushed in, seeing his panic, taking his hand again and assuring his son he was there, and he was not leaving. Mark pinned his eyes shut, convincing himself to stop fighting the ventilator and to just bury himself in the Realm.

January knew that was what he chose to do because, in a few moments, it seemed as if he had fallen unconscious again. In another few minutes, they started preparing to take him into another surgery. January shot up to his feet the moment they started moving him. "Save his arm!" he ordered at the top of his lungs. "Do not take away my son's arm!" His demand had to be met. They couldn't make any drastic decisions.

XX
WHY EMILIE HATES

No one could speak in the face of bad news. Upon arriving, they were met by January outside Mark's room with a soft warning, "It was a very rough night." Sil pushed past, but Emilie held his arm, letting Marissa in first, laying eyes on her son in intensive care, once again unmoving and under the artificial lungs of the ventilator.

January pulled Sil aside at the door with a firm hand on his arm, not allowing him to enter. "I need to talk Shadows with you, but I don't want to worry anyone," he whispered, keeping his gaze on his wife as she fell into tears.

Sil nodded hastily, and Emilie finally let him free but followed January a block away from the room. January was sleep deprived but remarkably composed. "He's going to lose his arm," he whispered, only conveying urgency in his tone. "Unless we do something, they're going to have to make a decision in the next day or so. Strength is doing this to him. It's making him weaker, and I overheard this morning they think his body isn't capable of processing food, which is what he needs to get strong enough to heal."

Sil pulled a bit but hesitated when he caught sight of Mark though the entryway. Even with the new bandages binding his shoulder, the state of it was burned into his mind. At the location of the injury, Mark would lose his whole arm, and probably a good portion of his shoulder. What was being implied was small procedures to cut out the infection, and hope it was enough for Mark's body to recover. But Sil knew better, the Shadow was in his blood now, and if Mark was rejecting it, there was no real way to get that poison out of his system. Strength was devouring him at his weakest places—his shoulder, his lungs, his heart.

January growled under his breath. "Strength is supposed to be a powerful Shadow, right? He's supposed to have the power of strength or something? So why would it be eating him alive like this?"

Sil stared at the floor in shock. "I don't know... I don't know anything about Shadows this powerful. I barely know anything about Shadow Hope as it is." He glanced to Emilie, looking for something, any help.

She was equally panicked, holding her arm and hovering an inch off the floor. "Wasn't he getting better? He was awake, he just needed to get his strength back. Why is this happening?"

January didn't release Sil's arm, holding it tighter. "Find something!" he demanded softly. "You have to find a way to stop this Shadow!"

Nodding shakily, Sil pulled his arm free, thinking frantically through his options. "Keller," he whispered, "I'll talk to Keller. His Shadow might be able to inhibit Strength, and at the very least, buy Mark some time."

Giving a glance to Emilie, Sil turned away and ran back down the hall. "Where did Ocie go?" he asked as they dashed for the elevator to get out of there. With a quick tone in the Realm, Sil found her still in the hospital, and they honed in on each other somewhere in the middle.

Ocie stepped into an empty waiting room, guiding them inside to talk in private. "I called my dad early this morning. He's on his way up, and he should be here tonight."

"Good..." Sil panted in relief. "Did he have any suggestions?"

Ocie shrugged. "Not much. He's bringing the inhibition serum he used to heal Kip, but it might not work since the ASI has never worked on Mark."

"Is there..." Sil hesitated, "...a way for us to take Shadow Strength out of him. Like with our own Shadows?"

Ocie shook her head. "It's bound to his element, so it'll always find a way back to him even if we take it a hundred miles away. And we can't even do that because, right now, it's spread throughout his system, disjointed and volatile, and I think that's why it's acting so poisonous. It's not a complete Shadow, it's... broken."

Thinking this over, Sil grimaced. "Mark said Strength is broken into four parts, Geoffrey had one, and Mark has another, and not even Geoffrey knew where the other two parts are. We could try giving him another part of Strength."

"You want to stab him again?" Emilie blared.

"No!" he insisted loudly, garnering the stares of people outside the windows of the waiting room. "I mean Infusion, we could... I don't know, de-Infuse the sword."

"Or re-Infuse it," Ocie crossed her arms over his chest. "We could take the Shadow out, and re-Infuse it to the sword. That'll bind it there and not to Mark. He'll still have a small connection, but he won't be able to use it until he touches the sword."

"That could work," Sil nodded hastily.

"But... that means we have to go get the sword, back at Geoffrey's place." Emilie fretted, and Sil shuddered at the idea.

Someone very driven passed the windows outside, but did a double-take at the sight of Sil's white hair and the girl whose feet didn't touch the floor. The woman stopped, and Sil recognized her. "Um... Emilie... your mom is back."

With her back to the door, Emilie let out a curse under her breath.

"What is your problem!" Hellen screamed, barging in on them.

Emilie turned in the air, nonchalantly, portraying her truest form, as a petty bully. "That's a new record for finding me," she mocked.

"I chased after you as soon as you snuck out, and I knew where you were going!" Hellen argued back, meeting Emilie's spunk surprisingly well. "Would you quit avoiding us and go get in the car!"

Poising her hands on her hips, Emilie smirked. "I'm not going." The defiance in her voice was the final straw.

Hellen snapped, lashing out and grabbing hold of Emilie's ankle. "I didn't want to do this, but you don't weigh anything, and I can drag you." She turned for the door and started charging out.

"Hey!" Emilie shrieked, trying to kick her leg free, but it physically wasn't strong enough to fight. "What are you doing! Let me go!" She looked back to Sil for help but he just stood there watching her be dragged through the air with a slightly bemused smile on his face.

He leant over to Ocie and chuckled. "I think she's met her match."

Emilie paled, her floating body now gathering the attention of various hospital staff and visitors, immediately singling her out as a Shadow. Embarrassed, she dropped to the floor, forcing her mother to fall with her if she intended to hold on. Finally, she kicked Hellen's wrist with her other foot hard enough to make her let go.

"Do not do that again!" she howled angrily.

Hellen stood up over her. "Do *not* run away again!" she screamed back, making a scene. "I'm tired of chasing after you. You've been completely ungrateful of everything I've done to try and make your life better! I'm doing this for you. I called Greg because I wanted you to have a father. I told him to push me to declutter and get my life in order, and I told him to not let me give up. We are *this* close to a better life! And I won't give up until you've at least seen it!"

Her voice lightened slowly. "The house is so beautiful, nicer than I could ever afford, and it has slanted windows you can fly in and out of as you please. You can sleep in the loft. You can have so much freedom!"

Emilie lay on the floor in shock, too afraid to reinstate her Shadow, and thus too weak to stand up. She cringed, clamping her knuckles on the white tile. "Fine..." she hissed under her breath.

Sil ran out after her and helped her up just as she activated her Shadow. "I'll let you know if we get any news." He pushed her, guiding her to stick to her word.

She forced herself to pretend to walk out of the hospital. She didn't know why she felt so insecure, but she didn't want people to notice her. She felt gravity's full effect as she sank down into the car once more, and her mother didn't turn onto the highway in the direction of their little house an hour away. Instead, she drove into the city.

New York was dull in the grayness of early spring. The skyscrapers only made Emilie want to get out and touch the sky herself. To fly up there and annoy people through the windows. She wanted to have fun and let herself loose on the city, but the encasing heat of the car held her down. Traffic was frustrating, making the roads slow and unbearable. She could fly out right now and be there in an instant, but she didn't. She let the long wait keep her away from the apartment.

All she wanted was to stay with Mark right now, to be fighting to figure out a way to heal him and keep him alive. She could go back to Geoffrey's house and get the sword. She could potentially save Mark, but right now she had to be here. Cringing, she bit back tears in her eyes, masking emotions, and covering them in her nasty temperament. She had to be a monster right now, the rudest bully she could summon. She couldn't allow any feelings or vulnerabilities to show. She was a monster.

She expected the apartment to be a little window or two up on a high floor of a skyscraper, but instead, the building was only four stories high, and it was all one residency. The house was huge. They pulled up and stepped out onto the street, but Emilie rose up a couple feet, her eyes locking on the highest floor, at the wide street-facing window and the tower of slanted windows on the roof.

"I told you you'd like it," Hellen mused, popping the trunk and fetching the first round of suitcases. "Will you give me a hand?" She trudged up the apartment stairs, out of the sidewalk, and showed a little trust in Emilie to do as she was told.

Emilie picked up one measly bag, effortlessly able to carry more, but she refused. Faking a proud walk up the stairs, she stood behind her mother as she knocked on the door. She inhaled the cold March air, fixing herself with the mindset: *I am a monster.*

Greg answered brightly, lighting up when he laid eyes on his daughter. "You finally made it!"

Emilie tilted her hips and smirked. "No thanks to the injury in the family and my cousin almost dying."

Greg paused, caught off guard, and looked to Hellen for some kind of response. He already knew, Emilie could see it in his eyes, and he was playing dumb to keep attention away from Mark. He gestured them inside, and though Emilie didn't want to let her feet move, Hellen pushed her in through the threshold.

"The basement connects to the parking garage," Greg explained as they started up the first flight of stairs. "Our bedroom is here," he directed them around on the third floor once they reached the crest of the stairs. Out of the stairwell, they peered into an open space with windows on either long end of the room. It was decorated for a man's tastes, but some of Hellen's boxes were already piled at the foot of the king-size bed.

Emilie quickly realized this house was taller than it was spacious. Hellen ditched her bags, and they started up the final flight of stairs into the main floor. Emilie didn't like stairs, floating up them the whole way but keeping level with her parents to seem like she was cooperating. The first thing that touched her was the light, and then her eyes drifted to the front windows, even bigger than she had assumed. The sunlight flooded in and a few of the glass panels were open, letting the windy city air stream in through flowing, white curtains.

She rose up unconsciously, her gaze following the ceiling at the slanted windows, each with opening panels she could slip out from. She gradually let her gaze drift about the actual kitchen and living area. Everything had an open layout, with a gorgeous center island that had granite countertops, lush green plants growing along the shelves above the cabinets and above that a loft with a bed for her.

Emilie flew straight up, unobstructed by the twenty-foot ceilings and peered into the loft space she knew was her room. Best of all, it had no walls. No doors, no locks, just a staircase leading up to the space with direct light from the slanted windows. For a moment, she could live here. She could love it here.

"I found a buyer for your place," Greg broke into her excitement, speaking to Hellen. "They're willing to gut the place and do all the renovations at their expense. In a week or two, it'll be out of sight, out of mind."

Hellen nodded eagerly and took a seat in the living room, staring out the windows at the view in awe. "Thank you... so much," she breathed. "Without you, I never would have gotten out. I feel... free!"

Free. The word resonated with Emilie a few more times, and she placed her feet on the floor in the loft. The bed was a thin mattress set upon painted wood pallets decorated with indoor plants, and upon the crisp bedspread laid a little black box with a note on top.

Glancing over her shoulder at her parents talking downstairs, Emilie approached the gift nervously. Her name was on the note, she confirmed that first, and then lifting the paper, she cautiously unfolded it.

"Heard you have a great throwing arm," it said.

Sinking down onto the bed, she sat and opened the top of the black case. Shiny silver illuminated from the light above, and for a moment, she thought it was jewelry, but then she noticed the points. Inside formed molds was a set of seven throwing stars. Her mouth fell open slightly, eerily disturbed for a moment. Mark had been offered a weapon, and look where that had gotten him.

But with these, she could be unstoppable. By manipulating gravity, she could program those tiny things as she threw them to hit any target she wished. It was her match, her personality in seven shiny objects. She didn't know how Greg could give her something so perfect.

Very slowly, she picked one up and brandished it in her fingers, reluctant to get any fingerprints on it. Between her fingers, she spun it in her hand, watching it catch the light as its eight sharp points reflected her face like a mirror.

"Those are made of silver." Greg's voice came from the stairs, still three steps down and technically outside her room.

Whirling, she dropped the star into her bed and her back stiffened. *I am a monster!* she reminded herself. "They're not Shadow-Infused, are they?"

"What?" Greg puzzled, still seemingly playing dumb. He had to know what Infusion was. How could he be ignorant? "Look..." He started climbing up the last stairs and approaching her. "I know we got off on the wrong foot. And I know you need your freedom to come and go. So, let this be your place to rest, and you can have that freedom."

Emilie rose up out of the bed, floating to remain defensive. In her heart, she was terrified. Her father, a random Shadow who had appeared in her life, was offering her a weapon just like Geoffrey. All her suspicions suddenly became real when he reached out and took her hand. Upon making contact, she was paralyzed, hot terror seeping through her body.

She jerked away as quickly as she could. "Don't touch me!" but he held her hand tight. She shook his hand again and flew a few feet higher, but his grip remained. "Let me go!" Was this a nightmare? Was she even awake right now?

Relinquishing gravity, she raised him up and threw him toward the banister, but he held on, stumbling just before he saved his fall. "What do you want? To fight? To give me a Shadow like Geoffrey did to Mark?" Emilie rose up toward the slanted windows, keeping her ankles up out of his reach but as she looked down over the banister, she saw her mother, collapsed into the new couch.

Her eyes widened. "What did you do to her?!" she roared.

Greg glanced over his shoulder. "Nothing, she fell asleep."

"No way." Emilie shook her head frantically. "You're lying! You did something to her!"

"Calm down…" he soothed, "nobody is trying to hurt you here."

"Then why'd you grab my wrist?!" she screamed. *I am a monster!*

"I just took your hand, I didn't…" He paused, looking over her, and suddenly fear appeared in his eyes. "Are you hallucinating?"

"What?" Emilie howled in disgust. "Don't try to play with my mind! I know you're taking advantage of her, manipulating her to come here so you can get to me!" In her fury, the thought did enter her mind. What if she was seeing things? She was so psyched out after what had happened to Mark. Maybe she was paranoid.

Terrors started to rip through her being, and she sank slowly, closer to the floor. She saw Mark getting stabbed, over and over! She heard his scream through the glass, and she was right back there on that night. She had to be in control, she had to protect her family, the ones who really mattered to her, the Shadows.

She grasped up the seven stars and tucked them into her boots, but the moment she had her back turned to Greg, he grabbed her shoulders and yanked her down, or maybe he tried to hug her, she wasn't sure. She bucked, rising up and throwing him off, this time hard enough to get him over the banister, hurling him down into the kitchen so that he landed hard on the granite counter.

Hellen sat up from the couch abruptly and screamed when she saw him impact the stone. *"Emilie!"*

Rising up with a cold expression, it took a second for Emilie to realize Hellen *had* been sleeping. Tensing, she blinked a few times, coming to reality and realizing just how high the fall was. Greg laid motionless on the counter, slowly gasping and trying to rise until Hellen rushed for him.

All the blood rushed out of her face when she realized what she had done. Maybe he *had* tried to hug her. Maybe she *was* hallucinating. Flying up toward the slanted windows, she panicked while watching Greg open his eyes again, slowly, staring up at her. His pale eyes were bloodshot, and his breath resembled Mark's, choppy and faint.

Hellen lifted his head, trying to help him sit up and get off the counter, but she stopped and stared at her hand, coated in slick blood. Hellen let out a scream, and Emilie shook in terror, losing control of her Shadow for a second.

She had perfect control of her Shadow. This never happened! Flying was all she knew but she fell a full two feet lower. She had done that. She had hurt him. She might even had cracked his head open. But all she could think about was that moment of weakness. She refused to let herself show vulnerability again. Flying was the only thing she knew. Emotion, fear, impulse, they fell by the wayside.

Something sparked in her Shadow that held fire. Hatred welled inside her. She didn't care that she had hurt him. She didn't care if he never walked again. He deserved it because *he* made her lose control for just a second. Her Shadow took a firm grip on her being and she seized, suspended under the windows like a chandelier. Her lightning green eyes flashed and then faded as a muted blood red overcame them.

Hellen cried softly as something changed in the room, and Emilie's being shuddered. Emilie felt it in her heart. She could make herself stronger. She could choose to let her Shadow control her and blindly fall into its innate memories. Certainly, her Shadow had hundreds of wielders, but deep within it she could sense just two. Shadow Feather had only ever been wielded twice in all of time. And she was the third.

She granted it control. Her consciousness faded into a red mist. Glowing red sparks flung off her limbs, and anything they touched started to float. The life and wind in her Shadow died away, replaced with a dark visage and the memories of her other two wielders. *This is what I wanted. I wanted this! I am a monster!*

She was the beast to be feared.

Red dripped off the end of her hair, dyeing the ends crimson, and the rest of her brown hair was left darker, close to black like Mark's. Her red eyes solidified, menacing and bright, and her entire appearance took on a fiery crimson like blood. A smile came to her lips, and she took one of the stars from her boot and looked down at Greg. She had created herself, an unfeeling, inhuman creature, and enacted one proof in the face of her parents.

Taking the silver star between her fingers, she cut herself from the bridge of her nose to her left cheek.

Hellen stared up in horror, holding onto Greg's shoulders as he faded, but she flinched when Emilie threw the seventh star down upon the counter, sinking it deeply into the stone.

Without a human emotion left alive in her, she took off to the sky, not even opening the window but smashing through it, only covering her face with her elbows. As her presence left, all suspended items dropped to the floor and shattered. She didn't care how she cut her arms or sent glass raining down on her parents. In a red comet, she took off over the sky, ascending up through the clouds, above the skyscrapers, into freedom.

She was fire in the sky, a red shooting star whizzing across the skyline. In that moment, every emotion ceased, and she didn't even think about what she had done.

She flew through a cloud and was suddenly drenched in a flash rainstorm, cold intermingled with sleet that pelted her body like needles. She could see the midnight lights of the bustling city. The air was freezing up high, but she was numb to it all. Nothing hurt, not the cold, not the sleet, not even the cut on her face.

Abruptly she realized it was indeed dark out, and she had been flying for hours. She was unconscious to the whole day! Flying in and out of the clouds, between the towers. Everything was a blur. She had been away from Mark this whole time, unable to know if he had awoken or gotten worse. The blood on her face was frozen, and the rain caused it to melt and continue dripping down her cheeks, pushed by the wind. She didn't feel any pain, not even a twinge of sensation. She couldn't feel *anything*.

She flew out of the city, away from the chaos, the lights and the insanity. She fled for home but then realized her home was gone. Below her, she became aware of the dotting houses, the communities and cul-de-sacs, and of course, Mark's house. She dropped out of the sky, plunging into the backyard and collapsing down through a tree. The blackness of the night shrouded her, and she knelt on the ground, only holding herself up on her hands and knees as the mud seeped into her clothes.

It wasn't cold. It didn't sting. It didn't hurt.

"What's happening to me?"

Lights were on within the Halos' home. Some of them had come home to rest, and for a moment she thought she could be safe here. Rising up, she escaped the ground, the frigid rain dripping off her legs, and then she stopped and took to the sky. She couldn't face anyone right now, not for shame or for fear, but with that nature she had given herself, unfeeling, brutal, lifeless.

She flew to Geoffrey's, angry and maybe revenge-driven, she didn't know, but the redness in her eyes burned when she saw there were lights on in there too. A tarp had been hung in place of the wall, a barricade around the driveway, and an unsettling quietness in the neighboring houses. There was a car in the driveway.

Her chest expanded and her joints locked, but she dove in, unrestricted by the petty boundaries. There were boxes on the floor, numerous cases strewn about, and a huge blood stain on the floor in the center of the room. Emilie set her feet on the wood and dizzied, sick at the sight of Mark's blood. Someone stirred from amongst the boxes and rose up, a burly man, with old gray hair and verdant green eyes.

He stared at her, and she couldn't move. It wasn't Geoffrey, but it might as well have been him, snagging up the last of his weapons and making off into the night. However, his eyes calmed when he recognized her, and a faint, sorrowful smile appeared on his lips. "Feather..." his voice was warm and fatherly, more loving than any man's voice she'd heard in her life. "It's been a long time."

"Who are you?" she yelled, rising off the floor a few inches.

He set down one of Geoffrey's weapons, tucking a small copper dagger neatly into a cloth. Emilie only caught a brief sight of it, but it glistened with crested rhinestones all over its carved hilt. "You probably don't know me yet," the man whispered. "I promise I don't mean you or Mark any harm. I'm just taking Geoffrey's collection to a safer place."

"Where is Geoffrey?" she seethed.

The man shrugged a little. "He was gone when I got here, and I believe he ran off soon after Mark was taken to the hospital."

"You mean he's still out there! Shouldn't we be trying to find him, to make him pay for what he did?" Emilie felt her heart grow tighter, all the rage burning like a crimson flame.

Shaking his head, the man sighed and lowered himself gradually to the floor, grunting as his joints looked too feeble to get back up again. "Geoffrey has done what he was ordered to do, and it is very unlike Strength to follow orders. He can die in peace with a clean conscience."

"What!" Emilie howled. "How can—clean conscience! This was the most evil thing I've ever seen anyone do!"

Relaxed and composed, the man did not look at her. "You will do far more heinous things in your lifetime." Emilie tensed in the air, her thoughts flowing back to her father's bloodshot eyes. The man took note, a light appearing in his eyes. "Unless, you've already done it."

Grinding her teeth, Emilie backed away slowly. "How do you know about that? And who are you? How do you know so much about me, a-and Mark?"

"You can calm down," he assured. "My name is William. I'm the one keeping the ASH afloat right now. I've taken care of any questions the police had. I'm just here cleaning up Geoffrey's mess, and if I have enough left by the end of the month, I'll be able to pick up Mark's medical bills."

"If he even survives!" Emilie protested. "You clearly know everything that's happened, so help us find a way to save him."

William shook his head coldly. "I can't interfere, but I think you came here for a reason." He gestured to one of the piles at a lone padded case atop the stack.

She neared it cautiously, not daring to touch it. "Mark's sword?"

He nodded. "He'll have to pick up where Geoffrey left off in the search for the other two swords. I'll hang on to Morglay for now. But I can promise you— he's going to be okay. Trust your instincts, and trust the Shadows."

Hesitantly, Emilie took hold of the case's handle and relinquished gravity's hold to lift it. She denied the sword its weight and drifted back. "Where will I find you?" she asked softly, the wind and the rain picking up behind her.

William gave a little smile. "I'll be around."

"No," she said sternly. "Where can I find you?"

He tensed a bit but ultimately his eyes remained tender, and under the howling wind, he conveyed his home address to her in the Realm.

She smirked, poising her hand on her hip. "You don't trust anyone enough to say it out loud, but you trust me? Why?"

He returned to packing up the many swords and Infused weapons. "Because the wielders of Shadow Feather before and after you all have one thing in common." His eyes flared that lightning green her eyes had just lost. "Their ability to keep secrets."

Blood. The red hit her, and she jumped back. *The blood on the floor, the blood in her father's sclerae, the blood in her face.* It only faded when she washed it away under the heavy rain. Her consciousness blurred as she passed through the downpour, half-aware of the absence of light, and unaware of all sensations.

Her senses were blackness. Nothing to be seen, heard, felt, or thought. But everything cleared as if the rain stopped instantly. Her first comprehension was warmth, then cotton, and she opened her eyes. She was resting, deeply asleep a moment again, and lying on her side in a stale, stiff bed.

She heard movement and jumped, ascending vertically and taking the covers with her as a hand entered the corner of her eyes.

"Easy, Emilie, it's just me..." Marissa's soft-spoken voice drained into her mind, concerned and distraught. "You've got a big cut on your face. I was trying to clean it."

Wincing, Emilie suddenly remembered it. She had cut herself, and she hadn't even felt it, but the high of whatever she had done was wearing off, and physical sensations were returning.

"What happened?" Marissa asked, reaching up to dab the cut with a cotton ball. "You showed up here an hour ago looking like a zombie. And with that sword of all things."

Her eyes widening, Emilie sat up fully, kicking off the blanket. "The sword! I have to get it to Mark!"

Marissa jumped up and held her down, pushing her back into the bed, which startled Emilie beyond measure, but for some reason, she didn't retaliate. "It can wait until tomorrow!" Marissa insisted, "Keller arrived a few hours ago. Using his power on Mark seems to be helping a little, and they took him off the ventilator again."

Her chest filled with hope at the realization. Mark was breathing again. Keller had indeed bought them some time. Her head fell against the pillow, thoroughly exhausted. She was able to curl on her side and forget about her body, the aches and pains, her spindly limbs, and the scar on her face. She felt free of her bonds, but with that feeling came a deep hate. She had become a monster, and she was acutely aware of that. The hate in her heart burned hotter with each second, lulling her back to sleep.

XXI
AIR

March 11, 2031

A twinge of stimulus tugged on Mark's consciousness, pulling him up out of the Realm and to the real world for air. He gasped a little, fighting past his faint breathing and holding on to alertness. Someone was in the room with him. He felt them grasping at his thin blanket and drawing it away from his bandages. There was a slight gasp, but it wasn't his own.

He blinked his eyes open to the gaze of a young woman he didn't know. She was horrified, her hands hovering away from his shoulder, staring only at the bandages Mark couldn't see. She flustered a little when she saw his eyes were open and a deep muted mahogany, not quite red. "H-how are you feeling?" she stammered through the question, not quite sure how to cope in the face of a Shadow.

Mark took a deep, slow breath. "Scared..." he whispered hoarsely, "I can barely move anymore." He let himself cough slightly, having done all he could to hold it back, but from the lack of air he just felt like he was choking for a few minutes. Coughing also made him aware of the feeding tube as it simply added to his discomfort.

The woman muted her emotions to not worry him. She did her job, checking his bandages and packing some new gauze into his shoulder, but she didn't draw attention to the action. "What is the Realm like?" she asked sweetly, a kind voice Mark hadn't heard from any of the doctors yet.

He didn't know if he could summon enough breath to answer, and his throat felt so swollen up he wasn't even sure if he could produce a sound. "I'm trying to go deeper. But the deeper I go, the further from consciousness I get, and even my own body." He struggled to inhale, lifting up the mountain that was his chest with all his might. "As I leave, the pain disappears. I can feel the stars embracing me, and I'm afraid if I get too close, I won't be able to leave them."

"The stars?" the girl muttered, curious and open-minded.

Mark nodded and swallowed hard, pain ripping down his throat. "They're Shadows who have died, I think."

She drew her brows together and lowered her hands from the bandages, concerned. "So, if you go to be with them, you'll die, won't you?"

He made a very slight nod, red, bloody tears welling in his eyes. "I'm scared... I don't know what's going to happen. And all I can do is hide." He paced his breathing again, sinking away and closing his eyes for a few moments, and by the time he had recovered enough to look around again, the nurse was gone, and he felt someone holding his hand.

January sat there, staring at him, praying silently. Mark held his gaze for a few seconds before January reacted and scooted forward. "Hey, can I get you anything? Some water? Maybe I could turn on the TV?"

Mark blinked a few times, dazed and delirious.

Sighing heavily, January sank back down. "The Shadows want you to be awake for a bit today. I thought getting you to do something might help."

Finally, Mark inhaled sharply and shifted a little. "Okay..." he forced, long and slow. He could see in his father's posture how terrified he was. The last time Mark had spent the night without a ventilator, he had stopped breathing. January hadn't slept in days, watching over his son vigilantly, with his hand always near the call button.

"Can I speak with you?" Someone asked from the door frame, and Mark didn't bother turning his head to see who it was. January's face filled with terror. He didn't want to leave, but he forced himself to stand, just for a few seconds. Obviously, whatever needed to be said, they didn't want Mark to hear.

The door opened a moment after it closed, or at least it seemed quick in Mark's warped perception of time. "Good morning," a soft voice called before its owner came into view, and he managed to open his eyes. Sil circled around him, a warming smile and his wild white hair tied into a ponytail, which swayed behind his back.

"Oh, you *are* looking better," Another voice came, and Keller stepped up.

Mark summoned a smile for the man. "Hey... Keller!" he wheezed happily.

The man pulled up a chair and ruffled Mark's already crazy hair. "Inhibiting your Shadows has definitely helped," he observed. "You were asleep all day yesterday, so I'll try to get you up to speed. Think you can stay awake?"

He nodded, shifting and trying to lift his back slightly. Sil did him the favor of raising the bed to help him sit up, and from that angle, he was able to see Ocie had come in behind her father. "Strength is different from most Shadows," he said, "in that, instead of latching onto your element first and then spreading from your heart, it spreads like a venom where it was injected. I'm guessing Geoffrey was going for your heart as a cleaner transition for the Infused sword, but he hit your shoulder first."

Mark sucked in a breath, blinking erratically and trying to stay awake, but to them, it probably looked like another nod, barely comprehending the information.

"I heard about the Strength from the last generation. He was a temperamental boy, and Strength attacked his psyche. These class three Shadows, the sentient ones, have a knack for screwing with their wielders' perception. Hope feeds on despair and Strength on weakness. So, right now, Strength is making you *need* it."

"You just described Geoffrey," Mark whispered, barely a sound from his voice, but at least his snark was coming through.

Keller smiled confidently. "So here's our plan. I've already called up a bunch of Shadows from the ASH, and we're going to perform another Infusion on you, a much stronger one. *Oce* did a darn good job on you the first time, but there's only so much you can do with the power of four Shadows. After the Infusion, you should be strong enough to activate Strength and let it finish working through your system. It's not going to kill you. It'll just be another Shadow you have to refine. But I think you'll acclimate to it quickly. You'll make a fine Shadow Strength once you get the hang of it."

"Okay..." Mark got out again, blinking away the tears from the pain. "What about..." He gasped mid-sentence. "...my arm?"

Keller's brows knitted together and grew much more stern. "We'll do what we can. But I promise you won't lose it." He grinned warmly and reached out, touching Mark's cheek lovingly to reassure him. Had it been a few months ago, Mark would have been disturbed, but right now, he couldn't describe the comfort he received from the touch.

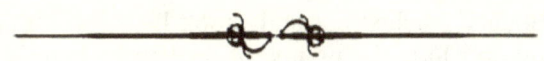

"He's hemorrhaging again," the nurse whispered. "The infection is eating away at his shoulder, and if you don't make a decision soon, you're not going to have any choice left."

January gritted his teeth, hardly able to accept this news, and bearing himself up was the only thing he could do. Stand there like a coward and take it.

"He's a minor," the woman reminded him. "You have medical authority over him. And right now, cutting out the infection will work, but that window is closing very fast as it spreads. Another day or two and amputation will be the only option."

Cringing, he shook his head. "Give the Shadows a chance. Just let them buy him a little time," he urged.

The nurse sighed, indignant but truly worried for Mark. "Time is against him right now."

January clenched his fists. Mark couldn't endure another surgery. His arm was already permanently disfigured, and he didn't even know it yet. He needed time. They just needed time. The Shadows had a plan now. All would be fine if Mark could keep his head up for a day more. The nurse turned away awkwardly, leaving January alone in the hallways, his feet quaking.

If this failed, Mark was going to die. This one hope was all he had left. Clearing his throat, January pulled himself together, refusing to let the bad news show through. He made himself go back in there. He made himself smile down at his son and lie to him as he rested in that bed, hemorrhaging, and with every second, losing his arm.

Keller sat by Mark's bed with a playful grin, rattling off stories and keeping Mark awake, but he stopped when he noticed January reenter. "Oh, excuse me. We haven't officially met yet. I only saw you in passing last night."

January reached out and shook his hand. "Likewise." He couldn't hide the twinge of disdain he had for Keller. The man had taken hundreds of Shadows from their homes, children, Mark included, and though he had done some good, January had a hard time accepting this. He couldn't hold eye contact with Keller for long, but the moment his eyes returned to Mark, Keller let go suddenly and leant in close.

"Jan?!" he gaped.

Reeling back, January tried to step away. "Uh... yes, January Halo."

Keller's mouth fell open, hastily looking him over from head to toe. "Oh my—It is you!" He gave a shriek and suddenly burst forward to give January a hug.

Jumping back, January scurried free. "Hold on just a second—"

"It's me, Ian!" Keller burst with a big smile. "I haven't seen you in twenty years. I thought you were dead!"

Falling pale, January feared his legs would give out. "Twenty... years?" he gasped quietly.

Keller still pressed forward, slapping his hand down on his shoulder, a little friendlier than January was comfortable with. "I guess it's been a little longer than that now. Last time I saw you... well... I guess it was right before... you know..."

January cringed, utterly disturbed. "Know what?"

Lowering himself, Keller smiled a bit bashfully. "I suppose you're still angry with me. That's fair. You have a family of your own now, and you clearly didn't want Mark in the ASH with me."

"Wait. What?!" January finally screamed. "I don't know you! I've never met you before!" He couldn't contain how his voice cracked, even though it drew Mark's attention. It pained January to think of his son watching as he cried out.

"You don't... remember?" Keller frowned, pausing for a moment and glancing to his daughter, simultaneously catching Sil's eye.

"He can't remember anything beyond twenty-two years ago." Sil stepped forward, fiddling with his ponytail.

Keller stepped away from January, silently shocked for a few agonizing seconds. "You don't remember *anything?*" he breathed. January shook his head a little. Keller exhaled, disgruntled, running a hand over his scraggly five o'clock shadow. "We were... Jan, we were best friends back then. I met you when you were fourteen, and our difference in age didn't matter. You were so full of life, you were a wildcard, you were... powerful. I couldn't—"

January shuddered. "No!" He frantically pressed himself to the wall by the door. He didn't want to run away from Mark. "I was living in a crap apartment. I hit my head on something. I probably immigrated when I was young or snuck into the country. I'm nothing, I'm not—"

Sil's shoulders dropped in awe. "You're a Shadow!"

"No!" January insisted, practically screaming.

Keller pushed forward. "I don't know how you lost your memory, but I have an idea. It was when I first put up the ASI around our home. Half the Shadows fought to stop me. They thought it was dangerous..." He hesitated. One shaky breath filled his voice with heavy emotion. "You were one of them. I guess you went into hiding like the others. You probably didn't want any trace of your Shadow so your test would be negative." He smiled brightly. "And I bet whatever you did, it bled through to Mark and that's why his test was negative!"

"No!" January insisted again. "That's impossible! I don't know anything about Shadows!"

"Hey..." Keller's voice grew softer. "Calm down, I'm not trying to attack you. Frankly, I'm just happy you're alive."

"What may or may not have happened to me *frankly* doesn't matter," January yelled. "Just help my son. That's all that matters to me!" He stormed out, rushing down the hall and not even realizing how hard he was trembling until he stumbled into the corner of a corridor and clung to it.

He sank, his legs finally giving out, and he embraced the floor, holding onto the one sturdy thing in his life. He tore at his hair, days of no rest had disheveled it, letting the wavy ends frill out rebelliously. The stress was turning him grayer by the day. His tears hit the tiles. He ignored the passersby and sobbed, alone.

There was nothing he could do to save his son. He couldn't even protect Mark from getting caught by the ASH. Maybe if he had known, if he had somehow not forgotten his past, he would have been able to protect Mark when he found out he was a Shadow. Maybe that could have been a bond, not a wedge between them.

It couldn't be true! He was the reason Mark's test was negative? How? Just how?

His hands formed to fists on the sterile white floor. He *couldn't* be a Shadow. He *hadn't* come to a Shadow settlement. He *didn't* know Keller. That was impossible.

"Jan…" Keller's voice returned from behind him, and hastily he knelt on the floor with him. "Listen to me." Tenderly, he laid his hands on January's shoulders. "I don't know how you lost your memory, but I remember you. Just a plucky little ginger doing his best to survive, running to the only place he had hope. You were annoying above all else, nobody could understand your crazy accent, and you had the strongest fight in you, of anyone I've ever met."

Giving a little chuckle, Keller took his hands off him. "Now look at you. You got what you always wanted, freedom and a family. And now you're a father who's been more loyal to his family than I've ever been able to be for Ocie."

The words stuck with January, bitterly sinking in. "None of that can be true…" He hung his head. "I have brown hair. I've always had brown hair," he insisted.

Keller just smirked and shook his head. "The last time I saw you, you had white hair." He leaned in close and smiled widely. "You've never been opposed to change, and that was your strongest trait. Try to trust me. Try to believe me when I say I know where you come from."

Frowning, January dried his face quickly. "Do I have a brother? Maybe he's the red-head, maybe he's the Shadow, and maybe he's the one you remember."

"That seems highly unlikely," Keller scoffed and jostled his shoulders heartily. It wasn't much, but it was friendly. "I can hear it in your voice. I know that accent. It's faded, but I know it's you, and I remember when you first told William your name—January, after the month you were born. That was the only name you had."

Gradually, January was able to meet eyes with him, fighting back tears. He was no one. He was nothing. He was an idiot teenager barely scraping by when he lost his memory, and after he lost it nothing changed. His life was constant, change wasn't possible.

"Dad!" Ocie screamed at the top of her lungs as she sprinted towards them. "Something's wrong!"

January's feet slipped out from under him when he shot up. He fell, but he ran, bumping into the nurses as a handful of them flooded into Mark's room. Sil was standing over Mark, holding down his right arm and doing his best to not put pressure on Mark's chest or shoulder as it was all he could do to control him as he lay there convulsing.

Everything in January's head, heart, and soul inverted. It was all too much. Near him, a nurse screamed loud and clear, "Seizure!"

Sil was pushed back, and the second he let go, Mark started flailing. His back arched and his muscles spasmed. He wasn't breathing. The whole time, he didn't draw air, and Sil gasped when Mark's lips started turning blue. His eyes remained open, glassy and lifeless, and blood bubbled in his mouth as the tremors further injured him.

They forced him onto his side, letting the blood drain out so he could breathe, when he started breathing—if he started breathing. The tremors slowed, and Mark inhaled deeply through his nose. His tongue rolled around the taste of blood, but he didn't have the strength to swallow or clear his mouth, so the nurses syphoned the blood every few minutes.

"What happened? What caused this?" Sil panicked, rushing toward Keller.

Keller's eyes dashed with all possible causes related to Shadows. "Blood loss, the poison reached his brain or is breaking down his muscles—No!" He turned his attention to the nurses. "Everything is filtered through his heart, then through lungs. He has a new Shadow, and it's trying to latch onto his element in the left chamber of his heart. There's a clot blocking blood flow. Embolism. Check for pulmonary embolism!"

The doctor stared at Keller with incredible shock at his ability to diagnose such a thing. "If we put blood thinners in his system, he'll bleed to death, and he can't survive another surgery right now."

January ran to Mark's side, kneeling by him and stroking his hair back, shushing him as he whimpered and cried. "How much longer?" he glared at Keller.

Cringing, Keller tightened his fists. "We can't give him another weak Infusion. We need at least twenty Shadows, and we'll be able to heal everything. He just has to make it until tonight!"

Shuddering, January found the doctor's gaze. "Can you put him back on the ventilator so he's not having so much trouble breathing?"

"Not after that," the man denied, then snapped at his nurses, "but put him on elevated oxygen." They scrambled to do so.

Mark's eyes fell shut, blood coating his lips, and January had to let go as a mask was placed over Mark's face. It didn't really do much. Mark's chest rose and fell.

His whole body shuddered, but he was breathing, just barely breathing. When he was unconscious, they slowly removed the feeding tube, not causing him to gag or cough, he was too weak to do either.

XXII
WHERE BROKEN GLASS
ULTIMATELY ENDS UP

Even in the shortened daylight of early spring, the day wore on long and painful. January called Marissa to bring June, and to just be there for Mark. They had expended their options. Mark's lungs were losing the power to fight, and he couldn't receive any more treatment. His arm was mangled, and all they could do for it was change the dressing and wait for that one to be saturated as well.

Sil and Ocie stayed open in the Realm, waiting for any hint of the Shadows getting close. "How long is the drive?" Sil asked Ocie softly.

She crossed her arms, leaning in the window shelf with him, just staring at Mark. "Six hours."

"Where are they now?" he added. His range wasn't far enough to even feel out of the state.

Ocie drew in a long sigh through her nose. "Pennsylvania somewhere…"

"How much longer?"

"Two hours, give or take."

Mark's parents sat beside each other at his side. Marissa cradled her little boy, brushing her fingers through his hair to keep him with her and at least slightly conscious. Her free hand was nestled tightly within January's. Sil stared at their loving contact coldly, knowing they were desperate and guessing this trauma was pulling them back together, but he still scowled.

Do you think he's going to tell her? Sil whispered through the Realm to prevent anyone else but Shadows from hearing them.

Keller perked up, overhearing it, but Ocie just let out her breath and shook her head. January was too terrified to tell anyone he was a Shadow. He probably still didn't fully believe it. Ocie wasn't even sure if he could hear in the Realm, much less enter it. Keller had spent the last twenty years believing his friend was dead, and for a moment, Ocie had never seen her father so happy.

Someone left the Realm beside them, and Sil nearly jumped out of his skin when Emilie materialized. "What happened to you?" he yelled, forgetting to keep his voice down.

Emilie flaunted her boots with a pair of very short summer shorts and a skimpy pink camisole, practically nothing to shield her from the cold, and Sil knew she had flown here. "I went a little nuts with the hair dye," she lied, tossing her braid over her shoulder and keeping the left side of her face on her opposite profile, unsubtly avoiding eye contact.

Sil looked her up and down to see her black hair and dyed red ends and scoffed. She looked like she was trying to mimic Mark. "Isn't that a little morbid?" Only then did he realize she was holding the case containing Mark's sword. "Lot of good that's going to do," he blared, leaving it at that. Maybe it was the red ends, but he wasn't sure if he saw the cut across her face.

He grumbled, quietly counting the Shadows in the room. Himself, Keller, Ocie, Emilie… Mark, and maybe January. Just five Shadows to Infuse Mark, and not even that. If January didn't know how to use his Shadow, or couldn't, he didn't count. But the most terrible part was that knowing, with that slight change, January *could* help them.

Sil shivered, getting a bad feeling from all this. Underneath the amnesia, Sil knew January had done this to himself, to hide from the ASH, and these drastic measures were his conscious and informed decision. Sil wanted to bet January had known exactly what would happen and intentionally erased his memories. The scariest thing was the possibility that January was a lot more powerful than they knew. It was something they all didn't have a lot of experience with: refined, adult Shadows.

He only recently discovered Keller was a Shadow, and Keller had effectively blocked himself out of the Realm for twenty years. He knew Kimberly was a Shadow, but she intimidated him, even though, until the Exodus, her powers had been dormant. Shadows weren't normally hereditary, but it became clear that Mark was part of a very powerful line of Shadows and might even have inherited some of his own father's strengths, if January had any.

Mark opened his eyes a little and shifted, seeming a million times more comfortable on his side, and the moment he moved, Marissa lit up. "Hey… hey… look at me, baby. Stay with me. I'm right here." Mark settled tiredly, but he did look very content.

Sil once again scowled. Mark only looked comfortable because he was so drugged up with morphine. That was the only thing keeping his pain manageable.

Marissa pulled the blanket up a little higher over Mark's shoulder to prevent him from catching any sight of the limb. Sil had seen it without bandages. What had been a very small incision had been cut open three times, wider and wider, and now, Mark had long tears all over his left quarter and a train track of stitches.

Infusion wasn't going to be able to save his arm. Sil didn't know very much about Infusions, but he knew it had to be focused on something, like his heart. It would heal the muscles, and the surface level scars, but that severed nerve—there was no way Infusion could completely fix that. He couldn't really know that for sure though.

Ocie pushed off the ledge and slowly walked around the bed toward the chair on the opposite side. Sil expected her to plop down and stare into the light, but instead, she sat down on Mark's bed behind his back and joined Marissa in brushing through his hair. Mark was able to keep his eyes open for longer, and with her touch, she enveloped him in Shadow Hope. In her deepest despair, the weakest moment of the day, she gave him the last of her hope.

She smiled a little as his breaths deepened. "You know, Emilie told me you have a crush on me," she whispered down to him sweetly. "If we don't go out after this, I think she'll drop me off a building. So as soon as you get better, let's go on a date. Sound good?"

He looked up at her with just his eyes, acknowledging her in his own way even though he was exhausted. She smiled, leaning down over him and giving him a kiss on the cheek. She laid down behind him, careful to not jostle his left arm but staying close enough to let him know she was there. He settled to sleep, but Marissa kept whispering things to him to keep his attention and keep him awake.

In all that time waiting, Sil found himself nodding off, lulled by the heavy, hoarse, and unsteady sound of Mark's breathing, shallow though it was. He just had to know it was there. The light started to fade outside, and finally, they had to turn on a few lights. No one had eaten, no one had slept; all they could do was wait.

Hearing a sudden commotion outside the room, Sil perked up. He stared at the door in hope, praying desperately, but when the sound died down, a little flash of green light appeared in their midst, keeping to the dark side of the room. Rita. She raised her eyes slowly, locking on Ocie lying there with Mark, and she cringed, fighting back tears.

"I heard you needed as many Shadows as you could get... so I found their van and brought them all here."

No sooner had she said this when the door was thrown open, led proudly and powerfully by Kip. A flood of young Shadows flooded in, all of room 13-15 where Mark had first been introduced to the Shadows, a particularly annoying Shadow that Mark had met once in the ASH, and of course, Kimberly. "Sorry about the wait," she declared, trying not to bring down the atmosphere. "Traffic was terrible. We weren't going to make it if it wasn't for Rita."

Keller took her hands gently. "We're just thankful you're here."

Sil scurried out into the crowd, counting everyone. There were fifteen from the room, including himself, Rita, Emilie, and Ocie. Kimberly and Keller made seventeen, and that idiot, Cesckim, who was normally accompanied by his prank buddy Mickey, but the kid was nowhere to be seen. That made eighteen. His breath fell short. "Just eighteen..." he paled and met Keller's gaze. "Only eighteen Shadows."

Kimberly threw off her coat and cracked her knuckles. "Really, I count twenty, including Mark," she said, her eyes locking solely on January.

He tensed, jumping up and prying his hand from his wife's grip. "I can't. I wouldn't even know how!"

Marissa looked up, concerned. "Jan... what's going on?"

He pushed away from Mark's bedside and got away quickly. "Eighteen is going to have to be enough. I-I can't help!"

Keller rushed toward him, confident and self-assured. "No-no-no, don't talk like that. You can do this! You just have to remember!"

January batted his hands away. "I *can't* remember!" he yelled. "My Shadow would be dormant just like Mark's was. I can't use it!"

"What?" Marissa shrieked, getting out of her seat and cornering him with Keller. January could see the betrayal in her eyes.

"We can't settle for less," Keller insisted. "That's the amount that puts a class three Infusion at the height of its power. We need you!"

While January protested and pushed them away, Kimberly closed the distance, rushed in between Keller and Marissa, and took his gaze. Mystic and beautiful, Kimberly spread her Shadow over him. "Quiet yourself, and remember." She exhaled, misting him with her dark aura, her gentle Shadow of mind control.

January ran into the window shelf, grasping it for support, but he slipped and stumbled, staring onward, only at his son.

Suddenly a loud and ringing wave swept over him and he gasped. Mark's eyes were locked directly with his, and he felt it. Mark was calling out to him in a silent voice. Mark was awake. "Dad..." he choked out, tears of blood drifting over the bridge of his nose.

January ran to him, tripping all over his legs and grabbing his hand with all his might. "I'm here! I'm here!"

Mark mustered all his strength to grip his father's hand, rolling onto his back into Ocie's arms. He filled his lungs, crackling through the blood. "White..." January tensed. "White flames..." January's eyes went so wide he thought the pain would blind him. Mark inhaled again. "White flames..."

January let go and stood up, hastily backing away from his son. Mark knew. Mark had known for a while now, but he just hadn't had the strength to say anything. Mark choked, trying to bring in more air, but he let out all he had with a third whisper, so faint his lips could only be read, "White flames."

"Wait! Wait!" Ocie grasped Mark's cheek as his head fell. "No, no, Mark! Stay awake! Stay with me!" She patted his face a little, but it did nothing. "Come on, Mark, wake up, just a little longer!" He didn't breathe, giving in to everything and losing consciousness. "No! No! Dad! We have to do it now!" she shrieked at Keller.

January backed right into Sil, clattering over him and falling to the floor under the window. All the Shadows watched him with ethereal eyes, and he finally gave in to Kimberly's touch. His mind fully opened to the voices in the Realm and the enormous new world, and he covered his ears, overwhelmed. His eyes flared as his Shadow came alive in him and his brown eyes sparked, flashing with white and not fading from that pale silvery glow.

He clawed at his hair, crying out as hot white flames raced across his arms, and when the fire reached his hair, rather than burning it, the brown façade melted away, turning his hair completely white. Keller rushed to kneel with him, and with a cautious smile, he took January's hands. "Shadow Ignition, it's good to have you back!"

January looked up, still panicking, no closer to his past, his memories, or the truth, but this was real. Keller pulled him to his feet, and for just a second, January stood shocked, and Shadow Ignition was given new life in his body.

"Do it now!" Ocie screamed. "Mark's not breathing! Please!"

Keller met January's gaze very sternly, and before taking the chance to teach him, he pressed his palm to January's heart and ripped out his newly awakened Shadow as well as his own, and he started the Infusion by combining their two Shadows. The rest of the Shadows did the same, rushing together and pressing them all into one. Finally, amongst them, Kimberly placed her fingernails upon Mark's bandaged breastbone and drew out his Shadows, Fire and Strength, orbiting each other like a binary system, red and gold. With her own, she added this to the fold.

At twenty strong, the light burst, hot and white like a star within the hospital room. Keller guided it with January's hand to lower it into Mark's heart, letting it reach its utter climax and fill the entire room, the entire hospital, entire city, and entire state. The light turned night to day.

As soon as all the Shadows were absorbed into Mark's heart, the light began emanating from his body alone, enveloping the Shadows and blasting over them so intense they had to shield their eyes. Mark was completely lost in the brightness. It intertwined with his broken body and mended all it could, working fast, for he was drifting away.

When the Infusion finally died down, and January was able to unshield his eyes, the eighteen Shadows cleared the bed, giving plenty of space to Mark as he became visible again. Marissa uncovered her face and rose up, staring into the sheets were Mark lay, where Ocie still held him in her arms. A fearsome, deathly silence filled the room, unbroken even by breaths.

Mark laid in the hospital bed, still as stone. His skin was colorless, and his expression was empty, but the blood had vanished. The scar on his brow was the first thing January noticed as he neared. It was completely healed, without the palest pink line beneath the stiches. His chest wound had all but vanished, leaving a faint but noticeable scar.

Ocie peeled off the bandage on his shoulder, which had turned white as if all the blood had been magically cleaned from it. There was no swelling, no redness, no bleeding, and no pain, but there were scars, long ridged tears in the muscle where it had been sewn back together, and the stitches remained. But the wound looked years older now and fully healed. Even the cut on his opposite shoulder was gone.

January took his first step forward, peering down at his son, but he cringed and fell at the bedside in utter pain and sorrow. Mark wasn't breathing at all. There was no life left in his body.

Ocie drew him up into her arms, jostling him gently. "It takes a minute," she assured from her own experience. "It just takes a minute! He'll wake up!" His head fell back in her arms, and a freakish feeling crept into her heart, restraining her breath. "It takes a minute..." she kept repeating.

Kimberly neared the bedside cautiously, before anyone else could dare to, and she brandished something in her hand. The Shadows watched, confused, cautious and still hopeful. With fluid movements, she gently lifted Mark's head and placed a thin gold chain around his neck with a precious pendant lying directly over his heart. "I can't give him much," she said. "You give him love," she turned from Ocie to Sil. "You give him strength, and I can give him hope."

She stepped away ethereally, giving January a chance to see the pendant bore a pair of wings with two gems set on either wing, one as red as Shadow Fire, and the other black as onyx. "He'll need that for when the Novas arrive..." she whispered cryptically, then surrounded herself in magenta flames and burned away, vanishing in some kind of teleportation.

January took another step forward, touching the sheet on Mark's bed and peering closer. He reached out with a limp hand, wavering, hesitating, then he touched his son's arm. He was cold, all warmth had left his body, and in the instant he felt his skin, January could sense the fire within Mark's heart had gone out. Tears swelled up in January's eyes, and he found himself having trouble breathing, hyperventilating, and too terrified to move or let out a cry.

He placed his hand over Mark's heart, hoping to feel Shadow Fire, the crackling flame, fighting to burst, but he couldn't. Mark was cold through his core. Marissa touched his shoulder just as his knees caved and he fell into her arms, sobbing. Together, they sank to Mark's bedside, and Marissa touched his face, crying harder when she laid her ear against his breastbone. January filled with dread. It had to be the most horrifying sound, her head against a human chest, hearing nothing at all.

Holding onto his pale face, Marissa kissed her son's forehead, pulling him into her arms and cradling him. In the jostling movement, a pair of tears fell from his eyes, sliding down his cheeks as two trails of pure blood.

It didn't work.

Marissa held onto him, January hugged his arms and huddled into himself, conscious of everyone else's cries, how they grieved, and as the hours of the night piled on, he barely registered when they eventually had to leave. Begrudged though it was, the Shadows were teleported back to the ASH, leaving the family and Mark's best friends with him. Sil sank down to the floor, holding his head. Ocie sat on the other side of the bed, stroking Mark's left hand as she cried. January didn't know how Sil or Emilie were taking it. They were gone already. June was gone too, probably spirited away by Sil's parents, assuming they had come to get him. January tried not to worry for her absence. There was no point it making the little girl see her brother's lifeless body.

Part of January's heart still had hope. He lost concept of how time passed, but he was almost certain, any minute now, Mark would gasp, fill his lungs, and everything would be okay again. But then, reality pinched him, and January realized it was only his own lungs protesting, and he gasped. He had to stop trying to hold his breath until Mark came back.

January let go of his wife and moved to the chair beside Mark's bed. He was exhausted. His eyes were heavy and lifeless. There was nothing left to do. He was gone. He didn't want to, but he rested his eyes, and after the nightmares took hold, he slipped away, feeling the tears still drying on his eyes. This time, there was nothing else left to try.

XXIII
THE CHERRY INFUSION

March 12, 2031

The light finally dimmed down to a pale white, cool and crisp, leaving Mark with an unforgettable sight. He was no longer in the hospital. The sky was the palest blue he had ever seen, and though white clouds dotted the sky, they were spread thin like a blanket over him. The temperature matched his own body, warm and dry. The air was cool like spring, but it didn't feel like spring, and yet, to him, it smelled like winter.

He lay on the ground in the softest grass, but its color was gray and hardly green. Still, it was like lying atop a fleece blanket. He was on a slight incline, his head higher than his feet, and there was a hard lump under his upper back he assumed was a root. Turning his head, he felt no pain, and suddenly his muscles came alive and he shifted his entire body. His left arm jerked and stretched out, obeying when he raised it above him.

He sat up quickly and realized all he wore was a pair of jeans and his chest was otherwise bare. His left shoulder was covered with netted scars, but nothing hurt. He clenched his fist and loosened his shoulder, but it felt no different from before. This felt like a dream. It was too good to be true.

He looked out across the horizon and was met with an endless field covered in muted gray grass. Something touched his head and he shook it off, catching something small and fragile in his hand. He stared at it, a soft pink circle so pale it was almost white. Another one fell on him and he whirled about, his eyes falling on an old twisted cherry tree in full bloom.

The silence was so tranquil, the endless expanse so freeing, and for a few moments he felt he could sit under this tree and meditate in the Realm until he starved, quite happily in fact. Flower petals snowed down on him, filling him with peace, and finally he tested his voice.

"Is this the starfield?" Everything was muted, even his own voice traveled out dull, like the air was thick. Wherever he was, this wasn't Earth.

"Look up, you're well beneath the starfield." A sweet feminine voice came closer behind him, and he turned hastily to see a young girl sitting under the tree, clothed in a flowing white dress. She was innocent and pristine with curly black hair that rained down around her like a veil, and she had a pure smile.

Mark gazed back up into the heavens at the pale blue sky, and deep within the expanse, made out small glittering lights visible in the endless daylight. He was in the Realm, far deeper than he had ever gone before, and this place was tangible.

"Who are you? A Shadow? Or..."

The girl chuckled playfully and fiddled with her sleeves. "Asha," she introduced herself brightly. "It's so wonderful to finally meet you."

Mark heard something slip from behind the broad trunk of the tree, and he rose up, finding his feet were lighter. He had infinite energy here, and his body felt almost entirely weightless. "Is someone there?"

She looked over her shoulder, easily seeing behind the tree and reaching out at another being. "Come on out. There's no need to be shy." Mark saw a light reflected on her hand, then slowly, a torch of sturdy golden flames was placed into her palm. She stood up and held onto that fire, coaxing it out. It was a hand in hers. The arm attached to it was made entirely of fire, followed by the rest of the body, creeping out around the tree and gazing at Mark unblinking.

He tensed, it was a boy, completely enveloped in fire, a figure of pure magma, alive and hotter than the sun but not burning anything. He appeared wobbly on his feet, unused to movement or exertion and clearly even weaker than Mark. "He's been so lonely here, even with my company," Asha said. "It will be good for him to have a brother."

Mark trembled and gasped. "Is he dead?"

Frowning, Asha nodded. "In a sense... his body is high above us, among the stars, and he is bound here, unable to join it. Your body is even higher, far out of your reach, but you are not without hope. You can continue living, free and unencumbered by the weight of the human world. You can stay here with us."

Shaking his head hastily, Mark stepped back, but he traveled no farther, as if the ground moved under him toward the tree, keeping him trapped where he was. "I can't stay here! I have to wake up!"

Again, the girl frowned. "There is a heavy price..." she whispered, holding gingerly to the boy's flaming hand. "Tell me, what is it you want most, for the Shadows?"

Mark furrowed his brows, confused. What was this? Some kind of wish-granting vision? He shrugged haphazardly. "I don't know... freedom. Unity? Hope or Strength."

The boy tensed but shrank back, his flames dimming as he hid behind the tree again, seeming overwhelmed with sadness. Asha's gaze lowered as well. "I'm sorry, that's the wrong answer..." Slowly, she rose up to her feet and reached into the branches of the old tree. "You can't stay here with us, but you will have to return to become a part of the tree. For now you can go back. Use your time wisely. We'll be waiting for you."

"Wait..." Mark gasped, his voice stopping. "That was a test? I... I didn't know! What did I do wrong?"

Delicately, Asha plucked one of the flowers and brought it toward Mark, slow and ethereal. "Do not trouble yourself with answerless questions." She held out the little cherry blossom, offering it to him. "Rest while you're here. Savor the peace of this place." She tucked it into his fingers, then looked back to the boy hiding behind the tree. "Don't be sad. It's not every day someone reaches into the class four Infusion. You two should get to know each other."

Tensing as the boy slowly came out again, Mark's feet trembled. "Class four? But... they were performing a class three Infusion. What happened?"

Asha sat down in the grass, guiding Mark and the boy to join her. "It was the same Infusion that brought him here." She touched the boy's flaming shoulder. The heat didn't affect her in the slightest, while Mark felt it across the distance. "A tradition carried down by the winter's protégés, a skill that can only be shared by one of the protégés himself. And I believe it was your father's powers linked to the class four Infusion. When he was young, he performed the most powerful healing Infusions with only his one Shadow, and with one more Shadow added, he triggered your class four Infusion."

She looked between the two of them on either side of her. "Indirectly, he's the reason both of you are here."

Mark dug his fingers into the dirt in frustration. January had absolutely no memory of Shadows. He couldn't have known this would happen. Not much of what Asha said made sense, but what did was the fact that January could create full-strength healing Infusions by himself.

The glowing figure of the other boy rose up, pointing to Mark's fist containing the cherry blossom he had already crushed. He didn't seem to want to get closer, as if he was scared of his own power, but for the first time, he summoned his voice. "Don't... forget me," he whispered, desperate and alone. Mark didn't know how long he had been trapped in here, but from the one sound in his voice, Mark knew just how lonely he was.

Mark pressed his lips together and nodded. "I won't," he promised.

Asha took his wrist, gently raising his hand and opening his fingers. "You must take care of this now. It is your life force, and it's not as strong as it looks." With a wave of her fingers, the cherry blossom in his hand burned up into a glowing pink orb, like a Shadow, but bright and lovely. She took this power and held it over his heart, pushing it against his chest.

"You will leave here soon," she whispered, taking both his hands and pulling him to his feet lovingly. The air swirled around them, the wind rose, and the cool air seemed to get hotter, picking up the blossom petals and flying around him in a spiral. In his last seconds, he savored the sight of the gray grass, the pale blue sky, and the cherry tree. Each petal that touched him turned his skin to white blossoms, which were ripped apart in the gentle wind, cascading up into the tree and vanishing into particles of the air.

It was a state of regaining consciousness and finally opening his eyes. Drawing his breath like awakening from sleep, Mark's eyes flickered open to the cold room and the warm, white sunlight. The morning light kindly touched his face, and he could see the tips of tree branches outside caked in snow, but finally budding with the first spring blossoms.

He wasn't aware of any bandages, not even any pain, only aware of the pure white covers pulled up to his chest. He groaned a little as he sat up and looked around the hospital room. His body still felt incredibly light, but his joints were weak. Even so, he warily set his legs over the side of the bed and tensed. His left arm was moving naturally.

Awe filled him as he stared down at his arm and gradually raised it forward, flexing his fingers and bending his elbow. *How?* He'd overheard everything. There was no way to repair nerve damage like that! Keller didn't even think Infusion could heal his arm. This was a miracle. He gulped a little. It was probably the power of class four Infusion.

Geoffrey had been reluctant to warn him about higher class Infusions, and how dangerous they were. All Mark knew was that he had tipped the scale into the higher end.

Setting his feet on the floor, he shakily put a little weight on his legs. He was careful to support himself, but when he used his left arm for support, he winced and simultaneously realized his fatigue was a lot deeper than he anticipated. His legs gave out and he stumbled, sinking back onto the bed without any strength. His left arm couldn't bear any weight, sore and weak, but at least he could move it.

January slept soundly, facing the bed, and Mark smiled a little when he laid eyes on him. His father's hair had turned pure white, and it was more disheveled than ever, frilled around his ears and mostly in his face, long and lanky.

Doing his best to hold onto the bed railing, Mark tried to stand up again, slowly, taking his time and reaching out with his left hand to nudge his father's arm. "Dad... wake up." Reaching so far sent a bolt of pain through his shoulder, and he recoiled the moment January jumped a little, partially alert.

He opened his tear-stained eyes, rubbing his face tiredly until he looked up and his irises shone clear and bright, a pure white color untainted by brown or even blue. He had white eyes.

The moment Mark saw it, his father's eyes filled with tears and he stood up abruptly. "Mark!" he gasped, barely a breath in his voice as he started crying in terrible distress. He reached out. His hand shook, but he touched Mark's left arm, first confirming the warmth in his skin and shuddering. "H-how?" he rasped just before throwing his arms around his son, fully enveloping him tightly. "You were dead! You weren't breathing all night! How? How is this possible?"

Mark fell into his father's arms for support, completely overjoyed as his eyes regained their full, bright crimson. "It's okay..." he whispered. "I'm okay." He finally pulled away, grasping the bed rail and gasping. He laughed nervously as he watched his dad cry. "You're a Shadow?" It finally sank in. "You're actually a Shadow!"

January wiped his face, disheartened, but nodded weakly. "I don't know how you knew."

"Knew?" Mark blared, his full voice returning, his breaths easy and incredible. "I was suspicious from the moment I found out *I* was a Shadow. But it was when I saw you in the Realm. Around normal humans you just look like one of them, but around Shadows! That gave you away!"

January cringed, still very distraught. "You think I was hiding it?"

Mark nodded easily. "Definitely, but from yourself too. I don't know how, but you must have cooked up something crazy to hide your Shadow that well *and* erase your memory."

"I still don't remember anything." He winced a little. "This is new to me. Just like it was for you..." He stared down at his hands, remembering the flickering white flames, and he despaired, completely terrified. He gulped hard past his fears and finally looked up. "Will you help me?"

Lighting up, Mark nodded eagerly. "Of course! And you've got all the Shadows now! We'll help you get your memories back. And now we know it was definitely caused by Shadows, which means there has to be a way to reverse it."

January smiled, leaning back at Mark's enthusiasm in amazement. "You haven't changed, right back to your same old self..." he whispered, slightly bemused.

Mark stumbled a bit but held on tight to the rail. "I want to see your Shadow!" he begged, only then realizing how much he sounded like Kip.

Hesitating, January looked at his hand again. Mark could see the struggle in his eyes, he knew exactly what it felt like from his own experience. With no focus or clue on where to concentrate, January's hand was coated in a soft white combustion that was just slightly warm and very calming to look at. "I can feel the Realm now," he whispered. "I felt the Infusion... I had... full control over it. And even though I thought it didn't work, you were still completely healed."

"I know," Mark beamed. "I could feel it too. You were that Infusion. You were the power behind it." He thought about it for a moment, but he didn't dare mention the fact that it had been a class four. He didn't even know what that meant himself. Wobbly on his feet, Mark plopped down into the chair next to January's and leant back comfortably. There was absolutely no pain. It was incredible.

Remembering the cherry blossom, he touched his heart and tensed a little when his fingers graced the scar and something cold. Looking down, he caught sight of the pendent placed over his neck and he stared in surprise. "Where did that come from?"

"Kimberly gave that to you," January took a seat beside him. "She said you'd need it for when the Novas came."

"What does that mean?" Mark puzzled.

January drew his brows together. "I don't know, I assumed it was some Shadow thing and Keller would be able to tell me, but after you didn't wake up, everyone left, and I didn't think there was any point in asking."

"I'll find out then," Mark nodded to himself. "So where is everybody?"

Inhaling deeply through his nose, January sank back into shock, letting reality wash over him. "Grieving... they all still think you're dead. The Shadows went back to the ASH, Sil and Emilie went home, I don't know where your mother got off to with June, but I think Ocie and Keller are still around."

Mark mimicked his father, taking in an effortless deep breath. He felt good, utterly glad the simple task of breathing was no longer so painful. Frankly, the only discomfort he felt at all was that he was ravenously hungry. He wanted to get out of the chair and run for it with all his might. He wanted to go find out all of Strength's secrets and get it to its full potential, but for some reason, he also really wanted to burn something and watch it decompose in the fire before his eyes.

He massaged his shoulder, the dull ache was barely noticeable, but the muscles were still tattered within his skin. The scars were long, and there was definitely still some healing to be done. But he could be patient. He needed to build up his strength after lying limp for so long, but his legs refused to let him exert himself.

He pushed himself forward, supporting his weight on the armrest and staggering to his feet to walk on his own.

"Where are you going?" January burst, jumping up to help him.

Mark threw him off, smiling brightly as his eyes glowed crimson cherry. "First things first, I want out of here!" He was unstable on his feet but ever so happy as he raced to the door. January tried to run after him, to make sure he didn't hurt himself, but Mark wanted no help.

As soon as he threw the heavy door open, he was blasted with the sterile light of the hallway and on the threshold outside his room into the corridor. He saw a black and white analog clock. He chuckled at the irony, reading it aloud, "Six-fifty-five."

XXIV
THE CHOICE

Mark ran down the halls happily, trying to go faster and faster to get away from January and be free of any helping hands. He refused to succumb to weakness, too happy to let it hinder him. He was shivering, the halls were utterly freezing, and after a few minutes, it occurred to him he wasn't wearing a shirt.

He continued glancing behind him until he finally lost January and slowed to a more comfortable pace. His legs were getting stronger already, that or it was just Shadow Strength in him, driving him forward. On the first floor of the hospital after navigating an elevator in this state—he still hated elevators—he spotted Emilie in a waiting room right near the door. She wasn't alone either, keeping guard over Marissa and June as they slept across the uncomfortable chairs, and Ocie as she sobbed with dark eyes.

Mark went into the Realm, sneaking up on them, but Emilie sensed him in the door frame, reacting first by clobbering him. Knocking him to the hard floor and right out of the Realm. He laughed hysterically when she pinned his right arm behind his back.

"Oh, my goodness!" Marissa woke with a start at Emilie's sudden attack, but only then did she realize who was under her boot.

"Don't you know better than to sneak up on me!" Emilie growled down over him.

Mark just laughed harder, effectively pinned to the floor. "You do realize, only six hours ago, this would have killed me!"

Like a blast of energy, he felt fear and a screaming echo out in the Realm from Ocie. Disbelief in what she was actually seeing, her words rang out at all the Shadows in her range.

He's Alive!

"Mark!" the three other girls screamed in unison, and together Ocie and Marissa fought to pry Emilie off of him.

"Wait, don't!" Mark yelled, a big, dumb smile still across his cheeks, and Marissa's gaze met with January as he finally caught up with Mark. "I want to get her off myself!" he requested, fully latching onto Strength and letting it fuel him.

Emilie cackled. "Good frickin' luck with that!" she sneered, pressing down harder on his back. "I can manipulate gravity!"

Not answering, Mark tested her, making tiny movements to find all her pressure points, searching for any weak spots. With only one quick movement, Mark sprung up and linked his leg around Emilie's, taking advantage of her weightlessness to fling her off him, pinning her to the floor evenly, all while babying his left arm. Emilie let off her fight in shock. Mark had actually done it. In a physically weakened state, he had beaten her.

Just as quickly, Emilie threw him off her and sat on the floor indignantly. "Twice, I gave you my Shadow, and I'll do it a thousand times more, but don't take advantage of me like that, you hothead!" She smiled slightly, finally wrapping her arms around him in relief.

January stepped into the waiting room with a weak grin, pausing at the sight before taking off his coat and dropping it over Mark's shoulders. "Let's go find you some clothes," he suggested and helped Mark to stand.

Finally, he met eyes with his mother and Ocie, and he watched her excitement overflow as she rushed and threw her arms around him. Within the embrace, she playfully gave him a little kiss on the nose. "How are you feeling?"

"Hungry!" Mark laughed. Marissa and June got their chance, and June nearly clobbered him again, not even slightly traumatized by how she had hurt him last time. He lost his balance when they let him go, falling into his father's arms and laughing heartily at his clumsiness.

"Jan..." Marissa addressed warily. "Are *you* okay?" she asked, stepping toward her husband and trying to make some small physical contact with him.

January frowned a little, but nodded. "I guess Mark was right... I'm a Shadow. I guess I have been the whole time we've been married."

"But you still don't remember?" she whispered, on the edge of tears.

Pressing his lips together, January shook his head.

"Oh, come on, don't make me go back to that room," Mark complained as Ocie guided him a few steps back toward the elevator.

She held his left arm and rubbed his back to stabilize him. "You need a little more rest before you'll be back to normal." She reverted to taking his hand, acknowledging how much stronger he was, and her fingers slipped in naturally between his own.

"Oh, that reminds me," Mark sang as Ocie made him take it slow down the corridors. "You promised me a date!"

Her cheeks lit up pink. "You remember that?"

He nodded with a beaming smile. "But seriously though, there are some things I want to talk to you and your dad about, plus I'm starving, so lunch?"

Ocie let out a pure laugh and hugged his arm lightly. "Fine…" she hummed happily, "lunch it is!"

Mark winced a little at the pull on his arm, but the discomfort was absolutely nothing compared to what he had endured, so he was able to ignore it. The lights were still off in the hospital room when they arrived, and Ocie hit a few of them before forcing Mark to sit. Not a fiber in his being wanted to lay back down, but she convinced him by taking a seat herself. He laughed playfully, feeling perfectly ridiculous with his dad's coat around his shoulders and no shirt on underneath.

Ocie giggled in response. "You're so pale!" she made fun of him.

Awkwardly, he glanced down and back at her, then gave a lopsided grin. "So what? I just spent the better part of a week bleeding out. I just need to get out of here!"

"Show some *patience!*" Ocie slapped his knee as he crossed his legs, sitting up fully in the bed.

The best part of being alone with her, though the *alone* part was certainly delightful, was having that broken by a nurse on her rounds, who hadn't quite gotten the news. She gasped at the sight of him sitting upright, perfectly healthy and joking around with that snarky grin. The poor woman didn't know what to do with herself.

Keller arrived to satiate her, ushering her out and finally placing his hands on his hips to shake his head. "I have never seen an Infusion take that long to solidify, and I can't believe… your dad… with no memory of Shadows, guided that Infusion to heal you."

Mark perked up and set his feet over the side of the bed. "So, you felt it too!" He beamed. "Was my dad really good with Infusions when you knew him?"

Raising an eyebrow at Mark's enthusiasm, Keller took a seat in one of the many chairs surrounding his bed. "He had a knack for them, yes. But I'd really prefer not to reminisce on our old life before the ASH without him here. He deserves to know too, understand?"

"Okay," Mark accepted quickly, uncharacteristically quickly, which startled Keller. "I've got another question for you. What do you know about class four Infusions?"

Keller tensed and paled. "There's only three classes."

Mark denied hastily. "No, I'm sure of it. The Infusion used to heal me was a class four!" he insisted, but then saw it in Keller's eyes. He had lied.

"Dad?" Ocie muttered worriedly.

Keller's face clouded over. "The Forbidden Infusion," he gave in. "You saw it, didn't you?" His back straightening starkly, Mark nodded. Keller cringed and hung his head. "I've only read about it in the oldest of records. The last person to ever survive a class four Infusion called it the Field."

Mark nodded eagerly. "Everything was muted and soft, like colors were off, and there was a girl there! She seemed like... I don't know, in charge."

Covering his mouth, Keller nodded. "Asha?"

"Yeah!" Mark gasped. "Who is she?"

"I have no idea." Keller groaned. "But the records just said she was there."

"Did they say anything about a test or cherry blossoms? What about the fiery figure?" Mark's questions continued whirling about in his mind, unable to form together into words fast enough.

"Mark, I don't know!" Keller insisted. "The records just say to never attempt a class four Infusion and the process is a closely guarded secret."

Mark crossed his arms over his chest. "So closely guarded you'd give it to an amnesiac to forget?" he deadpanned. "Dad's the one who performed it. Maybe he'll know more when he gets back his memories." He stopped himself, seeing the surprise in Keller's face.

"I can only tell him what I know, not the secrets he kept."

Mark fell silent. January *was* hiding something— something he had wiped his own mind to forget.

Reaching out, Keller grasped the bed sheet to gather Mark's attention. "Jan had many secrets. He only told us his name, his country, and the Shadow settlement where he was from. The same one Rita is from. He was only fourteen when he came to us, and, like you, he was so much more powerful than he allowed people to see."

Mark fidgeted with the bed sheet restlessly, but Keller stood up and patted his shoulder. "Give your dad some time. If I know him at all, he'll warm up to his new situation."

Mark frowned a bit but nodded.

"If I know you." Keller nudged him in the shoulder. "You certainly warmed up to it." He laughed, but Mark winced, jerking up to protect his shoulder and laughing when the slight pain wore off in seconds. "Sorry!" Keller apologized hastily. He just needed to not strain it for now. He was lucky his arm wasn't still paralyzed. However, as he laughed, he spied a slight flash of green beyond Keller, and for part of a second, he thought he saw Rita's darkened expression before she teleported away again.

January charged in, blowing past the residual mist and dispersing it without even noticing. "I brought you some clothes," he declared, passing a little stack of fabric into Mark's lap, but he didn't meet his father's gaze, instead waiting to see if Rita would reappear. "Is everything okay?" January puzzled, gathering his attention.

"Yeah..." he forced quietly. "I just thought I saw Rita."

January pressed his lips together, sensing Mark's worry, but he sighed and made it more obvious he was hiding something behind his back. "I think this might cheer you up a bit." Playfully, he revealed a big bag of fast food to spread around.

Mark tied back his hair into a ponytail as he stepped out of that dreadful building for the first time in almost a week. His left arm strained to reach so high, but he was still just thankful to be able to move it at all. The air was crisp but much warmer than it had been last week, and he was comfortable enough to not wear a coat as he followed his father out to the car.

His legs were tired from just the walk through the parking lot, but he refused help, confident he'd get his strength back soon. Even so, he leant on the rental car, waiting for January to unlock it, which seemed to take forever. He looked back when January didn't immediately get into the car and noticed his father opening the hatchback and loading in a long black case.

"Is that—"

"—Lævatein?" January confirmed, shutting the trunk briskly. He didn't say any more about it, not how he knew its name nor how it had come from Geoffrey's house to here. He unlocked the doors finally. Mark slouched in, physically drained, but he didn't know why. Maybe it was being in bed for so long, maybe it was the heavy meal, but he almost dozed off as they finally left the hospital.

"So…" January broke the silence, "why were you wondering?"

Mark rubbed his eyes but forced a chuckle. "I guess I forgot it was mine." He hugged his shoulder uneasily. He was permanently scarred by Strength, and he couldn't help but think maybe Geoffrey had endured the exact same betrayal from someone who had trained him. Maybe it *was* his father. Maybe that man had been a lie Geoffrey had concocted. Mark couldn't know for sure. All he knew was that the moment Geoffrey had done what he set out to do, his confidence was shattered. He had immediately regretted doing this to Mark.

So he couldn't hate him. Geoffrey was another Shadow Strength, just like him. They shared the same Shadow, and it was possible there could be four wielders of Strength at a time. Now, Mark just had to find the other two swords.

He laughed a little. "Geoffrey tried to train me, but he did it so it would be more fun for him when we fought, a little challenge for him." He didn't know why it was so easy for him to find humor in that. "That fight was so unfair, and he knew it."

January focused on the road, a little disturbed, but trying to laugh it off. "Well, you were really hanging on there," he mused, nudging Mark's shoulder with his fist.

Mark reeled away, protective of his arm. January stopped smiling and gaped, now mortified after his careless gesture. The utter silence ate at January's psyche, and he panicked for a second, waiting to see if he had actually hurt him. Mark couldn't hold his breath any longer and finally cackled. "I'm not that fragile!"

"Then why'd you flinch?" January jabbed harmlessly.

Loosening his shoulder, Mark tested his limits. There were still some restrictions, but it felt so much better. When they finally got home, Mark let out a sigh of contentment. It felt like it had been ages since he was happy to be home, and he took Lævatein out of the back himself to carry it inside.

He almost anticipated opening it, to see the red sword again. It felt strange to actually want that, but he didn't get a chance to look on Lævatein like he had Morglay, and he saw how Geoffrey treasured it. Marissa came running when they entered, smothering him tightly and showering him with kisses, but she prevented June from doing the same.

When he was finally released, he hurried back to his room, bearing the case low as he closed himself off. Half-consciously, he flicked his light switch to illuminate his dim room. It startled him, realizing that while he had been in the hospital, someone had finally changed the lightbulb. He was tired, he still didn't have all his energy back, but a little rest would do him good. The door latched as he leant into it and sank to the floor. Lævatein came with him, and he found peace in the solid *thud* as it hit the floor.

Cradling his left arm, he opened the latches with his right, and gradually lifted the lid, peering inside. The luster of the gold had not diminished, it seemed to almost have a glow from Strength Infused into the weapon, and the tinted red blade did not bear a single blemish. Mark sighed again, perfectly content. This was *his* sword. Gold and rubies, valuable enough to trade for a fancy car, and it was his. He wouldn't trade it for the world, especially with the price he had paid for it.

He and the sword were connected now, and he smiled; somehow, it was worth it. He was following a long tradition, and now that Strength was fully intertwined with his element, he was excited to see what he was capable of.

For now, he was tired. He slipped into the Realm, spiraling into the darkness and peace and leaving his home behind. He slumped against the door, passing out on the carpet in minutes. Real sleep welcomed him, not struggling to breathe, or lying in that death-like state. He was so tired that the floor felt like a mountain of feathers and he forgot his body.

The light waned and the first warmth of spring faded, and after dark, January knocked on Mark's door. The silence made him worry. He tried to hold off for as long as he could, but he couldn't fight the urge to stand outside Mark's room, making sure he was really in there. A quiet fear inside him told him that Mark had snuck out through the window again, that he had run back into danger, that maybe he wasn't even breathing in there. He knocked again, softly, hoping for some tiny confirmation, so that he could leave him alone.

"Mark?"

He placed his ear against the door, listening for the faintest sound of wargames or music in Mark's headphones, but when he got no response, he tried to go in. His heart leapt into his throat at the memory of it being locked. He wanted to ban Mark from ever locking his room again. The doorknob turned, but something was blocking it when he pushed it open. He couldn't cool his nerves or stop himself from panicking. He pushed harder and peeked inside. Mark sat there, slumped against the door panel, and January lost his mind with worry.

Squeezing in, he knelt to his son, about to lay his hands on him, but he stopped, noticing Mark's deep and content breaths. Mark's right hand had wrapped around the hilt of Lævatein, and his left was curled to his chest tightly. His face was so relaxed, so serene, January couldn't make himself disturb him.

With a little effort, he pried Mark's hand away from the sword and very carefully raised his teenage son off the floor to carry him to bed. January wasn't a very strong person in general. He took it slowly, managing his own klutziness to lay Mark soundly in his bed and pull the warm, heavy covers over him.

Mark didn't stir in the slightest, his mind so deeply dug into the Realm that he no longer felt anything physical.

The door hung ajar behind him, and when he turned slowly to leave, Marissa was in the doorway, hugging her sides. January tried to ignore her knowing gaze and bent down to tuck Lævatein into its case and close it up. Marissa wouldn't have it. "It's been a full day now…" she whispered, following him with her gaze as he set the case at the foot of Mark's bed. "Have you even had a chance to look at yourself?"

January paused in the center of his son's room. He didn't want to do this here, not where Mark could wake up and see them. But if he stayed here, maybe the fight wouldn't happen. Marissa huffed and turned away, giving

January a brief moment to look over at the mirror. He looked leaner, taller, and much more confident. His white hair was still shaggy, as he hadn't gotten the chance to brush it back yet, and his white eyes pierced the dim light in Mark's room.

January couldn't shake it, but the most startling change was the diminished wrinkles in the corners of his eyes, and the lack of age to his posture. Easily, he looked two or three years younger. Finally, he shuffled out, leaving the door open to keep an ear out for any movement.

Marissa had already resigned herself to the kitchen, starting some coffee to help herself stay up all night as well. "I first noticed it this morning. You already look younger than me."

He followed her in slowly, taking a seat at the kitchen table as she frantically measured the coffee grinds. He waited as she hastily shoved the coffee machine in the corner, violently switching it on. She gripped the countertop, holding back tears. "Marissa..." he whispered, "we need to talk. We haven't really talked since October."

Turning slowly, she cringed but nodded and took a seat across from him. Black, bitter water dribbled down into the coffeepot, and the sound was the only tangible thing that kept her from crying. He reached across the table, lovingly pleading for her hand, and with some reluctance, she gave it. "How are you taking this?" he asked softly.

The tears slipped away, and she clenched his fingers. "I had to keep it together for Mark, but he nearly died, and you were the one who was there for him. I couldn't do anything. And now... you're a Shadow... there's a lot of things I'm still trying to accept."

"But will you accept me?" January lowered his gaze. "Amnesia and all?" He conjured a little smile to assure her he hadn't really changed. "I don't understand what's happening to me, and our family is changing, so can we work together to accept the things to come?"

Marissa leant back in her chair and let go of his fingers, jaded and worried. "You're getting younger," she glowered. "Mark hasn't noticed yet. I don't think anyone else has, but when you got your Shadow back, you started aging backwards." She clenched her fists. "You're going to find out what happened, how you lost your memories, and by the time you do, you'll be the same age as when you lost them. And I'll be left behind."

Gasping, January rushed around the table. "No!" he took her arms because she wouldn't give him her hands. "I love you, I will always love you, and whether I get my memories back or not, I'm—"

"Don't lie to me!" she cried out.

January flinched but pressed himself to continue. "I don't know anything about Shadows. I'm so confused, and I have to have my questions answered. Keller can fill in some of the blank places."

Marissa scowled. "You still don't realize there are *blank places* in your memory from since I've known you? You've forgotten people you've met, places we've been! Moments in our life we're never going to be able to get back! Jan... I'm happy you have this one answer, but I don't want your priorities to be just with Shadows. I need you here, present, in this family! You can't completely change!" She sobbed loudly.

It was too late. January already knew that. The change had started, and he needed to go after the truth. Grimacing, January sat back down, his eyes drifting off to his jars of tea and all his regret. He sighed and gulped down his insecurities. "I'm leaving..." he breathed softly, causing Marissa's eyes to widen in terror. "I'm going to go stay in the ASH for a while, and I think Mark should come with me. We both need to be with the Shadows."

"Jan..." Marissa choked up. "I—I didn't mean it, please! Don't go."

He frowned, shrinking into himself and refusing to look into her heartbroken eyes. "It won't be forever. I just need some time." Gradually, he stood and returned to her. "I will come back," he promised and kissed her head.

XXV
BLOWING CHERRIES

March 13, 2031

Morning came slowly, and as the first light touched the window blinds, January rose early to start packing. Sleeping on the couch wasn't as painful with the promise of leaving today. As quietly as he could, he slipped into his bedroom to start gathering some clothes together, but navigating the dark room proved difficult. Marissa didn't stir, but January still didn't want to take that risk.

He heaved the pile of clothes out to the living room, only then noticing the empty plate on the table with remnants of egg left out beside an accompanying fork. Beyond that, January spotted the porchlight on, and the back door open a crack. Throwing down his stack, January stomped over. "He'd better be close!" he swore under his breath, praying Mark hadn't run off to Sil's or something at this hour. Or worse, that he might have gone off with Rita.

The misty morning light muted the concrete, and the golden gleam of the porchlight worsened the obscuring fog, which January realized smelled of smoke. He saw a tempered crimson flame and Mark's left arm coming out of the cloud, and he seemed completely focused and unaware of January's presence. In his right hand, Mark brandished his sword trailing the fire along its red blade.

Mark's eyes were bright and full of fire, showing vividly through the smoke. He wasn't wearing a coat, and he barely wore a shirt, resorting to a very thin, red, compression tank top. January frowned a bit, able to see the netted scars along Mark's left shoulder.

He practiced against an invisible opponent, remembering all of Geoffrey's training, everything the man had been able to teach him. Mark was immersed in this world now, content, having found his truest passion.

January stepped out behind him, still feeding his arm through the sleeve of his coat. "What are you doing up so early?"

Mark jumped, scampering off the edge of the concrete into the grass and lowering Lævatein. He grasped his heart with his still flaming hand. "You scared me!"

Smiling a little, January drew his collar and shivered in the cold. "Funny, I'd think you'd never want to use that sword again." He plopped down into the metal deck furniture, which was completely frigid.

Mark seemed absolutely unaffected by the cold, contently swiping up a black sheath from the ground and returning Lævatein to it. "Yeah, have it and not use it," he chuckled, hesitating with his hand still around the hilt. It seemed more natural to him with every second he held it. "I think it'll come in handy."

January shivered despondently, not looking forward to the day to come. "Oh, yes, because sword fighting is so handy."

Giving a smirk, Mark placed his hand on his hip. "You know, you can use Ignition to make yourself warmer," he mused, revealing from his bright cherry eyes that he was using Shadow Fire, even though it didn't manifest as flames.

"And did you figure out how to do that on your first day?" January deadpanned, but with a smile, Mark nodded optimistically. January just sank back and grumbled. The worst part of this was a quiet nagging feeling that he was relearning how to walk. This wasn't his first time honing Shadow Ignition. Either he was going to be frustrated, or he would get it fast.

For now, he hugged his coat and sighed. The faint light was beautiful, the smoke starting to clear, and Mark was just about to draw Lævatein again. January inhaled through his nose, catching the scent of smoke, but it didn't bother his lungs. "I'm reverse aging," he revealed softly.

Mark turned quickly, lowering his sword again. "What?"

January's eyes flared. "I don't know how, but I'm reverting back to the state I was before my Shadow went dormant." He gazed out past Mark into the tree line behind their house. "I don't know how fast it'll happen. I'm just pretty sure it's going to get a little awkward when I start looking like a teenager again."

With a twisted grin, Mark neared calmly, leaning his sword against the table so that one of the cross bars linked into the metal mesh. "Don't worry," he assured, resolute and honest. "No matter what happens, no matter how you change, I'll always respect you."

A little relieved, January stared at the gold hilt of Lævatein, wary of it. "Let's get inside. We've got a little packing to do."

"Packing?" Mark shrieked excitedly.

January glanced over his shoulder, and with a tone in the Realm, he affirmed where they were going. *To the ASH.*

Mark's eyes widened fully to hear his father's voice in the Realm. Already, after a day of knowing he was a Shadow, January was able to use the Realm without entering it. Mark's heart raced in pure exhilaration. Geoffrey was right. He said that Understandings were the one hereditary thing in the Shadows, that family members tended to have the same Understandings. Mark knew it was too early to confirm, but January had to have the Understanding of the Realm, just like him.

Charging back into his room, he ran headfirst into someone coming out of the guest room. "What the—"

"Where are you charging off to?" Emilie blared over him as he hit the floor.

Mark blinked a few times, startled to see her. "What are you doing here?" he asked, rubbing his forehead.

Emilie smiled wryly and floated up, her dark hair braided loosely, letting her bangs fly free without gravity. "I live here now. You offered me the guest room, remember?"

Staring dumbstruck, Mark got to his feet warily. "Since when?" he yelled. He could barely get his reaction off the tip of his tongue. What about her mother? What about moving to a new house? What happened?

Emilie flew down to him, that cruel smile still on her lips, and he made out the cut down her cheek. "Better get used to it. I'm gonna be hanging around you for a long time."

Thoroughly intimidated, Mark inched his way around her back to his room, closing it off to keep Emilie out. Finding a backpack he had to dump burned computer parts out of, he stuffed most of his clothes into a bag. He strapped Lævatein into its case, selected the *very* few random things other than clothes he wanted, and for a moment, he stared at his TV and game console.

He shuddered, very hesitant to come to a decision. He couldn't take it with him, but more so, he couldn't ever continue his addiction. All that mattered to him were Shadows now. He had to leave gaming behind. He had to finish learning how to sword fight. He had to leave his old life behind too. This would bring him peace.

He ripped the zipper, forgetting his own strength as he tried to close the backpack, then he slung it up onto his back, hitting himself squarely in the left shoulder. He knocked the wind out of himself, stumbling and stifling a curse, but his yelp was enough to draw in his father.

"Are you o—"

"I'm fine!" Mark yelled, not quite angry, just shocked from the pain. "I got this. I don't need any help!" But it wasn't his father.

Sil stood there, staring onward, utterly shocked, and in silence. His eyes dashed about Mark, clearly searching for the bandages, the blood, and the deathly paleness in his complexion. Sil backed away slowly.

The backpack slipped out of Mark's hand and he sank, his shoulders falling. "Sorry... I'm just a little—" Abruptly, Sil rushed in and thrust his arms around him, embracing him tightly. In that moment, Mark felt Sil shaking. "Hey..." Mark choked out softly. "I'm okay, it's okay!"

Sil released him, his eyes dark, and he tried to mask tears. "I know... I just couldn't fully believe it until I saw you." He looked terrible. Mark knew how cold it was, and Sil had evidently run over here without grabbing a coat, not that the cold bothered him at all. Even so, his face was a little more frostbitten than normal, and as always, his hands were like ice. It took a moment for Mark to realize, for a fact, Sil had been crying.

The icy bully, who had tormented him on his first day in the ASH, had been grieving. Sil stealthily rubbed his face, emotionally exhausted. "I guess you're probably sick of getting asked, 'How are you feeling?'"

Mark chuckled lightly and plopped back on his bed. "Yeah a bit." He smiled and offered for Sil to join him.

Managing a grin, Sil leant into the bedpost, "Is it too far to say, 'I told you so?'"

At this, Mark let out a real laugh. "Well, you know me! I gotta go all the way before I figure out this is a huge mistake."

Sil folded his hands together awkwardly, and for the first time, Mark thought he really saw Sil as younger than him, even if it was a few months. Sil was very sheltered from the real world. He was prudent, if a bit anti-social, but terrified. If this was the real world, and danger like this could catch them at any moment, Mark figured Sil wanted nothing more than to hide at home.

Sil raised his eyes to the light fixture. "Honestly, I kinda panicked when I heard Ocie in the Realm."

"Really?" He probably shouldn't have interrupted, but Sil nodded absently.

"I wanted to go back to the hospital, but it was still really early. I don't know why, but I couldn't make myself get up and go wake my dad. By the time he realized what was going on, I was a wreck. I didn't want to believe my own senses, and I couldn't let him convince me to go see for myself. He told me I should just wait until I calmed down and that ended up being a whole day." He seemed to have a touch of guilt in his voice, lowering his eyes and scratching at his palms. "I... think I had a panic attack."

Mark perked up a bit, concerned. He didn't know what to say. Sil was... strong. He was... untouchable. He couldn't visualize his friend afraid. Geoffrey's words were stuck in his head, belittling Sil. Because he thought they were all just jabs to get him fired up, but now he knew for certain that Geoffrey had been manipulative, gaslighting to try to drive a wedge between him and his family, and his friends.

Finally, Mark found the words, they made sense after all the times he had heard it. "Are you okay?"

It was what Sil needed to hear, he could tell. Just enough validity to make him feel safe. "No," he mouthed reluctantly, and his breath fell, shuddering. "But... I think I want to make myself stronger, like you. So, I don't have to worry about people like Geoffrey."

Mark offered a reassuring smile for him and leant closer. "Well, I've picked up some tricks. I'd be happy to teach them to you!"

Sil chuckled. A smile looked good on him, and he nodded to accept, but he pushed Mark away. "Yesterday you were too weak to stand!"

At this, Mark punched him in the arm rather harshly and Sil shirked back in surprise, "I could beat you easily now! Don't test me!"

Rubbing his arm, Sil paused, slightly disturbed by the power in Mark's fist and his utter obliviousness to how he'd actually hurt him. "Dude, you need to chill."

Mark got up again and went for his backpack, attempting to continue packing. "Sounds like my dad and I are going to the ASH for a while. You could come too."

Sil's gaze followed the floor to the black case containing Lævatein. As wary as he was of Mark's vigor, he was more afraid of the prospect of other, more fantastical, adult Shadows who would soon come into their lives. Keller had given them something good, a safe home to learn their powers, protected from people who would use them or discriminate against them, and from the fighting that had occurred early in the generation. If anything made Sil feel safe, it was going home.

"I'll talk to my dad, but... I think that would be good."

March 15, 2031
Mark caught sight of her right on the edge of the balcony, staring out over the warm, sunny grass. "Rita!" Mark charged up after her. "Stop avoiding me!" The Scottish red-head started, catching his eye then jumping from the marble balcony and teleporting away. "Rita!" Mark yelled again, but she was already long gone.

The ASH was bustling with Shadows, some who had grown up there, and some who had come out of hiding to help rebuild the settlement. Rita was without a home again, but for the second that he had seen her, she seemed content.

Mark let out a curse and angrily tied back his hair into a ponytail.

"She's still not talking to you?" Sil puzzled, following him up the stairs.

"I'll try again later," he grumbled, stretching his shoulder and cracking his knuckles. "In the meantime…" He smirked, implacable, insane and itching for a fight.

Sil's shoulders fell in dismay. "Oh lord, here we go again…" he groaned, hastily dodging as Mark threw a fist at him. "Why do you keep doing this?"

Mark lit his hands on fire and drove him back. "Come on! This would be much more fun with wooden swords! You've got to try it!" Sil managed to block his fist, reluctant to touch the fire, but in spite of how scary it was, Mark's flames had no intent to burn, and Sil knew that. "Besides, you were the one who was so quick to fight me when we first met."

Sil scurried for the stairs. "That was before you got Shadow Strength and became an insane edge-lord and adrenaline junky! I didn't realize you'd get this into it." Mark cackled, absolutely overjoyed when Sil fought back, carefully grabbing his right wrist and sending Mark tumbling down the stairs. Very light on his feet, Mark saved his fall, kicked off the stairs, and jumped the remaining steps to the sidewalk below. Sil had been careful not to yank on Mark's left arm, but he was still utterly amazed by the quick save. *Amazed*, but he was only sure he wouldn't hurt Mark because he'd already done it four times.

"I don't get it." Sil shook his head slowly, as Mark prepared to dash back up the stairs. With a wave of his hand, he coated the marble in ice, stopping Mark just before he jumped. "How are you so good at this? Just a few days ago you were too weak to move."

Mark tensed, Sil saw the foolhardiness rising in him. He thought he could climb the slick stairs, and he was going to try. "I'm not weak!"

Brashly, Sil created bars around the stairs, blocking the insane fireball from even attempting it. "I forgot." He grimaced. "You can't stand it when anyone even implies you're weak now."

Mark redirected, overconfidently immersing himself in the power of Shadow Strength. It didn't make him physically stronger, or even mentally stronger, it made him crazy! When he used Strength, he had the impulse control of a ten-year-old, and more often than not, Strength gave him the edge to actually not get hurt when he tried stupid things.

With all his might, Mark jumped and grabbed the slanted, smooth stone handrailing, and somehow, he had the grip strength to not slide off as he hung off the edge of the balcony. Of course, he supported most of his weight with his right arm. Sil gaped at the sight as Mark climbed up onto the balcony, a good fifteen feet off the ground.

"You're nuts," Sil stammered.

"Now give me a real fight!" Mark shouted with a big, beaming smile and sprang off the railing.

"Would you two please stop trying to kill each other!" Keller wandered out, exasperated by all the screaming. "At this rate, you're going to get hurt, or worse, damage my building!"

Mark stood fully and leant against the stone wall of the ASH behind him. "We're not fighting. It's sparring."

Keller crossed his arms. "Well, it looks like you're maniacally bullying Sil, which now that I say it out loud, sounds really weird. Sil, since when are you not the one antagonizing people?"

Giving a snarky grin, Mark gestured with his thumb. "He called me weak, so I tackled him." Sil punched him in the arm in response. "All right... you win..." Mark winced, babying his left shoulder.

"You really should be taking it easy," Keller warned. "Your arm needs time to heal, and you should consider yourself very lucky to still be able to use it." Mark opened his mouth to dismiss it, but Keller interrupted him, "And keep in mind that Strength wants you to be dependent on it. It wants you to look weak, so you need to actually eat to keep up with the energy it gives you."

Mark's eyebrow twitched as he heard that word again, and Sil laughed at Mark's manic behavior. "So, let me get this straight," Mark screeched. "Strength wants me to look puny?!" Overcome with frustration, he blew past Keller into the ASH blaring, "I need to gain some weight!"

Sil covered his mouth to stifle his laughter. Mark had already been slight of frame before Strength, but a couple days of fasting and then being in the hospital hadn't helped. He was still as pale as a sheet of paper even in the warmer climate of Virginia.

Mark's heart was strong, undamaged by Strength's wound, and as far as anyone could tell, the new Shadow had fully assimilated into his bloodstream. It was so much faster than Mark's first Shadow it was uncanny, and Mark continued to catch on to the challenges of his Shadow very fast. Sil felt a little left in the dust.

Maybe it was genetic. Shadows weren't hereditary, but it was very clear to Sil they were attracted to other powerful Shadows. Either to become their wielders or their offspring. Sil guessed Mark was a Shadow for the same reason anyone else was, but he was powerful in the Realm and in refining his Shadow because of January. It didn't matter what January was hiding, Sil could guess what it was and why. It went back to that power of Infusions. January had a dangerous skill; he knew it somewhere, deep down, and erasing that knowledge was all he could do to keep it from falling into the wrong hands.

"Beautiful, isn't it?" Kimberly stepped up behind January as they watched Mark and Sil from the window of his new room.

Straining, January nodded. The drive down had been exhausting, and upon arrival, he had taken straight to bed. But the moment he woke up, he had been flooded by questions from the young Shadows in the mess hall. He glanced over his shoulder at her, puzzled by her apparent compassion. "Thank you..." he murmured. "For saving his life."

Kimberly took a glance around his new room, at the lonely bed and the slight unpacking he had managed. "You have no one to thank, it was all you. But I do have you to thank."

"Me?" January puzzled.

Giving a little laugh, Kimberly tossed her strawberry red curls over her shoulder. Seeing him again was like going back in time. He was older but it was still his eyes, his skepticism, and his guarded stealth. He didn't even remember what he was hiding from. "Yes, I know you have no memory of it, but you taught me how to perform the Infusion to save someone I love. Now that you have your powers back, I wanted you to know I was grateful."

Graciously, January lowered his head. "You're welcome, I guess." But then he paused. "Was it... class four Infusion?"

She nodded, and her smile did not fade. "You should go join the Shadows," she reverted, offering her advice freely as she had to Mark. "Be around them. Maybe that will help spark your memories."

January affirmed, reluctant to leave the quiet, the familiar, to surround himself with the world Mark had been sucked into. Kimberly followed him out, ushering him into the bustling halls, and she watched him disappear down the stairwell, accepting his new life as Shadow Ignition.

Kimberly turned from him, stepping toward the banister overlooking the lobby from this floor, and smiled contently. She strode the halls with her children, mothering them and patting their backs as they played and bickered. She made her way down the stairs, greeting the Shadows snacking in the mess hall and chuckling as Mark raided the kitchen for something high in protein.

She left them, the smile not fading until she reached the infirmary, sinking into the room she had spent so many waking hours in. Her sorrow surfaced, opening herself in the Realm and diving in deep through the layers of blackness, the corporeal plane and the incorporeal, down into the starfield. Within it, she had hidden a golden orange star, a hot burning ember that still had life in it, preserved just before the moment of death.

She touched the star, revealing the physical form of the body this soul was attached to. She had placed him in the Realm to protect him, and to preserve him. He had no consciousness, but the expression of pain was frozen in stasis across his brow. He was alive, but he couldn't survive even another second in the real world.

He moaned, unaware of the amount of time that had passed or that the Realm was keeping him alive.

Kimberly touched his face, stroking back his hair and kissing his brow. "Shh... it's okay, Irwin. I'm here. Not much longer, just hold on a little longer."

The pocket door slid open, and she left the Realm instantly. In the doorway, Rita slammed the door and locked it. Kimberly straightened her back, startled. "What are you doing here?"

Rita teleported closer, and Kimberly noticed the tears in her eyes. "Is my Nova ready yet?" she demanded, heartbroken.

"Rita..." Kimberly consoled, bringing her arms around the girl she had cared for and watched over among the Shadows. "Not yet, but it will be soon..."

Rita fell against Kimberly's chest sobbing, completely overwhelmed. "I cannae live with this anymore. I did that to him. I almost got him killed! I led him to Geoffrey! What happened... it's my fault!"

Kimberly shushed her lovingly. "It's all right, I promise. It'll be all right. This Nova will make that guilt completely disappear, and when I'm done, they'll make the Shadows completely flawless." She peered into Rita's face, nudging her chin to gather her tearstained gaze. "Hey, you could actually talk to him. That might help? Might not even need to make the Nova in the first place."

"No!" Rita denied quickly, pushing away from her. "I want my Nova, I need it! Don't try to convince me otherwise. Just finish it!"

Sighing, Kimberly nodded. "You're strong enough on your own. You don't need to bring yourself down with this." Rita didn't need this Nova. She was just too overwhelmed by a petty emotion. Nonetheless, Rita would serve as the perfect candidate for the first experiment with the Novas.

"I don't care!" Rita screamed, her accent strong and deep. "Just... please! I cannae face him after what I've done!"

Kimberly's gaze sorrowfully drifted down at the little bookcase next to the old television, at the books *he* used to love. "You always were strong. I just wish you'd give him the truth, like he deserves. You love him. I know you do. Don't give up on that."

Rita pressed her lips together, biting back tears. "I do love him..." She whimpered. "But he doesnae care about me... I'm invisible to him."

A caring touch was all she could give Rita right now, another hug and a kiss in her red hair. "Just a little longer," she promised.

About E. Kathryn

Writer, Illustrator, musician, humanesque creature who doesn't get enough sunlight and lives solely on tea, E. Kathryn started writing The Shadows when she was thirteen years old. Brought up in northern Virginia with her six siblings and tons of animals, she was homeschooled and given the freedom to write to her heart's content. When she's not writing incessantly, E. Kathryn enjoys drawing, playing the violin, and collecting and consuming way more tea than she needs.

Stay Connected
EKATHRYNSSHADOWS.COM
Twitter @EKsShadows
Instagram @e.kathryns_shadows

Book 3 of The Shadows:
Halo's Rag Doll